THE PINK HOUSE AT APPLETON

Jonathan Braham

THE PINK HOUSE AT APPLETON

Matador
9 Priory Business Park
Kibworth Beauchamp
Leicester LE8 0RX, UK
Tel: 0116 279 2299
Email: books@troubador.co.uk
Web: www.troubador.co.uk/matador

ISBN 978-1-84876-745-4

A Cataloguing-in-Publication (CIP) catalogue record for this book
is available from the British Library.

Typeset in 11.5pt Book Antiqua by Troubador Publishing Ltd, Leicester, UK

Matador is an imprint of Troubador Publishing Ltd

Printed and bound in the UK by TJI Digital, Padstow, Cornwall

For my sister,
Kimberley Ashbury Portland-Tobiaz,
who would have loved Yvonne.

CONTENTS

PROLOGUE

Some things you cannot forget, even those you think you've deleted permanently. The slightest impulse brings them back, every detail, every sound and smell, the deepest feelings in digitally enhanced, high definition reality.

Boyd Longfellow Brookes lived his special memory, planted in him over forty years ago, in Technicolor. A tragedy, it recurred even in dreams, in the dead of night, sometimes with such force that he lived the ordeal as a child, before it became memory.

That October afternoon it was the music that triggered it. He sat at his Apple Powerbook G4, trading stock on Schwab-Europe.com, tapping into the black keys, mouthing into the black telephone, sipping from a glass of red wine. He liked these pleasurable wine-satiated afternoons at home for they, peculiarly, heightened and sharpened his risk-taking.

Beyond the window, restive trees rustled, yellow leaves soared and fell away, and the first grains of rain landed on the windowpane. Out on the King's Road, Routemasters 11s and 22s passed like red shadows. The rousing wind, setting the trees in a rhythmic dance as the sky darkened, ruffled the feathers of the late pigeons as they dashed for home and Trafalgar Square. And suddenly the rain came down in white, belligerent streaks.

He quit the Apple Powerbook and ran to the balcony, enveloped in a sudden frisson of expectation. Stopping impatiently in the kitchen, he poured hastily from the half-empty bottle, a tasty Chateau Figeac, resting on the corian worktop. He supped the wine but did not reach the balcony. Music stopped him: the Saint-Saëns Violin Concerto No 3 in B minor, the *Andantino quasi allegretto*. Out from the little Bose radio on the bookshelf poured the haunting strains, heard over forty years ago in silence and distress. He stumbled onto the rain-swept balcony, the wine glass heavy in his hand.

He was eight years old again in the house at Appleton Estate, petrified. In that dark scene he stood alone in the drawing room, Mama weeping while Papa raised the strap and said, 'Boyd, did you molest Susan?'

The world stopped. Mavis, lovely Mavis, smelling of garlic and escallion, rushed from the kitchen, protesting his innocence. 'Lawd, have mercy!' And when that wasn't enough, she accused them. 'But who could say such a thing, sar?'

Mrs Dowding could, that small-minded gossip, their next door neighbour, who thought the *Tropic of Cancer* was a *sex* book, a *bad* book. Evadne could, Ann Mitchison's maid. She saw any association between a boy and a girl as *lust of the flesh*.

The world turned against him the moment the alien word, *molest*, slid from Papa's lips. He did not know the true meaning of the word but saw it in their eyes, his family, gathered in the room around him, the one word, *guilty*. And something else too – the realisation that he, Boyd, was capable of such a monstrous thing, that all his living had been meaningless, untrue.

He could not tell Papa *what it meant to see Susan's eyes like pretty marbles, inhale the scent of her, see her pinkness and her gingham dress. It was impossible to tell Papa about his big feelings, his secret thoughts, the inner sanctum where the music came from, the part of him that had gone out to Susan. That was what Papa wanted to know, the very things he himself could not talk about.*

He had run from the room that day because he could not explain. And that night, distraught, alone in his room, he heard the heart-clutching music from the Mullard radio.

And there was a certain comfort in hearing the music, lying in bed, knowing of the anger and indignation that prevailed, knowing that he had been utterly condemned, and knowing that he was totally innocent. But it was the events of that day that had quickened the end of Appleton because, after that day, the disaster was unstoppable. Papa, the great man, could not prevent it. He was involved in the destruction from the very beginning, as the facts later revealed.

In the final days, Papa never once returned home from the club till the grey of dawn. The Land Rover deposited him to the pink house, full of Appleton rum and a singular vision of the future for his family, his knee-length socks in heavy brown brogues, short khaki trousers crumpled, cotton shirt drunk with Royal Blend tobacco. He put the key in the lock, made a noise in the pantry to signal his arrival and continued down the hall in the dark to the bedroom where Mama lay, dried tears on cheeks, questions unanswered. And he mounted her in the dark under the covers, her flesh hot like the virgin sugar in his hands at the factory.

Papa thought not of Mama but of Miss Chatterjee at the club, whose smooth thighs rippled as she stroked the tennis balls. Miss Chatterjee, small of ankle, with the lipsticked mouth and a womanliness only travel, education and class could confer. It was Miss Chatterjee who Papa penetrated during the early months at Appleton, while Mama gave everything that she knew to give, and would have given more if asked. She was there to serve. But it was Miss Chatterjee who Papa saw and felt beneath him until the English family, the Mitchisons, arrived. Then it was Ann Mitchison with her quivering, seductive, kiss lips, all through the summer. Ann Mitchison changed everything.

At nights, unable to sleep, Boyd listened and heard the trembling music, whatever the hour that Papa arrived in the Prefect or the Land Rover, and Mama's submissive moans and cries as if she called out to him. Very often he was at their bedroom door in the dark, seeing their contortions, the moonlight splashing the sheets and silver-lining the dark furniture. And always there was Papa's vigorous back, bringing the music to an abrupt, discordant end, drumsticks and cymbals clattering down to the ground.

Standing and looking out from a rainy balcony in Chelsea, in October 2003, that was what he remembered. But that wasn't everything.

PART ONE
The Beginning

CHAPTER 1

They lived in a pretty little house in the heart of the Black River valley, on a grassy slope overlooking Appleton Estate sugar factory in St Elizabeth parish. The house was painted in deep green and cream gloss, popular colours of the period and for houses of that sort. Papa said that it was a gingerbread house. Mama didn't think so and she should know; she was born in a gingerbread house, chalk-white with fanciful fretwork, deep in forty acres of gardens in St Catherine. Mama's mother, Grandma Rosetta, still lived there along with Mama's two brothers, Uncle Haughton and Uncle Albert.

When Mama left the gingerbread house as a young married woman, she moved to an estate house set in a field of pink bougainvillea at Worthy Park. Later, as Papa's prospects advanced, they moved to Appleton, driving a hundred miles in a single day in the grey Ford Prefect with the three children in the back, through the dusty roads of Clarendon, Manchester and St Elizabeth, to this house with front and back verandahs and balustrades. Papa was thirty-one and Mama twenty-nine years old. It was 1957.

In that year, Jamaica was still a British colony. Sir Hugh Foot, in starched white ceremonial uniform and exotic plumed hat, was governor of the island. Norman Manley, the Oxford-educated Jamaican lawyer, was Chief Minister and tireless advocate of "full internal self-government". But independence was still five long years away. In those days, the sugar estates teemed with white English managers and other professionals and their families, living for the most

3

part in pastoral civility with their black Jamaican counterparts.

'We Brookes are first rate,' Papa boasted at the dinner table in their little Appleton Estate house. 'Don't let anyone tell you otherwise. We are not one of those hurry-come-up families, and there are plenty of them about, especially in Kingston, with little education and no background. The name Brookes means something. And Pratt, too,' he added, making a concession to Mama's side of the family. Mama's family were landowners, small farmers. Papa's were plantation managers, professionals. He believed that the Brookeses had the edge in social ranking because they were sophisticated and skilled, not because, like the Pratts, they had had vast acres of agricultural land handed down to them.

Papa's smile was mischevious and as broad as his forehead, but there was hardness in his eyes.

'Where's that boy?' he asked, looking about.

'Go and get Boyd,' Mama said quickly.

The little girl left the table instantly and they could hear her rushing feet on the polished wooden floor of the house heading in the direction of the drawing room.

'Didn't you hear the dinner bell?' the little girl asked the small boy curled up in the chintz armchair with a book at his face. 'Perlita rang the bell five times.'

The boy didn't hear for he remained curled up, forehead furrowed, not moving.

'Didn't you hear the dinner bell?' his sister repeated impatiently. Then she said cunningly, '*Papa* wants you,' the stress on *Papa*.

The small boy reacted at once, took just enough time to fold the page at the correct place then leapt out of the armchair and hurried out of the room behind his sister. At the table their big brother sat upright, not amused. As they took their seats Papa paused and said, 'Hmm.'

'I didn't come to Appleton to fool about,' Papa continued, everyone at the table giving him their full attention. 'Education, ambition, hard work. That's what it's about. Some people only know how to waste time and not apply themselves. We Brookes will leave our mark here at Appleton.' He was an only child, the last of that line of Brookeses, without any property to his name and, although he would never admit it to anyone, he believed that he was a man alone against the world, but born to win. His three children, from the earliest days, heard the words of Longfellow from their father's lips at breakfast, lunch and dinner, and sometimes before bed:

The heights of great men reached and kept
were not attained by sudden flight,
but they, while their companions slept,
were toiling upward in the night.

The Appleton sunset painted a soft crimson upon the windows and against the white, freshly ironed cotton tablecloth. It added a dramatic edge to Papa's firm brown face. Through the French windows a valley breeze brought the tantalizing smell of boiling sugar, the exotic perfume of sugar estates, and quietly in the background the Mullard radio whispered *Love is a many-splendored thing*.

Mama, dressed in light maternity clothes, looked up. She had brothers and sisters aplenty and felt no passion, perhaps being a woman, about her family name, or about having to prove herself. She certainly didn't believe that there were any battles to be fought. But she wanted to leave her mark. She wanted to become somebody, an ordinary somebody, but somebody of her very own, not just a housewife and mother. But she said nothing. When Papa had the floor, impassioned and impatient, delivering his little lectures, it was best to listen, even if she had heard it all before.

'Brains, intelligence, class,' Papa reminded them, his big, even teeth bared in a self-congratulatory smile. 'Gawd! That's what we Brookeses are made of. I could run the whole shooting match down here.'

The move from Worthy Park Estate was a timely one. As deputy assistant chief chemist, Papa's chances of advancement at Appleton were good. His ultimate objective was to leave Appleton after a few successful years and take up a senior appointment, possibly as chief chemist or general manager, at another big sugar estate like New Yarmouth or Monymusk. But the move was good for another reason. It put a lot of distance between him and a certain matter, an indiscretion, which took place in an outlying district, Lluidas Vale, one reckless night almost eight years ago, after he'd been drinking a little too much. He was not proud of it and, in fact, had only known about the result of his misdemeanour shortly before he left for Appleton. He didn't think Mama knew about it – there was no way in which she could know. But women had a way of knowing.

'It's nice here,' Mama said tentatively, now that the lecture was over. 'Doctor, dentist, pharmacy, shops, a reliable train service, the nursing home at Maggotty, good hospitals in nearby Mandeville, and a design academy too.' Her eyelids fluttered like a bashful girl's. This bashfulness, this little-girl quality in her, was what appealed most to Papa when they first met. But now, after many years, he found it debilitating and was impatient with it. He wanted a little haughtiness from his wife. He wanted just a teeny-weeny bit of snobbery, a little malice, which should bring about the sophistication and the fascination he so wished she possessed. Mama was far too trustworthy, too innocent. He wanted stimulation, challenge, but all he got was fidelity, devotion.

'Nice?' Papa said, thinking it a strange word to use to describe a place that would determine their future.

Mama paused, not quite knowing how to deal with Papa's reply. 'Will the electricians come tomorrow?' she asked, changing the subject. 'There's no light in the pantry. And we could do with an outside light by the ironing room and the laundry room.'

'Dixon will see to it,' Papa said brusquely. 'Didn't I say so? He'll do it, or send one of his lackeys. They have nothing to do but stand about.'

'And the stove smokes. It makes poor Perlita cough and sneeze.'

'Cough and sneeze? She should be so lucky. Can't she get, what's his name, Delroy, that brother of hers, to look at it? Lazy son of a gun. He's always idlying about with his long hands at his sides and that lazy look in his eyes. I don't understand these people. They can't do anything without being told? And what is he doing hanging around the property day after day for? If he wants to be a yard-boy he needs to get to work.'

'He doesn't come here anymore. Perlita said he got a job with the Public Works Department, breaking stones on the road.'

'I'd like to break stones on his head, that lazy good-for-nothing,' Papa said. Then he sighed. 'All right, Victoria. I'll see to it. Probably hasn't been cleaned since the day they put it in. People don't seem to understand that the only way to maintain anything is to clean it. That kind of attitude can only hold back the country.'

'I could bring back the gloss with a little Vim and steel wool,' Mama said.

Papa's response was swift. 'I didn't take you all the way from St Catherine to Appleton to clean house. That's maids' work.'

Mama, aghast, opened her mouth to speak but closed it as a sudden movement caught her eye. The curtains at the door parted and Perlita appeared, having been listening keenly to the conversation from her place in the kitchen. From habit she wiped her hands carelessly and lethargically on her apron. She was a St Elizabeth rural woman, not given to speaking with care and restraint.

'Mr Brookes, sar,' she said with insane boldness, 'who going to deal with the travelling salesmen, sar? They come from off the road, through the gate and right up into the

7

verandah, sar. Three, four of them a day, selling things Mrs Brookes don't need. And them don't take no for an answer. Them is hooligan, sar. Poor Mrs Brookes have to deal with them all the time, and she is expecting. The house too close to the road, sar, too close.'

Papa considered this interruption shocking impertinence and paused long enough to demonstrate it. 'Don't you have work to do in the kitchen?' he asked, glowering.

'Yes, sar, ma'am,' Perlita said, bowing slightly as she left.

Papa's expression was one that Mama knew well. Perlita was walking on thin ice.

'It's your job to train her,' Papa hissed, leaving the table. 'Do you expect me to do everything?'

Papa, who at first liked the new house, had quickly grown to dislike it. All he heard from the brief interlude with Mama and the hapless Perlita were house problems. The house did not say *Harold Brookes*. It did not say *Home of the Brookeses, a first rate family*. It said *ordinary*. Papa wanted a house in a pastoral setting, with a garage, gardens, an expanse of lawn and a long driveway. His house should reflect not only his status on the estate but the level of his intelligence, his *savoir-faire*. And, frankly, he did not expect to wait forever. He learned from his father, the great Lascelles Brookes, banana plantation manager, dead now, that prosperity did not come to the meek, to those who stood in line.

* * *

Appleton was green and blue. Vast fields of sugar cane stretched into the distance, their green shoots steady in the wind on the valley floor. All day long the lemonade-sweet heat shimmered across the valley. Blue mountains crouched on the sunny horizon and green hills reached up from the open spaces, cut through by the snaking Black River. In the warm perfumed evenings the sunsets were radiant pink, painting the powdered faces of the estate wives sitting on the terrace at the club drinking Babycham and gossiping, while ignoring their restless husbands lined up at the bar. And at night a million stars, like golden sugar crystals, crowded the sky.

On the grassy slopes stood the big houses of the managers, smaller houses for staff on their way up the management ladder and houses for others just beginning the climb. Papa's house was in-between. It was solidly built, facing the road and the sprawling, silver, steaming factory: a giant engine down in the heart of the valley. In the mornings, as the sun crept up the hill, the verandah lay in soft shade. The three Brookes children liked to sit there and wave to the people who passed. The children.

A small, glossy, perforated black and white photograph of them in the family album showed the eldest child, Barrington Winston Brookes, looking grave and grown-up at eleven years old, the plumpest of the three, in pepperseed trousers and starched white shirt. He held the hand of his sister, Yvonne Elizabeth Brookes, the youngest at five years old, forehead round and intelligent, hair pulled back, polka-dotted dress well above dimpled knees, a mischievous smile about her lips. Boyd Longfellow Brookes, the smaller of the two boys, dressed in short linen trousers buttoned to a white shirt, stared into the camera, brows knitted, enquiring, troubled. He gripped his little sister's hand tightly. His feelings and his thoughts, mostly in grey and blueberry-blue, dwarfed him. He was eight years old.

Every morning at this new house at Appleton they looked at the people passing by: the estate postmen who arrived on rickety red bicycles, zigzagging across the road, shirt-tails flapping in the breeze. The Bible women, dressed in dusty black, who relentlessly tried to save souls, having the front door slammed in their faces by Papa or an enraged Perlita. Mrs Moore, the chief engineer's wife, with a pretty parasol, flowery dress, and a hat encrusted with artificial fruit, who waved and waved even when they thought she'd stopped waving. Miss Casserly, the young teacher with the sun on her face, cotton skirts like spread hibiscus, and always picked up by a punctual car long before she got to them. Mr Dixon, the electrician with gloved hands and tools sticking out of his pockets, who lived at the Bull Pen, the batchelors' residence, but was to be found on the hill daily, fixing fuses, plugs and switches, wrapping black tape over wires and joking extravagantly with the maids. Mr Tecumseh Burton, the tailor from Balaclava with the American accent (Perlita called it a 'twang') who, touting for business with his nephew, Edgar, drove up in a black Chevrolet with bales of cloth, took Barrington and Boyd's measurements and delivered well-cut short trousers a week later, saying to Papa, 'At a good price, suh'. Mr Jarrett, the sprayman, his magnificent brass spraying equipment heavy on his shoulders and his fragrant, gorgeous smell. He visited often to pump up his apparatus and spray the air. The children loved him the most, because he was tall and thin with sleepy eyes and praying-mantis features. They smelled him before they saw him. His aroma was of the lovely spray fumes and DDT. As he slowly passed, the sun glinting off him, they breathed deliciously, waving deliriously. He always turned to look with mock surprise as if seeing them for the first time, his cigarette never leaving his lips. Sometimes he presented them with sweets: Mint Balls, round and white with pink stripes down their sides and covered in white sugar, vivid pink and white coconut candy that crumbled in their hands, sticky Staggerback that clung joyfully to their teeth and Paradise Plums wrapped in crackling greaseproof paper. The Paradise Plums he took out one by one from a paper bag like a naughty but wonderful magic trick, each one pink on top and yellow underneath, as the children trembled with unsurpassed delight.

Other people passed by too. The maids in pairs, chattering and gay, laughing like carefree birds by the water's edge; and *higglers*, market women, their breasts heaving and their bottoms in a shocking rhythmic romp, *bankras* heavy on their heads. And there were gardeners in overalls, more casual in their walking, handymen and beggars and peculiar people whose business they could not determine. And there was one other person.

This person wore dark clothes and rode by the house on a black bicycle every day just before ten o'clock. The only thing that was not dark about him was his machete, two and a half feet of steel, white sharp in the light, strapped to the bicycle frame. The children found him mysterious. They had their eyes on him every day, daring him to look so that they could wave, but they never waved because he never looked.

'He's not nice,' Yvonne said, exasperated, after five mornings in a row fixing him with a steady eye and getting no response.

'You mustn't say that,' Perlita cautioned, a picking finger up her nose. 'Him is as straight as a arrow. Everybody say so.'

'But he's not looking at us,' Yvonne remonstrated, not interested. 'He's blind. And deaf and dumb too!'

'Don't be stupid,' Barrington told her. 'Blind people don't ride bicycles.'

Watching the dark figure disappear down the lane, Boyd knew why he didn't look. It was for the same reason he himself didn't always look people in the eye. Papa said it was because of *lack of confidence*, but it wasn't anything of the sort. The eye revealed everything. People could look straight into you, deep down into the secret pinkness where you lived. The bicycle rider concealed things he did not want anyone to know about. Boyd knew. He had secrets too. *Great Expectations* lay opened on his bed at a certain page. He couldn't wait to get back to the book and to the two fascinating characters in it: the pretty girl, Estella, who made his heart flutter, and the boy, Pip, who really was Boyd Longfellow Brookes. And so, as he hurried away, he did not hear Perlita's final remarks.

'Him keep himself to himself,' Perlita said of the bicycle-rider. 'Him don't drink at rum bars all night like some of the good-for-nothing men. Him don't smoke or gamble. Him is a strange man but him don't busy himself in other people's business.' Perlita said he arrived at the factory at ten o'clock every day and left at six every evening. People set their watches by him. His name was Mr Ten-To-Six.

'*Ten-To-Six!*' Yvonne laughed, unbelieving.

* * *

It was wonderful at first, this standing about on the verandah of the new house, waving cheerfully at all and sundry. Yvonne even pretended that the balustrade was a bucking horse and rode it, shouting 'Giddyap, giddyap!' brown legs and feet in misbehaving imaginary stirrups.

'Those lovely little children,' Mrs Moore said. And the maids commented to their mistresses, who mentioned it to their husbands, who repeated it, in their way, at the club. Papa got wind of it, interpreted it as only he could, and put a stop to it forthwith. Driving home early from work one day he towered over the children, scowling, in short khaki trousers, knee-length socks, and heavy brown brogues smelling of Nugget polish.

'Get inside the house. You're not little vagabonds. If I ever catch you out here again fooling around, I'll put you on the streets to beg your bread!'

The words were so shocking that the children stumbled backward into the house. They knew (from peering out the rear window of the Prefect) what it was like to beg for bread. Mr Rawhog, the local vagabond, did it. And look at him – forever crouching in the gutters, dirty, his crotch wet and smelling of wee, always hungry and desperate-looking, no home to go to, always at the mercy of the rain, and no roast beef, rice and peas, cabbage and fried plantains cooked by Perlita for Sunday lunch.

'Get out of my sight!' Papa marched after them. 'Here I am trying to teach you *values and principles* and there you are trying to drag me into the gutter. You want to behave like *those people?* Go on. You'll see where that will get you.'

Papa was *values and principles.* He talked about *values and principles* at the dinner table when everyone was there to hear, and in the car when no one could get away. He said that *those people* would never amount to anything because they lacked two very vital ingredients, *values and principles.* *Those people* were degenerates who had children (little bastards) in every town and village and who walked away from their responsibilities. *Those people,* Papa had said, lowering his voice, were all busy committing *adultery,* which was all they were good for. None of the children knew what *adultery* meant. But they guessed it meant something bad, and because Mama seemed very uncomfortable, never dreamed of asking her. The dreadful people committing *adultery* were so disreputable that they made no plans for their children's education. That, Papa said, was the most irresponsible thing of all. Large numbers of them were leaving Jamaica for England by banana boat. Good riddance.

From the safety of their bedrooms they heard Papa's strident voice. Mama's was low and whimpering. They heard Papa's heavy brown brogues firm and quick upon the red Polyflor-polished wooden floors. Hidden behind drawn curtains they saw him lurching in the yellow Willys jeep down the winding road, back to the factory with its white steam that said *Shhhhh, Shhhhh, Shhhhh* day after day, and the pervasive smell of boiling sugar that lulled everything into pastoral calm.

When Papa was gone, the children came out from their rooms and Mama came to them. It was in that magical period of the morning between nine and eleven o'clock. At that time fathers were at work and maids dusted and polished and the Mullard radio played *Housewives' Choice,* music by Harry Belafonte, Doris Day, The Platters and Jimmie Rodgers *(Oh, Honeycomb, won't you be my baby, well, Honeycomb, be my own).* The verandah opened upon the world and Mama herself wanted to be in the world, not locked away in an estate house. But that was where Papa wanted them to stay, not standing idly about on the verandah like common people. Mama herself now watched for the yellow jeep with its big, baby-round headlamp eyes and warned the children as it laboured up the slope. But she was sad.

Mama did not want to end up like her mother, alone in that house in St Catherine, unfulfilled, with only death to look forward to. She wanted to realise her little dream.

'A dressmaker!' Papa said, shocked, when she first brought it up. 'You want to be a dressmaker?'

'More like a designer,' Mama calmly suggested, desperately wanting Papa to show just a flicker of genuine interest.

'You've never said anything before.'

Mama was silent, thinking about Enid, her sister. Enid led a fantastic social life, had a smart house in an upmarket district of Kingston, knew people, had travelled abroad and had the sort of experience Mama could only dream about. Enid had realised her dream.

'And where would you do your dressmaking?'

'I would work from home,' Mama replied eagerly, immediately seeing orders for her clothes being dispatched by train to *Daphne's* and *Issa's* in Kingston, and Sunday newspaper articles raving about her designs.

Papa had laughed and stared at her hard. You are a mad woman, his eyes said. Papa knew about dressmakers. They were small-town, peasant women, who sat before aged Singer sewing machines in the untidy front room of their modest little houses, surrounded by cheap-smelling materials and half-finished clothes for even less dignified women and various odd people. It was not an image that complemented his vision of big house and garden and servants, and delightful evenings at the club. He found it hard to believe that Mama could contemplate such a thing. He wouldn't hear another word about it after that.

14

CHAPTER 2

After that dressing-down from Papa, the children kept well away from the front verandah. Mama too. She felt as if she'd received a dressing-down herself, and decided that if she couldn't go into the world, she would invite the world in. So she invited Mrs Moore for a chat one morning. Boyd peeped in at the door, sniffing and savouring the drifting woman fragrance of Mrs Moore. It was a spicy-camphor sort of smell, nothing like his Aunt Enid's frangipani scent. The radio played *Que Sera Sera, Whatever Will Be Will Be* while Mrs Moore talked in her older woman's voice. And she showed ankles and smooth upper arms that stirred feelings and thoughts that Boyd had never known.

'Victoria, you must come up to the club and meet the rest of us,' the older woman's voice of Mrs Moore said. 'You can't stay shut up in the house forever.' She laughed and Mama laughed too, liking Mrs Moore with her colourful hat, encrusted with artificial fruit.

'I see you've already got yourself a maid,' Mrs Moore observed. 'It took me six months to get anyone decent. Good maids are hard to come by in St Elizabeth, and you have to teach them everything. Is she any good?'

'Oh, she seems fine,' Mama replied, not wanting to mention Perlita's frequent nose-picking and the many nasty little habits she was fast discovering, like the endless hawking and spitting. Mama was tired of telling Perlita to wash her hands before she kneaded the dough for the dumplings. Perlita didn't think much of that advice. She went to the bathroom to do number two and didn't wash

15

her hands there either, and she coughed and sneezed at will. Sometimes wriggly strands of her hair were found in the sauce at dinner. Perlita was on borrowed time. One more slip and she was out, to beg for her bread on the hot, dusty roads of St Elizabeth. That was what Papa said.

'Hmm,' Mrs Moore murmured. 'Never let anything fester. If they have to go, let them go.' She slapped her fleshy thigh to make her point and Mama's head snapped back. 'Get rid of them. On the spot!'

'She seems fine,' Mama repeated meekly. 'Very pleasant.'

'Without a good maid,' Mrs Moore told Mama gravely, 'it's difficult to run an estate house, as you know. And it's more difficult here in St Elizabeth with the poor quality of the maids. The laziness. The gossip! Everyone on the estate knows your business. It's all they're interested in. And the thieving! They'll steal the clothes off your back.'

Mama giggled and Mrs Moore smiled and added, 'If you let them.'

At that moment, Mama knew that she had a friend. Mrs Moore leaned forward and spoke with a tone and expression of pure wisdom. 'Victoria, you will not settle until the right maid is in the house. Don't feel sorry for them. Remember, you cannot help every poor girl who comes to the door looking for work. You'll know when the right one comes along and, believe you me, quite a number of them will come along. Hmm.'

There was a pause in the conversation as Mrs Moore sipped her coffee, her huge breasts formidable and reassuring. Boyd's eyes widened. Then Mrs Moore disappointed Mama. 'We won't be staying here long,' she said, looking swiftly and approvingly about the room. 'Stanley plans to work for a big engineering company in Kingston. We'll take Icilyn with us. She'll be cheaper than the Kingston maids and more respectful too, after all the training I've given her. Appleton is good for us – free house, furniture and everything – and you can live like a king on a few pounds. But our home is in Kingston. And there's not a lot to do here. Yes, there's the club, the odd party, dinners and so forth, and some people getting up to mischief, as they always do, Victoria.' Mrs Moore laughed loud and long until she wheezed. 'And sports for the younger ones. Young people need sports. And the Crop-Over Dance, of course, when the bigwigs come up from Kingston and people let their hair down. My niece, Pepsi, comes up on school holidays to keep me company. A bright, lovely girl with a magnificent head of hair. Wait till you see her, just wait. But you must come to the club, Victoria, show yourself.'

Boyd, moving quickly away from the door at the sound of chairs being pushed back and seeing shocking images of the heaving udders of Mrs Moore, wondered with great imagination at the coming of a girl named Pepsi, and could not wait.

* * *

When Papa entered the hall that evening, Boyd was slumped in the armchair breathing hard, *Great Expectations* opened in his lap. Deep cello music came from the recesses of the Mullard radio nearby. Boyd was thinking, with delicious torment, about the beautiful and heart-breaking Estella, so ruthless towards Pip. He had reached the part on page eighty-nine where Estella takes Pip into a corner and says "You may kiss me, if you like." *You may kiss me!* It was so breathtaking for a girl to say a thing like that. But Estella was cold and didn't mean any of it. Boyd felt Pip's hurt and yet, especially because of her cruelty, felt a deep and burning attraction for Estella. Even the sight of her name on the page sparked passion, pain, pleasure. He'd felt the same about Lydia Parsons, that haughty girl at Worthy Park Prep, who took away his crayons and never gave him the time of day. Night after night he'd had torturous dreams about Lydia Parsons for that reason alone. She and Estella were the same. He wondered if all pretty girls were like that.

'What's the matter with that child now?' Papa asked Mama, closing the bedroom door behind him.

'Who?' Mama asked.

'Boyd. Who else? He's sitting by the radio sniffling again.'

'Nothing's the matter with him,' Mama said, her tone suddenly assertive.

'You could fool me.'

'He's just a thoughtful child. Little things affect him.'

'I see,' Papa said. 'He stands naked in the rain like a little savage. Sometimes he just sits on the verandah looking into space, and when you say anything to him he bursts into tears. What's going on in that head of his?' But before Mama could answer, Papa carried on. 'He has to learn not to dwell on things. You think I allow this, that or the other to get to me at the factory?' Papa gave a sarcastic little laugh.

Mama faced him, surprised. 'He's only a child.'

'And he'll remain a child until he learns to manage his feelings.'

'Did you understand your feelings when you were eight?'

'I certainly didn't dwell on them. Sometimes you have to put feelings aside and get on with life. And he's aways hidden away in the garden, doing what, no one knows. Now, that is strange.'

'A little sensitivity doesn't harm anybody.'

Papa rolled his eyes and left the room just as the dinner bell went.

During dinner the small spotted dog, standing outside by the kitchen door, uttered pitiful sounds, lamenting his absence at the table. Not more than six months old, he came with the house, waiting on the front steps, tail whipping in a blur on the day of their arrival. He had sidled up to Boyd, who promptly named him "Poppy".

Now Boyd waited impatiently to get to Poppy and the back verandah. The back verandah received the red sunset in late evening. Very often he stood alone in the warm dark, breathing the evening scents, roseapple and jasmine, feeling the quiet and strangeness of a new place, listening to the cautious night noises, and watching the fireflies, the *peeny-waalies*, approach from the darkness behind the maids' quarters. And he always wondered, as he stood there, what Perlita was doing in her room with the door closed. Sometimes, from the darkness outside he peeped in, flat against her window, standing on half a brick, expecting to see her slowly undressing, expecting to see a pink slip, her woman's heavy titties and thighs, slow self-conscious movements, like Mama. But Perlita never took her clothes off. She seemed busy with other things.

As he waited, Boyd saw the gathering darkness, the *peeny-waalies* nervously watching, the flowers waiting to breathe their night breath, all awaiting Papa's departure. He waited too, for Perlita to undress, for Pepsi to arrive, for his tangled feelings to turn into pretty common sense. And from the bathroom he heard Papa's unrestrained voice, *Beecaause you come to me, because you speak to me, beecaause...*

Throughout dinner Yvonne had given Boyd mischievous little glances. Now, as Papa left for the club, his grand tenor waning, his lime-green Limacol cologne wafting in his wake, his brogues firm upon the wooden floor she turned to Mama, who was staring wistfully at Papa's departing back.

'Mama, Boyd took out his teapot and pee-peed on the ants. And he's eating the flowers again.' She was only five years old. At that age every thought turned into words. Barrington, as impatient to get to his scrapbook of footballers and cars as Papa was impatient to get to the club, quickly left the table.

'Eat your pudding,' Mama told Yvonne, imagining Boyd's discomfort.

But Boyd only saw himself in the fragrant darkness of the garden. He was alone with Pepsi, whose face was already the face of a girl he knew, whose strawberry-red lips spoke impossible things, just like Estella.

Mama saw Boyd in the garden too, but he did not see her. Watching from her bedroom window one day, she had learned something about her son. And she wondered what Papa would say if he knew about Boyd's peculiar habit.

* * *

The first time he tongued the flowers was in the garden at Worthy Park, in a quiet place where no one could see. It was almost like sucking Mama's titties in the lily-scented bedroom on a hot afternoon. He didn't know when he stopped sucking Mama's titties but it wasn't long ago.

On that day the roses hung ripe, soft-fleshed, and so mouth-watering that he had simply fallen upon them, the music alive in his head, his skin hot and tingling. He thought of pink tongues and lollipops, and then warm, firm titties, full for sucking. The warmth of the earth rose up and smote him and all around flowers of every colour spread a path for his approach. The hibiscus came first, unwrapped lollipops to be taken in the open, translucent, exotic in the sun, silky and wet upon his tongue.

The first time tonguing, he did not hear Mama. She called him ten times that day and got no reply. But she was not cross with him when he finally entered the house, fresh from the garden. She was relieved. She saw the dark stains on his lips and judging that he had been gorging himself on otaheite apples again, pointed straight to the washstand where the pink Lifebuoy carbolic soap lay.

'Wash out your mouth,' Mama said then.

But there were other times. Mama did not say *wash out your mouth* when the rain tongued him, falling hard through the trees upon the grass, like horses on the rampage. He remembered the first day in it. The noise of the rain was like voices and music, Christmas paper torn and rustled, filling his ears. It was Mama's voice calling, but obliterated amid the rushing crystal-clear water. As the skies opened up, he had dashed out the back door, hidden in the violence and whiteness. It was shocking, joyful, making his heart churn.

'Boyd, get out of the rain!' Mama shouted frantically from the verandah, spying the small dripping shape, the first time it happened.

"E's soaked right through, ma'am,' the maid said, unbelieving, not understanding, grasping at him as he entered the kitchen.

Barrington said in code, *Stop acting like a fool, you. You're just asking for Papa to give you a beating.*

'Boyd, why did you stand in the rain?' Yvonne asked, genuinely concerned, as he was towelled down, and Bay Rum applied hurriedly and liberally about his body. She helped with the towelling, to prevent him getting pneumonia.

He only gave a half-smile, inhaling the Bay Rum. The question was impossible. Maybe when Yvonne was eight years old she would know the pleasure of rain, know what it was to be suspended in the universe, at the centre of things, with the mad rushing in the ears, yearning fiercely, deeply seeking, senses fired up, passions like red hot sunsets.

* * *

That night, following Mrs Moore's visit, he could not sleep. It was because of the new house smell, a trembling, delicate pink scent; the new feelings and the waiting for Pepsi. It was because of the moonlight silver on the verandah, the new dog asleep somewhere outside and the little slaps and cries from Mama's room. Mama and Papa had stayed up listening to the radio, the WINZEE station from America, and talking. He heard when they struggled off to bed in the late hours, when the sky was grey-blue. And he listened at Mama's door, as he often did, to the whispers and the strange sounds. He could see them clearly through the slit in the door. The moonlight came through the window and splashed the sheets on their side of the room. Papa was on top of Mama and fighting her, slapping her, hurting her. Mama was not fighting back. She was moaning deep in the sheets. He trembled barefoot at the door. He had thought that coming to Appleton would put a stop to it. He'd seen it happen many times at Worthy Park and wanted it to end. Now he knew there was no end to it.

He went back to bed. But it wasn't long before he walked dreamily out into the garden, into magnolia. The sun warmed his face and hands and he felt the urgent tug of the music, heard the voices whispering hush, hushh, hushhh.

When the music called, from deep in the pink core of him where feelings lived, he came into himself. During the evenings, at sunset, when he sat in the chintz armchair listening to the Mullard radio deep in arias and fugues and adagios and burst into quiet tears, he knew it would always be thus. Sometimes he was scared with the enormity of feeling, of not knowing, unable to find expression, drowning in melancholia.

'Miss Mama?' he remembered Aunt Enid saying.

Mama had two sisters, Aunt Amanda and Aunt Enid. Aunt Enid had the lemonade voice, frangipani scent and warm caresses. She was unmarried and without children, and loved Boyd. She exuded everything good. He had spent a week at her Kingston house where the garden was lush and a hammock hung from a St Julian mango tree. The days were nectar days and the sun like honey. The mango scents weakened his senses and Aunt Enid came to him in the warm afternoon in the garden, sat with him in the hammock so that they could look back at the house in the background and hear nothing. Her breasts were like soft toffee. He lapped at her and ate her and was smothered by her. And she took him to her without words. They were together in the silence. And there was no aching because there was no anguish. It was the first time he had been away from Mama and Papa. He was six years old.

'Miss Mama? Miss Papa?'

He smiled at her. She smiled back. She knew. And she stroked the soft part under his chin till he hung his head. He was in paradise, full of secret knowledge, in the music place where words were unnecessary. They slept together in the garden heat in the shade of the mango tree, and were only awakened towards evening by the maid, ringing the bell frantically for dinner.

* * *

Mrs Moore visited Mama almost every day during those first weeks at Appleton. She was a lonely woman, Papa said. All her cheerfulness and outward confidence was just a sham. But that meant nothing to Mama. Mrs Moore was a fresh breeze, a happy tune, the therapy she needed. At about ten o'clock each day the front door opened and in walked Mrs Moore, wearing her fruit-encrusted, camel-coloured felt hat and her spicy-camphor perfume. Under the drawing room window in the overgrown garden, Boyd heard the tinkle of cups, the clink of silver cake knives (Mama's wedding present from her father), the gushing conversation, Mrs Moore's jolly laughter and Mama's happy, girlish giggles. He heard the Mullard radio say '"Passing Strangers," by Billy Eckstine and Sarah Vaughan.' And the beat of his heart quickened because he heard the voices whisper the name of the girl who was coming soon, the girl whose lips were lollipop-red, *Pepsi, Pepsi, Pepsi.*

CHAPTER 3

Pepsi arrived at the beginning of the half term holidays. Her lips were lollipop-red, just as Boyd knew they would be, and black coils of hair sprouted about her head in magnificent profusion. She spoke about Mr and Mrs Moore as her "Abuelo" and her "Abuela", and about her school, Excelsior, on Mountain View Avenue in Kingston, where she was in the first form and very good at Spanish.

When Pepsi first visited, she sat, legs crossed, in Mama's bedroom, chin in hand, conversing like an adult while Eartha Kitt sang *Under the Bridges of Paris with you, I'd make your dreams come true.* Pepsi sang too. She was only twelve. When lemonade was served she did not pour it herself but waited, sitting upright, for Perlita. Not that Perlita minded. She was used to this type of behaviour from the alien visitors on the estate and from beatniks (her best description of Pepsi). Pepsi sipped her lemonade, unlike Yvonne, who took great gulps. She retreated to the bedroom with Mama where she hovered like a nurse, pretending that Mama had had the baby. She ran and fetched, applied Johnson's Baby Oil to all the places where it was to be applied, patted the pillows where they were to be patted and sighed with Mama as if she herself had burdens and unfulfilled dreams. When her job was done, Pepsi tiptoed behind Mama out of the room to languish on the verandah on the white rattan chairs. She languished there while the sun's rays crept lazily across the tiles, and while Barrington, who had suddenly developed a habit of being very attentive to

24

Mama, stood at the French windows with his hands in his pockets, watching.

Boyd lingered at the end of the verandah in the long grass, hoping to catch Pepsi's words, to glimpse her slender legs which ended in brown open-top shoes with loosely buckled straps, and sniff the adult scent of the Pond's Cold Cream that she wore. Her coming and her presence had already created dramas of epic proportions in his head. And in those dramas she fought with Estella and Lydia Parsons for his special attention.

'Pepsi!' a voice hollered from beyond the green hedge. 'Mrs Moore want you!' It was Icilyn, Mrs Moore's maid. 'Pepsi, where are you? Come now, you hear? Pepsi!'

Poppy rushed to the side of the house, barking hard, fazed by this reckless, disrespectful shouting in the quiet of mid-morning when the only sounds were radio sounds, the sublime voices and music of *Housewives' Choice*.

'Pepsiiii! Pepsiiii!' The voice seemed desperate.

Poppy was barking himself to death.

'Pepsiii! Mrs Moore want you. Come now. Pepsi! You hear me, chile?'

Pepsi took the steps down to the garden two at a time. Sunlight splashed her hair. Boyd, Barrington and Yvonne watched the thin-legged figure till it vanished in a dazzle of colour at the garden fence. What manner of girl was this?

The next day, in the long grass at the far end of the garden, hidden from the house, Pepsi came suddenly upon Boyd and Poppy. She found them gazing into air.

'Do you know what place this is?' Pepsi asked brusquely.

Boyd hesitated. They were a long way from the house, alone in the grass with Pepsi.

'This is where the slaves were beaten by the slave owners in slavery days,' Pepsi related. 'You live on a sugar estate and don't know that? They don't teach you these things at school because Jamaica is a colony and they want to keep you down, but my cousin who's at university told me. The women slaves were lashed with cat-o'-nine tails. Their clothes were ripped off.' Pepsi looked about. 'Have you ever seen a naked woman?'

Again Boyd hesitated, trying to make sense of the question.

'Not your mother. Everybody's seen their mother naked.'

Boyd didn't know what to say. He had his secrets and his reserve.

'Have you ever seen a naked woman who wasn't your mother?'

'Yes,' Boyd said. Poppy's tail waltzed slowly as if hypnotised.

'Who?'

He didn't want to say.

'Boyd, I said who? Who was it?'

Boyd was silent.

'It's your maid,' Pepsi told him.

Boyd nodded, with relief. He didn't want to talk about the fleshy, pink women in the encyclopaedia. He didn't know how to tell about them.

Pepsi laughed. 'Ha, ha. Boy. Spying on your maid. Disgusting. That is what you country boys do, spy on people. You were, weren't you?'

Boyd didn't answer.

'I said you were spying on her. Was it when she was undressing in her room? Tell me. I know what you people get up to.'

Boyd couldn't think, the air full of the women's lotion and earth smells.

'Did you spy on her when she was in the shower?'

Boyd nodded. She already knew. He had watched Perlita in the shower from a crack in the adjoining cubicle as she shrieked and gasped under the gushing water. It was her joyful shrieking and the rush of the water that had called him to her. He remembered the three tufts of black hair, her bouncing titties concentrating his eyes, the fleshy form that was woman, and he could not, did not want to stop looking. Later in the garden, in the sun amid the hot grass scent, he felt a wonderful but troubling excitement.

Pepsi laughed again. 'You quiet people are the worst. What did you see?'

Poppy had grown tired of the game and had gone off in a rush through the tall grass after a pair of game pea doves.

'I'm not going to tell anybody. I know what you little boys do. Whatever you tell me is between me and you, okay? When you spied on her, did you see her thing?'

'Yes,' Boyd replied slowly. He had seen many things.

Pepsi tittered. 'Do you know what the slave masters did to the slave women?'

'Beat them,' Boyd said quickly.

'Don't be stupid! It's what men do to women, don't you know? I'm not making it up. It's all in the books. The slave owner took out his teapot and put it in the slave woman's thing. Then she had babies. Did you know that?'

Boyd shook his head. He couldn't imagine how anybody's teapot could make babies. He only peed with it and knew that when he was bursting he had to go, that Perlita referred to the Vienna sausages at breakfast as "little boys' teapots", and that Mama always said, 'Did you wash your teapot?' after his bath if she didn't bathe him herself.

'It's how babies come,' Pepsi continued. 'Your mama and papa tell you that babies come from the stork? Well, that's a lie. Nobody comes from a stork. My cousin says that it's just to keep children ignorant. You put your teapot into the woman and a baby grows in her tummy until she has to go to the hospital for the doctors to take it out. My cousin studies biology and told me all about it. Every boy can do it, and every girl. It's how even dogs are born, but they don't have to go to the hospital. One dog gets on top of the lady dog and puts his thing into her, then after a while the lady dog has puppies. Your mama is going to have a baby soon. It's growing in her. But don't tell her what I told you.'

27

Pepsi drew close to Boyd in the grass. Her presence overpowered him. 'Show me your teapot,' she said. Her face was expressionless. 'Show it to me, Boyd.'

It was so sudden and unexpected that Boyd didn't hear it at first, especially as Poppy had reappeared, panting. Pepsi was so close to him that he could feel the hairs on her arms. But it was her eyes, forcing him down, that placed him where she wanted. His eyes fell upon small peeping lizards in the branches above. Their scarlet tongues jerked with astonishment at the scene beneath them.

'Show it to me,' Pepsi coaxed. 'I'm not going to tell anybody.'

Her fingers were at his trousers. They were surprisingly cool. Beyond the shade of the trees and the deep grass, out past the thick hedge where the house lay in radiant light, Perlita opened the kitchen door and Poppy, distracted by the possibility of food, raced away for the second time. Pepsi had raspberry breath; she was breathing with lips apart, and Boyd saw the pink of her tongue. Even if he could speak it would be impossible to ask her to stop. The buttons of his trousers were almost undone.

'Pepsiiii! Pepsiiii!' It was Icilyn at the fence again. 'Mrs Moore want you. Come now. Pepsiii! Pepsiii! Pepsi, you hear me? Don't be fresh, chile. Come now!'

The last Boyd saw of Pepsi were her slim legs, the wrinkled white of her shorts displaying grass stains, vanishing in the green. He stayed in the grass, in the close quiet, till the wind rustled the leaves, till the factory siren, the *cauchee*, screamed like a pig, lusty and terrible, dispensing the hot steam, finding a voice but not release. And Boyd pondered the many questions in his head but found no answers, only a deep bewilderment.

* * *

Mrs Moore didn't remain much longer at Appleton. At the end of the holidays, she and Mr Moore left with all their furniture piled high in a large Bedford truck, Pepsi waving long into the distance. Barrington wrote to her immediately, a letter of several pages, torn up and corrected a dozen times. Excelsior was the only school for him now, and come September he would take the train to live with the Moores in Kingston. It had nothing to do with Pepsi. Boyd was unruffled. The memory of Pepsi's lips, her lovely girl smell, girl laugh and girl looks, the seductive fearfulness and shocking danger of her were enough for him. He marvelled at the sound of her name, *Pepsi*, and the memory of the songs of the moment, "Under the Bridges of Paris", "Passing Strangers" and "Honeycomb", and he could not forget that instant in the long grass when time stood still.

Pepsi did not write back. Barrington returned to pretending to be grown-up, walking about with his hands in his pockets and looking serious with a furrowed brow. He also started to practise *dynamic tension*, something he'd read about in an advertisement featuring Charles Atlas, the body builder, at the back of a Roy Rogers comic.

Mama went back to listening to *Housewives' Choice* while she sewed and leafed through seventy-two pages of *Woman* magazine. But her thoughts were elsewhere.

'Nothing lasts forever,' she said to a pensive Boyd sitting next to her on the sofa. 'People come, people go. Everything comes to an end.'

'Why, Mama?' Boyd asked, feeling the weight of the words.

Mama, seeing his troubled look, tried to restrain herself, but was surprised as the words flowed from her, unstoppable. 'Well, darling, because it's true. Nothing lasts forever. Mrs Moore and Pepsi were here yesterday and now they're gone. We lived at Worthy Park and now we don't live there anymore. You used to see your Aunt Enid often but now we are too far away. I don't see my mother anymore either. And my father, your grandpapa, isn't alive anymore.' Here Mama stopped, aware that she'd said too much. Boyd said nothing but she sensed the enormity of his thoughts.

'Is Grandma going to die, Mama?'

'No, darling, of course not.' It was the only way to reply. She took him to her.

'Is Papa going to die, Mama?' Boyd's eyes didn't meet hers.

'No, darling!' Mama cuddled him closer and felt his tension. She kissed his cheeks. 'Papa will live to a hundred and that's too far away to even think about.'

'What about you, Mama? And Barrington, and Yvonne? And Poppy, and me?'

Mama gave a forced laugh, cuddled him even closer, and regretted having started the conversation. 'Don't be silly, my little *peeny-waalie*. No one's going to die. Little children don't die. Everything comes to an end but children are here forever and ever.'

Boyd said nothing more. But the words that mattered so much stuck in his memory. *Everything comes to an end. Nothing lasts forever.* And he remembered Grandpa Pratt, who they never saw again.

Mama wished she'd kept her silence, but she'd simply articulated what was uppermost in her mind. She missed Mrs Moore with her floral frocks and her jolly motherly talk and laughter. She missed the coffee mornings and the chance to use her silver service. She missed the social intercourse. And she started to complain that Papa never took her anywhere, not even to the club.

'What's the hurry?' Papa said.

'We've been here almost four weeks,' Mama told him, pained.

'People will think you have nothing to do at home if you're always at the club.'

'I don't want *always* to be at the club,' Mama replied, frustration breaking her voice. 'I just want to go there sometimes, meet new people, get out of *this house*.'

Papa grew tense at once and stopped speaking, hearing

the two words that infuriated him. He saw this as a direct criticism of his family management, of his implementation of the Brookeses master plan, which, as far as he was concerned, was receiving his full attention. *Some people would never understand.* He lit one of his Royal Blend cigarettes, breast heaving, dreadfully restrained, reading *The Daily Gleaner.* The only sound in the room was the vicious snap of the paper as he periodically turned the pages.

An hour later, at his bedroom window, Boyd saw parachuting dandelions fall into the oleander hedge as Pepsi walked away looking over her shoulder at him, her lips hot and beckoning. He also saw Papa get into the jeep and drive off in the direction of Siloah, the nearest town. At sunset, when the night noises were beginning to be heard, when the garden fragrances had drifted into the house, when The Chordettes sang "Eddie My Love" on the radio, Papa returned. He carried a small, mysterious package tied with silver string.

CHAPTER 4

Boyd saw Papa go to Mama, holding the small package behind his back as The Chordettes said, *Please Eddie, don't make me wait too long.* Later, he saw Mama standing in the middle of the room crying, just before Papa closed the bedroom door. The next day, they heard the news. Papa had bought Mama a bottle of *Evening in Paris,* her favourite perfume. *Soir De Paris, as lovely a perfume as money can buy,* the advertisements in the papers said. And finally, that Saturday evening, Papa took Mama to the club.

That night, Boyd heard when they returned. He heard their quick footsteps, muffled but excited voices, shoes falling to the floor. *Evening in Paris* drifted into his room. Soon he heard Mama call out. On tiptoe in the darkness he approached their bedroom door, peeped through the slit and saw Papa in his usual place on top of Mama. *They were making more babies.*

'The Moodies are very nice people,' Mama said at breakfast, looking lovely in a short-sleeved white blouse and round, white, clip-on earrings.

'They lived in England,' Papa said, as if the mere fact that they lived in England made them nice. Papa's respect and admiration for the English went deep. He accepted, a long time ago, that it was the unjust respect of the colonised for the coloniser, a matter of fact thing. It was the sort of respect that could only be righted or exorcised through true self-government or genuine social intercourse.

'We're having them for dinner on Saturday,' Mama gushed. She radiated such enthusiasm that the children sat open-mouthed. Yvonne, who could usually be relied upon for some irreverent comment, only wrinkled her nose. The visit to the club had worked wonders. Mama was blooming. At the club she had had several glasses of Babycham, loving the bubbles and the fizz and especially the picture of the prancing baby deer on the bottle's label. She talked excitedly about the interesting people she'd met. The children heard about Miss Hutchinson, poised and attractive, who wore clothes straight out of *Woman* magazine. She spoke with a cultured accent and had travelled widely in Europe, living in Paris and London. She smoked and drank, not Babycham but gin and tonic, and spoke French like the French, not like Jamaicans with dramatic flourishes and unusual nasal voices who thought they were speaking French. Papa said that she was a bohemian but a very nice bohemian. Then there was Miss Chatterjee, the youngest of the younger women, with a degree from London University. She, too, dressed in the most fashionable clothes, played better tennis than anyone, wore expensive perfume and was quite unattainable. All the men were in awe of her because she was impossibly haughty, but haughty in the manner of the young and impossibly beautiful. And one day at lunch a funny thing happened.

Mama said to Papa, 'Isn't Miss Chatterjee beautiful?'

Papa stammered uncharacteristically, almost choked, looked about guiltily, then back at Mama with lowered eyes. None of the children remembered whether he said yes or no, but they knew immediately that Miss Chatterjee had bowled him over too, like she did all the men, all of whom had sweet dreams about her. Mama had stared and said nothing, her lips suddenly drawn tight.

Other people at the club included Mr and Mrs Baldoo, a couple in their early forties, respectable and very well educated everyone said, always ready with gravely spoken sound advice. They clearly had *values* and *principles* in abundance, and Papa said so at the dinner table. There was

Mr Samms, suave, neatly turned out, and with very good manners ('A real gentleman,' Papa confirmed). There was Mr Dowding, tall, with a Clark Gable moustache; Mrs Dowding, ('A Betty Crocker cake mix woman,' Papa said. 'When she's not baking, she spends her time prying and interfering,') and their son, Dennis, who was mostly away at boarding school. The Pinnocks were boring and their daughter, Geraldine, was, 'A little show-off,' Papa said, because she played the piano in an affected manner. And finally there were the Moodies. Mr Moodie was the deputy assistant distiller.

Mama liked Patricia Moodie immediately because she felt safe with her. Patricia Moodie had no memory of yesterday and gave no caution to the present. She possessed a recklessness that Mama secretly admired.

'She's a flirt and only knows to dance the mambo,' Papa said mockingly, and then laughed as if he hadn't meant it. 'She doesn't belong in the country. Too pretentious.'

Mama had retorted girlishly. 'Well, I like her. She is a nice person, so gay, not stuck up.'

And so the Moodies came to dinner, driving what Barrington called a Buick. To Boyd and Yvonne, the red Buick was just an *American* car: big, flashy, with lots of sharp edges and pointed parts and much chrome, like the cheap, brightly coloured toys with *Made in Japan* printed on them. But it was a big talking point for Barrington. 'It's the only Buick on the estate,' he said, as if, somehow, all the other vehicles did not count. They could see that he was getting beyond himself because, as everyone knew, and Papa had said it, only English cars mattered. Only flashy people drove American cars. They stood out, both people and cars, drew attention, and were not to be taken seriously. Papa said it was like wearing plastic shoes when you could wear real leather shoes, made to fit.

Patricia Moodie laughed a lot, flashing white teeth and lovely large dark eyes. She wore small white gloves and a yellow silk dress. Her upper arms were brown and bare

34

and around her neck hung two strings of suckable pearls. She wore that deep-red lipstick with a hint of orange, just like Mama's. Boyd stared at her lips and felt that if they were sweets he would lick them and never stop. They were luscious lips, warm and seducing.

She caught him watching her with the longing eyes and said, smiling radiantly, 'Oh, hello, little Brookes,' embarrassing and exciting him all at once. She bent to stroke his cheeks and he saw her brown breasts and felt her mystery and bewitching. Memories of that day in Kingston with his Aunt Enid came back to him, the sensation of being so close to a grown woman in the scented heat.

Patricia Moodie's swing skirts swung about very much. Boyd imagined that there was an abundance of frilly cloth beneath her skirts. (Perlita later described the frills as *crinoline*, worn only by hoity-toity people.) His eyes strayed down, out of habit, to her agile ankles and the high-heeled shoes, *stilettos*, that said clip-clop every time she moved. He imagined her dancing the mambo and liked the movement of the swirling skirts, the rocking of the ankles and the tension in her calves. It was the last thing that he saw before Papa shooed him and Yvonne away to their rooms.

Stealthily, Boyd joined the night noises and the *peeny-waalies* in the dark under the window by the oleander bush. He caught the stream of Papa's Royal Blend cigarette and heard the clip-clop of Patricia Moodie's shoes.

'We take the diesel train into Kingston,' Patricia Moodie said from above him on the other side of the window. 'It's safer than going by car. And we always go first class to get away from the big-bottomed market women with their bundles of this and that.'

Boyd heard Mr Moodie roaring at something Papa said. The faster Mr Moodie drank, the louder his laugh became. His cigarette smoke and huge shadow shut out, for just a moment, the yellow light from the drawing room.

A quarter moon rounded the mountain so that the garden was no longer in deep blackness, as Boyd wished it, but in soft-blue blackness. He drew closer to the oleander bush, leaning hard against the warm, lower brick wall of the house.

'The Ward Theatre and the Little Theatre in Kingston for mainly local productions,' the clear voice of Patricia Moodie said from the other side of the room. 'Last year we saw Ivy Baxter's *Danse Elementale* and the Ballet Guild of Jamaica. Manjula Chatterjee was in the audience, such a nice surprise! And of course there is the Carib Theatre, which is really a cinema, for some international things. They sometimes use the hotels and the university auditorium because of lack of venues. In London there are so many theatres, so many concert halls, they're spoiled for choice. And they have good theatre, the best in the world. Moodie isn't interested in any of this. So uncivilised. *So uncivilised.* I don't know what to do with him. So many Jamaican men are without curiousity. Nothing interests them. Have you travelled, Victoria?'

Boyd didn't hear Mama's reply. Patricia Moodie did not wear *Evening in Paris*. She had lived abroad. But Mama, who had not lived abroad, did. It was her only perfume. *Evening in Paris* was for young mothers and nice girls. It was not frivolous or dangerous, but innocent, excitingly safe and loving. Patricia Moodie's risqué perfume came out of crystal bottles with gold tops and couldn't be bought at local shops.

Papa and Mr Moodie's shadows merged by the other window and Boyd moved closer.

'Harry, I know you know,' Mr Moodie said under his heavy gin and tonic breath. 'You hear the buggers at the club talking. You must have heard the rumours. I don't believe any of it, but, you know. That little shit.'

'Easy, easy,' Papa cautioned.

'No fucking shame! Loose! Loose!'

'Moodie!'

Boyd could feel Papa recoil. Mr Moodie had used a very bad word, the kind that the gardeners and labourers used when they thought no one could hear.

'She was dead set against coming to Appleton,' he heard Mr Moodie say. 'She's a town girl. Every day she threatens to take the train back to Queens Avenue. Dammit, if she wants to go back to Kingston, let her. Harry, I love it here. I am a country boy at heart. Estate life is good for me, you know what I mean?'

'I know exactly what you mean,' Papa said, after considering Moodie's question. 'But you've only been married a year. You need to talk. It's the only way. Women need a lot of sensitive handling.'

But Mr Moodie was no longer listening. He acknowledged to himself that it was rather a bad topic for the evening, a moment of weakness for a man like him, and changed the subject. 'I hear your name's down for the big house on the hill,' he said.

Papa laughed with relief. He had not been impressed with Moodie at all. Moodie needed to get a grip. He would much rather talk about his biggest project at the moment, upon which much depended: the new house on the hill. 'What else did you hear?'

It was Mr Moodie's turn to laugh. 'Harry, you deserve that house. Boy, you don't waste time. You'll probably get rid of that little American jeep of yours and get a Land Rover now, just like a proper estate *busha*.'

Papa chuckled. 'Maxwell-Smith's still on contract, but he's definitely going early. Moodie, that house was built for me. It was waiting for us. Gawd! Don't say anything at dinner, whatever you do. I haven't told Victoria yet, in case things don't work out. Y'know, no use raising her hopes.'

'Your secret is safe with me, *busha* Brookes,' Moodie said, downing another stiff gin and tonic and casting his wife a swift, glowering look.

That night Boyd dreamt of a house, set among perfectly drawn trees with leaves like green clouds, in a forest full of mystery, with a winding white road leading to it, the pink house of the Maxwell-Smiths.

CHAPTER 5

The Maxwell-Smiths were an English family. Papa said they were English because they said "Tay" instead of "Tea" and didn't socialise. To get to their pink house meant driving across the black metal bridge over the Black River. It meant driving up the white road between green pastures with guango trees and Brahman bulls on every side, up beyond the tree-lined path, through heavy whitewashed wooden gates on estate-manufactured hinges and onto a driveway, to the right of which lay an expanse of emerald-green lawn. Where the lawn ended there loomed the impressive pink house with the red roof. An English car, a Wolseley, burnished-grey with coffee-coloured leather upholstery, sat just outside the gleaming whitewashed garage in the shade of giant papaya trees.

This pink house, a delicate pink that appeared white in the heat, with its exotic red roof, gleamed and winked during the day. The children, on the verandah of their green and cream house on the opposite side of the valley, gazed longingly at it because it looked like a picture in a book. Papa contemplated it over his test tubes and Bunsen burner at the factory. He looked at it from the open-top jeep on the way home each evening. And he studied it from the verandah of the house he now despised, the house that did not do justice to his station.

'Inez going to Englan' with Mrs Maxwell-Smith,' Perlita announced breathlessly at breakfast, as she served up fried dumplings and burnt Vienna sausages for the fourth morning in a row. 'She travelling by BOAC, ma'am, by aeroplane!'

Papa and the children's heads went up in a single motion. The children were fascinated with the new dumplings, small, round, the size of golf balls. They loved them. Papa's head went up for another reason.

'Is that so?' he said, with magnificent restraint. He'd been struggling not to tell Perlita to pack her bags. But she was lucky that day. Perlita's younger sister, Inez, worked for the Maxwell-Smiths at the pink house.

'Yes, sar,' Perlita said. 'She buying grip and getting her passport. She going to Englan', sar, Englan'! The Queen, Buckingham Palace, Big Ben!'

'So when is she leaving?' Papa enquired casually.

'The first week of July, sar. It all planned. She going to bettah herself in Englan', where the Queen live. Travelling by BOAC, sar.'

Perlita held a dishcloth in one hand and a heavy wooden tray in the other. She smelled of Vim and coconut oil. It was her only smell; Vim from scouring the saucepans and the sweet coconut oil from all the frying. She wanted to talk and there was much to tell. Mama and the children were studies in curiosity. Papa ate, not looking up, the muscles in his temples working away.

'I see,' he said finally.

'Yes, sar, ma'am, she going to bettah herself. She can't sleep. The poor chile so excited. Mrs Maxwell-Smith leaving me some of her clothes, nice things, shoes and such. And Mista Maxwell-Smith is a very nice man, y'know, sar? Him leaving us a clock, crockery and other things as well. English people sooo nice.'

'Coffee,' Papa said curtly, giving Perlita one of his hard looks.

'Ah bring in the pot right away, sar.' And off she went, her flip-flops flip-flopping noisily against her bare heels.

Yvonne, forehead wrinkled, asked, 'Are we going to England, Papa?'

'England?' Papa eyed Yvonne with his customary mixture of pity and amusement. 'Only poor people go to

England,' he said. 'The kind who don't know how to use their knives and forks; people who sit with their elbows on the table, who speak with food in their mouths, who yawn without putting a hand to their lips. Did you hear me, all of you?'

'Yes, Papa,' the children said in unison, snapping to attention.

'Those are the kinds of people who pack their grips and go to England, to better themselves, as they say. And God knows they need to better themselves. The men have names like Delroy, Elroy, Glenroy, Alphanso, Adolphus and Wilfred. And the women are called Icilda, Delcita, Agatha, Esmeralda and,' Papa thrust his chin in the direction of the kitchen and lowered his voice, 'you know who.'

'Perlita,' Yvonne chirped innocently.

Papa glared at her. 'Eat your breakfast,' he said.

'Aunt Leah's daughter, Bunny, went to England, to Cambridge University,' Mama said, not looking at Papa. 'And cousin Astley, too. They're not exactly poor people.'

Papa pretended to scowl at her, putting up two fingers. 'All right. Only two types of people go to England. A few students to university. Mainly to London, Cambridge or Oxford. They are from good families and come right back home with their names in *The Daily Gleaner* against a BA, an MA or a PhD, and take up respectable positions in education, medicine, law or the government. All the rest, the great mass of them with their brown grips, their white shoes, the women especially, flashy hats and badly made double-breasted flannel suits, are poor people. English people think that these are the only Jamaicans that exist. They think that all Jamaicans are like you know who.' He glared at Yvonne. 'Can you imagine a thing like that? Gawd. They go up to England and disgrace the rest of us with their bad behaviour. It's always in the English newspapers. The best people stay at home and build the country. Poor people go to England to work. And they never go by BOAC, only by boat. Why? Everyone of them

40

as poor as a hungry mongoose.'

Yvonne laughed out loud and repeated, 'Poor as a hungry mongoose.' She would repeat it throughout the day until someone said 'Shh!' and 'That's enough!' She laughed then and everyone joined in, even Perlita, listening in at the kitchen door on one leg.

'Hmm,' Mama said. 'Men from Lluidas Vale have been going to England by boat for years, leaving their poor wives behind.'

'See what I mean?' Papa said. 'By their behaviour you shall know them. They leave their wives and children here in Jamaica, go over to England and shack up with English women. They have another half dozen children but never stay around long enough to accept their fatherly responsibilities. That's poor people for you, reckless, irresponsible.'

'They do well in England by the look of it,' Mama said. 'They send home money for relatives; a guinea here, a guinea there, which goes a long way. And parcels too, with English clothes, woollen hats and coats and furry boots.'

'Sending woollen hats and furry boots to a hot country,' Papa said with contempt. 'What they should be doing is getting an education. They don't have to pay for it in England, thanks to a Labour government. But I bet you tuppence that all they do is sit on their behinds in rum bars. They call them pubs over there. They're not going to England to become lawyers or doctors or big shots. Mark my words. A few may, if they buckle down. But most of them will go to what they know: cleaning houses, driving buses, lazing about at the betting shop and thieving. Why? Well, you can take a person out of the pigsty but you cannot take the pigsty out of a person. That is what poor is.'

'Is Inez poor?' Yvonne asked the question they all wanted to ask. They weren't sure about Inez and Perlita, who ate three meals every day, wore clean clothes and were given heaps of money in a brown envelope on Fridays. If anyone was poor it surely must be people like Mr Rawhog, who lived in the gutter with bloodshot eyes, wet, red lips and a stench so revolting that even dogs backed away. But he wasn't going to England.

'Well, she's going to England but she's certainly not going to university,' Papa said under his breath. Fresh coffee aroma drifted into the room.

'Where's the coffee?' Papa thundered.

'Coming, sar,' a high-pitched voice shot back from the kitchen, triggering utensil sounds, slamming of cupboard doors and the turning on and off of taps.

'Are we poor?' Yvonne asked, her confused face turned towards Mama, hoping to get an answer that was not suspect.

'Out of the mouth of babes,' was all Mama said, as if some fundamental question had been answered.

Papa laughed a whooping laugh, his voice echoing in the pantry, head thrown back. 'Are we poor? Well, we don't have stupid, frilly crochet stuff, glass animals and plastic flowers on our coffee table. And you don't go to government schools. You're not poor if you are educated, speak proper English, dress correctly and don't behave like *dark people.*'

Papa had strong views about *dark people*. They were people who were constantly leaning up against a wall, a tree, a door or anywhere. They didn't stand tall and straight. Such people were weak of character. They crowded outside betting shops with beer bottles in their hands, used bad words like *rass clart* and *blood clart*, and had little or no education. Jamaica was full of them. *Dark people* were decidedly worse than *those people* because, in addition to *values and principles*, they also lacked genuine ambition and were narrow-minded. In Papa's book they were the lowest of the low. Many of them, trying their luck, were taking the boat to England, to places like Birmingham and Manchester, dressed up in ill-fitting clothes and carrying huge brown grips. Good riddance to them too.

'You'll be poor if you don't study your lessons,' Papa

warned. 'All this fooling about on the verandah will get you nowhere. You'll end up like little ragamuffins.'

'They need a good school,' Mama sighed, 'as good as Worthy Park Prep.'

'You know it's at the top of my list, the very top,' Papa told her irritably. There's a Catholic prep at Balaclava but it's very expensive. That's the place I'm thinking of.' He turned to the children who were listening intently. 'Don't buckle down to your work and I will put you on the streets to beg your bread. Let me tell you, you and you.' He pointed a threatening finger at each of them in turn.

Hearing this, Perlita stepped forward. 'Sar, my niece, Ina, go to Teacher Fraser school in Taunton.' For a moment she'd hesitated, then she came right out with it, convinced she was helping her employer. 'Is a good school, sar. She get good eddication, sar, good eddication. Teacher Fraser is no fool.'

'Thank you, Perlita,' Mama said, hoping to spare her, anticipating Papa's response.

Yvonne's eyes lit up instantly. 'Papa, why can't we go to Ina's school?'

'Yvonne, look at me,' Papa said with a basilisk stare, his forehead deeply lined. 'There are other schools. You hear me, other schools.'

Yvonne seemed confused. 'But why can't we go to Ina's school?'

'That's not the school for you.'

'But, why?' Yvonne spread her arms indignantly.

'Because I say so.'

Yvonne persisted. 'But, why?'

'Go to your rooms and read your books,' Papa growled, waving them away.

'But we haven't done anything!' Yvonne was dumbstruck.

'You've done enough. Get away!'

* * *

That night, Mama and Papa sat on the verandah talking, a half-moon contemplating them. They sat in nocturnal warmth, breathing roseapple and guinep. Their words drifted into the room where Boyd lay in bed under the covers.

'Barrington will go to Munro College in September,' Papa was saying. 'And he'll eat well there because they've just advertised in *The Daily Gleaner* for a new catering matron. I'm not sending him to that government school at Taunton. Full of riff-raff.'

'But it's so far,' Mama said, thinking of Barrington living away from home.

'Baldoo thinks Munro is the best private secondary school in St Elizabeth, in the country; and the Balaclava Academy the best prep in the parish. It's where that young Miss Casserly teaches. A lot of Chinese and white children go there; the Lee's children, the Cadien's, the Lyn's and the Jureidini's. Boyd will start in September. Yvonne, next year.'

Lying in the dark, Boyd's excitement and anxiety grew.

'But the expense,' he heard Mama say.

Papa inhaled harshly. 'They think they're on holiday because they haven't gone straight to a new school. I'll get a private tutor to brush them up before next term and get Yvonne a few more books. Keep her busy with reading, writing and arithmetic.'

'When they go back to school they'll settle down,' Mama said.

There was a pause. Then Papa's voice took on a restrained, meaningful tone. 'Victoria, you know I'll always look after you. And I'm not saying this because I've been drinking. Yes, you know I can sometimes be a bit hard, but that's only to make sure the children understand that life isn't a bed of roses. They think everything comes easy. As long as you are a black person in this country you have to work three times as hard as other people to get anywhere. English people with half your experience and brains come out here and before you know it, they take over. In two ticks they're in charge. It's not right.'

'You work very hard, I know,' Mama told him. 'Harold, I want to help, I can –'

'Victoria, you cannot help. This is my responsibility as head of the house. And that's not complaining. It's just a fact.'

'But you have us!' Mama was emphatic. 'Harold, you are not on your own.'

Papa chuckled. 'I don't need help. My father knew what he was doing when he spent all the money he had on my education and all the time he had on his women. With education you can go anywhere, face anyone. You can stand on your own two feet. I disowned my mother and her side of the family because they chose to be peasants, without ambition. I am a motherless child, Victoria, a loner. I want the best for the children. They will be everything we have ever dreamed about. I'll work my fingers to the bone, for you, for them. I have my faults but, in the final analysis, I will succeed because I take my responsibilities seriously, you know...'

Papa's voice trailed off, replaced by Mama's reassuring words. 'Harold, I know. You do your very best. You're a good man.'

The clink of glasses came to Boyd's ears and he breathed Papa's Royal Blend cigarette, the ultimate adult scent. From the drawing room the Mullard radio and WINZEE brought the music of America into his room, the melodious tones of Dean Martin, *Memories are made of this*. The music was like a warm caress.

And that night, Boyd, made apprehensive by Papa's words, surrendered to the soft caress of the pink women from the pages of the *American People's Encyclopaedia*. His dreams, ecstatic, were of a school full of Chinese and white children, of pretty girls like Pepsi and teachers like Miss Casserly. And fleshy pink women were on every page of his reading books. Throughout the following day, in the quiet of his room he sought out these voluptuous creatures hidden away in the heavy volumes. These were not the

45

Lydia Parsons, Pepsis or Estellas who made his heart leap and imbued his thoughts with the scent of lilies and pretty music. The pink women frightened and impassioned him. They called him to them day after day and made him very guilty of acts that he had no knowledge of. Their pink bodies, like untouched flowers in the heat in a secret place, astonished, tormented and absorbed him. And they made his head hurt with a fever. But he wanted to be with them, to feel the pain of pleasure and misery. That was what they did to him.

Papa said the *American People's Encyclopaedia* wasn't half as good as the *Encyclopaedia Britannica*. Even the name was more authoritative. The *Encyclopaedia Britannica* was the encyclopaedia to have, as all educated people knew. But he bought the *American People's Encyclopaedia* one evening from a travelling salesman who had demonstrated that any of the volumes could be suspended by holding on to a single page. Boyd had witnessed the impressive demonstration with Papa after supper. The salesman had stroked the demonstration copy of the encyclopaedia full of the knowledge of mankind, covered in sumptuous burgundy leather. The smell filled the room.

'Let your boy have a look at the book, suh.'

The salesman had handed over the heavy object, sensing, from the moment he arrived, the eyes of the small boy upon him and the contents of his grip. He understood children and knew that they could make the difference between a wasted journey and a productive one. 'The encyclopaedia is a university, suh. If you want it, suh, it's in there, everything, more than the teachers themselves know.'

Papa made up his mind on the spot, taking delivery of the *American People's Encyclopaedia* two weeks later. And Boyd lived in the books after that. He spent hours gazing with shocking curiosity and longing at the *Birth of Venus* and at the other nude women among the pages. These women with their lolling breasts, fleshy buttocks and thighs reminded him of Mama. There were many pictures of babies clinging to breasts, in pensive poses, eyes dreamy, full of contentment from the full titties, reminding him of himself when he was little. Women were everywhere, in tight bodices with creamy breasts pouring out like dough. Some of the pink women had dark patches of hair at their vital spots. He did not know why but the thatch of dark hair on the women's bodies triggered troubling enquiry and a curious yearning. He struggled to know their significance. And the names of the painters of these pictures fascinated him – Titian, Michelangelo, Botticelli, Goya, Raphael, Poussin, Clouet. They were names that he could not pronounce but imagined that he could. And always his thoughts were pulsating and hot. And Perlita was there too, her big titties bouncing under the shower, shocking, disturbing, wonderful.

* * *

That Friday evening at their green and cream Appleton house, Perlita washed up the dinner things and put them away after a day full of imperfections. She was in her room preparing for home when Papa appeared by the side gate, blocking her path. His hands were on his hips. Perlita must have known everything was up because she started crying – a terrible wailing and howling, so terrible that Mama rushed out wringing her hands. Dogs began to bark from miles away and others nearby joined in. Perlita dropped her bags and Papa, waiting for that very moment, pounced. Six large fried fish, red snappers, covered in onions and red peppers, presented themselves, wrapped in newspaper. They lay on their sides unhappily, eyes vacant.

'Why is Perlita crying, Mama?' Yvonne asked.

Mama did not reply, her eyes fixed on Papa.

Perlita appealed to Mama. 'We are poor people, ma'am. Ah have brothers and sisters to feed. It won't happen again, ma'am. Ah will pay for it out of me wages. Is only a few fish, ma'am.'

47

Big mistake. Perlita miscalculated. Those fish were not a *few* fish. They were a hundred thousand fish and they were not just fish. They represented Papa and everything he stood for. They were the shirt off his back. They were his fish, his children's fish, his wife's fish, his sweat and blood and everything else too, and nobody was going to spirit them off like that. Perlita was history.

'Ah beg you, ma'am, sar. Please, please.' Perlita's pleases tumbled out without self-respect. 'Please, sar, please, sar. Ah won't do it again, sar.'

Her begging made everyone uncomfortable. Mama turned towards Papa who was pointing to the opened gate beneath the logwood tree at the side of the house, dark now in the congealed, dying sun. She saw Papa's implacable face and knew that there was absolutely no hope. Perlita saw it too and in that moment revealed herself. Fierce malevolence came from her eyes.

'You black *Neaga*, you.' She glared at Papa. 'You wicked *ol' Neaga*. God going strike you down!'

'What is *Neaga*, Papa?' Yvonne's sudden question revealed her innocence. It was not a term used at the dinner table and not one that came easily to Papa's lips. People like him knew that such an expression belonged firmly in the vocabulary of *dark people*. Perlita was simply behaving true to type.

'She's ignorant,' Papa growled, his face blue-black with indignation. 'She means Negro. And she probably doesn't know that she's just described herself.'

It was the last time they saw Perlita, wiping her red snapper fish eyes as she gathered up her belongings, reduced now, and went out through the gate, not once looking back. As the gate closed behind her, the last weak streaks of sun disappeared, plunging the verandah into purple darkness.

CHAPTER 6

A few days after Perlita left, Poppy barked up such a racket that everyone ran for the front door. A woman stood on the bottom steps of the verandah with a huge grip in one hand. From where they stood, just inside the door, her perspiration assaulted their senses. Poppy sniffed the air noisily, haughtily. *Could this be the new maid?*

'Ah come for the work, mo'om,' Agatha said, for it was she.

'Agatha?' Mama asked, to make sure it wasn't someone else.

'Yes, mo'om,' Agatha answered. 'Agatta Mac, mo'om.'

The children noticed the maid's pronunciation of her own name. ('Put your tongue between your teeth to pronounce *th*,' Papa always said.)

'Did you come all the way from Santa Cruz?'

'Yes, mo'om. Ah took the bus halfway.'

'Come in,' Mama said.

Agatha's steps were ponderous and uncertain as she made her way through the drawing room. Barrington was nimble enough to catch a small vase as it fell in her wake. Corner tables and occasional chairs somehow got in her way. The curtains between the dining room and the pantry deliberately reached out to detain her. Once again it was Barrington, seeing the impending calamity, who leapt forward and prevented further damage. Boyd and Yvonne exchanged looks of alarm at this strange, unintentional recklessness, and fanned out before and beside her to protect her and the furniture. Poppy sniffed high and low.

When they got Agatha into the kitchen, Mama made ginger tea and sat her down at the kitchen table. Another piece of theatre took place. Agatha fumbled with the teacup. Tea splashed into the saucer. They saw her gnarled fingers, too big for the handle of the cup. Finally she got the cup to her lips, watched by four pairs of eyes. Only Mama had the grace to look elsewhere. Poppy was the main culprit, staring Agatha down, eyes following every action, head ascending and descending with each movement of her hand. He was also the first to recoil when she started to slurp. These were not reluctant slurps but vicious, deliberate slurps, the very things Papa warned against, the slurps of *those people*. 'They know no better,' Papa often said, referring to *those people* of whom Agatha was one, and at the same time giving notice that children didn't slurp at the table or anywhere else, and that if he ever caught them doing such a thing, well, they knew what. Agatha had already lost important points. Then she burped. Not once, but three times, each one fiercer than the first. And they knew she was doomed before she started.

After tea, Agatha clarified two things. She was Seventh Day Adventist and intended going to church every Saturday. 'To do God's work, mo'om.' And she insisted on Fab to wash the clothes. 'Is what them use in foreign, mo'om.'

Fab was popular with the maids on the hill. They liked it because it smelled nice and created sparkling white suds, not like the heavy brown soap bought in squares from village shops. Fab was the new detergent from abroad, from *foreign*, that the Queen at Buckingham Palace used, and film stars too, that *The Daily Gleaner* in its pages proclaimed as *giving the brightest clean. It just takes away the dirt.* All the maids wanted soap to "take away" the dirt. They didn't want to spend back-breaking hours over a scrubbing board and evil-smelling water. Fab was just so fab.

'Fab or Tide, whichever you prefer,' Mama said.

Agatha smiled. Mama couldn't settle the church issue, but Papa would.

When Papa arrived, the landscape gold, lamps glowing from every house on the hill, families settling down to dinner, Agatha was safe in her room reading her Bible. Her lamp cast broken shadows on the wall. Papa would interrogate her in the morning.

That evening, Mama served up hot Fry's cocoa and ginger biscuits in the drawing room. She read *The Star* while Papa read *The Daily Gleaner*. The children sipped their cocoa and barely breathed while on the radio, very softly, Cathy Carr sang, *Come down, come down from your Ivory Tower.*

'The poor man.' Mama reached a hand to her breast, horrified.

'What?' Papa did not look up from his paper.

'"Mr Donald Lee,"' Mama read out. '"Shopkeeper of Water Lane, Kingston, was shot three times in the chest by a burglar on Friday night last. Mr Lee and his wife were awakened in the middle of the night by noises outside the shop window and turned on the light to investigate. The burglar fired two storeys up, hitting Mr Lee. He died on the spot. Mr Lee leaves a wife, Esmie, two daughters and a son."'

'The mistake was to turn on the light,' Papa observed.

'The poor wife and children,' Mama lamented, on the verge of tears.

'If you should hear anything suspicious in the middle of the night, never turn on the lights,' Papa warned. 'Why? That is the excuse the criminals are looking for. You'll be in the light and they'll be in the dark. Shoot you down dead.'

'At least it only happens in Kingston,' Mama said.

'Out here in the country mad people will chop you up with machetes,' Papa replied.

'Don't frighten the children. The last time someone went mad was in Lluidas Vale and that was ten years ago, and he didn't harm anyone. Alphanso Robinson was his name. He was wandering about the district naked, for several days.'

'With a name like that no wonder he went mad,' Papa tried to joke. 'No family to look after him, probably all living in Birmingham, England.'

The children trembled. Boyd strained his ears to hear Mitch Miller and "The Yellow Rose of Texas" from the golden depths of the Mullard radio. The songs came from a magical place, far from their sombre drawing room. Outside, the night seemed to be crawling with burglars, waiting to shoot them down in cold blood or chop them up with the machetes the cane-cutters used. Poppy's plaintive cry gave credence to the picture building up. He barked low, frightened low, and kept on scratching against the back door.

'What's wrong with that dog?'

'He had his dinner,' Mama said, as if dogs only barked when they were hungry.

Papa was looking straight into the dining room and out through the green jalousies at the end of the room. Suddenly he bounded in a single movement into the pantry.

'Fire!' Papa cried out, in a new voice that they did not know.

He switched on the kitchen lights, flinging the back door open. In bounded Poppy, tail in a spin. In came the night air and out they all went behind Papa. The sky seemed like a red inferno. It was Agatha's room. Shadows leaped like demons behind the windows and red flames shot out from the opened door. Agatha herself stood away from the building, Bible in hand, praying aloud.

'Lawd Jesus! Lawd Jesus!' she kept muttering, oblivious of Papa, who rushed by her. 'Help me, oh Lawd! Help me, oh Lawd!'

Papa attached the writhing pink hose to the outside tap while Barrington, full of purpose, turned the handle all the way out. The water shot up in a white jet and they could hear it hitting the wooden walls. Papa got as far as the door but fresh flames leaped out.

'Back, back!' Papa commanded, wrestling with the hose. Everyone clustered round Mama on the back verandah as Papa, in a heroic stance, mastered the flames. Barrington crouched as if awaiting another call to action. Agatha remained in the shadows, slapping her Bible with open palms and stomping about on the spot. A dreadful, burnt-wet smell hovered in the air and settled into their clothes.

Agatha left at midday the next day, teary-eyed, her shadow slow on the ground. She did not hurl fierce malevolence at them, as Perlita had done, but went meekly, clearly filled to overflowing with the Biblical promise that the meek would inherit the earth.

As Agatha departed, the estate carpenters arrived, sawing, hammering and planing until a new building appeared at the end of the day. But Mama's brows wrinkled because she remembered Mrs Moore's words: *Without a good maid, it's difficult to run an estate house.* And Papa avoided discussing the matter because both his first and his second domestic appointments had failed spectacularly.

At this time, several very concerned older women at the club took Mama under their wing and described the difficulty they, too, had had in finding a competent maid.

'Oh, yes,' one woman said, 'there are plenty of maids about. But can they cook, wash and iron? Can they take instruction? What about their hygiene?'

'It's a tricky business,' another woman, more serious-looking than the first, said. 'You can find a girl who can cook like your mother but who has the most disgusting personal habits. And it's not unknown to find them as clean as Sunlight soap but with the brains of an imbecile. Most are as *dark* as anything, not having completed elementary school or worse, unable to read or write. Watch out for those. They are the ones who believe in *Duppies* and *Rolling Calves*. Send them packing at once!'

'The best way to go about finding the right sort,' the most concerned of the older women said, 'is to employ them and watch their every move like a hawk. Search their rooms when they aren't there. Keep a watch on their coming and going and the type of visitors they entertain. At the first sign of trouble, too much *Bush* tea drinking, food missing, bedclothes, cutlery and worse, money, fire them on the spot!'

These older women who advised Mama had spent an extraordinary amount of time on the subject of maids. It was the main topic of conversation at their dinner parties and at the club. Some of them, after many years at the estate, had still not found the right maid. A hardened group, the most serious of the concerned women, held committee meetings to discuss the maid problem, the one problem that completely bedevilled them. Mama listened politely and smiled a great deal, but she wanted to get away from their company.

And Papa reassured Mama, saying that they were bound to find the right maid soon. Thieves and Bible-reading ignoramuses just wouldn't do. And he made urgent enquiries at the factory through his dubious intermediaries.

* * *

Two maids came and went in quick succession, lasting only four days between them. The first, Edilyna, burnt through three of Papa's shirts during the ironing and burnt breakfast, lunch and dinner. Papa fired her after dinner on the first day. The second, Lurlene, took two hours to prepare breakfast and seemed completely exhausted on her feet. She fell asleep at the kitchen sink on the second morning. 'Sleeping sickness,' Papa said. Lurlene was given her wages on the third day when she was found seriously nodding off in front of the red-hot cooker. And then there was Melvyna.

Melvyna, the fifth maid, came up from Lacovia with all her belongings crammed in a large *bankra* on her head, and her face drenched in perspiration from the long walk.

Mama commented on the attractiveness of the *bankra* and said she had seen very attractive baskets at the Victoria Crafts Market in Kingston but none came close to Melvyna's. Melvyna was well pleased and promised Mama a *bankra* of her own, as her brothers back in Lacovia made the baskets themselves to sell at the local markets. She was quick of eye and swift of motion, preparing breakfast, polishing the furniture and getting down to the washing before anyone was awake. Mama had to restrain her. She made a promising start.

And so, on a Sunday evening with the scent of boiling sugar in the air, Melvyna pushed Yvonne's pram along the paved roads, with the children all round her in their Sunday clothes. She wore a floral dress that Mama had given her, a wide-brimmed, black straw hat and white shoes. Yvonne's big pink doll with the corn-yellow hair sat in the pram. Sometimes, when she got tired, Yvonne sat in the pram with the doll in her lap.

Barrington wanted to walk by Geraldine Pinnock's house. He didn't say so himself, he just walked in that direction as if he had no particular interest in going there, and Melvyna followed. Geraldine Pinnock was only eleven years old but she was going to be a concert pianist like Winifred Atwell. That September she was off to the Hampton School for Girls, which was not far from Munro College, Barrington's new school. All evening long she played the piano but didn't appear on the verandah. Barrington had his hands in his pockets and observed the house from under uninterested brows, but Boyd knew where his heart was. He and Yvonne picked roseapples near Mr and Mrs Moore's old house and paid no attention whatever to Melvyna's entreaties to be orderly and to pick, if they had to pick, only the ripe apples. The roseapple smell and taste mesmerised them. They had never seen so many lovely roseapples hanging from a single tree before.

They crossed the railway tracks to gaze down into the river, saw the strong current dragging long grass and reeds along the banks, and held Poppy tight to prevent him falling in. Poppy, excited to the full, made little darting movements between their legs as if he would rush headlong into the water but always pulled up at the last minute.

'If him not careful him will end up at Black River,' Melvyna warned.

'But this is the Black River,' Yvonne told her, pointing into the dark, swiftly moving water and glancing at Poppy with some concern. Out of the corner of her eye she could see that Boyd seemed hypnotised by the silent power of the water. None of them could swim and she didn't think Poppy could either. He was just a small dog. Maybe when he was a grown-up dog he would learn to swim.

'Black River is a town where the river go,' Melvyna told them. 'They sell ice cream in little white boxes from a white van in the street down there. And you eat the ice cream with wooden spoons.'

'Wooden spoons!' Yvonne was disgusted.

'Let your Papa drive you down there and you will see.'

'Ice cream spoons,' Barrington informed them authoritatively. He had been to the estate manager's garden party for big children. At that party, Geraldine Pinnock, in her white silk dress, dark plaited hair and black patent leather shoes with the button at the side, had played the piano. Everybody had eaten ice cream, not with boring old silver spoons but with cute little wooden spoons like they used in America. It was the latest thing. They even had Coca-Cola, that new dark drink in the curvy bottle.

'You know nothing,' Barrington told Yvonne.

By the time they got in sight of home, Yvonne was doubled up in pain. She was moaning and holding her stomach, her forehead contorted and sweating.

'Eating green roseapple,' Melvyna deduced, with a look of sadness. She knew her fate and was resigned to it. She would be blamed for letting the children eat unripe fruit while she was in charge. It was a sacking offence.

Mama put Yvonne to bed and told off Melvyna, mostly with bad looks.

'But ma'am, but ma'am,' Melvyna protested. She dreaded Papa coming home and finding Yvonne in her wretched state.

Melvyna went to bed early, but not before she begged Mama, almost on bended knees, to let her prepare hot *Cerasee* tea, a special concoction she knew of. Yvonne, the poor chile, would be better in no time. If that didn't work she knew how to make a *Fever Grass* drink, another special concoction. Mama said no. But, Melvyna desperately wanted to know, what about a little *Bissy* tea, or *Leaf of Life* tea with nutmeg? Certainly not, Mama told her. Not even a little *Bush* tea, ma'am? Melvyna was persistent: Yvonne would be better before you could say *hallelujah, tenk you Jesus*! Mama again told her no. Depressed, she sat up in bed reading her Bible. She and the house were fast asleep when Papa finally arrived well past ten o'clock. So she escaped his wrath that night.

'Man not made to fly in plane,' Melvyna told them, as she served dinner the following evening. There was a story in the newspapers about rich Jamaicans, especially those from Upper St Andrew, flying regularly to Miami to shop. It was all the rage. Buying clothes at *Couture Jamaique* or *Issa's* was not good enough for them. Melvyna seemed really put out. 'If God want man to fly he would give him wing, like bird.'

'You plan to go abroad, Melvyna?' Papa asked.

'No, sar!' Melvyna exclaimed, astonished. 'But if ah was to go to Englan' ah would go by boat.'

'By boat,' Papa smiled. 'So, that's okay with God?'

'You can laugh, sar,' Melvyna said, seeing the funny side. 'When God come we all have to answer, sar. *When the roll is called up yonder ah will be there.*'

'Another Bible woman,' Papa said under his breath when Melvyna returned to the kitchen. 'Where do they come from?'

'You should know,' Mama replied, knowing that Papa's contacts at the factory supplied the maids.

'I have nothing against a Bible-reading person,' Papa mumbled. 'I just don't want them knocking on the door day after day. We go to church, the *Anglican* church, and read our Bibles, on special Sundays anyway. It's those Pocomania people, y'know, and all that ignorant stuff they come out with that I'm really against. When they get possessed with the spirit you never know what they'll do. Remember Agatha? I don't want them coming here and filling the children's heads with all that ignorance. It's okay for those *dark people* who live in places like Look Behind, Quick Step and Pisgah.'

'And Lacovia,' Yvonne said.

The next day, after Melvyna had left the dining room, Papa reported something he'd heard at the factory: that she was active in one of the revivalist churches and could be practicing *Obeah*.

'What?' Mama's hand flew to her lips.

'What's *Obeah*?' Yvonne didn't look up from her egg custard, which was covered in cinnamon.

'It's what the Pocomania people do,' Barrington replied. 'Evil spirits.'

Papa was about to correct him when Melvyna appeared at the door.

'You call me, sar?' She stood quite still.

'No,' Papa said, startled.

'You sure, sar?' Melvyna was unblinking.

'Yes, yes, go back to your supper.'

'If you sure, sar.' Melvyna returned to the kitchen.

Papa shook his head, unbelieving. Everyone turned to him and back to the empty space at the door where Melvyna had been, expecting her suddenly to materialise. Not a sound came from the kitchen.

Just after five o'clock the following evening, Papa drove up with Corporal Duncan, a young police officer. They leaped out of the jeep and walked briskly towards

Melvyna's room, but Yvonne, standing on the kitchen steps, delayed them.

'She's in the kitchen,' Yvonne said, pointing.

'Who?' Papa asked.

'Melvyna,' Yvonne replied conspiratorially. 'She's cooking dinner. And Papa, she didn't wash her hands with soap. I saw her.'

'Go in to Mama,' Papa said, shooing her away and exchanging glances with Corporal Duncan, who seemed a little less commanding without his splendid police horse, the dark tan stallion, Cyrus, but visibly impressed with Yvonne's evaluation. She has a good police brain, his expression said.

No one knew what was found in Melvyna's room, if anything. But it wasn't long before she was summoned before Papa and Corporal Duncan in the pantry. She was suspicious when she saw Corporal Duncan in his splendid police uniform, all red and black and blue, with silver buttons and polished leather. But no one was going to bully her. She had Jehovah on her side. At first she tried to face them down but she couldn't because they didn't look her squarely in the eye, preferring to look at the floor, over her shoulder, or away just before their eyes locked.

'I want you off the premises,' Boyd heard Papa say.

'What, sar?'

'Pack your things and leave now.'

'Is what wrong, sar?' Melvyna looked from face to face, hoping for some explanation, some urgent apology for a tragic mistake hastily made.

'You heard me, pack your bag,' Papa repeated.

'But why, sar?'

'You know.'

'Know what, sar? Ah treat the missis with respect. You too, sar, and the children. And ah do me work – '

'Heh, heh,' Corporal Duncan chuckled. 'You can do that work somewhere else.'

'Is what you mean, sar? What you mean?'

'You heard your employer. Go to your room and pack your bag. Your wages are on the bed. Get going.'

'But, sar, as God is me witness,' Melvyna began, then stopped as Corporal Duncan moved towards her. She appealed directly to Papa. 'Call Miss Victoria, sar, call Miss Victoria. She will tell you ah'm a good worker. She said how good ah wash, iron and take care for the children. Ah'm a God-fearing woman, sar.'

Mama entered the room then and was the only one to meet Melvyna's eyes. But she, too, wasn't sure of Melvyna by then. She wasn't sure about *Obeah Women*. In fact, Melvyna had actually begun to look decidedly satanic since Papa's news that she might be involved in witchcraft. And so, because Mama wasn't sure, she wanted to let events take their course, however unjust it all seemed.

'Get going,' Corporal Duncan ordered. 'I don't want to have to arrest you.' He began to look very businesslike.

'But Miss Victoria, ma'am, is it because ah let the children eat green roseapples, ma'am? Ah warned them, ah told them, ah – '

'All right,' Papa said gruffly. 'Enough of this. To your room, now!' Together he and Corporal Duncan forced Melvyna out the door.

As Boyd watched Melvyna backing away, not afraid to face her accusers, he knew that Papa and Corporal Duncan were the villains in the books he read. Melvyna was the wronged heroine who would triumph, but only after a lifetime of pain and suffering.

Melvyna protested till the last.

'God is me witness!' she cried, pointing skyward, the hot tears wetting her cheeks.

CHAPTER 7

Papa was outraged. He came home in a foul mood and sat on the verandah all evening, smoking hard, flinging half-smoked cigarettes into the garden. Only Mama went near him. She soothed him and she comforted him and relayed the awful news to the children. It seemed that they would not be moving to the pink house after all.

The pink house had been promised to Papa and he had announced it triumphantly at dinner. He had taken Mama to the club to celebrate with the Moodies and bought yellow, red and green hula-hoops for the children, who hula-hooped all day and into the night. Now news reached him that the house was destined for another family, an English family, the Mitchisons, who were living at Monymusk, a sugar estate in Clarendon parish. The Mitchisons were ready to move to Appleton the moment the Maxwell-Smiths left, and the Maxwell-Smiths would be leaving in a matter of days. Everyone was disappointed, even Poppy. He'd been looking forward to running up and down the long driveway and chasing fowls and small birds on the lawn and into the back garden.

'I'll hand in my notice,' Papa said, face grim, lips set, eyes fierce. He turned towards the factory, a huge mechanical dragon in the distant darkness, hissing steam. Lights flickered in the distillery, in the boiler house, in the chief chemist's office. And he inhaled the beguiling odours that were his life – dunder, molasses, golden boiling sugar, fresh rum, estate vapours – substances for which he had a chemical equation registered in his head.

Mama stroked his arm, gently brushing cigarette ash from his sugar-scented khakis, encouraging restraint. Their future, the children's education, all that to go up in smoke?

'This could only happen in a blasted colony like Jamaica. A man has no respect in the country of his birth. As long as you work for someone, other than yourself, you are nothing. And these Mitchisons, let me tell you, are only getting the blinking house because they are English, for no other reason. English people come here, take what they want and don't give a shit. This country is racked with prejudice. The sooner we have self-government, the better. You see why I get behind the children, why I give them hell? Without a sound education, *a sound education*, Victoria, and a professional career, they may as well be slaves in their own country.'

'But – '

'But what, woman? Didn't you hear me?'

'They know you're good at your job,' Mama said calmly. 'Mr Mason said so himself. It's all he talked about at that little drinks party they invited us to. And you got that letter from the directors in Kingston, thanking you for your work.'

'What good is that now? It's all planned. They take decisions behind your back. If you're not white you're treated like trash. Gawd.'

'But you've always said that what matters is your ability.' Mama stroked his arms.

'Of course. But not everybody sees it that way.'

Mama paused. 'What did Mr Mason say?'

Undisguised contempt was written all over Papa's face. 'He's in Kingston at a managers' meeting.' He swallowed. 'Conveniently.'

'Oh,' Mama said, feeling a sense of relief. 'So nothing is certain.'

Papa stared at her with incredulity but did not reply immediately, switching his gaze down into the valley, back to the white lights of the factory. The night was dark and deep, the smell of the sugar, rum and heat pleasant and close. It was a scene, a sensation Papa knew well, scents he loved. He had powerful feelings he could not deny. Most of his life had been lived on sugar estates: Bernard Lodge, Worthy Park and now Appleton. He'd received sugar scholarships and studied in British Honduras and Barbados. He was an estate man to the core.

'Victoria,' he said, with an air of experience, 'I know these things. It's how they behave on sugar estates. But, you mark my words, I shall put my foot down. I'll not be walked over. I'm not some ol' *Neaga* from the cane-piece, y'know.'

'Of course you're not!' Mama scolded him.

'They don't know who they're dealing with.'

But they knew, because later that week, with much restraint, Papa announced that the pink house was still theirs. The arrival of the Mitchisons had been delayed while a new house was being prepared for them. The estate had dispatched its full complement of carpenters, masons and skilled craftsmen to spruce up the large but unfinished house down the road from the pink house.

Mama stroked Papa's arm and gave him a sweet look. A burden was lifted off the children's shoulders and they too looked at Papa with admiration. But the refurbished house for the Mitchisons interested them. Its dull-white walls could be seen across the valley, partly hidden behind a ridge in the shade of giant poinciana trees.

'It will be the most modern house on the estate when they're finished with it,' Papa said quietly. 'It has the new flat roof and I hear they'll put a telephone in there.'

'A telephone.' Mama did her best to contain herself. The children stopped eating. Next to a car, an English car, or preferably a Land Rover, and a very good maid: a telephone was the most essential thing on a sugar estate. It was what set them apart, the important people from the unimportant. Aside from the status telephones conferred, they were simply necessary for life in the countryside.

Those were Papa's very words. At Worthy Park only the top people had telephones.

'He must be a big shot,' Barrington blurted out.

'No,' Papa said slowly, picking up a tiny bit of white fish on his fork and placing it carefully into his mouth. 'Just the assistant general manager. Mason told me today. Everyone thought Mitchison was the new head bookkeeper. He is well qualified, with estate experience in Barbados and at Monymusk. And they say his wife is a live wire; probably the kind of woman who wants to know everybody's business.' Papa shook his head and grimaced. 'We have enough busybodys on the estate already.'

'Is there one at the pink house, Papa?' Yvonne asked irreverently. But she was bound to ask since the house was the home of the Maxwell-Smiths, the English family, who were the very opposite of *those people*.

'One what?' Papa didn't look up because he knew what. They all assumed the pink house had one. There had been no telephone at their Worthy Park house and none at their green and cream Appleton house.

'Telephone, Papa.' Yvonne seemed mystified. A house such as the pink house was bound to have a telephone. They had taken it for granted.

'I don't think so,' Papa informed her slowly. 'And if there is one there, I'll ask them to remove it. We don't need a telephone. Everybody wants a telephone. What did we do before there were telephones? Everybody wants this, everybody wants that. And a telephone is at the top of the list. It's a way to show off, to say I am better than you. We don't need it. We Brookes don't need to show off. If the Mitchisons have one, it doesn't mean we must have one as well. People with telephones spend all their time gossiping when they should be doing something useful. I'm not going to lower my principles and ask, or beg, for something like a telephone. Oh no. Other people can do that, not us. We are Brookes, and that means something.' He put his knife and fork down. 'Who are we?'

'Brookes,' the children repeated hesitantly, eyes darting about.

Papa said nothing more. They had no idea why he had changed his mind about the telephone. It might have been something to do with *values and principles*. Mama seemed to know, though she said not a word.

'There's a gardener at the house,' Papa told them later. 'He's worked there since he was a boy and is very good with the orchard and vegetable garden. We're keeping him on. Name's Vincent. He's a very good worker but,' he appeared grave, 'he has only one eye.'

'Yechk!' Yvonne said, and stopped eating.

Boyd stopped eating too. 'But why?' he asked, vaguely tearful.

'Why what?' Papa turned to him with amused curiosity.

The words would not come out. Boyd could not explain it although it was vivid in his head. A gardener was a gardener, used to gardening with all his gardening skills, good enough to be employed by the Maxwell-Smiths and now by Papa. He could see Vincent in the early warm-cool of morning, pruning, weeding, tending, planting little buds, spraying the beds of dark-brown earth with his watering can while small birds pulled at worms and little yellow butterflies hovered overhead. Such a man as Vincent, making his stitch in the fabric of nature, in tune with the rhythm of time and calmly going about his work in his place in the gardens, was almost as important as the Brookeses. What did the fact that he had *only* one eye have to do with it? Papa was gazing at him impatiently.

'You should say what you have to say,' Papa said. 'Don't be shy.'

Boyd felt that he had already said what he had to say to himself. The problem was that he couldn't tell it to anybody else. He couldn't get the words out, could not find the right ones from the multitude crowding his tongue. He glared at his plate, curled his toes tight and felt ready to snap. Mama smiled reassuringly. Papa didn't understand.

'One more thing,' Papa said, sighing. 'There's a coolie settlement behind the hill.' He saw Boyd suddenly look up. 'It's at the bottom of the valley but you can see it from the back of the property. I don't want any of you crossing the fence and going anywhere near there. They probably have yaws and chiggers and God knows what. And there are big bulls and prancing horses in the pasture and on the slope, so keep away from there. And I don't want anybody going near the river. It's not a babbling brook and none of you can swim. People drown in it every year. You hear me, Boyd?'

Papa might have said: *Pocahontas, Sitting Bull and Crazy Horse all live down there in their wigwams. And pretty dark-haired squaws come out at night gazing at the moon and at the pink house, waiting for someone.* Boyd couldn't wait to get to the coolie settlement.

* * *

They moved to the pink house on Friday July 15, 1957. White oleander blossoms flew up from the driveway as the Prefect, with Poppy hanging out the rear side window, roared up it. That evening, Harry Belafonte sang "Jamaica Farewell" on the Mullard radio while the lamps glowed amber in the drawing room. The Maxwell-Smiths had already left for England by BOAC, taking their dog and their maid, Inez, with them. But their smell still lingered in the house, an English smell of flannel and tea. The children discovered interesting articles left behind; binoculars in an old leather case which Boyd claimed, and a blue Lone Ranger pistol with silver bullets for Barrington. They got in the way of the painters during the week it took to paint the house, and grew to love the smell of pastel-coloured green paint which covered the drawing and dining room walls. They befriended the painters in their shapeless overalls, who lounged about at lunchtime with bulging necks and searching eyes, eating sardines and hard white bread and farting. And they met Vincent.

The first time Boyd and Yvonne saw Vincent, their eyes were glued to his face. Mama slapped their hands for being insensitive and rude. But it was because they had never seen anyone with such an eye before. Vincent's eye oozed runny custard, a pale eye that looked but could not see, a fish's eye, flat and wet and dripping. He was standing against the silver water tank by the kitchen with his machete in his hand while Mama conversed with him from halfway up the kitchen steps. Vincent cut a downcast figure and his smell was of underarms and old leather. Boyd didn't want to think it but Vincent was the Hunchback of Notre Dame, ugly and maligned, and he was instinctively drawn to him. Poppy was drawn to Vincent too, circling his ankles, making wonderful growling sounds and perfecting dramatic attacking movements, but holding back at the very last moment.

While they were getting acquainted with Vincent, Papa had driven up, vaulted out of the yellow jeep and walked quickly towards the kitchen steps. He barely acknowledged Vincent and spoke without looking at him.

'Give it a good wash,' he said, indicating the dusty vehicle. 'And when you're through, wash and polish the Prefect. And no skylarking!'

A pained expression clouded Vincent's face. Mr Maxwell-Smith had never spoken to him like that in all the years he had worked for him. He turned to Mama for consolation but all he got was an embarrassed smile.

* * *

Boyd wasted little time in exploring the grounds. He wandered along the fence in the back garden where, under the shade of a guava tree, he had a clear view of the brown cows in the fields. Their slow looking, their full titties, their languid presence and the rich gloss of their bodies drew him to the same spot day after day with Poppy at his feet. But the gardens of the pink house always called him away.

The pink women were forever there, lying casually in the grass, beckoning, smiling like the *Mona Lisa*, waiting for him.

One day, satiated with adventure from his roaming, Boyd wandered into Mama's bedroom after her bath. He saw how her titties with the dark nipples, her thighs fleshy and her skin smooth and shadowy, were just like the brown cows reclining under the trees in the pasture behind the house. Mama draped her slip about her when she saw him and smiled an awkward smile. But Boyd felt only the warm calm and heard the silent, enquiring voice.

This voice told him that Mama was like the paintings in the encyclopaedia. Two paintings in particular summed up Mama and the brown cows in the field: *Venus and Cupid on The Sea*, by someone called Luca Cambiaso, and *Love in the Golden Age* by Paolo Fiammingo. Boyd wanted to touch the ample flesh so real on the page. Another painting, *Lady in her Bath* by Francois Clouet, was of a baby at a woman's breast. A woman stood in the background with what appeared to be a water pitcher. The body of the pitcher seemed like a full breast, glossy and moist, waiting to be grasped and tongued. In the hot afternoons, as he pored over the picture in a kind of rapture, he felt himself sucking his own tongue. His earliest memories were of his puckered lips glued to Mama's nipples, face squashed against her brown titties. That was where life began, where memory started. The cows in their restful poses with their full titties hanging, the nude women and Mama all said the same thing to him. Mama was a lovely brown cow with warm, smooth breasts. At night he had dreams of being cuddled in the grass by these maternal brown cows, his lips at their warm udders, satiated with pleasure.

When he'd had enough of this adventure, Boyd took himself further along the fence to a secluded spot where he could see the curling blue smoke from the coolie settlement down in the valley. The coolies were the Sioux in the comics on his bed, exotic, mysterious, wronged. Their cooking smoke were smoke signals. The signals drew him to them and he gazed long at the brown barracks, nostrils open to the wind, trying to detect the scent of their living, seeing images of bashful dark-haired squaws. They were waiting for him. The urge to creep under the fence and into the ecstasy of the comic books was overwhelming. The comic books had come alive at the new house. It was useless to fight.

Towards midday, when Papa had left, when the sun was clean and hot, the air vibrating and scented, Boyd put *Drums of War* down on the bed and rose, summoned. The coolie drums sought him out, led him on to where the coolie girls waited in the shadows of their barracks. Down the verandah steps he went, out into the powerful music.

He hesitated in the fragrant heat as a black and yellow butterfly shot up out of the hibiscus. It flew above Mama's flowerbeds, swooped across the lawn, made as if to perch on the jacaranda but flew behind the house and over the fence. Boyd raced after it. Poppy, coming from nowhere, joined in the chase. Boyd had seen such a butterfly, a swallowtail, in the encyclopaedia. Excitement obliterated Papa's rule never to cross the fence where it separated the green pastures from the house, the gateway to the pretty squaws, the coolies down in the valley, whose drums were now beating like thunder.

Under the barbed wire fence Boyd scrambled, shirt momentarily caught in the rusting barbs, Poppy falling back, eyes fixed on the darting spectacle against the blue sky. On and on they went, downhill, gasping for breath, hoping their prey would alight in one of the low branches of the cashew trees dotting the slope. But the butterfly came down in a yellow patch of daisies, only yards from the fence separating the field from the dirt road and the coolie settlement. It seemed almost invisible among the daisies and Boyd crept forward. Suddenly the coolie barracks loomed near. Behind him, up the hill, the pink house seemed a long way away. The drums were silent now. And Boyd heard screams.

The noise frightened him, but he felt dragged towards it. Crossing the dirt road, he entered the coolie compound. Smoke came from behind the barracks. The screams came from there too, and people's voices and fearful sounds. Smells that tasted of dirt and death reached his nostrils. It was a pig squealing without dignity. It seemed to be struggling, fighting to break loose from whatever danger imprisoned it. As the screams rose to a bloodcurdling pitch, Boyd pushed forward and came upon a savage scene. A crowd of coolies in a courtyard surrounded a rectangular stone platform: old men and women with silver hair to their shoulders; naked little children with iron rust bodies and dark hair; pretty, pretty girls his age with dirt-stiffened dresses, fragile hairy arms and stringy brown hair. There were girls there like Estella with pouting full lips, dark of eye, calculating stares. The older people sat quietly in the shade. Some of the women were combing their hair with a languid air while the girls watched, their arms fine and elegant. But Boyd's attention was dragged towards the centre of the courtyard. On the raised platform, two slim, hairy coolies held down, on its back, a crusty black pig with a savage snout, the biggest pig Boyd had ever seen. He thought with horror that they had undressed and were holding down a *higgler*, one of the strapping, large-breasted marketwomen with enormous *bankras* on their heads who came to the house selling red beans. The pig was constantly breaking loose, shaking them off. A third coolie, shirtless and brandishing a long knife with a sharpened blade that flashed in the sun, stood a little apart, waiting his moment. That moment came as the pig, weakened momentarily, was forced down in a final burst of violence. The knife flashed once, came out red and plunged in again, swift and deep, killing deep. The pig, surprised, gave a hoarse cough as thick blood splashed everywhere. Other men jumped forward, keen to join in the butchering.

Quickly the coolies poured hot water over the black body. A horrible stench erupted. With sharp knives they set

70

to work to skin the animal in swift, practised flourishes. Each swipe of their knives revealed white strips of the pig's under-skin. Boyd inhaled terrible odours and retched. If only he had stayed with the butterfly.

'Me name Ramsook. Me kill the pig.' The tall, shirtless coolie pig killer was standing next to him. Coolie children and a few old women, fine-boned and elegant, approached. Boyd smelled their coolie smell. He couldn't speak.

'You live in big house?' The man pointed towards the hill.

Boyd nodded. The children stared, not saying anything.

'Your father big man at factory, make sugar, make rum,' the coolie said.

The coolie women had a philosophical air and did not look at Boyd directly but at something just over his shoulder. They had small faces and a beautiful demeanour. He could see them sitting in the Lloyd Loom chairs at the club sipping Babycham. If only they were clean, wore nice frocks and shoes and didn't sit as they did on the porch with legs wide apart. Some might even appear as pretty as Miss Chatterjee.

'You tell your father we want work. No work for us in cane-piece. Tell him to give us work. We cut cane, plant ratoon, dig trench, cart manure, hoe, weed.'

Boyd backed away, not understanding. Poppy was struggling defiantly on the ground with a coolie dog twice his size.

'Stop it!' Boyd cried out, imagining Poppy lying dead in the dirt.

'Away, Cutthroat!' the coolie said, waving his arms. A small coolie boy chased after Cutthroat, a dog with a slinking tail and a wicked eye. Poppy got to his feet barking vigorously, his coat covered in red dirt.

'You want pig meat?' It was the pig killer again. 'Take up to the house?'

'No,' Boyd said quickly, backing away, now that Poppy was no longer preoccupied.

'Tell your father what Ramsook say,' Ramsook reminded him as he left the courtyard with its smells, smoke and blood. The disgraced pig lay naked and white on the block, mouth open, showing discoloured teeth and a pink slit in an arc at its throat.

A light wind sprang up, shifting the red dust as Boyd made his way back out into the dirt road. A dozen silent coolie children and their dogs followed him, stopping as one when they got to the fence. The sultry coolie girls gave him lingering looks and one, the dead stamp of Estella, appearing as if she meant to go after him, stared haughtily, hands on hips. Boyd wrenched his gaze away. The air in the pastures was clean, the grass luscious underfoot. He ran all the way up the hill, not looking back until he reached the summit. Back down the hill, the coolie girls were still standing by their rusting barbed-wire fence. The vast cane fields behind their houses were blue-green, their small clearing like a spot of dried blood on the lush landscape. Boyd wished they had green grass instead of dust in their yard and that Mr Ramsook had not killed the struggling *higgler* woman in cold blood.

Boyd's worry was how to approach Papa about Mr Ramsook. He knew that Papa would not focus on getting Mr Ramsook a job. He would want to ask questions: 'What were you doing down there? Didn't I tell you never to cross the fence? What is the matter with you? What if you caught lice and hookworm from those people?'

Papa would want to cloud the issue.

'They just sit on their backsides all day and expect to get work. Lazy buggers. Ramsook wants work? Let him get work. And if I ever hear of you going down there again, I'll whip you so hard you'll wish you were never born. Now, get out of my sight.'

Boyd knew that it was impossible to mention Mr Ramsook to Papa, nothing about his silent promise to the pig killer, nothing about the coolie girls with their slender, hairy arms, their dark Estella looks. And nothing about how the violent and bloody killing of the pig had erased much of the exotic imagery of the squaws from his memory.

As he slipped back under the fence of the pink house, he saw the familiar form of Vincent, like a pliant hunchback, on his knees planting banana suckers in the moist dark earth behind the garage. And he saw someone else too. Far to the left of the hill against an open sky, he glimpsed a fair figure gazing with riveting interest at the coolie barracks, the wind ruffling her hair. It was a white woman, her cotton skirts thrashing about her creamy legs in the lively valley breeze. As he watched, she walked rapidly away, round the hill, behind a clump of trees, towards the big houses down the lane. Boyd did not move but continued to stare silently, inquisitively, at the place where the woman had been.

* * *

At the end of the first week at the pink house, Barrington, sitting quietly on the windowsill and dreaming of Geraldine Pinnock, while simultaneosuly imagining himself playing for Jamaica against the rest of the world in the greatest ever football match at Wembley, raised his eyes level with the emerald green hedge at one end of the lawn and discovered Boyd standing there, staring up into a blue sky. Barrington watched him for a long time and counted up to a hundred, expecting him to move, but Boyd didn't. Barrington counted to a hundred and fifty and willed Boyd to move as he didn't want to count any more. He wanted to ride over to the Pinnocks and show Geraldine his gun. But Boyd stood still with his arms spread wide, taking the sun, his features swimming in the heat. Then, as Barrington stopped counting, frustrated, Boyd fell backwards, hands straight out in front of him, into the deep embracing grass. Sage-green birds flew up in a cloud.

CHAPTER 8

Birds flew up as Boyd fell down into the deep, fragrant grass. He lay as if dead against the breathing earth, feeling the tingling passions, the delirious quiet, the secret music. There were many days like this. But that day something new happened.

As he left the grassy embrace, he wandered off to the far end of the garden, where the periwinkle fence grew. Here, where the fence ended, the private road began, leading to the big houses of the Mitchisons and the Dowdings. The sunlight came through the trees in soft gold spots upon his face. He put the binoculars to his eyes and gazed out beyond the green, across the private road, over the fence. He saw figures moving about in the garden of the big house. It was the Mitchisons, the English family recently arrived from Monymusk sugar estate, the family about whom Papa had raged. The woman he'd seen on the hill overlooking the coolie barracks was Mrs Mitchison.

Boyd saw a small figure on a blue and white bicycle held upright by their maid, a woman in a starched blue uniform. The figure on the bicycle was pink, with light-brown, short-cut, sun-touched hair, and wore a lilac gingham dress. As he watched, the maid let the bicycle go. After an awkward moment, during which everyone stood braced for action, the bicycle circled the poinciana tree in the centre of the garden and vanished round the corner of the house in a wink of pink. Mr and Mrs Mitchison and the maid followed, half-running. Boyd waited in his spot under the trees, unblinking. But she did not reappear. A sudden wind blew up from the valley, rustling the trees, sprinkling a potpourri of new scents which appeared in sad and exciting colour. And he went into himself, deep down where thoughts originated. Something had shifted in his firmament. Poppy was frantic at his feet, prancing, tail whipping about, breathing furiously, tongue lashing. His thoughts racing, redolent in hibiscus-pink, Boyd felt fascination of a kind he had never known. He couldn't wait to see the pink girl again.

That night at dinner, Yvonne said, 'Mama, there's a little white girl next door. I saw her peeping over the fence.'

'That will be the Mitchison's daughter, Susan,' Papa told them.

Boyd trembled when he heard this. What a name. *Susan.* It had music and heartbeat and the scent of evening primrose. And it was pink like the Appleton sunsets.

That night he stayed up late listening to the radio and the pretty songs, "Don't Forbid Me", "Moonlight Gambler" and "The Green Door." The peeny-waalies flew by the window and away into the night. And he was warm and dying, dying with gladness. No one knew. He just listened to the radio, the crackling Mullard radio, and through the whizz and the buzz and the miaow, heard the pretty songs from the distant place and thought of the people who had just arrived at the house down the road. The door to their house was "The Green Door" (one more night without sleeping, watching till the morning comes creeping). He couldn't sleep and longed for the next day when the figure on the bicycle would appear with the sun and the sugar smell of Appleton.

CHAPTER 9

One more night without sleeping,
watching till the morning comes creeping.

She did not appear at all the next morning, and not in the afternoon, the girl on the bicycle. *Susan.* That wonderful name. He repeated it over and over again until it became more than a name. And he was waiting for her the following day too, sheltered among the green things, the binoculars clamped to his eyes. When at last he was about to give up, she appeared from the side of the house with the sun behind her. She did not see him. Waves of warm air, in shimmering streams, separated the two of them. She continued walking towards the periwinkle fence on her side of the private road and seemed to be looking for something in the bushes. Boyd left the shadow of the trees. He saw her hair ablaze in the sun. She was pink against the green. Breathlessly he put the binoculars down.

Birds flew up out of the hedge and across the road. Instantly her head jerked back. She watched as the small yellow birds flew in a smooth, undulating motion and alighted on the fence opposite, where a small boy and a dog stood looking into the sky. She drew closer to the fence, surprised, not expecting to see anyone there. The boy was not looking into the sky but over her shoulder. His head was inclined obliquely. She saw him see her in that split-hazy moment. But before their eyes met, he quickly looked down, as if shy. Then he moved backwards into the trees. She stood on tiptoe to try to see over the hedge, but the boy, about her age, did not reappear. Through the sunshine-yellow haze she saw the pink house looming through the trees like a picture in a book. All was quiet. Susan Mitchison stood still. She heard the musical voices whispering *hush, hushh, hushhh,* and in her quietness was overcome with unspeakable joy. *It was just as she imagined it when Rosalind came upon Orlando in the Forest of Arden!* The book, Lambs' *Tales from Shakespeare,* lay opened on her bed at the chapter entitled "As You Like It." Susan's feelings and her thoughts, mostly in crimson, dwarfed her. She was seven years old.

* * *

Something had shifted in Mama and Papa's firmament also, but they did not yet know it. Late that night, as the dew appeared on the lawn, Mama faced Papa.

They had been talking on the verandah in the dark when it had come up in her, the feeling of desperation. Suddenly she'd seen the dull flash of ambition growing dimmer and dimmer and it frightened her. It would die soon. She faced Papa because he had commented, casually, about Ann Mitchison, the wife of the assistant general manager. He said that she had qualified in fine art at a college in London and was politically very astute, *very astute.* So, no longer was she an interfering busybody! He said she shared his views about Jamaica's political future. Full self-government, complete independence was the answer. Papa said he could not agree more. He had found her, at a meeting at the club over drinks, totally absorbing, *totally absorbing.* Here was a *woman who knew her mind.* And Papa had said no more, returning casually to his drink and looking into the *peeny-waalie*-filled night. Mama, not usually a jealous person, experienced what could only be described as a vague sensitivity. But as the moments drifted by, this passing sensitivity took hold. Here was a woman, Ann Mitchison, who had achieved something with her life, something Papa had no difficulty in appreciating. And yet, in his own house, his own wife's tireless begging for an opportunity for personal development fell on deaf ears. All she ever wanted was to be a designer of women's dresses and sell to selective shops like *Daphne's* in Kingston. Long before Papa came along, that was her dream. Some of her early drawings on creamy paper were at the bottom of her suitcase at the back of the wardrobe. None of her children had ever seen them; neither had Papa.

She faced Papa that night in 1957 at Appleton, the mother of three children and one on the way, feeling more than a bit desperate.

'I want you to listen to me,' she said, her voice wavering.

'What?' Papa sipped his third rum of the night, gazing up at the stars. His plans were falling into place but not fast enough for him. Two years. Two years, and they would leave Appleton for greener pastures. With the children attending the best schools, he could begin to plan for their university education. Only London, Cambridge or Oxford mattered. They would enter the professions: law, medicine, education.

'I want you to help me,' Mama said.

Papa laughed innocently. Stars flashed across the sky. 'Help you with what, Victoria? I need help myself. All the decisions I have to make at the factory, here at the house, this, that and the other. Life isn't a bed of roses, y'know.'

Mama rose from the chair. Papa could be so inconsiderate at times. The chair made an extraordinary screeching sound against the tiles. She'd never liked those chairs, heavy aluminium things painted in pastel green and white. But they were the latest thing in verandah chairs and the estate was full of them. She much preferred wicker chairs. Besides, they were never cold at night, didn't make silly, metallic sounds and weren't so heavy and *ridiculous*.

'I need to do something with my life,' she almost pleaded. Her white skirt appeared pale blue in the dark.

'Need to do something with your life? Victoria, what are you talking about?'

'I mean, I *want* to do something with my life.'

'I hope it's not that dressmaking business again,' Papa said, glaring, a clear warning that he was not interested. Mama didn't seem to understand his clear objectives for the family, the certainty that they would be achieved, that everyone should get behind him as head of the family, to ensure that nothing blew them off course. She didn't seem to understand that nothing, absolutely nothing, would drag him down.

'Harold, it's my life,' Mama stammered, lips now trembling uncontrollably.

'But you are doing something with your life,' he told her. 'You're expecting another child. I provide a good home. We already have three children. You are a good mother. You could be a lot tougher on them, but we're all human.'

Mama was exasperated. 'I want to talk about me, me.' She beat her breast. '*Me*! I want to talk about *me*!'

'Say what you have to say,' Papa replied, paying no attention to the anguish on her face. 'Speak up, Victoria. For Christ's sake.'

'I just want to – '

'What?' Papa snapped once more, as if admonishing a little child. When he was in that state all her confidence flew away.

Earlier, when she rose from the chair, she had felt a sudden surge of lightning confidence and clarity, but words were now clogging her throat. She was doomed, closed like a tomb, carrying a life, history and dreams that no one would ever know. Papa's nonchalance and aloofness, and then his aggression, brought her back to what she was, the girl from St Catherine who had never been anywhere. She was a mother whose children would remember her for doing nothing. They would continue to fear and respect their father because he made things happen, good or bad. She would be forgotten because she did not dominate their

79

moments, did not make the air swirl and shake and make their hearts beat, sometimes with fear. She was not that interesting someone who sent them to school, paid the fees, whipped their behinds and left the house every day to return at night smelling of the world. She would not be remembered because she did not leave her mark on them, she had only loved them quietly and constantly. All she had was the smell of home which, one day, they would all want to get away from. She did not want to be alone.

She had not envied the women at the club who had travelled and studied, who smoked and drank and were so sophisticated and confident. But now she thought of them as better than she was. She had not been to the club for drinks with Ann Mitchison and felt left out. She had not been because Papa had not taken her. It infuriated her that in the space of just a few days Ann Mitchison had gone from being a busybody to a woman almost worthy of worship.

Mama started to cry. Papa didn't notice at first but when she sat back down, he saw the round pearls of tears reflecting the moonlight. His instinct was to round on her with disgust. But she seemed so pretty, so vulnerable in the dark, in her white skirt, with her rising bosom, her muted crying, John Pratt's daughter. He was aroused. He took her into his arms. Instantly, vibrant images of Ann Mitchison assaulted him, shocking him to the core. Try as he might, he could not dispel the images, and so he succumed. He had only met her a few times at the club. She had impressed him as only few women could and he had instinctively camouflaged his appreciation. But he had not been able to ignore the expressive lips, the eyes that drew him in, her provoking presence. He had not been able to free himself from the embrace of British domination expressed in fair womanhood. Now Mama was Ann Mitchison in his arms. She went willingly into the bedroom, like a child, to the place that she knew. Papa felt like a lion, an estate lion, a lion of the cane-piece. Already feeling twitches of the burden of guilt, he sensed that he'd taken the first steps on the road to perdition.

The very next evening, with the red sun barely below the mountains and the sky full of dive-bombing swallows, Papa, dressed in cricket whites, knocked up some wickets and summoned the boys onto the lawn. They batted and they bowled. They fielded and they kept wicket and they shouted, 'Collie Smith!', 'Rohan Khani!' and 'Frank Worrell!' at intervals. They displayed their cricketing skills for Papa while Mama and Yvonne watched from the verandah. Vincent watched from the porch, shielding his eye from the sun. He ran for the balls that went too far and acted as a kind of outfielder although he wasn't in the game.

Later, they gathered on the verandah to listen to Papa's plans for the future yet again, to hear how Barrington had already left university with a first class degree, qualified as a lawyer and been snapped up by the top law firm in Kingston. They heard how he'd gone on to people the land with the first of the Brookes boys, grandsons for Papa and heirs to the Brookes dynasty.

'But I'm going to be a footballer,' Barrington protested, sipping bright green Kool-Aid as the night noises came on, as the *peeny-waalies* came out and as they breathed the evening smell of Appleton.

'You'll be a great lawyer,' Papa assurred him, 'respected throughout the country. You'll make a lot of money too, drive a Jaguar and live in a bigger house than this one.'

'What about me, Papa?' Yvonne had seen Barrington's eyes light up.

'Yvonne, you'll be a doctor, finding cures for the worst diseases known to man.'

'Diseases? But I want to be an explorer, Papa. Or a nurse, and – .'

'You listen to your Papa. You'll be a very famous doctor. Dr. Yvonne Brookes. How does that sound?'

Yvonne beamed. Temporarily lost for words, she turned

quickly towards Mama, then Boyd, whose future had not been told. 'And what about Boyd, Papa?'

Boyd, who had been watching Mama listen quietly to the conversation, like someone expecting at any moment to hear that she, too, would be a lawyer or someone of very high standing, looked round. But just before Papa spoke, just before Mama's or Boyd's future could be foretold, they saw the Mitchison's maid, Evadne, come through the garden gate with a note in her hand. Poppy immediately set upon her, worrying her ankles and nipping away at the hem of her dress, so that she dashed about, holding the note aloft. Eventually she reached the safety of the verandah. She handed the note to Papa and left, bowing, Poppy escorting her back to the edge of the garden. Boyd, seeing the maid arrive, the maid who came from the same house as the girl with the sun-drenched hair, the girl who was as pink as the pink women in the encyclopaedia, breathed new and delightful scents.

Papa read the note and handed it to Mama. 'Invitation to dinner,' he said, pouring himself another drink and looking pleased with himself.

'Tim and Ann request the pleasure of your company,' Mama read, then stopped. She immediately thought of the reciprocal dinner party, worried about meeting her neighbour and about the fact that she was still without a competent maid. She worried too about her lack of confidence and about Papa's sudden interest in Ann Mitchison. That night she searched Papa's face for the secret that she suspected was hidden there.

And that night Boyd saw her again in real life images. *Behind the pink house, in the shade of the otaheite apple tree, she sat on the swing, hands up, holding on to the thick ropes, feet lightly touching the apple blossoms covering the bare earth, in a slow motion rhythm, back and forth. As the rhythm quickened, she laughed, standing up on the base of the swing, knees bent, pumping hard. He stood in the dandelion bed nearby, watching as she fluttered out and in. It was quiet but for her quick gasps and the fluttering of her dress. Boyd saw her go far out, so far out that he could see the back of her, and so far in that he could see up under her dress. He turned away, not wanting to look, only wanting to see her hair and lips and her eyes and hear the flutter of her dress. But he wanted her to stop, not to swing so far out, to swing low and gently and then stop and run to him in the dandelion bed where Poppy was, and where the heat off them, in a suffocating potpourri, drugged and calmed their eyelids, limbs and their breathing.*

CHAPTER 10

As Mama's doubts ate at her, as Boyd's pleasures and anxieties threatened to overwhelm him, Aunt Enid visited. She brought essence of gladioli in her wake, bags of candy and a florin each for the children and grim news for Mama.

'Vicky, you've got to get it out in the open,' she urged when they were alone together. 'They say she's the dead stamp. Not more than seven years old. It would be right after you gave birth to Boyd, you see.'

'It's too late to do anything,' Mama told her nervously, seeing her sister's intervention as unbearable pressure, something she could do without. 'And he would have said something anyway. It's not like him.'

'You really think he would tell you of his own volition?'

'Of course,' Mama whispered. 'He really looks down on that kind of behaviour.'

Aunt Enid stared at her sister and shook her head. 'You're too trusting. Vicky, it's deception, plain and simple. You mark my words. If he's capable of this, he's capable of anything. He's just like his father before him. The Brookes men are great philanderers.'

But Mama wanted her to stop all the whispering and questioning. The fact was, she didn't want to believe any of it. Worthy Park and Lluidas Vale were in the past and should stay there. In any case, what could she do if it were true? Papa was her life and her future. And she had more urgent issues to attend to than something that might, or might not, have happened years ago between her husband and some woman.

Aunt Enid asked about Boyd. He was always the first to run and throw himself at her and she, as someone without children, loved to suffocate him to her and feel the warmth and innocence of a child who, everyone could tell, adored her. She often joked that she would take him away with her one day. But it was the first time she'd visited the pink house and had arrived without warning.

'Playing on his own somewhere,' Mama said. 'He'll soon come running.'

Memorable images of Boyd came to Aunt Enid. He'd spent a week with her in Kingston. She'd been undressing in her bedroom and turned to see him standing at the door silently watching.

'What is it, honeybun?' she'd said, covering up her bosom instinctively while trying to be casual about it. 'Is something wrong?'

'No,' Boyd had answered, coming further into the room and taking a seat on the bed. His eyes, completely absorbed, never left her. But they were gentle eyes, searching eyes, not knowledgeable eyes. There was no guilt about him.

She continued to undress and to chat with him as though they were in the garden on an ordinary day.

The following afternoon she'd popped out briefly and asked her maid to keep an eye on him. When she returned, Boyd could not be found. Her maid, a silly, gap-toothed woman with electric-shock hair, knowing her job was on the line, rushed from room to room screeching, giving the moment a level of danger that scared Aunt Enid.

Boyd was found minutes later in a corner of the garden, under the rose bush, sniffing and licking at the spread pink petals. He did not see Aunt Enid as she came up behind him, did not see the maid pissing herself with relief on the porch in the background, her job saved; but when he did, he just smiled. He said not a word and Aunt Enid, too, said nothing. She just cuddled him to her there in the warm sun, among the roses, next to the hammock under the mango tree, for what seemed to the maid an unnecessarily long time.

'That little boy of yours,' was all Aunt Enid said now.

'He always plays by himself,' Mama said quickly. 'But he has a secret little playmate now, the little white girl across the way. Susan, the Mitchisons' daughter. She's a quiet one too and lives in her own little world. Just like Boyd. I see him looking through his binoculars over the hedge, trying to find her. Sometimes she comes looking for him but he hides under the periwinkle fence.' Mama smiled. 'They're just children.'

'Well, what is she like?' The question came too quickly for Mama.

'Who?'

'Your new neighbour, the Englishwoman.'

Mama hesitated. 'I haven't met her yet.'

'What?' Aunt Enid registered both incomprehension and astonishment. 'You mean to say you weren't with Harold when he had drinks with her at the club?'

'No, but they've invited us to dinner.' Mama faced her sister meekly, as if guilty of some serious shortcoming. They said nothing for a while. Then Aunt Enid caressed her sister's arms and spoke to her, calmly, firmly and tenderly.

'Don't believe everything he tells you. Stand up to him.'

'I do, I do.'

There was a long pause.

'And don't let him keep you forever at home, Vicky, do you hear me?'

Mama stammered. 'He won't.' But it wasn't a very convincing answer.

* * *

That Monday morning, the children sat on the verandah of the pink house watching out for the new maid. The verandah was square-shaped, like the house, and almost twelve feet off the ground. Papa said the house was in the

Georgian style and Mama did not refute this because she did not want to argue. The children faced a sea of green: lawns, hedgerows, wild growing things that had been tamed. A week ago at the same spot, they had watched Mr Jarrett and his magnificent brass spraying equipment, as he sprayed along the sides of the house. He had been tamed too. They no longer received his sweets, the lovely Paradise Plums and the Mint Balls. Papa had forbidden it both in the children's and Mr Jarret's presence. Mr Jarrett had looked down at his feet, his face and shoulders sagging when he was told.

'Unmarried man like that,' Papa muttered mysteriously when Mr Jarret left.

But Mr Jarrett's scent was still so gorgeous that Boyd sniffed the air for him, watched as the fine spray from his equipment swirled and wafted away and reached the verandah. He watched the driveway when he knew Mr Jarrett was visiting so that he could meet his kind but now uncertain eye, to imagine about him, and most of all to reassure him. But Mr Jarrett was beyond reassurance. It was not the first time that men had misjudged him, mistaking his kindness and love of children for guile. He left quietly one afternoon and did not return. Feeling guilty, Papa made enquiries but no one knew what became of him. His little house in Taunton was locked up and stayed locked up. He had kept himself to himself so no one knew about him. Someone said he had taken the train to May Pen, since he had family nearby in Race Course. But no one knew for certain.

As the children looked straight down the driveway to the whitewashed gates, they could make out a bicycle rider and another figure balanced on the crossbar. Poppy bounded down the steps to cut them off with fierce barks. The man quickly positioned the fenderless Raleigh between himself and the fiercely snarling dog.

Mama, hearing the dramatic barking, came out, saw the two figures crouching defensively and seemed to remember something important. 'It's Adassa,' she said.

Moments later, Adassa sat in the pantry telling them that she had been educated to elementary school level and hoped to travel to England one day to study nursing, to follow in the footsteps of her sister, Desreen, who lived in Birmingham and was doing very well over there. On the covered porch by the kitchen, her man friend sat on a stool drinking ice-cold lemonade and surveying the premises with undisguised interest.

'Ah'm a good cook, ma'am,' Adassa boasted. 'Ah can cook callaloo soup, ackee and salt fish and rice and peas, ma'am. Ah'm a good cleaner, and ah can wash and iron. Ma'am, when ah clean dat floor you see your face in it. Ah don't make no fuss, ma'am, ah go about me work. Just give me the job, ma'am, and you won't be sorry. Ah not like some of the other maids, ma'am. They only want to use Fab and Breeze. They want dis and they want dat. They want everything. Not me, ma'am. Ah don't mind using the brown soap, ma'am, if dat is all you have. Ah use dat Reckitt's Blue, ma'am, to bring out the whites.'

'She a good cook, ma'am,' the man called out from his place on the porch. He'd been listening keenly. 'She is a God-fearing woman, ma'am.'

'Thank you, Mr ...?' Mama began, looking bewildered.

'Gordon, ma'am, me uncle,' Adassa said.

'Thank you, Mr Gordon.'

'Ah only telling God's truth, ma'am,' the man replied.

'Can you start today?' Mama asked, awkwardly.

'Today, ma'am?' Adassa burst into tears, shocking Mama. 'Ah can start right away, ma'am, right away.' She shouted to her uncle. 'Ah get the job! Ah get the job!'

Everyone stared in silence. And so Adassa, the sixth maid, was hired.

And that afternoon Boyd was again summoned, this time to the periwinkle fence. Everything led to her, the nodding hibiscus, the slender oleander leaves, the violet blue of the jacaranda, every blooming thing. When he got to the fence he could not see Susan, but felt her, and inhaled her pretty-scented fragrance. He imagined them lying in the grass, not speaking, feeling the music and the heat. Susan was now every girl he had ever known: Lydia Parsons, Pepsi, Estella and all the others who existed in his imagination.

In the joyous stillness of the afternoon, Susan's name panted into his ear, stirred his young wonderings, gave him fervent dreams. The music that rose up in him was distinct and beckoning. He wanted to follow the strains across the lawns, over the fence, wherever they might lead. They led only to one place.

And that place was where Mama and Papa were dressing up for, the home of the English family, the Mitchisons. He wanted them to go off to their dinner quickly so that he could be alone with the radio and hear the pretty songs. These songs of women's voices against a background of tinkling piano and golden horns talked a language promising beauty, sweet suffering, of hearts tossed and torn. The air resonated with expectation. He felt it in the breathlessness and the nervousness and the inexplicability of everything.

CHAPTER 11

Papa sat on the verandah in that lovely moment when the night had not yet closed in, when that delightful boiling sugar aroma drifted in from the factory, a pleasure known only to estate people, when early stars sprinkled the sky, and the radio, turned down low in the depths of the drawing room, played a song of evening. But Papa noticed none of this. His mind was preoccupied with thoughts of his hostess. He was in that place of indecision. It was not a place that he was familiar with. But then he was not familiar with a woman like Ann Mitchison, who, on the one hand, was the very essence of the great imperial power and yet, on the other hand, spoke to him in tones that he found stimulating.

For the third time that evening, Papa put his head round the door. There was Mama facing the large oval mirror above the bureau, dabbing at her cheeks with a small round pad, shoulders bare, elbows dimpled, earrings sparkling. Yvonne and Boyd sat at the foot of the bed, braced on their hands, eyes round. *Evening In Paris* filled the room.

'I'm ready,' Mama said, seeing Papa's impatient features at the door.

'So, what are we waiting for?'

Boyd inhaled, in deep gulps, Mama's scent, the scent of the dressing up and the going out for the evening, and followed her out to the verandah. There he and Yvonne watched Papa lead her to the garden gate near the periwinkle fence and down the path for the short walk to the Mitchisons. The darkness, lit only by the *peeny-waalies*, swallowed them up. Boyd quivered. Would Mama return with news of Susan? Would she ask Mama about him? What wonder, what revelations lay ahead! The feelings of exhilaration and perplexity; what did they mean?

He flopped in the armchair by the radio, passionately close, to hear the haunting "Wayward Wind" in the caramel light of the drawing room. In every word from the radio he heard the name *Susan, Susan*. It presented itself in beautiful forms, sunsets and moonlight, sublime thoughts. He sank deeper into the chair. *The wayward wind is a restless wind, a restless wind that yearns to wander.* It was cosy in the chair, and with the radio playing to him only, his thoughts crept away, airy and light, far away from him.

* * *

'Come on, go to your bed,' Papa said, speaking from out of the radio, out of WINZEE, out of the gloom. 'That damn woman; Adassa!'

Boyd had fallen asleep next to the radio. It was late. Mama and Papa had returned from their dinner. Mama, smelling of the wonders of another home, of new people, led Boyd to his bed. Bed was the door into the Mullard radio. Boyd dreamt many dreams, all extraordinary and torturous, and so did not see Mama and Papa lying at either ends of their bed late that night, not speaking, arms behind their heads, both with diametrically opposed views about the dinner and about one person: Ann Mitchison.

During the short walk from the Mitchisons', they argued.

'I don't know what you're arguing about,' Papa kept saying.

'You know damn well,' Mama repeated with a boldness that surprised her.

'I don't,' Papa replied with studied calm.

'Yes, you do.'

'I do not.'

And that was when they stopped speaking.

Mama remembered their entrance to Ann Mitchison's drawing room, the over-exuberance of their hostess. Mama thought she was better than good-looking, the most attractive woman in the room. But that was because Patricia Moodie was absent, and Miss Hutchinson, and Miss Chatterjee.

'How dreadful,' Ann Mitchison cried. 'We live only a few yards away and this is the first time we've met. Victoria, what must you think?'

Mama didn't have time to think. Tim Mitchison whisked her away and introduced her to a cluster of cravat-wearing bald men, the estate manager, Mr Mason, among them. They were standing in one corner of the room while their wives kept to another corner.

'Mrs Brookes,' Mr Mason exclaimed, thrusting out his hand, flashing a wide smile and kissing Mama's hand. 'You're looking as wonderful as ever.'

'More wonderful than ever,' the other men chorused, crowding round, making Mama bat her eyelids and look down shyly. The men loved this, the powerful effect they were having on her.

'That man of yours, where is he?' Mr Mason laughed, and the other men laughed with him. 'Don't tell me.' He laughed some more and the other men again laughed with him. 'Always in the company of lovely women.' The men roared.

Out of the corner of her eye, Mama saw Papa at the other end of the room, not in the company of lovely women, but in the company of one woman. Ann Mitchison threw back her head and laughed, white neck gleaming, tongue and lips vibrant, hair shimmering; and Papa transfixed before her. And Mama saw her white hand touch Papa on the shoulder.

At that moment, the bald men no longer about her, Mama felt a drink pressed into her hand and Myrtle, the estate manager's wife, next to her like a comfort blanket.

Myrtle was a woman who was happy with herself and her station and saw nothing in speaking for hours, it seemed, about such topics as maids and the trials of planning that year's Crop-Over Dance at the club. Mama wanted to get away while wanting, almost as much, to be near someone who wanted to be with her. Myrtle was one of those rare Englishwomen who had lived in Jamaica so long that she was more Jamaican than some of her neighbours.

'Harold's quite a live wire, isn't he?' Myrtle said during one of the few lulls in the conversation, observing Mama as she craned her neck to seek out Papa.

Mama laughed softly and sipped her drink, but she remembered the last time someone used that term of description. It was Papa, describing Ann Mitchison. After that she grew silent and let Myrtle talk. She couldn't bear to watch as Papa was sought out time and time again by their charming hostess. At one point they seemed to glide out onto the verandah in the dim light, like a courting couple. Mama cast her eyes about the room, expecting everyone to be astonished. But the laughter and the chatter, the social intercourse, carried on. She was the only person who noticed. She was the only one who saw them on the evening primrose-scented verandah, in the clinging warmth, under the watching stars, close to touching.

* * *

Eight shillings a week was what Papa paid Adassa. Boyd, standing behind the door wanting news of Susan Mitchison, overheard him say so to Mama in the pantry as he bent over his gun, oiling and polishing the barrel and stock in preparation for his shooting trip with Mr Moodie and Mr Dowding.

'Why is that man still here?' Papa asked, squinting down the barrel.

'Which man?' Mama's expression reflected pure displeasure.

'Adassa's man,' Papa said.

'Adassa's man? You mean Mr Gordon, Adassa's uncle, who brought her on his bicycle?'

'That's the man. What's he doing here?'

'Doing here?'

'He's outside,' Papa said calmly, pointing the barrel of the gun out the window and squeezing the trigger.

Mama clutched at the table and groaned. 'You mustn't do that, Harold,' she said with gritted teeth. 'You know I don't like you having that gun around the house. The children – '

'It's not a gun. It's a shotgun. And you know I keep it in a safe place, away from them. It's impossible to do any harm in the house. Look, he's talking to her right now, her "uncle", if you can believe that.'

'Where?' Mama thought Papa was being silly.

'Look out the window.'

Mama looked and there was Mr Gordon, he of the Raleigh bicycle without fenders, from Accompong. He was partly hidden by the crotons, talking to Adassa on the steps to her room. He took the large paper bag she offered him and put it hastily into the brown crocus bag at his feet. Then he hoisted that up on the handlebars of his bicycle and rode off. Adassa appeared at the door of her room, glanced towards the sky, seemed to sniff the air, came down the steps and continued along the path to the kitchen.

'Oh,' Mama said to Papa, as if it was all clear to her now. 'Adassa told me he was bringing her some personal items. She wasn't certain she'd get the job, you know, and so didn't bring all her personal belongings with her.'

'Oh,' Papa mimicked Mama. 'So this is the last we'll see of him.'

Adassa could now be heard in the kitchen.

'Was that Mr Gordon, Adassa?' Mama called out.

'Who, ma'am?' Adassa seemed surprised.

'Mr Gordon. Was that him?'

Adassa entered the pantry, saw the gun and shrunk

back. 'Is something wrong, ma'am?'

'Adassa, no.' Mama said the words slowly. 'Was that Mr Gordon?'

'Which Mista Gordon, ma'am?' She seemed even more alarmed.

'Your uncle.'

'Mista Gordon?' She gave a short, awkward laugh. 'Oh, you mean Mista Gordon, ma'am. Yes, him come to see how ah doing. But him gone, ma'am.'

'Is he coming back?' Papa asked, still squinting down the barrel of the gun and remembering how she'd left the children unsupervised.

'Coming back, sar?'

'Yes, that is what I said. You understand English, don't you? Is he coming back on the premises? Yes or no?'

'No, sar,' Adassa stammered, knowing that that was the required answer.

'Good,' Papa said, having a mind to fire her on the spot. The impulse, a reflex one, was simply because he was in a quandary about Ann Mitchison. She was in his thoughts and could not be put aside. He wanted to pull the trigger, release the strange pressure that had built up inside him.

Adassa remained rooted to the spot, eyes on the gun.

'It's all right,' Mama said gently, indicating that she could return to the kitchen.

'Yes, ma'am,' Adassa said, bowing and leaving, eyes wide. She was quite shaken.

Mama faced Papa, shocked. 'Are you saying her uncle can't visit her at her place of work?'

'I know these people.' Papa was very casual, giving his full attention to the gun. 'You lived in that gingerbread house all your life till you met me. You don't know them the way I do. You see people. I see shenanigans. I'm telling you, Victoria, that man's no uncle of hers. Keep a sharp eye on her.'

'Not her uncle?' Mama pretended not to hear the reference to the gingerbread house and her inexperience, a not very subtle continuation of the after-dinner argument.

'No,' Papa said, and changed the subject. 'Radcliffe, the tutor I told you about, is coming here tomorrow. He's got a BA from the University College of the West Indies, y'know. We agreed four hours a day, three days a week. Get them in shape before they go back to school.'

Mama remembered, during the only moments they were together at dinner, Ann Mitchison's comment about the Balaclava Academy, the prep school Papa had chosen for Boyd. She intended to send her Susan there too, based on Papa's recommendation.

'See that he gives them the full four hours. That Barrington needs to buckle down, set an example. He spends all his time riding about all over the place like a circus monkey. Get behind him, Victoria. I'm not throwing good money away.'

Mama thought Papa very devious, talking about the children's education rather than concentrating on the issue of immediate concern. She despaired at his insensitivity. Hadn't he been the slightest bit conscious of the attention Ann Mitchison was paying him, and imagined the effect that it might have had on her? And, even if there was nothing in it, why couldn't he be just a little understanding? She felt abandoned.

Papa cleared his throat. 'Anyway, I'm off to the mountains tomorrow.'

'You take care,' Mama said. 'You always hear of someone getting shot by mistake.'

'Moodie and Dowding are good shots. Anyway, make me a nice packed lunch. Don't let Adassa near it. Does that woman ever wash her hands? You do it, Victoria. I don't want her near my sandwiches.' And Papa gave Mama a warm smile, so affectionate that Mama smiled back. Her face softened and her troubles subsided.

Boyd, seeing this display of affection, left his place behind the door and wandered off into the flowery warmth of the garden, where he frolicked with Susan all afternoon, ecstatic with the lovely distress. Her eyes were marbles and her lips rose petals.

That night in bed his thoughts tumbled about. Ever since the dinner at the Mitchisons, he'd wanted to ask Mama about Susan, but there was never a suitable moment to raise the question. And when Papa or Mama or Yvonne, even Barrington, made some reference to the Mitchisons, he had been too self-conscious to say anything. Now Susan was too important to mention.

Mama tumbled about in bed too and could not sleep. She thought she saw Ann Mitchison's face on Papa's pillow. She sat up in bed like a jack-in-the-box. It was then that she knew that she had gone too far. She berated herself: she was wrong, was dreadfully silly and would have to make it up to Papa. Ann Mitchison had simply been the most marvellous hostess. It was true that she had spent a lot of time with Papa. Mama had never seen another woman respond like that to Papa, standing close to him, looking into his eyes, speaking intently. But as the wife of the assistant general manager, of course it was her duty to get to know the competent deputy assistant chief chemist, soon to be assistant chief chemist. Just when Papa was really getting ahead, she, the one person who should provide every possible support, had not been up to it, had behaved like a silly girl, full of jealous impulses. She accepted that it was all because of her inexperience of life, quite unlike the other young women on the estate, who had excess of it. She would stop it at once, that very night, and support her husband.

* * *

When Papa returned from his shooting trip, he was surprised to find that Mr Radcliffe, BA, UCWI, had not turned up. But Barrington was more surprised to find that Papa had returned with only a dozen sad little birds. He couldn't imagine what Papa and his friends had been up to.

If it had been him, the whole family would be feasting on big birds for weeks. Of course, he said all this when Papa was safely at the factory, but he said it all the same. Adassa presented bird for supper two nights in a row.

'Can I have pudding instead?' Yvonne asked on the second evening.

'You don't know what you're missing,' Papa said, forking her tiny bird onto his plate. 'All that sweet pudding will rot your teeth.'

'Adassa, pudding please,' Mama called out to the kitchen.

'You call me, ma'am?' Adassa came halfway into the room.

'Yes, can you please serve the pudding.'

'Pudding, ma'am?'

'Yes, Adassa, pudding.'

'But – ' Adassa spread her hands and pretended to look silly.

'What is it now?' Papa said sharply.

'Nothing, sar. There's no pudding.'

'No pudding?' Mama said, shocked. 'But you baked several yesterday.'

'But, ma'am, you know the children like their pudding and ah cut a slice every now and again, and before you know – '

'Blaming the children now,' Papa muttered, concentrating on his bird, chewing the small brittle bones into pulp.

'Poor Yvonne wanted just a small slice,' Mama despaired.

'Ah get her custard, ma'am. Ah use the half dozen eggs from the laying hens.'

'And ginger beer too.' Yvonne chose her moment effectively.

But puddings were not the only missing items that evening. Mama could not find bed linen – a pair of embroidered pillowcases and two flat sheets. Everyone suggested that the items might have gone astray during the move.

'But I packed everything away carefully,' Mama said in her worried way. *Only the devil could have spirited away the clothes.*

The children were instructed to look again in the cupboards, under beds and in the laundry basket. Adassa searched every inch of the laundry room and when she was through, had to do it all over again. She searched in the grass beneath the clothes' line and in a twenty yard radius. Did the wind blow the clothes off the line? Did Poppy, in a moment of insanity, drag the clothes off and secrete them under the house? Vincent was dispatched to find out. Armed with a broomstick ('Anything could be under the house, like *Duppy*') he searched every dark corner in two minutes flat and emerged, looking over his shoulder. No clothing found.

At dinner the next evening, to everyone's surprise, Papa complimented Adassa on her cooking. She'd prepared Fricassee Chicken, baked breadfruit and a sauce thick with baby onions. The meal was not particularly outstanding.

But Papa said, 'You know, you are a good cook.'

Adassa was astonished. She hung her head. 'Yes, sar?'

'And you bake the best puddings, too.'

'Is true, sar?' Adassa was glowing.

'Yes, it's true. Why don't you bake sweet potato puddings this weekend? Cornmeal puddings too. Use lots of coconut milk and raisins.'

Adassa walked on her toes after that, bursting with confidence.

* * *

Mr Radcliffe BA, UCWI, finally sent word that he couldn't be more sorry. He really had been looking forward to teaching the children and spending time on the estate, but an opportunity that he could not let go had come up – the post of junior master at Cornwall College. Papa was livid. An agreement was an agreement. Radcliffe might have a university degree but he was still one of *those people*. He wouldn't amount to much.

It was such a disappointment, Mr Radcliffe not turning up. All three children had been readying themselves for the first session with him and felt badly let down. Barrington had planned to talk about football and Pele, a Brazilian footballer who was only seventeen years old, and Denis Law, also only seventeen, from England. Their pictures were in the Sunday papers and now in his scrapbook. He'd planned to surprise Mr Radcliffe with page after page of arithmetic, and astonish him with textbooks from Worthy Park Prep. Yvonne planned to recite *Ride a Cock-Horse to Banbury Cross*, and *Hush-a-Bye Baby on the Tree Top*. She had also assembled a pile of books including *The Water Babies* to read to Mr Radcliffe. In a quiet moment she might show off her collection of "pretty lady" pictures, dressed up in an assortment of frocks, cut from the Sunday newspapers and from Mama's discarded *Woman's Own* magazines.

Boyd wasn't at first looking forward to meeting Mr Radcliffe. The wretched man would only make it more difficult for him to muse about Susan. But Papa had said Mr Radcliffe would arrive and so, at the last minute, he too made his plans. He would read passages from *Gulliver's Travels* and *Robinson Crusoe* because these were the sort of books Mr Radcliffe would probably expect him to read, children's books. He would recite "Excelsior" by Henry Wadsworth Longfellow and "Silver" by Walter De La Mere. And then, since Mr Radcliffe's degree was in English which Papa had praised at the dinner table, describing Mr Radcliffe as a man of literature, he would talk about *Tropic of Cancer*. Miss Hutchinson had mentioned the book at the club when talking about her life abroad, the things she'd done, visiting Sacre Coeur, the Louvre, the Left Bank, and having her portrait painted by the street painters of Paris. Not many people had read the book, Miss Hutchinson had said, since it had been banned. But she'd managed to get a copy. It was revolutionary, a real *masterpiece* of literature.

When she said masterpiece, Boyd had been intrigued because of what he imagined such a word to mean. He'd asked her, in a quiet moment, if he could borrow the book. She'd smiled sweetly and bent down for a hug, her breasts spilling out like frolicking puppies about his cheeks.

'I promise,' she said. 'When you're older.' And she kissed him.

After that it was difficult to tell her that he had read *Great Expectations (about Pip, Estella!)*. He just wanted her to know that he wouldn't find it extraordinary to read grown-up books, that he read them all the time.

'You said it's a masterpiece,' was all he said, bottom lip trembling.

Miss Hutchinson smiled warmly. 'It is. A book about life.'

'I want to read it. I can.' He had begged like a child, sensing, too late, that that was the very thing he shouldn't have done.

'I know. You are a very bright little boy, Boyd. One day you must come round to my house and read my books.' And she'd left him in her lingering fragrance contemplating that incredible invitation.

A book about life. That was what he had intended to say to Mr Radcliffe. If they'd got along, as Boyd hoped they would, he might have talked about the new feelings in him, the bewildering Susan feelings. Maybe Mr Radcliffe understood them and could explain.

* * *

Adassa started her baking early that Saturday, buoyed up by the compliments Papa had heaped upon her. As Boyd left the house for the gardens, he heard her singing "Brown Skin Gal" in a voice that radiated pure happiness. But when he returned that afternoon, drunk with secret pleasures, Corporal Duncan's horse, Cyrus, was tethered to the lime tree by the water tank. A bad sign.

He entered the pantry just in time to see Papa and Corporal Duncan, in his squeaking police riding boots, walk grim-faced out the door. The mouth-watering aroma of sweet potato pudding filled the pantry. Mama, Barrington and Yvonne stood silently looking out the window. From the radio in the drawing room a voice sang out, *You made me cry, when you said goodbye, ain't that a shame.*

Through the pantry window, Boyd saw Corporal Duncan and Papa at Adassa's door, Poppy frantic behind them. Corporal Duncan must have knocked a devastating police knock, for Adassa came to the door instantly, her arms flung wide. There was a flurry of movement. Adassa fainted on the steps but came to as suddenly as she went out, helped up by Corporal Duncan. Then they all disappeared into her room, Poppy close behind.

Soon Adassa emerged, weeping noisily. Papa appeared, big bundles in his arms. They saw him throw the bundles onto the grassy verge. The objects rolled about and came to rest in the dirt. Poppy was upon them instantly, savaging each one in turn.

'It's the puddings,' Yvonne breathed.

'How many did she bake?' Mama stared, baffled.

Later that evening, as Adassa left the house for good, a *bankra* on her head, she was a sad figure in the creeping darkness.

'Why can't she leave in the morning?' Mama asked, deploring Papa's hardness. 'How will she get to Accompong at this time of the evening?'

'She should have thought of that when she was busy thieving,' Papa said with vehemence. Mama turned away, exasperated at such reactionary logic.

They watched as Adassa struggled down the driveway on her way to Accompong, ten miles away, with night approaching. Their hearts went out to her. But no one saw the dark figure of Mr Gordon, her "uncle", standing up against his bicycle, waiting impatiently at the end of the road. He had waited there many evenings before under the tamarind tree. As she came towards him, he smiled roguishly, then hoisted her upon the crossbar, placed the last of her bundles across the handlebars and rode off. The Brookeses were not the only people trying to find the right maid. The pretty Indian woman, Miss Chatterjee, was searching too, his spies told him. He would ride up to her house the very next day with Adassa on the crossbar of his Raleigh and try his luck again.

The following afternoon, unusually for him, Papa stayed at home reading the newspaper. He seemed uncharactersitically restless. As it was Sunday, the house was quiet, but because he was home, it was extraordinarily quiet. Mama kept to her room. The radio played Bach's *Jesu, Joy of Man's Desiring*, as on so many Sunday afternoons. The quietness and the music enthralled Boyd, as he sat on the windowsill with the binoculars focused through the trees upon the Mitchisons house, seeing vivid images in pink and feeling wonderful palpitations. And so he did not see Papa pause suddenly in the hall, stare at him hard and walk away shaking his head.

That evening, Papa slapped on more lime-green Limacol cologne than usual. Mama noticed this but said nothing. And even when, just as it got dark, Papa announced, much to Mama's consternation, that he was visiting Tim Mitchison on estate business and left the house with indecent haste, she said nothing. Boyd, staring out the window, full of deep urging, consumed with pleasure and melancholy, longed only for tomorrow.

CHAPTER 12

Tomorrow arrived with a new maid looking so smart that Mama looked her up and down. Her name was Mavis. She came from the district of Taunton where Mr Ten-To-Six lived. Boyd saw at once that she had swelling breasts that moved about and a bottom that wiggled under her dress. She had dimples at the back of her knees and his eyes wandered there. Once she caught him looking and pushed out her tongue and wagged her little finger. 'You little cutie,' she said. They giggled.

Mavis radiated a scent that he did not know (she called it *Essen*) and on weekends wore bright red paint (she called it *Cutex*) on her fingernails. He spent much of his time watching her from behind curtains and doors, through louvres, from behind trees and from other places. Sometimes, when he thought she wasn't looking she turned unexpectedly and showed him her wet, pink tongue. She came with music too. Every day, from the first day she arrived, "Since I Met You Baby" echoed throughout the house.

'Is Ivory Joe Hunter,' Mavis said, when Yvonne asked, before bursting into song, breasts bouncing, skirts shimmering.

Ivory Joe Hunter came from America. He crooned from the small brown radio with the cream knobs in Mavis's room all day and all night: *Since I met you baby, my whole life has changed, and everybody tells me that I am not the same.* They had never known a maid to own a radio. This surely must be the best maid of all.

During the week, Mavis smelled of the kitchen, thyme and rose water, Ajax "the foaming cleanser", Jeyes and stewing and baking things from the black Caledonian Modern Dover stove. The aroma of detergent, baked pork and fried plantain wafted from her in complex whiffs and draughts. But on weekends, starting on Friday nights, she changed, becoming a sweet-smelling lily-of-the-valley. She became pink powder and red lipstick. She was *Essen*, drifting cleanliness and *Cutex*. Her scents told of exotic nightlife, thumping music in dance halls, the world of film shows, blazing guns, people embracing and kissing. The children knew this because Mavis told them so as they sat on her bed, listening rapt to her adventures as she dressed. At weekends she was romance and danger, provocative, exuding mounting excitement about what men did to maids on a Friday night in the dark, hot places out of reach of the coloured lights. She came out of the radio at weekends just like "Since I Met You Baby". And she took Boyd's breath away. Even Susan took a back seat that first week. It was because Mavis reflected, vaguely, some of the characteristics of Lydia Parsons, Pepsi, Estella and the pink women.

At the end of the second week, Mavis left the house before it got dark, when the sky was bright orange and the swallows were out. When she left her room to say good evening to Mama and Papa, she was powdered, lipsticked and *Cutexed*. She was a new person in floral skirts, oiled calves smooth and firm, black high-heeled shoes loud on the polished floors, white earrings clipped to fleshy lobes and *Essen* all about her. It was an event, and the children hung about to witness it. Mavis's breasts were as moist as her lips, and when she walked, so confident on the polished floor, her bottom made her skirt shudder. Boyd looked up at her with feeling, his senses enveloped in *Essen* and thoughts of the beautiful evening. Mavis, looking round, bent down low to caress his cheek, and her breasts smothered his face.

'Will you be back before ten?' he heard Mama ask.

'Ah don't know, ma'am,' Mavis replied.

'Well, when?'

'About twelve, ma'am. Ah getting a ride back.'

'All the way from Siloah?'

'Yes, ma'am.'

'The dishes washed and everything put away?'

'Oh, yes, ma'am.' Mavis's breasts rose. Her high heels made little clicks on the floor and *Essen* came off her like steam from horses galloping in the rain.

'And everything ready for tomorrow? Peas shelled?'

'No, ma'am. But ah can do that first thing in the morning.'

'Are you sure?'

'You know me, ma'am.' Mavis smiled confidently.

To the children listening, this was unfamiliar territory for Mama. If Mavis said that she could manage to shell the peas first thing in the morning, everyone knew the job would be done. They suspected a hidden hand in Mama's questioning. The words, though spoken by Mama, belonged to Papa. Just then, in that moment of quiet between Mama's question and Mavis's answer, a passionate voice from the radio said, *I want you to taaake me, where I beeelong, where hearts have been broken with a kiss and a sooong.*

'Is Fats Domino,' Mavis breathed at them.

Boyd, overcome with passions, watched her from behind the curtains of his bedroom window as she walked down the long driveway to her evening of indulgence. He saw himself leaving the house, like Mavis, as the day ended, to meet a waiting Susan silhouetted against a crimson sunset. And the Black River valley was the valley of tears, *where hearts have been broken with a kiss and a song.* Vincent watched too, standing by the door to his room, his arms hanging straight down at his sides, his loins on fire.

Papa said, 'Is she gone?'

Without waiting for a reply, Papa rose from the sofa,

keys in hand, and went out the kitchen door. The children, sensing drama in the air, followed. Mama stayed behind. When they trooped past the ironing room and past the maids' bathroom, Mavis's smell of fresh Lifebuoy soap was still there, as were the soapsuds in the gutter. It was a decent scent. They got to Mavis's room and Papa opened the door. *Cutex*, *Essen* and the smell of straightened-hair met them at the door. There was a guilty air about as Papa went through Mavis's things. What he was looking for, no one knew. They stood back, breathing in her *Essen*. Her bed was made but slightly ruffled; the state of young women's beds everywhere who go out for the evening. Pink talcum powder from a pink box was scattered over one half of her small side-table. Hair curlers, a black comb, white plastic brush, two small bottles of *Cutex* and her hot-comb full of pulled black hair covered the other half of the table. Her brown plastic Bush radio with the round cream-coloured knobs was in the middle of everything, looking enchanting and important because it brought foreign voices and bewitching music into her room. Papa saw it and raised his eyebrows. He opened her drawers and her wardrobe, searching between hanging dresses. He searched under the bed, the cardboard grip in the corner and looked towards the ceiling. He found nothing.

'All right,' he said at last. 'That's it.'

'That's it?' Yvonne was disappointed. She'd been expecting them to find secret boxes filled with puddings, bed linen and other things stolen from under their noses.

Papa ignored her, closed Mavis's door behind them and returned to the house. They could see Vincent sitting on the doorstep of his own room roasting cashews. Boyd stayed back. Vincent's fire was red and orange and gave off twirly blue smoke with a delicious odour of dry burning leaves. Although his eye was lowered, Vincent observed Papa closely, his brows Rasputin-dark, breathing like a trapped volcano.

* * *

Mavis was outrageously half-naked but that was nothing to her. Yvonne and Boyd sat on her bed and listened to her talk excitedly about a world they did not know. In that world were dances, gambling, goings-on everywhere and films (*The Robe, Billy the Kid, Red River, High Noon*). Boyd had been to the pictures only once, to see a western called *Ride, Vaquero!* Papa hadn't wanted to take them as they would have to mix with the riff-raff, people rank with sweat and cheap perfume. But Barrington had begged because Robert Taylor was in it, and finally Papa had given in. That was over a year ago but Boyd remembered the gripping movie music, "The Melody of Love", precursor to the unforgettable images, the kissing, the galloping horses, the shoot-out, the sudden death.

Mavis spoke eloquently of the Roxy, where the screen was full of crimson writing dripping in drama, music extracting emotions so powerful that she did not always know who she was when she emerged from the cinema. She mentioned names they had never heard of, in a tone surpassing worship – Randolph Scott, Joel McCrea, Ava Gardner, Victor Mature, Gary Cooper, Robert Mitchum and Jennifer Jones. These people were film stars and were "starring" in the films, which were in something called Technicolor. She told them about the films she'd seen, films of romance, westerns, about cowboys dressed in black. She talked engagingly about how women and men kissed (she hugged herself to demonstrate) in stunning and intimate close-ups: lips squashed together, the women's lipsticked lips quivering like a red beating heart, writhing as the music rose with their tortured breaths filling the cinema. *And they kissed with their tongues.*

'Why do they kiss with their tongues?' Yvonne's brows were wrinkled.

Mavis gave her a compassionate but pitiful look. 'You too young to know.'

But Boyd knew at once. Kissing was the closest thing to sucking the flowers and Mama's titties. He wanted to do it too, enveloped in *Essen* and *Cutex* and movie music and passion. He wanted to do it with the squashed red lips of someone, in Technicolor. He wanted to do it at sunset or in the afternoon in the shade, do it hidden in the rain, do it in the grass on a bed of crimson blossoms, do it in the fragrant heat. He wanted to do it when there was no one about, only her, and he wanted to do it soon. Kiss was a crimson lollipop on his tongue.

Sitting on Mavis's bed with growing intimacy, it felt as if they were at the cinema hearing the breathless voices, seeing the stunning close-ups. The sweet scent of kiss was everywhere. And the perfume from Mavis's beauty bottles, cachets and vials and the music from her pretty plastic radio evoked a palpable sense of drama.

'Who's in it?' Yvonne asked.

'What, sugar?'

'*The Robe.*'

Mavis flashed her hands to dry her *Cutex*. *The Robe* was the latest film she'd seen. Her titties bounced. 'V-i-c-t-o-r M-a-t-u-r-e!' She pronounced the name with wonder and adulation. 'It's about the robe that Jesus wore before he was crucified. God is coming to take his world. There will be fire and brimstone. Mark me words.'

'When?' Yvonne asked excitedly.

'When? When? When him ready.'

'But why?'

'Why?' Mavis said, looking with genuine sadness at Yvonne. 'Why? Because man wicked.' She looked at herself in the mirror. 'God said, "Follow me and I shall make you fishers of men." But what did man do? Turn to wickedness, turn to adultery.'

Yvonne and Boyd looked up instantly. It was Papa's word, *adultery*, the thing that *those people* who were going to England were only good for.

'What is adultery?' Yvonne glanced sideways at Boyd.

'What? What? Wickedness. Man turn to wickedness, drinking and gambling.' But Mavis did not finish her recitation. Her pretty plastic radio spoke to her. 'Johnny Cash!' she cried, snapping her fingers, arms in the air, body twirling, eyes dreamy.

A deep voice on the radio growled, *Because you are mine, I walk the line.* The voice was accompanied by a big guitar and Mavis repeated every word of the song. They regarded her with awe and thought that *adultery* wasn't so bad after all. Mr Moodie was always drinking and gambling and he certainly wasn't one of *those people.*

That evening, Mavis wore yellow nylon panties and very red lipstick. Her mouth was like a full red kiss. The dance halls of Taunton and Siloah waited for her with their shadows and sound systems. And men from districts far and near, with their rum breaths, gold teeth and sly looks waited too. As the children watched, she combed her hair, applying more *Essen* under her armpits, behind her ears and between her breasts. Then Barrington entered the room, scowled at them and pretended not to see Mavis.

'The *Cutex* not dry,' Mavis said, flashing her arms about as she sat on the small stool, thighs splayed. The music from the WINZEE station came clean and true. Johnny Cash departed and other voices replaced him: Lloyd Price, Professor Longhair, Gene and Eunice and Della Reese. The children crowded round, drunk with excitement. Boyd felt as if he was inside the radio, in the heart of the music. Endless bliss lived in Mavis's room.

'This is nice *Essen*,' Yvonne observed, using Mavis's term, taking her finger from the oblong bottle, touching her ears and sighing dramatically. 'I'm going to wear this.'

'When you older,' Mavis said.

'When I'm older?' Yvonne responded with astonishment. 'I'm five!'

'You not old enough.'

'How old are you?' Yvonne sniffed the *Essen* and dipped her fingers into a tub of pink Cashmere face powder.

'Older than you,' Mavis said, slipping on her party dress, wriggling her bottom to get the dress in place. Her slip and brassiere straps stood out against her bare, dark shoulders, which were so smooth and polished that they shone.

'Tell us,' Barrington said, breaking away from the window where he'd been gazing intently towards the driveway through the trees. He'd been half expecting the Prefect to come roaring up to deposit a menacing Papa by the garage door, giving them no time to get away from Mavis's room. 'Let me catch you in there again and I'll give you such a whipping!' Papa had warned them, the muscles in his jaws giving powerful meaning to every word. But Mavis's room was enticing even to Barrington, who, as the oldest child, was expected to set an example by obeying Papa. Unfortunately, he couldn't obey all the time. In fact, he was so good at obeying that Boyd and Yvonne, although not saying so, felt a special pleasure at his presence. It gave their presence legitimacy.

'Eighteen,' Mavis said.

'Eighteen,' Yvonne whispered in disbelief, her face now puce with the pink powder. 'You are old.'

'Not older than your mama,' Mavis replied, zipping herself up, the daisy-patterned frock tight around her waist.

'Do you have any babies?' Yvonne asked.

'Babies!' Mavis exclaimed. 'What ah want with babies?'

'Mama is having a baby.'

'You don't know anything,' Barrington told Yvonne, eyeing Mavis as she pulled up her dress around her smooth thighs.

Boyd looked about self-consciously, wanting to tell them what he knew about babies coming out of his teapot, about how Mama and Papa made babies in the night, but restrained himself.

'Ah'm not ready to have babies,' Mavis said. 'Ah'm seeing man.'

Again they all stared at her, doubly shocked. They knew the words were meant to be shocking. They resonated with Papa's own words at the dinner table, that maids were *loose* and always *going off* with men who meant them no good.

Papa had banned them from singing "Marianne," the song that talked about *taking man*. It was the forbidden song whose words should never cross their lips. They had no idea why the song should be forbidden but since it was, they lost no time in trying to find out why. But their investigations produced nothing. Mavis knew that Papa had banned it, having listened to the talk as she went from dinner table to kitchen. She was saying nothing. A line from the song, performed by a local band, went, *Marianne, down by the seaside taking man.*

'What is *seeing* man, *taking* man?' Yvonne brows were now contorted. Mavis was bound to explain it to them just as she had explained about adultery.

But all Mavis said was, 'Hush your mouth.' And that was the end of it.

Mavis left the house as it grew dark. She was going off to take men, dance and drink in places where there were coloured lights and thumping music. And men who meant her no good would hold her tight, writhing into the night, smudging her red lipstick.

No one heard when she returned home, but she did, because breakfast was on the table the next morning when they got up, the sun brilliant orange outside the window. Boyd examined her for signs, anything that would give an indication of what happened the night before at that place where she was *taking man*. He searched her out – first her eyes, then her breasts, arms, calves, neck. Was she the same Mavis, their Mavis? He wanted to see the dress she'd worn the night before – was it crumpled, full of alien scents? He knew how Papa's clothes smelled when he was out all night – rum, cigarette, Brookeses sweat and unknown adult odours. He would go to her room.

His chance came during the afternoon when Papa left for the factory. The Sunday sun beat down, the sky as clear as glass, reflecting purple bougainvillea. It reflected the sand-coloured quarters where Mavis pottered about in her slip, sipping electric pink Kool-Aid, trying to recover from the exertions of the night before. Her little Bush radio was tuned permanently to WINZEE not to Radio Jamaica. Her hair was in curlers and her legs folded under her on the bed as she applied new red *Cutex* to her fingernails.

'Hello, cutie,' she said, as Boyd entered the room.

Boyd sat on the bed next to her. The dress she wore the night before was hanging in the opened closet, crumpled. It burst with mysteries. Her shoes, cast aside, worn out, lay under the closet. She made space for him beside her on the bed, drawing one leg up and sticking out her pink tongue. The strap of her slip slid down her arm revealing a firm breast. She eased the remaining strap down. Then she closed the *Cutex* bottle and placed it on the little side table, fanning her fingers in the air. His eyes never left her titties.

Realising that his eyes were glued to that one place, Mavis jiggled and bounced her titties about. As his eyes widened, she laughed and he giggled, drawing back in a shy way. She thought he looked like an enquiring puppy, darting eyes following a bouncing ball, small body without history, incapable of knowledge, unsullied, like breast milk. She placed a frolicking finger in the centre of his forehead and watched as his eyes narrowed.

Boyd saw the red *Cutex*, sniffed its red scent, felt the warm finger turning in a circle on his forehead. His hand went up involuntarily, slid along Mavis's smooth arm, and reached out, grasping for the taut brown breast. Mavis's giggle was like a prolonged sneeze, and Boyd took away his hand, alarmed at her giggling. Then, with a mischievous gaze, he gingerly returned his hand, patted and stroked her fleshy baubles, softly, gently, delicately, until Mavis stopped giggling and grew quiet. And her radio said, *Even little children loved Marianne, down by the seaside sifting sand.*

At breakfast, Mavis gave Boyd looks that he could not appreciate. She stroked his cheeks as she passed behind his chair and giggled when their eyes met. Mama saw this and smiled affectionately.

* * *

Under the bright Appleton sun, Boyd and Poppy eyed Mavis as she hung the clothes out to dry. They were not alone. Vincent's eyes were upon her too. They watched her against the blue of the sky. *This is the way we wash our clothes, wash our clothes, wash our clothes. This is the way we wash our clothes, so early Monday morning.* Mavis hung out great white sheets, whiter than white from the Reckitt's Blue; sheets that billowed and flapped, their brightness making Boyd and Poppy blink. She held wooden clothes pins in her mouth and her hands were full of damp clothes still smelling of Tide soap flakes. Because the clothes pins prevented her singing, she hummed and moved her head about in wordless rhapsody. Her own skirts billowed up in the wind and she kept bending in a funny dance to hide her exposed knees and thighs. She made Poppy bark with the dance. And when she stared down into the valley where the river reflected blue sky, Boyd stared too, in calm repose, drugged with tranquillity.

Down over the fence he looked, down where the splendid brown cows stood proud in the rolling Appleton fields, so brown and so splendid that they glistened and bristled in the clean Jamaican sun. He looked down past the grey wooden fence and into the white road stretching into the distance, before it vanished in the green of guinep and cashew trees. There in the distant whiteness, like a spot on stretched clean sheets, appeared the dark figure of Mr Ten-To-Six on his black Raleigh bicycle, his head held low.

Mr Ten-To-Six rode on by the lightning-struck, weather-beaten tree at the junction of the estate road and the road from Taunton. He rose up in the saddle as the road ascended two hundred yards to a plateau, descended steeply past the black bulls and the meadow full of daisies and buttercups, down to the rivet-filled bridge over the Black River. Mr Ten-To-Six reached the plateau in a steady zigzag of concentrated brute force, seemed to rest

114

momentarily at the top then free-wheeled down to the bridge, white dust rising behind him. Over the bridge he went and was immediately swallowed up by the embracing cane leaves. But just before he was swallowed up, the sun caught the blade of his cutlass for a split second, and Boyd and Poppy were amazed at the violent flash of white heat that engulfed him. It was as though fire and brimstone had sought him out and struck him to the ground, pulverising him into white dust. Then the road was quiet again and they returned their attention to the exotic figure of Mavis, her frolicking breasts and flamboyant pink tongue, and to Vincent spying on her from behind the trees.

* * *

With the arrival of Mavis, Vincent seemed a new person. He was transformed from a distrustful hunchback into a kindly dwarf.

One day, from his hiding place in the garden, Boyd saw Vincent peeping into the maids' shower room. But Mavis wasn't there. Boyd could see her entering the house. He knew the scene Vincent expected to see because he himself had already seen it: Mavis naked under the shower. She was like the women statues in the encyclopaedia, firm and without blemish, and she had the same three tufts of dark hair, like Perlita and Mama. Unlike Perlita, she didn't shriek under the gushing water. She just hummed.

Vincent's behaviour intrigued Boyd so much that that afternoon he and Poppy observed him keenly as he worked. Vincent worked quietly, head down, at intervals expertly flicking a finger across his lined forehead to clear the perspiration. He was bent at the knees now, weeding the flowerbeds under the drawing room windows, paying particular attention to Mama's forget-me-nots. His short trousers, of a thick green khaki, reached to his knees, showing off huge, rock-hard calves and rough, hairy shins.

115

He was only twenty yet could pass for forty.

'Does it hurt?'

Vincent turned towards Boyd but said nothing.

'Your eye,' Boyd explained, pointing.

Vincent was surprised. People never expressed concern about him. Grown men tripped him up when he wasn't looking and little boys took aim with their slingshots when he walked the streets. It was all about his eye. People always assumed that his eye was all there was about him, that he was his eye. It was the only thing people saw when they looked at him. He knew how people made him feel, and it was only because they viewed him through his eye. To them he was a *one-eyed* person. He was much more than that.

'No, it don't hurt,' he said, straightening up and smiling.

'Did you get it in a fight with hooligans?'

'No, ah'm not a fighting man.' Vincent chuckled.

'How then?'

'Ah was born wid it.'

'Born with it? But how?'

Vincent wasn't used to this. He shrugged, not knowing what to answer. There was a long silence broken by the sound of a distant aeroplane. Both Boyd and Vincent gazed upwards. Vincent thought, as he often did, how great man was to put a metal machine in the sky. But you wouldn't catch him going in an aeroplane. Not even that BOAC. He left that to foreign people.

As if reading his thoughts, Boyd asked, 'Are you going to England to better yourself?'

Vincent smiled. In spite of his natural reticence, the words poured out.

'Heh, heh. Ah not going to Englan'. Ah staying right here. One day ah will have a little house, a acre of land and a few chicken. And maybe a young woman in the house.' As he said this he glanced slyly towards the kitchen where Mavis was preparing lunch.

Then Boyd asked a question he instinctively knew could

be asked of Vincent: Pepsi's question, which could never be forgotten.

'Have you ever seen a naked woman?'

Vincent, startled, carried on weeding. Since Boyd, he guessed, was only seven or eight years old, he couldn't possibly have asked such a question.

'Not your mother,' Boyd continued. 'Have you ever seen a naked woman?'

This time Vincent faced Boyd with an expression of sheer incomprehension but remained silent. Again he returned to his gardening.

'I saw Mavis under the shower,' Boyd said.

As Vincent looked up, Mavis came down the kitchen steps, her breasts and bottom in a jolly romp, heading towards her room. They all turned to look, in silence, their movements frozen. Poppy left first, as if trailing a scent, his tail in the air, and Boyd quickly followed. When they were gone, Vincent relaxed a bit, staring with juvenile lust at the receding back of the young maid. He swept perspiration from his forehead with a quick flick of his index finger, sighing with delayed astonishment.

Vincent didn't mind at all that Mavis paid him not the slightest attention and was thoughtless in her responses, ignorantly referring to him on one occasion as "That one-eyed Cyclops". He was grateful to be on the same premises as her, grateful that he could behold her day after day, grateful for the pleasures she stimulated in him. A time would come when he would be able to enter the rum bar in his district of a Friday evening when it was crowded and have those people, the ones who talked behind his back, treat him like a man. But he was rendered invisible without a woman, lacked status, bereft of everything that made a man a man in the place where he was born. Mavis was the woman who could change his life for the better. She was also the pain in his heart. The more she trampled him underfoot, the more he welcomed the pain of her abuse.

After only a month, Mama announced that Mavis was a

"good, clean girl". She had found her maid at last. Papa was well pleased. He knew, from searching Mavis's room, that she was not a thief, from her meals that she was a good cook, and from her behaviour that she was the perfect little companion for Mama. In her first week in the job, Mavis slammed the door in the faces of two Jehovah's Witnesses. And three other women who, judging by their peculiar attire, could only have been Bible women, were sent packing with the words, 'Mrs Brookes don't need no Bible, clear off!' Papa rejoiced.

He marked the occasion by spending all night at the club, only coming home in the wee hours, quite drunk. He was so drunk that, in the morning, Boyd sniffed the awful vomity fumes as he lay stretched out in the guest room in his sleeveless vest and blue striped boxer shorts, senseless, his nocturnal deeds unknown. Next to the chamber pot of vomit on the floor lay his soiled clothing.

That Sunday, the sun beat down crisp and clear and white oleander blossoms fell like magic snowflakes along the driveway. The valley and the garden gave up fascinating fragrances and on the radio a choir sang, *All things bright and beautiful, All creatures great and small, All things wise and wonderful, The Lord God made them all.* But Mama stayed in her bedroom, sewing quietly, unable to disguise her deepening anxiety, unable to restrain the creeping jealousies. When she came out for lunch, the children saw that her face was terribly drawn. And Boyd was filled with deep remorse because his secret pleasures were immense, his head full of pretty images of the pink girl, full of things bright and beautiful. But that evening, for the first time, he didn't watch the sunset and the darting swallows from his place on the verandah. He stayed in his room wondering at the nature of Mama's distress, not understanding his own.

And that same evening, as the orange sky changed to vermilion and the swallows came out, Susan Mitchison rode gingerly down the road, eyes fixed on the pink house.

His name was Boyd, the boy who lived at the pink house, her mother had said, and he would be going to the same school as her in September. She stared long and hard up the driveway and at the empty verandah. If only he would come out and play with her instead of hiding behind the shrubbery and the trees. They would ride down the lane and along the river road together. And what a lovely little dog! It would be so nice to run up and down the garden with them, somersault down the slope, swing from the branch of a tree, ride to the riverbank and watch the mongoose, hide in the canes and feel the sugar-scented heat. And at night, while her mother talked with Mr Brookes, she'd often seen them, they could snuggle up in bed and tell stories. And she would tell him about "As You Like It", the story in her book, Lambs' Tales from Shakespeare. She would tell him that he was Orlando and she was Rosalind, that Rosalind liked Orlando the very first time she saw him in the Forest of Arden. She would tell him things she couldn't tell anyone else.

CHAPTER 13

In the morning, Boyd, troubled still by Mama's unease, wandered behind the house overlooking the valley, near to the spot where he had seen Susan's mother gazing down at the coolie settlement. As he gazed into the distance, he saw Papa's Land Rover racing along the valley road away from the estate in the direction of Maggotty. Behind it raced the Land Rover of the Mitchisons. The vehicles disappeared together in the blue-green expanse of sugar cane. Boyd watched the white road for a long time, the only sound the testing calls of crickets in the thickets, then calmly walked away, head down.

Moments later, from another strategic spot in the gardens, he spied someone on a bicycle in the shadows of the private road – a pink figure, hair tossing in the sun. Realising immediately who it was, he rushed madly out into the sun towards the fence, keeping very close to the trees. Susan was on her own – a stabbing emotion among the apple-green leaves. Her face was hot and glowing, her hands grasping the handlebars tightly, hair in motion. Her uncertain legs pumped at the pedals from under a yellow printed cotton dress. Boyd's head hurt with incomprehension and wonder. He watched her get off the bicycle and look in his direction. She did not see him. Was she thinking of him? Turning round, she rode back up the road towards her house, looking desperately through the trees. Boyd did not move. She was looking for him. He did not know what he was feeling because he had not felt it before. But he knew he was frightened.

'Boyd not eating, ma'am,' Mavis said to Mama. 'Is the second day in a row he leave half his lunch on the plate.'

Mama went to Boyd's room immediately, closely followed by Mavis. He was lying on the bed, looking out the window.

'You're not well,' Mama said, feeling his forehead. 'What is it?'

'Nothing, Mama,' Boyd said, taken aback with the sudden attention and with Mavis staring, her big girl's eyes crystal clear.

'P'rhaps me cooking don't agree with him, ma'am,' Mavis suggested over Mama's shoulders, not masking her worry.

'No, no,' Mama replied reassuringly. 'He loves your cooking- your rice and peas, your ginger cakes, your dumplings, roast beef and carrots, everything!'

Mavis exchanged warm looks with Boyd. 'Maybe he eating too much fruit, ma'am,' she said. 'Too much of one thing good for nothing.'

'Are you, Boyd?'

'No, Mama,' Boyd said, weakening, having a sudden rash impulse to tell them everything, about the Susan feelings, the fever, the sweet mystery, other things that he knew. But he did not know how to say it. The feelings had no matching words, were just flutterings, palpitations, sublime music, like "The Melody of Love", played on the gramophone at the cinema just before the showing of a film.

'Well, I think it's all that fruit,' Mama said. 'Maybe green plums? You need to eat properly and grow up to be a big, healthy boy.' She took her hand away from his forehead. 'My little *peeny-waalie*.'

'Yes, Mama,' he said, loving the fact that he was her *little peeny-waalie*.

Mama thought she saw panic in his eyes but she couldn't be sure. Boyd watched them go, Mavis with her dimpled back-of-knees and bouncy manner and Mama gliding and cool in her maternity clothes. A soft breeze rustled the curtains, bringing fragrances of Susan. And cool shadows crossed the lawn, heralding an evening of dramatic images and beautiful anguish.

On the third day, he came down with a raging fever.

'Ah'll have to make him mint tea right away,' Mavis said, hurrying off to the kitchen the moment she found out.

'No,' Mama told her. 'Ginger tea, Mavis. Fresh ginger.'

'Yes, ma'am,' Mavis said, pausing in mid-stride. 'We have a heap of fresh ginger. A good thing Vincent bring some in from the back garden this morning.'

Boyd spent the afternoon in Mama's arms, his temples burning and his body sickly hot. He felt Mama's tummy where the little baby was and breathed Mama's scent, comforting and good, but hearing notes of distress. And he listened for the voices of the garden, and they came to him in rich, wonderful tones, repeating only one name.

Over at the Mitchison's house at about that time, Ann Mitchison felt Susan's forehead not once but twice. Susan was sitting up in bed, gazing out the window at the magic garden. A copy of *Lambs' Tales from Shakespeare* lay on her pillow opened at "As You like It". Above her head the mosquito net was tied in a single knot, just like the knot that prevented her breathing, just like the knot in her stomach. Her head hurt, but it was pleasant lying in bed with her mother's warm hand on her forehead. Susan had big feelings too, feelings that words could not describe, feelings that came with music and colour, feelings that overwhelmed her. *She was snug in bed in the cottage in the Forest of Arden. And she was awaiting Orlando's arrival. He would come to her out of the forest.*

'It's all right, darling,' Ann Mitchison said. 'Mummy's here.' And she took Susan in her arms, seeing the weepy face and remembering the time, in Barbados, when she had last seen that expression. On that day they had been unable to find Susan. They searched everywhere, the maid and gardener joining in, scouring beneath the house, combing the adjoining fields, calling her name. And when the men from the estate heard that she couldn't swim, they ran even more frantically up and down the banks of the river at the back of the house shouting out her name. Finally, when they were exhausted and desperate, thinking the worst, the maid found Susan sitting quietly under overhanging bushes not far from the house, at the point of tears, gazing intently into the heart of a beautiful red anthurium and fingering its leathery flower. She had heard nothing.

It was the same week during which Papa returned home from the club two nights in a row, so late that not even dogs barked. When he came to bed, Mama detected stale perfume. But she dispelled the thought, a wicked, wicked thought, immediately.

'Late drinks session at the club,' was all Papa said on both occasions, getting into bed and falling asleep almost instantly.

On both nights, Mama lay awake, unable to sleep.

* * *

That Sunday evening, the Moodies visited to celebrate Papa's promotion. The pink house stood big and handsome in the midst of luxuriant greenery. Papa was standing on the clipped green lawn, back to the sun, hands on hips. He had been pointing out parts of the house to Mr Moodie.

'This could be the manager's house,' his after-lunch voice boasted. He spread his arms wide as he spoke and bared his teeth in a wide smile.

Mr Moodie laughed, slapped Papa on the back, and both retired to the green lattice table and chairs on the lawn with bottles of gin and rum. Papa talked about how Appleton was good for ten thousand tons of refined sugar that year, about quotas and the world market, boring Moodie to death. Then Papa mentioned the new assistant general manager and his wife.

'She's not a bad-looking woman,' Moodie observed,

coming to life. 'But married to a man like that! He could be her father, the age on him.'

'You don't know what you're talking about,' Papa said dismissively. 'Most Englishmen look like that. They bald before their time. It's the weather over there. They're a decent couple, with the right values.'

'Harry, what do you care?' Moodie stared at him.

'A little bit more than you do. She's not your typical Englishwoman come out to the colonies, full of ignorance and prejudice. She genuinely gets involved. She's trying to get work for some of the coolies down at the settlement; that bugger Ramsook and his hordes. And she talks sensible politics too.'

'You think because she is English it's okay for her to flirt the way she does? If our wives were to behave like that we wouldn't tolerate it for one minute, not one minute, Harry. You know I'm right.'

'For Christ's sake, man, she's not flirting. She's being sociable. She's just not stuck up. I've worked on sugar estates where the wives of foreign managers look down their noses at you. She's good for Appleton.'

'Mitchison evidently doesn't agree with you. He spends most of his time away from her, supposedly on business. People say he may have a woman in Kingston. The maids are talking too. And they always know a thing or two.'

Mavis drew near with the ice bucket and they stopped talking.

Papa and Mr Moodie sat in the shade, where the jacaranda blossoms formed a blue carpet on the bottle-green grass under their feet. Mr Moodie was dressed in flashy two-tone shoes, white trousers, lime-green shirt and dark-green sunglasses. This was not his usual attire, and later Papa said he was only trying to keep up with Patricia Moodie. The children were fascinated by the dark glasses because they were mainly seen on people in magazines and on film posters. If they didn't know who Mr Moodie was, they might have thought he was a visiting film star.

As Mavis returned to the house, Mr Moodie continued. 'They certainly know a thing or two, the maids. And another thing, Harry, she might not be your typical Englishwoman, Ann Mitchison, but I bet you she's already fooling around.'

'Christ almighty, man!' Papa turned away in disgust.

'You take it from me, I know women. She looks the type. She'll play, and she'll play discreetly.'

'So you think everybody's at it.'

'Harry, I know women.'

'You don't know what the hell you're talking about.' Papa was clearly put out and Mr Moodie wondered at this because there was no basis for it.

Papa knocked back his drink and called out for Mama to join them. Mama was busy with Patricia Moodie in her bedroom, talking nineteen to the dozen like young girls. That day, Patricia Moodie seemed like an actress herself, 'Like Audrey Hepburn,' Mavis told them. She was dressed in an apple-green swing skirt that moved with a life of its own, sweeping the furniture and the children who stood around. But most of all it was her perfume ('Good *Essen*,' Mavis said) that made Boyd swoon. He'd been swooning ever since she arrived in the red open-top Buick.

'What's buzzing?' she said when she arrived, flowing into the house, sunglasses perched on her forehead. The children had smiled sheepishly and Yvonne walked immediately behind her, copying her walk, extending her arms with fingers splayed, her bottom in a quick left-right, left-right motion.

Papa's guests laughed long into the evening. When their spirits soared impetuously after several gin and tonics, Patricia Moodie suggested driving up to the club.

'To the club! To the club!' She darted away, white teeth flashing, neck like a swan, arms flailing the air. 'Catch me, Moodie, catch me!' She was as restless as the wind.

'Go as you are, Victoria,' Papa said quietly as a compliment, not looking at Mama, who sat back, horrified.

She was wearing a floral frock with a single string of pearls and seemed casually elegant. But going to the club meant dressing up.

'They're so happy,' Mama murmered, observing her guests embracing against a pink sunset. She didn't face Papa, who said nothing.

'Live for today!' Patricia Moodie cried, returning from her little run, free from the clutches of Mr Moodie, visibly intoxicated. 'Let the good times roll, Daddy-O.'

'The good times are already rolling for Harry and Victoria,' Mr Moodie said. 'The house, the Land Rover, whitewall tyres for the car, young Barrington off to Munro. And did you see their new maid?'

'She's so young,' Patricia Moodie breathed. 'And such lovely skin.'

'But not as lovely as Ann Mitchison.' Mr Moodie roared mischievously in his gin and tonic voice. He winked at Papa, who winced.

'She's refreshing,' Patricia Moodie said to Mama, not appreciating Moodie's joke. 'She could really improve Appleton.'

'Yes?' Mama said, looking suspicious.

'Oh, yes. You need a woman like that in a place like this. Did you know that she set up education classes for some of the poor young girls at Siloah?'

'Oh,' Mama said.

'One helluva woman,' Mr Moodie said, chuckling.

After a brief silence, Papa got up. 'Well, let's go,' he said.

Poor Mavis was forced to cancel all her plans for the evening, cajoling Vincent, who didn't need much cajoling, into running four miles with a message to her family in Taunton, while the Prefect, reflecting the blazing red sunset in its rear window, roared off down the driveway and to the club.

Boyd watched from the verandah as they left. He was tortured with feeling and went deep into himself. *Papa and Mama had changed. He could feel the space between them and hear the words that they were not speaking. That evening, the Mullard radio whispered "The Blue Danube Waltz". He wanted to creep into the radio, drugged with passion. He was Boyd, but he was nothing. And then he was everything and did not wish it and was overwhelmed with the music and saw beautiful things and started to cry. He just wanted Mama and Papa to talk to each other again, for Susan to come riding up the driveway and smile and say 'Hello, Boyd'. But the music wrenched at his heart and wouldn't stop.*

* * *

Papa had shocking news at dinner a few nights later. Patricia Moodie had left Mr Moodie.

'Walked out on him,' Papa said grimly. 'No gratitude.'

Mama's hand flew to her opened mouth. 'No,' she gasped.

'Yes,' Papa confirmed.

The children stopped eating their boiled bananas and mackerel, onions and tomatoes. Papa, brows wrinkled, related how a man had driven up to the house that morning while Mr Moodie was at work and had driven off with Patricia Moodie, leaving a disbelieving maid on the verandah and all Mr Moodie's clothes scattered on the lawn. Mama wept. Papa thought Mr Moodie had done everything he could to please Patricia Moodie, even dressing like a film star and driving that ridiculous car. But, at last, he was on his own, free again, riding his horses on Sundays and drinking at the club till the wee hours. Throughout this talk, Mama looked long into the distance.

'She wasn't right for him,' Papa said, quietly observing Mama.

'I thought they were just right for each other.'

Papa seemed shocked. 'It was doomed from the beginning.'

'You couldn't tell,' Mama stuttered and clasped her

127

hands together. 'There wasn't anything outward for anyone to tell that they were unhappy.'

Papa considered this. 'She didn't care for him,' he said. 'She's heartless. Moodie's better off.'

But Mr Moodie didn't feel better off. News reached them that the first thing he did after the shock of the news was to send the keys of his Appleton house by courier to Patricia Moodie all the way in Kingston. He couldn't let her go. She'd gone into him deep. He wanted her to know that she still had access and would always have access, because she was special, the only woman he had opened his heart to, that he would never let her go, that he was nothing without her. He didn't wait long for an answer. The keys were returned the following day without a written note, without an oral message delivered by the courier, just the cold keys on their own, alone, like he was. It was the lowest point in his life – he was abandoned, discarded, tossed aside, of no significance. He was not even history. It was as if she had erased him from memory, when he so much wanted to be remembered. He cried like a baby all night.

Boyd dreamt of Patricia Moodie, her swirling skirts, her supple calves, the high heels, the red-lipsticked lips, the pearls falling into the secret part between her breasts, her warm presence. *How could it be that she didn't last forever? He knew her scent and the music from her. If she, someone he knew so well and was so passionate about, didn't last, who could?* In these Technicolor dreams he was tossed and torn and felt the searing pleasure of her heartlessness. *People come, people go, nothing lasts forever.*

And in the days after her leaving, he saw a drooping Mama still with no real friends, listening to *Housewives' Choice* day after day, pondering her own future and talking to Mavis, fascinated with her gossip. For a maid, Mavis seemed to know more about the goings-on at the estate than Mama; about the Mitchisons, the Dowdings, Miss Chatterjee, what happened at the club, the Bull Pen over the weekend, who did what, when and how.

'All the men fancy Miss Chatterjee, ma'am,' Mavis gushed.

Mama rolled her eyes.

'Every single one of them, ma'am,' Mavis laughed.

Mavis reported the demise of Mr Dixon, the electrician who lived at the Bull Pen. She had news long before Papa announced it at the dinner table.

'Ruby throw kerosene oil all over Mr Dixon last night and strike a match,' Mavis said. 'While him sleeping in bed, ma'am. Sleeping in bed!'

'What?' Mama asked, astonished.

'Yes, Miss Victoria, ma'am. Mr Dixon scorn her and take up with another woman. Ruby, the woman him scorn, so vexed she went straight to the Bull Pen when she know him sleeping. Set him alight in the night, ma'am. Poor Mr Dixon burn bad, bad. And Ruby in the lock-up now, mad as a dawg.'

Before Mama could draw breath, Mavis carried on. 'And Mrs Mitchison always at the club, planning this, planning that and chatting with Mr Brookes. If she have anything to say, she say it to Mr Brookes. She respect him, ma'am.' Seeing Mama's look of disbelief, she asserted, 'Yes, ma'am, is true. So Evadne tell me. Her cousin, Ralstan, is the bartender at the club. And when Mrs Mitchison have her lunch at the club she take little Susan with her. Evadne have the run of the house from ten o'clock every day when Mrs Mitchison drive off, ma'am. And…'

Mavis didn't understand Mama's sudden silence and her fixed stare into the distance. She knew that Mrs Brookes was a very thoughtful woman. The nicest and the best women were.

As Boyd heard Susan's name mentioned, a sudden warmth spread from his cheeks down to his toes. *And Susan came to him. She came to him suddenly. Mama did not know. Papa did not know. He frolicked about with her in the sun. They climbed trees together, sweated and laughed and sat in the shade and chatted. They dashed about in the gardens till late in the* afternoon and felt each other's heat and breath. Sometimes they watched, close together, not speaking, the evening shadows growing long on the cooling grass, and forgot to hear the dinner bell and so had to be pulled apart by the cloying hands of Evadne and Mavis. Susan was all the pretty girls in all the books he'd ever read. And she was Estella. Pretty, heart-breaking Estella, growing more alluring each day with absence. Susan was sitting next to him with her legs drawn up under her berry-red gingham dress with the puff sleeves. She was a pink hibiscus. He just wanted to run his tongue slowly up the silky petals and down deep into the pink centre. He wanted to feel her lips like he felt the petals. He wanted to kiss just like in the movies, lips squashing against lips, eyes closed like babies at titties, the music rising while the sun turned to Technicolor red, hearts beating amid hard breathing.

And it was while he was drugged with these torrid thoughts that the idea of a scheme came to him. The boldness of it made him sit up. *He would go to her and do it in Technicolor. He would end the waiting and go over to the Mitchison's house and do it there.*

PART TWO
The Middle

CHAPTER 14

The Mitchisons sat on the verandah of their new home. It was eight o'clock, a warm night and the stars were out, starlight-white in a night-blue sky. The scent of orange blossoms drifted in from the trees at either end of the garden, and there were other scents, too, that they did not recognise. They loved the new house. It was modern, airy and painted in sober, cool colours, appropriate for the tropics. It was much bigger than their house at Monymusk in Clarendon, and more stylish, with the modern flat roof that was all the rage. The gardens were very well-kept, too well-kept for their liking. They would teach their gardener, Adolphus, how to make it more unkempt and interesting, the way they liked it. Susan, their child-fairy, fast asleep in bed, needed a magic garden, not a golf course.

'Good man, Brookes,' Mitchison said. 'The sort of man you need on an estate like this. Full of ideas, very competent and always punctual, something most of his countrymen have yet to learn.'

'He's impressive, isn't he?' his wife agreed. 'And so polished.'

'Polished?'

'You know, all-efficient in a management kind of way.'

'A great talker, too. If you have nothing to say, keep away from him. I see he cornered you at drinks the other night and wouldn't let you go. What was it, politics or sugar production?'

For some reason Ann blushed, a deep pink, which in the darkness of the verandah appeared as radiance. 'Both, actually. And, for the record, I cornered him. I heard he supports Norman Manley's case for self-government. I wanted to hear exactly what his thoughts were. He quoted from Manley's speech in the House last year on full, internal self-government. Great speech. He's absolutely fascinating.'

'So is Victoria,' Mitchison said.

'I meant Manley, the Chief Minister.'

'I see. Isn't Brookes?'

'Of course. The most charming man on the estate. Almost as charming as you.'

Mitchison laughed. 'Save your flattery. What do you think of Victoria?'

'Very quiet, doesn't say much. Seems decent, though. She's expecting their fourth child. And it hardly shows.'

Their maid, Evadne, appeared with a wooden tray on which were two glasses and a crystal pitcher. She was beaming.

'Thank you, Evadne,' Ann Mitchison said.

'Thank you, Evadne,' Mitchison repeated.

'Tenk you, ma'am, sar,' Evadne returned, combusting with bliss. She was not accustomed to being thanked so much by her Jamaican employers, and never for doing her job. 'Tenk you.'

When Evadne left, Mitchison spoke carefully, registering a change of tone. His hair was receding, leaving his forehead wide and smooth and ochre-red. The remaining hair was dark and brushed hard back, revealing a hint of grey around the temples. The smooth flesh of his forehead caught the diffused light of the drawing room. Ann was convinced his forehead was getting bigger all the time, transforming his head from one that was respectably ageing into something grotesque. She had never mentioned it and did not intend to, since he was so sensitive about losing his hair, but the forehead was so conspicuous that nine out of ten times she found herself looking at it rather than listening to him.

'What's that, dear?' she said now.

'Christ, Ann!'

'I'm sorry, I was miles away. And you were almost whispering anyway. Do please tell me again.'

Mitchison sighed heavily. 'What I said was, I don't want you getting too close to these people.'

'Oh, dear,' Ann said wearily, giving him her full attention.

'You know perfectly well what I mean. At Monymusk you single-handedly ran the Crop-Over Dance, you took charge of the library and any social function at the club and took it upon yourself to visit every disadvantaged family in the district. You are not the social welfare officer, you are not a social worker, you are not the estate party planner and you are not a political activist. You are my wife.'

Ann sat open-mouthed, her fleshy lips trembling, but not through distress. She was shocked and irritated. 'I had no idea you felt that way. For goodness' sake, Tim, why haven't you said anything before?'

'I want things to be different at Appleton.'

'I thought you wanted me to get involved. You've always encouraged me, made it quite clear you didn't want a stay-at-home wife.'

'I'm not saying you should disengage completely. At Monymusk things got out of hand.'

'Out of hand! But you said nothing.'

'At Monymusk things got out of hand. I'd come home and you were never there, always at some women's group or some poor person's house. Be the wife of an estate assistant manager. That is what I want.'

Ann sat straight up in her chair. 'I thought that that was precisely what I was doing, what I do. Tim, we cannot simply live here like typical English people, the ones you used to despise, keeping ourselves to ourselves. We've always said we would never be narrow, that we should always mix. This is yet another opportunity for us to get to meet people of all backgrounds.'

'That is what I'm afraid of.'

'That is what you're afraid of? Can you imagine what they already think of us? Whatever you want to think, we are representatives of the colonial power, to use their term. You know the history. You're familiar with the politics. If we remain aloof, we run the risk of giving the most dreadful impression of ourselves, and also of being completely ineffective at estate management. Well, you're the one who'll run that risk. You're the manager. We've been through this before in Barbados after you became junior manager – I thought you were genuinely concerned that I was taking on too much.'

'Ann, I'm simply saying ...'

'It's the tone, Tim. And I simply don't understand what you mean by *getting too close to these people*. You haven't made that quite clear. Who are *these people*?'

'No need to get so het up.' He was used to her forthrightness. Her entire family was like that.

She fixed her grey-blue eyes upon him. He looked away, uneasy because it was not what he had intended. He had wanted simply to make a statement and for her to understand. Evadne was closing the shutters in the pantry. Soon she would come out to the verandah to smile her smile and say goodnight.

'Tim, ever since Barbados you have changed.'

'Now you tell me.'

'That's where it started. I don't know what's happened to you. Where's the generous, inclusive man I married? I'll tell you. Slowly going the way of all Englishmen who work in the tropics. Exclusive, intolerant and selfish.'

'That's cruel. I don't accept that at all.'

'You need to listen to yourself sometimes. Don't you think that people like Samms and Brookes see exactly what you are? They're not fools.'

'Stop it.'

'No. Look, I think I know what this is all about. We haven't talked about it but I know perfectly well how you felt about not getting the estate manager's post in Barbados, especially after the excellent job you did as junior manager. It wasn't your fault. We should keep doing what we are doing. We weren't long enough at Monymusk. You're a good manager. I think we can really make a home in Jamaica and at Appleton. But that means being part of society, not living in a glass bowl. And Susan, for all her independence, needs consistency and a sense of permanence.'

'I'm going to bed,' Mitchison said, getting up, visibly upset.

'Oh, don't be silly, Tim. This is just what we need to do.'

'What?'

'Talk.'

'You can talk. I have a long drive into Kingston tomorrow.'

'Not again?'

'That's what the job's about.'

'Well, please don't get delayed in Kingston again. Remember, we're having dinner at the Brookes'.'

But Mitchison had already left the verandah.

Ann surveyed the darkened grounds, felt the sweet, warm air of the estate, and relaxed. She loved the sugar estates. Tim was a bit of a worry but he would get over it. Her assessment was that he seemed to be losing his confidence. Three estates in five years, and still only assistant general manager. It was tough but she knew the remedy. It was to focus on the job at hand and engage with people, buck up and manage. They could not keep moving from estate to estate with nothing to show for it. And moving back to England was not an option. Making a go of it at Appleton was such an exciting prospect. She was looking forward to the Brookes' dinner and joining Harold Brookes in conversation again. And she viewed it as much more than intellectual stimulation.

CHAPTER 15

On the evening of Mama's dinner party, it was not intellectual stimulation that absorbed Papa, although he was stimulated beyond belief. It made his heart pop and his senses tingle and, Christ; it was a wonderful thing for a man. But he hadn't gone out of his way to seek it. All of a sudden it had come upon him, snared him, made him feel young and vigorous and dangerous all over again. It could not be denied. He knew it, absolutely. What manner of man would walk away from such a prospect? The tension drove him too; it was what he thrived on. He would confound the risks and manage them as he managed his life.

The first of the guests to arrive was Mr Samms, all spit and polish, wearing his recently trimmed Clark Gable moustache. In the early night light, the tight black waves of his hair glistened. He sat with Papa smoking and tossing cigarette butts into the hedge circling the verandah, the very hedge Vincent had laboured to trim and tidy up that day, including removing a hundred cigarette butts, lollipop wrappers and dead leaves.

Miss Hutchinson arrived next, wearing a black dress that showed off her slender honey-brown arms, smooth shoulders and firm, ripe bosom.

'Get to your room, all of you,' Papa commanded the children when she arrived, assuming they would be up to mischief during dinner and making sure to put a stop to it before it started. But she came to them with her double string of pearls and her effervescence.

'*Tropic of Cancer*,' Boyd whispered in her ear as she bent

down to kiss him. Intoxicated with her woman's scent, he wanted to touch and snuggle up but held back.

'It's for big boys,' Miss Hutchinson whispered mischievously, stroking his chin. But she smiled encouragingly. 'Soon, very soon.'

On the verandah the Dowdings arrived to a gentle, relaxed reception. Then Boyd was conscious of much activity, of an unfamiliar but elegant bouquet sweeping into the house. Ann Mitchison had arrived. He crept down the hall in the dark, wanting to hear the swish of skirts, the unmistakable sound of pearls and other jewellery, the constant murmur of voices, the clink of glasses. Most of the action was taking place on the verandah where Miss Hutchinson's stylish laugh could be heard. But then there was a lull in the flurry of sound and Boyd heard footsteps trooping into the dining room. He shrank back out of sight, catching the first thrilling wave of new woman scent, more ravishing that Patricia Moodie's.

As he watched from the darkness, the seated diners seemed like a grand painting in their rich colours and deep shadows. There was Ann Mitchison, the mother of Susan Mitchison, sitting next to Papa, light-brown hair like polished horse's mane, cheeks like the pink of a ripened mango, teeth straight and white and even. Her eyes were grey-blue like Mama's crockery, but the part of her that held his attention was her lips. They were Mama's red lips but not firm and round like hers. Ann Mitchison's lips were luscious, with fleshy lines, heavy from end to end; they moved with every word she uttered, parted and poised, quivering, sensual and alive. And the burnished red of the lipstick gave her lips drama and romance in the light of the dining room. They were film stars' lips.

Boyd remembered little else but those lips; not the powder-blue linen dress that the owner of the lips wore, not even the striking baroque earrings of pearl and light-gold mounted on black enamel. There was little memory of Mr Mitchison, whose yellow-gold wristwatch flashed in

139

the light, but whose face had been obscured by the vibrant head of Miss Hutchinson. Papa's eyes had been hooded, his own lips eagerly smiling, jousting and parrying, unable to get away from the relentlessly seeking lips of his guest. He had seemed cornered. And Boyd remembered one more thing – the name of Mr Ramsook, the coolie pig-killer, of all people, spoken by Ann Mitchison, bringing a knowing nod from Papa.

'They are good people,' Ann Mitchison said. 'Mr Ramsook only wants a chance. He's willing to work and there's work that needs doing.'

Papa just kept nodding.

Boyd imagined that he had been at the pictures, seeing Ann Mitchison's fleshy wine-red lips filling the screen, dripping in Technicolor, mouthing adult words, waiting for the embrace, waiting for the passion and the kiss music. The memory only made him more excited about his ecstatic designs upon Susan. *That night in bed, the windows wide open, the curtains streaming, he climbed in through her bedroom window. And they licked pink lollipops, threw the crispy wrapping paper on the floor and touched. And Susan's scent was strawberry.*

CHAPTER 16

They met up at the coolie settlement in the afternoon heat, two Land Rovers parked in the red dirt of the estate road under the trees at the gate. Papa got there before her and, hands on hips, was speaking to Mr Ramsook, who was dressed in a soiled, sleeveless vest and washed-out dungarees pushed deep into black waterboots. Two other men with him showed their respect by looking down at their shadows, black hair falling over their eyes.

Ann Mitchison approached, looking out of place, Papa thought, in such desperate surroundings. Her creamy hand held onto the straw hat on her head. A flowery blue and white cotton handkerchief hung about her neck and the sleeves of her pink striped cotton shirt were rolled up at the elbows. All the coolie women came out to look. Never before had the wife of any manager visited the barracks. Papa turned from Mr Ramsook to confer with his companion, who, under the full sun and in such a rude open space, seemed extraordinarily young and vulnerable, in spite of her self-confidence. When it was over, Papa settled with Mr Ramsook, who bowed first to Papa and then in the direction of his benefactor. The other men kept on bowing as Papa walked away.

Under the trees in the dust at the gate between the parked Land Rovers, Ann Mitchison smiled with gratitude and drew near to Papa. Her faint perfume reached his nostrils and, in the heat, evoked outrageous juvenile lust.

'Thank you so much, Harold,' she said. 'Will you stop by this evening for tea? There's so much to discuss.'

Papa seemed to hesitate for just a moment.

'Close any loopholes,' Ann added.

'Yes, of course,' Papa assured her. And he heard himself say words that were not calculated. 'Far better than going up to the club.' But he'd hesitated because he knew that Tim Mitchison was in Kingston and that he would be alone with Ann if he took up her invitation.

Ann gave a girlish laugh. 'How nice,' she said, smiling self-consciously, the kind that told of growing intimate knowledge. Papa's smile said the same. It was not the first time they had met up under the Appleton sun in some undistinguished place in the twelve thousand acres of the estate.

* * *

That hot August night, Mama sat with Mavis in the pantry, the coolest room in the house, going over the grocery list. Barrington was demonstrating his fast-draw action, in the manner of the Rawhide Kid, to Yvonne and Vincent out on the porch between the kitchen and the laundry room. But Vincent's eye rested only on Mavis and his heart overflowed with deep desires.

Boyd's heart overflowed with desires too as he stole away in the pretty darkness to the periwinkle fence. Glancing back at the house, he saw the yellow light from the opened windows gushing onto the lawn. He heard the Mullard radio: *All day all night, Marianne, down by the seaside sifting sand, even little children loved Marianne, down by the seaside sifting sand.* In the darkness no one could see him. It was the best time to do it, in the dark. The pictures in his head, as he came upon Susan, were romping voluptuous, like the pictures in the encyclopaedia.

Creeping stealthily towards the fence, he barely got through it before he heard, just barely, a vehicle approaching. Surprisingly, the headlights were switched off. The vehicle came in sight, a lumbering dark shape.

Boyd peered out from the darkness expecting to see Mr Mitchison, but it was a familiar Land Rover passing slowly, surreptitiously.

His quest aborted, Boyd returned to the verandah, heart pounding, breathing hard. He wondered why Papa had been driving without headlights towards the Mitchisons and looking around so suspiciously. And he instinctively thought of the unsuspecting Mama in the kitchen, deligently preparing the family's grocery list with Mavis.

Later that night, among the crotons, Boyd sniffed the streaming *Essen* from Mavis's room and heard her music, *Day-ho, day-ho, day dey light and me want go home.* If only he could go to Susan as he went to Mavis. If only it was so easy. He saw Mavis pacing about in her panties and brassiere, saw the sensuous shadows in her room, heard the knock at the door and saw Mavis turn to open it. Vincent stood there blinking.

'What you want, big head?' Mavis seemed extraordinarily casual.

'Is who singing?' Vincent stammered, staring.

'Is Shirley Bassey, from foreign.'

'Harry Belafonte sing *Day-ho*. Who Shirley Bassey?'

'You deaf or something? Ah told you is Shirley Bassey from foreign.'

'So, Harry Belafonte don't sing it no more?'

'You ask too many damn fool questions. Is what you want?'

'Where you get radio from?'

'Don't be fresh. You going to stand there staring at me all night?'

'If you say so,' Vincent returned, his witty reply shocking him.

'No, ah don't say so. Ah don't say so at all. If is woman you looking for, go and get your own. You not going to find any around here.'

'Ah don't have no woman,' Vincent confessed, looking up, sensing opportunity.

Mavis laughed in his face, kept on laughing and had to hold on to her sides. When she stopped laughing, she gave him a pitiful look, wiping the tears from her eyes.

Vincent hung his head like a scolded child. He had never lived next door to an attractive young woman, never felt the kind of unruly sensations that coursed through his body at that moment. 'You can get Fats Domino on it?'

Mavis fixed him with a vile stare. 'Ah get Fats Domino, Chuck Berry, Professor Longhair, The Coasters, everybody.'

Vincent looked at the floor. 'You going out?' he asked her in a cowed voice.

'Is none of your business,' Mavis told him. 'And stop knocking at me door, you lickle fool. Go and get a woman. Clear off!'

Boyd, hearing Vincent's cruel dismissal, cleared off too, running back to the periwinkle fence, hoping to see Papa returning from the Mitchison's. But back at the fence, no Land Rover appeared, only the winking lights of the *peeny-waalies* meandering through the night. But he waited.

When Mavis pulled the door shut and returned to her dresser, shaking her head, she did not see Vincent's smile. It was impossible for her to know that he had experienced dizzying heights of sexual delight during their little encounter. Vincent thanked his employers. He thanked his good fortune. He thanked God. Mavis had not, as he had feared she would, slammed the door in his face. No. She had engaged with him. She had let him watch her in a state of undress. No other woman would have allowed that. No woman in his whole life experience had let him come even close; just one look at his dripping eye had turned them away. Vincent believed that for all Mavis's bluster she had feelings for him. He'd heard that women were like that, saying no when they meant yes. Why else would she have allowed him so much latitude?

And so, in the extremes of his delusion, Vincent returned to Mavis's room a little later. He knocked gingerly at the half-opened door and made as if to turn away when there was no answer. But he knew she was there because he could hear music, the words of a song that, in his dreams, came from his own lips: *Since I met you baby, my whole life has changed.* Brushing his fear aside, he pushed the door wide open. Mavis had discarded her brassiere and now wore only panties, lying on her bed, looking out the window at the yellow moon. She turned, smiling, but seeing who it was, scowled horribly, sprang up and pointed a malevolent finger.

'You again! Get out! You idiot. Get out!'

'But,' Vincent started, remembering the moment when so much seemed possible.

'Get out, you Cyclops! Get out, before ah call Mrs B.'

'But, but.' Vincent was confused. *She had let him watch her half-naked.* The encouragement, the hidden show of feelings for him, those little looks, meant nothing?

He got his answer as Mavis slammed the door more violently than ever, shaking the rafters, sending him slinking back to his lonely room. Hurt and dejected, he barely made out, from the corner of his eye, the form of a man approaching Mavis's room. Vincent stopped in his tracks. He saw the strange man lean his bicycle against the side of the building in the dark, enter Mavis's room unhindered and close the door quickly behind him.

When Boyd finally left the darkness at the periwinkle fence, instead of returning to the house, he turned again towards Mavis's room. Mavis was going to a dance. She had spoken about it when she served dinner.

'Just you watch out for the hooligans,' Papa had advised her.

'They never bother me, Mr Brookes,' Mavis replied.

As he carried on to Mavis's room, Boyd heard Poppy's growls of alarm and saw the dim light of a bicycle lamp. A man was approaching up the back path. They breathed the scent of a bold cigarette, Four Aces probably, and vulgar cologne. They saw the man enter Mavis's room. Boyd bounded away on light toes and took up his position by the frangipani bush further down the path. Soon the dim light of the bicycle appeared. Mavis sat cross-legged on the crossbar, the man hunched above her, his gold teeth flashing, talking low. He was not wearing bicycle clips and his turn-ups were big and awkward as he pedalled. They seemed very happy, Mavis giggling, eyes flashing, her *Essen* pervading the night. She had never spoken about this stranger.

Vincent saw it all. He'd seen them earlier together in the room in an encounter that outraged him. He'd seen them from his latest discovery that night of a hole in the wall between his room and Mavis's. He felt forsaken, and there was a scene in the dark drama unfolding in his head, in which he put up two vicious fingers at the bicycle rider. He knew he would see the man again later that night when Mavis was danced out, when they would roll about on her single bed. The man was no good. There were dozens like him in the parish, wanting only one thing. If only he could make Mavis see that. As the drama in his head grew darker, he fought to keep out the inhuman acts that should strike down the stranger, acts that he knew he was capable of.

CHAPTER 17

That hot August night, Mama waited up for Papa, wishing to be magnanimous, wanting to be tender and kind, to dispel any imagined obstacle that might have come between them. But Papa was late coming home as usual and she fell asleep. When he arrived, in the early dawn, she awoke. And when he came to her in bed, he was unnaturally fierce, like a mountain ram.

After lunch the next day, Mama cornered him in the bedroom and asked him tearfully, 'What have I done, Harold? What is the matter? Tell me, I want to know.'

'Dammit, nothing's the matter,' Papa retorted, walking quickly out of the room. Minutes later, Mama saw him speeding away, the dust violent and scathing behind him. She couldn't help it and burst into tears. Ever since the Mitchisons' dinner, it seemed not a single day passed without a row, even though she went out of her way to be accommodating.

In those days, Papa quarrelled with everyone in the house, including Mavis, Vincent and Poppy. He glared at them and ignored them and held them in contempt. He imagined they were on Mama's side and that was enough. Weren't they all together at the house while he was away at the factory? They were all in her camp, every single one of them. He was the outsider, always outnumbered, never receiving any support, a stranger in his own home. And all the time he was slaving away at the factory to put a roof over their heads, clothing on their backs, food in their bellies, what did he get? She was poisoning them against him, his own children. That was what was going on. See the way they huddled and broke away at his approach? See how they kept away from him, their own father? See how they looked down, always suspicious and guilty, whenever he called them, in a firm voice, to come to him? Ungrateful wretches, every single one of them.

The children kept well out of Papa's way during these internecine wars, quietly reading, fidgeting in their rooms and longing for him to leave the house. When he did leave, in a thunderous walk down the hall and out the kitchen door, they hoped Poppy would be sensible enough to remain under the house or, if he happened to be lounging on the patio near the kitchen, remain motionless, not giving eye contact. Twice before Papa had found his presence obtrusive, frankly disrespectful and threatening. Poppy had felt hard brogue leather about his ribs on both occasions. And Mavis, going about her business conspicuously in the kitchen, was always given the cold shoulder. Vincent, crouching by the flowerbeds on his knees, always kept his back to Papa and his head down.

Whenever Mama and Papa made up, the sun seemed more radiant. Everyone helped the mood. Mavis's washing up in the kitchen took on a musical sound. Vincent whistled as he worked under the windows. Poppy barked a joyful bark and chased invisible mongoose. Papa's face shone brilliantly too, like the moon in Yvonne's drawing book, with a smile so wide it cut his face in two, laughing loud and long and showing perfect teeth. This Friday evening in late August was typical.

'You little angel, you,' Papa said, suddenly appearing in the drawing room and pinching Yvonne's cheek. When she presented the other cheek, he pinched that too, swept her off her feet and took her to Mama, where the noises coming from the bedroom were the same as from a school playground. Papa was like a little boy, cuddling and tickling and shocking everyone. He chased Yvonne around the room so that she could feel the gritty hairs on his chin.

She shrieked and ran to Mama, only pretending, running back to Papa and falling into his arms for another feel of the bristles.

'Boyd, you'll be a great man one day,' Papa said, walking fast down the hall. 'Just look at you. You've got great written all over you. A chip off the old block, I tell you. You shall have the best education, you and Barrington and Yvonne. We were destined to be great, we Brookeses. Like father, like children. You shall be as great as your Papa – no, greater – and carry on the family name, my son!' He slapped Boyd on the back, and Boyd sniffed the Royal Blend, the sugar, the contents of test tubes, that Papa aroma, and believed every word. And in that moment, all his doubts about Papa disappeared, especially when Papa said to Barrington, 'My *big* son, shake your Papa's hand!' And Barrington, smiling proudly as only big sons do, put out his hand in that pretend adult way with a boyish grin.

Papa, rushing down the hall singing, *Beecaause you come to me, beecaause you speak to me, beecaause,* gave instructions to Vincent to have the car washed and polished within the hour.

'Put your back into it,' Papa said good-humouredly.

But Vincent, feeling low after his encounter with Mavis, took it badly. The only person who seemed to have reservations about his diligence and the quality of his work was his current employer. He missed Mr Maxwell-Smith with every passing day.

'We're going to the club,' Papa announced, 'as a special treat.'

The house exclaimed joyously at this announcement. Boyd immediately inhaled the scent of delicate pink lilies. Beautiful music filled his ears. He and Barrington dressed in their pepperseed trousers, tailored by Mr Tecumseh Burton of Balaclava, and applied palmolive pomade to their hair. Yvonne wore black patent leather strap shoes and a cotton dress gathered at the front. Mama wore club clothes, her two-tone shoes of cream and brown and dabbed *Evening in Paris* behind her ears, under her chin and several places on her arms. Pleasures smote Boyd at every turn: the sunset, the *Shhh, Shhh, Shhhing* of the factory, Mama and Papa speaking again, Papa singing *Beecaause*, Mavis competent in the kitchen, the car polished and waiting. Somewhere, distant but near, Susan waited all nervy and trembly in torrid loveliness. He hoped intensely that she would be at the club too. *Beecaause you come to me, Beecaause.*

White birds flew into the sunset as they left the car after a brisk drive and walked up the steps to the club enveloped in Mama's *Evening In Paris*. Miss Chatterjee and Miss Hutchinson were the first to greet them. Boyd's heart raced. Miss Hutchinson was the curling blue smoke from a poised cigarette, the intoxicating drink from a sparkling glass, the perfume in a hand-cut crystal bottle that savaged the senses, the look that carried deep, powerful meaning. But she was no match for Miss Chatterjee, who simply stepped out of a book, an undying sensation. Miss Chatterjee was exclusive, although quite friendly with Patricia Moodie, as they both came from the same suburb of Kingston. Men avoided her because she was a perfect picture, only to be looked at, never touched.

There was no sign of Susan yet. But Boyd knew that the Mitchison's Jaguar ('A cream Mark II with red leather seats,' Barrington said) was at that very moment making its way across the bridge and to the club. He would turn casually and there they'd be, coming up the steps to the terrace, Susan with shining hair, wearing little white gloves and smelling like pink lillies. And the evening would be dramatic, like a film, full of crimson skies and seductive music. *And he would try to get her away alone and do it then.*

Older women than Mama sat at green wicker tables in the gardens, in perfume and evening shadow, shielded by clipped green hedges against a soft sunset. The evening breeze buffed their tender skins, dark skins, caramel and pink skins, while they showed glimpses of thigh and crinoline petticoat. They were all of flashing eyes, pearly teeth and pretty lipsticked mouths, and Boyd completed dramatic stories in his head about them all.

At the table on the terrace with Mama, he watched Miss Chatterjee between cream soda bubbles. She was teaching Barrington, who would rather have played football, how to grip a tennis racket. She laughed and moved towards his brother, putting her arms about him to demonstrate the correct racket position. Earlier, when they'd arrived and everyone kissed, Boyd had been overcome by her *Essen* and the look in her eyes, and found himself pulling away from her embrace, unable to manage his exploding feelings. Now the same sensation overcame him as Miss Chatterjee giggled, smacked the ball with elegant arms, the poise of a ballet dancer in tennis skirts, dark hair flying, smooth thighs subtly rippling. She brought her own racket with her, Slazenger Challenge or something or other, withdrawing it carefully from its case each time. Everybody else used club rackets.

Boyd moved to the edge of the terrace, looking down on the court as men at the bar downed liquor in small chunky glasses. The men who had lived abroad drank Johnnie Walker Scotch whisky (born 1820 and still going strong). They watched Miss Chatterjee out of the corners of their eyes and propositioned her in secret.

They eyed young Barrington with impatience, disdain even, thinking that, if given the chance, they wouldn't stand about like a moron. The fact that he was a boy meant nothing – they saw themselves in his place and berated him in their hearts for not behaving like a *man*. They would do something, anything but let a fine opportunity slip by. Through a haze of liquor, boiling sugar aroma drifting up from the factory, that mixture of sensations that only estate workers who spend their time at the club know, they dreamed. But some things were only club dreams. The men had experienced a moment of recklessness. They returned to their rum and ginger, their whisky and water. Miss

Chatterjee's squeals and giggles, a red-blooded reminder of their youth, fleeting fast. But Boyd, only eight years old, sniffing the warm sugar smells, seeing the radiant sunset, studied Miss Chatterjee and saw the future.

'Have some salted biscuits and cheese, darling,' he heard Mama say as she placed her Babycham on the table, bubbles bursting silently.

Mama was sitting with Miss Hutchinson, charming Miss Hutchinson with the shapely calves, who, people said, had pulled down her panties at the club during the last Crop-Over Dance while drunk and dancing on a table. She had stopped only when the music stopped, gin and tonic in one hand and panties in the other. Mama and Papa arrived at the estate the following year so hadn't been present.

'People will say anything,' Papa had remarked. Mama, clearly in agreement, confirmed by saying, 'Did you know she speaks three different languages?' Boyd had heard every word, lurking behind the living room door, picturing the fascinating half-naked Miss Hutchinson. Miss Hutchinson was laughing with Mama now and smoking a cigarette, Senior Service, legs crossed, eyes half-closed and mouth sultry. She wore what Mama called "tropical clothes", and when she blew her cigarette smoke it was done with the sort of sophistication that people who depended entirely on posing and vanity lacked.

When Mama wasn't looking, Boyd wandered down the hall to the men's room, basking in the ubiquitous attention of powdered, plump women with big pearls, on their way from the women's room. But the Mitchisons were nowhere to be seen.

On his way back, he saw Edgar, Mr Burton's nephew, fondling a pretty girl in the parking lot. Edgar's cigarette smoke rose up from the pink oleander bush, a young man's cigarette smoke, not adult like Papa's Royal Blend or Miss Hutchinson's Senior Service. Edgar probably smoked Four Aces, the cigarette of a man on the make.

'Men like him have a baby in every parish,' Mr Samms

once said at dinner, shaking his head. 'Not to be let loose on nice girls.' And yet certain girls ran to Edgar like bees to honey.

When Boyd returned to the terrace, every vibrant face was Ann Mitchison's, every seeking, small face was Susan's. But they were not on the terrace or in the garden. Barrington sat next to Mama, bored, while Yvonne picked her nose and listened loudly to Miss Hutchinson. Miss Chatterjee sat three tables away, her skin glowing, eyes glancing repeatedly towards the club's entrance, tense, waiting too.

'Mama, will Miss Chatterjee teach us to play tennis?' Yvonne asked.

'You're too young, darling.'

'Oh, they're never too young,' Miss Hutchinson said quickly. 'Dennis Dowding can teach them. He's up from Munro now. If he can't do it, we'll get young Pamela Carby. She's very good.'

Mama smiled reluctantly.

'She was teaching Barrington,' Yvonne quickly pointed out.

Barrington grimaced, more bored than ever. He would have preferred talk about Wembley and English football, or Brazilians like Pele and Garrincha. He'd been watching the terrace and couldn't see Geraldine Pinnock anywhere, but he hoped that the Pinnock's car would arrive at any moment. They drove a grey Riley with brown leather upholstery.

'She's far too busy,' Mama said. 'She won't have the time.'

'She wasn't teaching,' Miss Hutchinson said. 'She was just playing about. Anyway, she goes off to Kingston almost every weekend these days. We'll get Dennis or Pamela to do it. Since their Senior Cambridge exams, they've had nothing to do. They'll teach you so that one day you'll be as good as Althea Gibson.' Miss Hutchinson threw back her head and calmly blew blue smoke stylishly towards the heavens.

'Who's Althea Gibson?' Yvonne asked.

Miss Hutchinson smiled and tickled her arms. Yvonne shrieked and threw up her hands, displaying frilly white bloomers. Mama's eyes went immediately to the white bloomers, and seeing that they were clean, displayed maternal calm.

'Althea Gibson? She's a black American girl. She played at Wimbledon, the big tennis tournament in England, and beat everybody. She's the best woman tennis player in the world.'

Barrington looked up. He knew something about sports but he had never heard about this Althea Gibson who was the best in the world. *The world.*

'In the whole world?' Barrington asked the world the question.

It was impossible. They knew Miss Chatterjee, who was a great player, and Dennis, who beat everybody at Munro College and boasted about it incessantly at half-term. Pamela was very good too, even Miss Chatterjee said so. She used to be the captain of the lawn tennis team at her school, Hampton. And yet Althea Gibson was better than all of them! But, surely, no one could beat Miss Chatterjee with her Slazenger Challenge racket. The children were quiet for a long time and then, just when they were about to pepper Miss Hutchinson with questions, Papa said it was time to go. It was eight-thirty.

The Mitchisons had not appeared. There was talk among the men that Mr Mitchison was in Kingston yet again, at the Sugar Manufacturers' Association headquarters. Poor Ann Mitchison was alone at home. Boyd saw some of the men whispering mischievously and laughing behind their hands.

'Mrs Mitchison can come out on her own, surely,' Miss Hutchison said with conviction, as Mama rose to go. 'She has a maid to keep house.'

'It's okay during the day, but how would it look at night?' Mama said, never having left the Brookes' home to go anywhere on her own in her life.

'How?' Miss Hutchison did not understand. 'She can drive herself here and drive herself back.' And she spewed smoke above her head, while giving Mama a probing smile. 'I do it all the time.'

As Boyd said his goodbyes, he glanced at Barrington, who was even more downcast than he was. The Pinnocks' grey Riley had not arrived.

They kissed Miss Hutchinson, whose eyes were pink and lovely under the lights. Mr Samms arrived, kissed her on the cheeks, called her Cynthia in a soft voice and sat at the table eyeing her up. Manjula Chatterjee was nowhere to be seen. Someone said she had already left, as she would be taking the diesel train into Kingston for the weekend. She always seemed to have theatre engagements or tickets for the Ivy Baxter dance concerts or Madame Soohih. And she would probably meet up with Patricia Moodie for dinner. Mr Moodie arrived just then, stinking of white rum from the distillery, smiled at the children, waved at Mama and winked at Papa, who pretended not to see.

They bundled into the Prefect, feeling snug and warm in the delicious, leather-scented air. Papa drove brisk and hard but bumped erratically over the railway tracks just the same, catching Mama's look of reprimand. They bounced over the black metal bridge, glimpsed the moon-spattered water, roared up the winding white slope, dust billowing behind, into the driveway with its yellow light and parked just outside the garage before anyone had said two words. The children just had time to see Poppy's eyes in the headlights and hear his tail whipping the door of the car when Mama said something sharpish, which they didn't catch. But they did hear Papa's calm, perhaps too calm, reply.

'I have to go back out.'

'Out where?'

'The factory. Some problem's come up. Moodie's been working flat out since seven this morning. I have to look after him, y'know. He's still coming to terms with the break-up. Children, go inside.'

They tripped over Poppy, and after an extraordinarily long time, it seemed, Papa and Mama joined them in the house. Mama's hair was out of place.

Papa left quietly, driving back under moonlight to rescue Mr Moodie. Boyd, on the verandah, saw the headlights of the Prefect meandering in the distance, past the giant flame trees at the factory gates, speeding away from Mama.

Back at the club, the men, and a few women, were getting ready to drink seriously. Ralstan, the bartender, had arranged for a suckling pig to be prepared with an assortment of fine yams and breadfruit. And there was to be soup, the kind the men liked – pepperpot, heavy with calaloo, scallion and dumplings, and hot to shrieking with red *bird pepper*, the kind that grew wild. This sort of food gave the men backbone and sometimes made them take unnecessary risks.

Curled up by the radio, Boyd dreamt about what might have been had Susan turned up at the club. Mama glided by in her nightgown, unsmiling, while in the faraway world where Althea Gibson was the greatest woman tennis player, LaVern Baker sang, *Two hearts, do-wap-de-doo, beat like one, do-wap-de-doo – my happiness, my happiness...*

'Get to your bed!' Mama snapped.

Boyd's tear-stung eyes met her's as he dashed from the room. Much later, when the house was very quiet and the only sound the barking of dogs, worlds away, he listened for the Prefect. The light was still on in Mama's room, streaming in a yellow flood on the flowers beneath her window. Papa still hadn't come.

The Prefect left the club early that night, much earlier than Papa's companions expected, which surprised them, as he was not known to leave their ribald company early. The Prefect returned across the bridge and mounted the slope, past the sleeping pink house and came to a stop outside the Mitchisons' property, where the servants had already retired. Ann Mitchison sat in the warmth on the darkened verandah, alone, breathing white oleander, the distant lights of the factory reflected in her grey-blue, waiting eyes.

CHAPTER 18

During the night, Boyd had fantastic dreams of Miss Hutchinson dancing atop a table at the club during the last Crop-Over Dance. The thought of her removing her panties in public shocked and thrilled him. It was comparable to the fleshy pink women hidden away in the encyclopaedia walking out of the pages and displaying themselves on top of a table at the club for the men to see. It was impossible to believe that Miss Hutchinson had stood, drunk, in front of everybody, and while they all watched, lifted up her dress to pull her panties down. That a private bedroom act could be presented in public, in such a manner, at such a place, with such daring was extraordinary. Her performance was as impossible as his licking the flowers in Papa's presence or having his secret thoughts about Susan exposed for everyone at the dinner table to see. Miss Hutchinson impressed and bothered him; she provoked in him sympathetic feelings and unbending adoration.

Still intoxicated with the dream and his secret quest, Boyd lay on the orchard side of the fence under the navel orange tree. Kiss music was in the grass. Poppy lay flat on his belly beside him, head cocked to one side, listening, waiting for their moment.

'You take your time,' Boyd heard Mavis say.

'Ah come as fast as ah could,' Evadne replied, as if reprimanded.

'Give me the red *Cutex* and ah'll give you the pink one, okay?' Mavis handed over a small bottle with a white top. Evadne did the same.

'Ah can't stay long,' Evadne said, peering at the bottle in her hand. 'Mr Mitchison at the house.'

'Is good *Cutex*,' Mavis informed her. 'Give it back tonight.'

'No,' Evadne said. 'Ah can't do it tonight. Mr Mitchison going to Kingston later this morning and not coming back till next week. Mrs Mitchison give me the night off and ah going up to Lacovia to see me family.'

'You mean Mrs Mitchison give you the night off even though she going to be on her own?' Mavis asked, unbelieving.

'Is not the first time,' Evadne replied airily. 'Everytime Mr Mitchison go to Kingston. Sometimes, for no reason, she even ask me if ah want the evening off.'

'And what you say?'

'What you think ah say?'

'Well, ah know what ah would say.'

'Ah say the same thing you would say,' Evadne laughed.

'Okay,' Mavis said, thinking Mrs Mitchison a strange woman. 'But don't leave it until weekend. Ah going to a dance at Taunton, Saturday, and ah want pink *Cutex*.' She turned away. 'See you later, alligator.'

'After a while, crocodile,' Evadne returned, walking off rapidly in the opposite direction, concealing the small bottle in the deep pocket of her uniform.

Boyd rose on his elbows as Mavis vanished up the garden path. He knew what he had to do. As expected, Tim Mitchison, grim-faced, roared by in the Jaguar. As the Jaguar vanished down the hill, he and Poppy crept into the orchard and came to a secluded spot overlooking the Mitchison property. Hidden in deep grass, they had a clear view of the open windows at the rear of the house, where frilly white curtains streamed. And they felt the first drops of light rain. But they waited.

Birds called out in the quiet and Boyd ducked down again as another vehicle thundered past. It was the Mitchison's Land Rover, Ann Mitchison at the wheel. Susan was now alone at home. She was alone and Evadne and Adolphus didn't matter.

Breaking free from the trees, Boyd and Poppy scurried across the road. The white curtains still flowed free at the windows. Boyd could feel the hibiscus in his hand, sense the silkiness on his tongue. Through the gate he crept, crouching now, and carried on to the curtained window, feeling the sprinkling droplets of rain. Her scent came to him, singular among the many others, whispering, guiding him. He would climb in through the window, part the curtains, step into the room, head towards the bed. The kiss music, the writhing lips and the garden perfumes would erupt like the last flash of sunset.

Hard rain tore into them, hurled down fruit, blinded their eyes. They put their hands against their faces, but it was useless, the rain was relentless. His clothes were wet and tight about him and his feet danced about in the rising crystal-clear water. He heard a multitude of voices but not his own voice, which was washed away. He heard Susan's voice, shrieking, full of intensity, calling, seeking, until their voices, far away, found one another and came back. In that moment, he tore off his shirt and trousers, stretched out his arms as little streams of steam came off him. Through clear water he saw Susan. She was pink all over, having removed her clothes too. Her wet hair hung in dark strings about her face, and her arms, like his, flailed about, steaming. They were hot in the rain, feverish, and in the falling whiteness of it and the impenetrable noise, felt safe, as if they were alone in their bedroom. They did not speak. There was no need for words.

The tension was too great. Poppy barked in the powerful silence and every eye turned upon the creeping figures. Poppy, sensing the attention like an ant under a microscope, barked again with discomfort and tried to clutch at his tail. A door opened and a dark adult shadow appeared. Boyd turned and dashed back through the fence and into the orchard, Poppy at his heels, his heart in his mouth and the rain crashing down upon them.

160

* * *

That Sunday evening, Miss Hutchinson visited to announce that Dennis had agreed to give them tennis lessons at the club. Mr Samms visited too, on his shoe-polish-brown horse, which he tethered next to Miss Hutchinson's car. As the small, calf-coloured Hillman Minx came to a stop, Poppy and Boyd rushed forward. Miss Hutchinson kissed the tip of Boyd's nose as she gave him the great news.

'Soon,' she whispered. 'Soon you can visit me.' It was as if, between them, there were deep secrets. When she joined the others on the verandah, he was left dreaming of the thrill of going to her house to read *Tropic of Cancer*. It seemed such an impossibility. But tennis at the club was the more urgent thrill because it meant only one thing. Susan. Boyd could not wait for Dennis to arrive.

On the verandah, Mr Samms roared at one of Miss Hutchinson's jokes. He seemed to have eyes only for her that evening and Boyd wondered what Mr Samms did the night Miss Hutchison lifted up her dress. Papa had described him as a man of *substance*. The fact that he rode up to the house on a horse when everyone would die to arrive behind the wheel of a car, set him apart. They said he came from a good family in Kingston but had been badly let down in love and, although outwardly confident, was weak on the inside.

'Putty in women's hands,' Boyd heard Mr Moodie tell Papa one afternoon.

As Mr Samms fawned over Miss Hutchinson, Papa put on one of his long-playing records, Earl Grant. *We kiss in a shadow, we hide from the moon, our meetings are few and over too soon! We speak in a whisper afraid to be heard, when people are near, we speak not a word!* The music, adult music, gushed over the voices on the verandah. Papa, animated after several drinks and oblivious of Mama's look of disapproval, placed one of his Louis Prima records on the record player, music he reserved only for drinking sessions with Mr Moodie. These long-playing records had sleeves with titles like *The Call of the Wildest* and *The Wildest Show at Tahoe*, and songs that burst with energy and audacity. On went Papa's favourite, "Angelina Zooma Zooma," music that got shoes tapping. *I eat antipasta twice, just because she is so nice, Angelina, Angeliiinaaaa, the waitress at the pizzeria.* Boyd heard the bellowing delivery of Louis Prima, the trombone and the deep drumming. But Mama had her way and the music ended with a sudden scratch of the record. Darkness descended, the fledgling stars came out and the voice of Earl Grant returned softly. *We kiss in a shadow...*

In the comforting blackness, Boyd tongued velvet roses as Miss Hutchinson's voice floated down from the verandah. He heard the words *Liberté, Egalité, Fraternité.* And because she had become quite emotional, the timbre of her voice rose like someone singing a difficult note. When she'd finished, no one said a word. Mr Samms spoke first, mumbling something about sugar estates being a legacy of slave society. Papa replied, too loudly perhaps, so that his voice hung awkwardly in the air.

'All the more reason why we must govern ourselves. Good God, man!' Papa must have said those words a million times.

Crickets shrieked as if to drown out the awkward silence and several *peeny-waalies* danced about the verandah, but Papa dispelled them all.

'We are men,' he said, 'responsible for our own destiny. Men, not mice!'

Miss Hutchinson giggled and that encouraged Mama, who didn't need much encouragement, especially when the talk turned to issues she did not fully understand. Mr Samms gave one of his thunderous *Ha, ha, haas*, as Mavis came with new glasses and ice and a humorous but respectful comment. The voices resumed in subdued tones with an occasional *oui* from Miss Hutchinson.

As if Miss Hutchinson's *oui* was the signal, Ann

Mitchison appeared like a white shadow from the bottom of the garden, gliding across the lawn and up the verandah steps. Her scent wafted in the dark warmth and her voice, when she reached the verandah, cascaded. Mavis hurried about with new glasses and ice. The men restrained their voices and the women laughed out loud again and the atmosphere became quite jolly. And Boyd heard Ann Mitchison speaking.

'I attended political meetings in England,' she said.

'Political meetings!' Mama was astonished.

'Oh, yes. My father saw to it. He believed that if you lived in a democracy it was important to be involved, express yourself and confront injustice openly and responsibly. He was international in his outlook. I would describe him as anti-colonial and, of course, he had a very strong impact on my political views. Going to political meetings never did me any harm as a child. I learned a lot from them.'

'Anti-colonial?' Papa seemed confused.

'Of course,' Ann replied breezily. 'The fact that you are English, or British, doesn't mean you are hell-bent on colonizing most of the world. In any case, we are no longer the power we were. The war saw to that. I wonder what my father would say today, gosh.'

The women laughed and Mr Samms joined them. Papa remained silent, smoking. He would like to hear Ann say *Rule Britannia*, shock them all and inflame his passions. He wanted her to retain her cachet. That was part of the attraction.

Then Miss Hutchison was talking, about meetings that she, too, had attended in London, about the famous people who attended them and about the ensuing press reports. Papa talked a lot about politics but had never been to a meeting or engaged in any activity. His politics were strictly in his head. Everyone listened earnestly to Miss Hutchinson and Papa's cigarette butts fell into the garden slowly.

Boyd knew that it was no use trying to get to Susan that night. He would wait for the tennis lessons. Susan was bound to be at the club when he would have every opportunity. He moved away in the scented night, embracing the warm wall of the house, staring at the stars. As he approached Mr Samms's horse, the kitchen door opened and Mr Samms and Miss Hutchinson came down the steps.

He saw them in the moonlight by the wall next to the kitchen. Mr Samms had Miss Hutchinson up against the wall, his hand on her bottom. Her own hands encircled his head and made caressing movements as he kissed her very hard. Frightened alarm froze Boyd to the ground. He heard Miss Hutchinson gasp as she broke away. Then they were at it again, grappling in a tight dance. Suddenly Mr Samms was dragging Miss Hutchinson, who seemed quite drunk, to her car. She got in, one leg out, chin raised. Mr Samms held her hands in a dramatic pose, slowly releasing them. He shut the door, looking deep into her eyes and blew her a kiss. She started the car and drove off, the headlights like yellow fingers pointing out trees, the eyes of a cat secretly watching. Mr Samms sprinted towards his horse, mounted and galloped off at a respectable pace. Boyd stood where they had been, dazed, breathing Miss Hutchinson's lingering perfume.

From the verandah, Papa's cigarette butts continued to fall more rapidly now, like shooting stars. He sat alone with Ann Mitchison, Mama having been called away by Yvonne, and felt the electricity between them. However nice she appeared, Ann was the imperialist maiden, to be captured and subdued.

On shaking legs, Boyd wanted to stand beneath the verandah in the undergrowth and listen to what they were saying, but it required bravery of the fatal kind. So he returned his thoughts to Susan, tennis at the club and Dennis.

* * *

164

Dennis was due to arrive in just over an hour. In his heart Boyd thanked Miss Hutchinson. And in his pocket he felt the secret note, words that would say everything, words that he had written carefully that very morning in a trembling hand, words that would lay the way for the ultimate act. He saw Susan waiting by the tennis courts in the early heat and her scent touched his nose, foretelling of pleasures to come.

'Eat up,' Mama said, observing Boyd struggling with his sausages. She sensed the tension in him. 'Look at Barrington, that's the way to eat.'

Barrington was not at all pleased to be the subject of attention. He ceased chewing and glowered. The tennis lessons were not top of his agenda, but the opportunity to get out of the house was not one to miss.

'I can't go,' Yvonne wailed, dispirited, forehead furrowed. Mavis stroked her smooth, small brown arms soothingly.

Papa had said 'Only the boys,' and Yvonne knew there was no point in arguing. Papa knew that although Dennis was a decent enough young man, he lived away from home at boarding school and only God knew what shenanigans he got up to there. Barrington and Boyd would go up to the club, play the fool, and the following day it would be all over the place – his boys behaving like hooligans. Papa knew boys. He didn't want to hear about any mischief, no monkey business at the club. If anything, any talk, ever came back to him, Barrington and Boyd knew there would be hell to pay. He expected them to behave themselves like well brought up children, like *Brookeses*.

Dennis drove up in a battered Land Rover exactly at ten o'clock. He swung out of the vehicle and pointed to his new Timex watch with the brown leather strap and the perfect stitching. It was the same watch Barrington dreamed of owning. He had completed the coupon at the back of the Gene Autrey comic and had been saving his pocket money, but his wrist was still bare.

'On the dot,' Dennis bawled. He was wearing his school khakis, a polo shirt, brown loafers and had that lanky look of boys between youth and adulthood. He wore his hair in a Tony C. This hairstyle, popular with boys his age, had been adopted from the film star Tony Curtis, whose hair jutted out in a coiffured quiff at the front. Dennis could often be seen using his slim plastic comb to maintain this quiff. He, and boys like him, called the hairstyle a TC. Barrington himself was secretly cultivating one for when he went to big school.

Mama took a worried look at the old vehicle parked in the yard and smiled graciously at Dennis. After all, he had volunteered to tutor the boys, although only after substantial kindnesses from Miss Hutchinson.

'It may be old but it's reliable,' Dennis assured Mama. 'It will take us there and back. And it can't turn over. It will stick to the road like a bulldozer. Mrs Brookes, you know you can trust me with the boys.' Dennis beamed, seeing the effect on Mama. The mothers on the estate approved of him.

There was no time to waste. The open road was waiting, the sky clear, the hot boiling sugar smell everywhere, wild flowers bright in the rolling fields, and the tennis courts lay in green shade, empty. But in the mounting excitement, Boyd saw beneath Mama's smile, saw the anxiety, saw that other face that would appear once they had gone. He was torn.

'I'll teach you to be Pancho Gonzales,' he heard Dennis say.

Dennis got in and slammed the door. They waved to Mama and to Yvonne, who was now racked with self-induced sobs. Mavis, standing behind Mama, poked her tongue out at Boyd. Her tongue appeared bright pink in the shade. Boyd, thinking strawberry ice cream, turned quickly away only to lock eyes upon a solitary Vincent leaning against the side of the garage with an air of total abandonment. Poppy followed them as far as the gate. It was a new experience driving in an open-top Land Rover, white dust billowing behind, Dennis's excited voice chattering as his sweating hand mangled the gears. *It could not be stopped now. They would be alone in the shade behind the club and he would do it there.*

'You don't have rackets?' Dennis said, surprised. 'Don't worry, we'll use the ones at the club. Remember, all the best players have their own rackets. When you're older and come up to Munro, you'll see how we play tennis. You'll see the way we play the other houses. Beat the daylights out of them all the time. When you walk out on the court wearing your Lacoste shirt with the little green crocodile – not every Tom, Dick or Harry will have those you know – dressed in all your whites and the girls from Hampton are cheering from the stands, oh man! You boys will find out one day. You have girlfriends? No, you're too young for girls. When I was your age – well, your age, Barrington – I used to fool around with Pamela Carby. Her old man didn't know a thing. The maid found out, though, but kept her trap shut after I gave her a look. I used to feel up her breasts – Pamela, not the maid – at the back of the house. Girls love that. You wouldn't know what it's like to feel up a girl's breasts. Jeez. Your time will come. Maybe today, eh, Barrington?' Dennis laughed his braying laugh, head thrown back, and narrowly missed a mongoose rushing across the road for the safety of the cane-piece.

'I sent a note to Geraldine Pinnock,' Barrington said, so brazenly that Boyd was embarrassed for him. Barrington just wanted to be like the big boys who had no restraint.

'A note!' Dennis hollered. 'What did you do that for? You need to go to her house when her old man's not there. Mrs Pinnock's nice, just like Mrs Wilson in *Dennis the Menace*. She'll give you cornmeal muffins and let you sit on the verandah with Geraldine. While Geraldine plays the piano, put your hand up her dress. See? Learn from the master. Go to her house, man.'

Boyd and Barrington exchanged shocked looks. They

knew such an act was impossible. If Papa ever heard about it, he would kill Barrington for certain, who would deserve to be killed, doing something like that. A note was safe.

'She knows about football,' Barrington said. 'I swapped her my football cards at the club.'

'Football cards? You goofed, man, you goofed.' Dennis laughed so raucously that both boys joined him, helplessly, laughing in the sun and the wind and the open air in the rickety Land Rover, laughing so hard they cried.

'Do you play football?' Barrington asked, when the laughing was over, thinking to get one up on Dennis, even though he wouldn't have minded carrying on with the conversation and learn from Dennis how to feel up Geraldine Pinnock. He wished that Boyd wasn't present. Boyd didn't know anything about girls. He only knew to gaze up into the sky and fall into the grass like a mad person.

'Do I play football? Ha, ha, ha. Do I play football. Barrington, Barrington, you are joking with me, man. You are talking to the king of football. I'm on the school team. Outside right, that's my position. I score from twenty, thirty yards all the time, ask anybody. They fear me at Munro. I have what they call *ball sense*. If you don't have that, you'll never be a footballer. One of these days we'll have a Boys versus Men's match. Mr Moodie is good. Lived in England in a place called Sheffield where silver cutlery comes from. They have professional football clubs up there. They *pay* you to play football. Can you believe a thing like that?'

Barrington warmed to Dennis and spoke rapidly about the football pictures he had collected, about Wembley stadium and Pele.

'Who?' Dennis said.

'Pele, Pele.'

'Pele what?'

'That's his name,' Barrington cried triumphantly. 'They say he's the youngest Brazilian footballer. The youngest! He plays for Santos. I have a picture of him in my scrapbook, and Denis Law too. He plays for Huddersfield

Town. They say he's a wonder-boy. I saw it in the *Daily Express* at the club.'

'A wonder-boy.' Dennis glanced at Barrington, nodding his appreciation. 'You are a football brain,' he said, appraising Barrington, who took on a look of very great importance, deliberately not looking at Boyd, whose eyes, he knew, were on him. 'What does Boyd play?'

'He doesn't play,' Barrington said quickly, with a "didn't you know?" look. 'He only reads books.'

'Reads books?' Dennis looked with interest at Boyd, sitting between Barrington and the gear-shift and holding on tight as the Land Rover bounced and swayed. 'What kind of books?'

'Every kind,' Boyd answered.

'Such as?' Dennis persisted.

Boyd knew that Dennis, although a senior boy at Munro with moustache hair already darkening his upper lip, wouldn't understand. Dennis was only interested in his Ivy League trousers, brown loafers and Vitalis for his hair. Boyd knew that he couldn't talk about *Great Expectations* to Barrington and Dennis. They would probably laugh at him. If only he could talk about the moment he met Estella at Miss Havisham's house, that quiet house with its weather-beaten gate and unkempt garden. How could Dennis and Barrington understand that he was Pip, or that he could easily be Pip, because all Pip's feelings, his anxiety, his vulnerability were his, Boyd's? *You may kiss me*, Estella had said. To hear such a girl say such a thing was utterly unimaginable. Yet it happened. He had been there, in the depths of that garden, in that house, facing Estella, completely overwhelmed by her. *In the same way in which Susan now overwhelmed him.* How could they understand, caring only for football and feeling up girls, about the big feelings that *Great Expectations* produced in him? He thought it best to remain silent.

'I bet you only read comics,' Dennis jeered.

169

'He reads lots of comics,' Barrington informed Dennis. '*Hopalong Cassidy, Kid Colt Outlaw, Superman, Heckle and Jeckle,* and *Johnnie Mack Brown.* And he likes to smell them.' Barrington laughed, seeing Boyd cringe. 'It's true.'

'Smell them? What for?' Dennis asked. 'I knew you were a comic reader. You can read my *Tarzan, Archie* and *Rex Allen* comics. You can smell them too. Ha, ha. I have a room full of them, maybe two hundred.'

It hurt Boyd that they didn't appreciate the scent of the comic pages, those lovely bright red splashes, the truest blues and yellows, the scorching blaze of a six-gun, the smell of America and of adventure. How could anyone not be intrigued by what lay among the pages?

'I'm going to read *Tropic of Cancer,*' he forced himself to say, not wanting Dennis to think he was just a comic reader. But the moment he said the words, he regretted it because he didn't want to be considered a show-off.

'Say what?' The Land Rover swerved, registering the impact of Dennis's surprise. 'What do you know about *Tropic of Cancer*? It's a bad book.'

'No, it's not,' Boyd said, feeling Barrington's weighty stare. 'It's about life.' He experienced that confidence, superiority too, of believing he knew what they didn't know. But he felt outnumbered.

Dennis laughed horribly. 'About life? Where have you heard all this stuff? It's about sex, sex! I shouldn't be telling you this. I promised Mrs Brookes to look after you boys. But it's strictly for adults, that book. It's banned. You're not supposed to read it. It's the baddest book around. When I say bad, I mean bad.'

'Miss Hutchinson's going to lend it to me,' Boyd said defensively, aware of Barrington's eyes upon him with that adult expression he liked to assume when he thought something was outrageous or verging on the ridiculous.

'Cynthia Hutchinson?' Dennis laughed some more, quietly now, as if he knew things they could never know. 'You little so-and-so. So *Miss Hutchinson* has a copy and she's going to lend it to you. You just make sure your father doesn't know. Jeez. If my old man knew I was reading a book like that, well, I won't tell you what he would do. They'd probably expel me from school too. My mother wouldn't talk to me again. She says it's dirty, a sex book.'

'But it's a masterpiece,' Boyd pleaded.

'A masterpiece! What do you know about masterpiece? Of course it's a masterpiece. It's a masterpiece of sex. It's about what men and women do, and it's not for little boys. It's banned. My parents haven't read it, I haven't read it, your parents haven't read it. I don't know anyone who's read it. Only intellectuals read it. People at university, people who live abroad, in places like Paris and London.'

'How do you know it's about...?'

'Sex? Can't say the word, eh?' Dennis laughed again. 'You don't even know what sex is. Everybody knows it's about sex. That's why it's banned. I could tell you things I've heard but you're too young. Too young! *Tropic of Cancer*, Jeez!' Dennis shook his head in disbelief. 'Miss Hutchinson is a bohemian. Look that up in your dictionary. A different kind of a woman, the kind men like. A woman of pleasure.'

'I know about bohemians.' Boyd was indignant. Nevertheless, a *woman of pleasure* appealed to him immediately and made Miss Hutchinson even more alluring. In his mind her colour changed immediately from amber to scarlet, and the fact that the book was considered *bad* only made her more compelling.

'I bet you do, Professor,' Dennis said, laughing and punching him playfully in the ribs. 'Only intellectuals and bohemians read that book.'

They were now approaching the club. Every vehicle in Boyd's eye was the Mitchison's Land Rover, every approaching car the Mitchison's Jaguar, cream and lean with the wire wheels and the big round headlamps. But only three supply vans and two other vehicles were sitting in the parking area. Bertram, the watchman, stood on the

171

entrance steps, his baton hanging low at his side. Bertram was always at the club, night and day. When did he sleep?

'Well, boys, today you become tennis champions,' Dennis cried, parking and vaulting out of the Land Rover. 'Come with me.' He slung his tennis bag over his shoulders and marched up the steps, winking at Bertram. Barrington and Boyd followed. Dennis took them to the bar, where he threw down the tennis bag.

'Bartender, a drink for my men,' he commanded in an unusual voice, the sort of voice heard at an end-of-term school play.

Barrington grimaced. In some ways he seemed more grown-up than Dennis. He cast curious looks at Boyd, as if trying to make his mind up about him. He wanted to ask about *Tropic of Cancer* but decided against it. He would stick to football and cars, subjects about which he was the undisputed master.

Ralstan, the bartender, stopped polishing the three dozen chunky glasses before him and viewed Dennis with amusement.

'You mean cream soda,' he grinned.

'Whatever my men want,' Dennis continued in his unusual voice.

Out on the main court, a game was in progress. From the length of the rallies and the crispness of the volleys, the players were obviously not novices. Dennis cocked his ear in the direction of the court, hidden by giant evergreens. He nodded every time the ball made contact with the racket, acknowledging that unmistakable *pock! pock! pock!* in the relative quiet of the day.

'You boys will be playing like that in a day or two. No, better. Remember, you'll be getting the best teaching available.'

'Miss Chatterjee taught Barrington,' Boyd said.

'Miss Chatterjee?' Dennis paused, his face a picture of undisguised admiration. 'Manjula Chatterjee. You hound dog, you,' he said after a time. 'She's good. Well, she has to be good to play at the Liguanea Club. Not everybody plays there. I'll teach you the finer points, how to win. In time you'll be good enough to go to Wimbledon or the US Open. Did I tell you I play for the school team? You don't get to play for Munro unless you're up there with the best. Didn't they tell you I got a mention in *The Daily Gleaner* sports page, picture and everything?'

'No,' Barrington and Boyd answered.

Ralstan brought the drinks and dramatised the entire exercise, setting the tray down on a side table, wiping their table with a blue cloth then setting out the drinks with a flourish before backing away with an affected bow.

'Take one for yourself,' Dennis informed him over his shoulder.

'T'anks. Too early,' Ralstan said.

'Well, have it when the time is right. And go for the strong stuff. Have a double. I'm paying.'

Ralstan smiled benignly. They knew he only drank *John Crow Batty*, the most potent white rum available. Only the strongest with cast iron stomachs drank *John Crow Batty*, or the very foolish.

'Well, you know, put it in the book.'

'Okay,' Ralstan said, wanting to get back to his glasses.

'Ralstan, Ralstan,' Dennis called after him, motioning vigorously with his hand. 'Who's on the court?'

'Miss Carby and three of her friends from Kingston,' Ralstan said. 'We preparing lunch for them. Table over there.' He pointed.

They scanned the far corner of the covered terrace, Dennis's face already in a crafty grin. One of the larger tables was covered in cream damask with polished glasses facing down. Green cotton cushions were puffed up on the chairs. A small card in the centre of the table said *Reserved*. A smaller table, further away, also had a reserved card.

'Who's that for?' Dennis asked.

'Mrs Mitchison,' Ralstan said, with an air of pride. 'She having lunch with her daughter or with one of the ladies,

173

ah believe. You never know who she going to have lunch with.'

At the mere reference to Susan, Boyd's thoughts exploded like balloons, pieces slapping him in the face. The crimson sound of movie music, "The Melody of Love", enveloped him. He gripped the arms of his chair tight and kept his head down, hoping that Dennis and Barrington had not noticed that *Susan* was written in big bougainvillea pink across his face. Tiny beads of sweat like dew formed on his forehead, on his nose, on the smooth flesh of his upper lip. Did no one see?

Dennis had grown silent, his hands twitching, his feet impatient.

'Well, boys,' he said at last. 'Meet me down at the side court. Barrington, you take this bag and don't leave till I get back. You're in charge. I'll just have a word with Pamela – be back in a jiffy.'

Then he seemed to slither across the tiles, bounced down the steps and was swallowed up in an instant by greenery. They knew they had lost him.

'I'm getting out the football,' Barrington said calmly. 'You stay here.' And off he went, taking his homely big brother scent with him. As he left, girlish laughter shattered the air from the other court hidden in the greenery.

A warm feeling overcame Boyd, left on his own. He sat in the green canvas chair at the edge of the green court in the green garden with *woman of pleasure* in his head, visions of Susan about him and the scent of white jasmine up his nose. The place where he sat was the place of Miss Chatterjee.

She stood under the floodlights at the service line in her tennis skirt, the flesh of her thighs tantalizing. She was taking up the serving stance, for the twentieth time probably, he could not remember. Once more he took up the incorrect position so that she had to run towards him, thighs trembling, to put her arms around him from behind to coax him into an acceptable stance. He felt his back and neck and shoulders being massaged by her titties and soft arms, her hair tickling his cheeks, saw their shadows meeting on the ground, and felt silly-awkward. Her fragrance radiated in the heat as she ran back to the service line to receive his balls. He tried hard not to look at her flouncing buttocks and the dainty sideways motion of her run, peculiar to all pretty women. He would serve and she would return with a ballet dancer's pirouette and a joyful laugh. He hoped to make a great many mistakes so that she would be onto him every time.

'All of them is *rass clart*,' a voice said, waking Boyd from his reverie. The curse words hissed like searing steam in the quiet. It was Rufus, the club gardener, pushing his ancient green lawnmower. They saw each other at the same time.

'Sarry, baas,' Rufus said, putting one hand on his heart. 'Ah never see you. Ah sarry, bass, ah sarry.'

Rufus, who people said was on *John Crow Batty* from mid-morning, had been offended. That was the reason he had used the dreadful curse words, *rass clart*, words less repulsive than *bombo clart*, the vilest words anyone could utter. The *John Crow Batty* smell came off his clothes like fresh fumes from the distillery.

'Ah mind me own business,' Rufus told Boyd. 'Ah don't interfere wid no one. Ah figger dat no one should interfere wid me. Right, baas?'

Boyd nodded.

'Doin' it right dere in me tool shed.' Rufus raised his eyes skyward. 'Right dere in the middle of all me t'ings. The crocus bags dem scattered all over the place. Ah was only gone 'alf a 'our to pick up some provision from the factory. But no, dem couldn't wait. Like two stray dawgs. *Two stray dawgs!* No shame. Ah expect better fram Miss Pam, but dat Dennis?' He shook his head and dropped his mouth in a grim expression. 'Dat boy only know one t'ing.'

Rufus walked off, still speaking to himself and shaking his head.

'Ready for the tennis lesson?' It was Dennis, face radiant, coming out of the greenery. Behind him, Pamela Carby's own face was radiant. Before Boyd could answer, Dennis massaged his shoulder affectionately.

'But it's up to you,' Dennis said. 'Barrington's playing football and you could be eating ice cream and a gingerbun. They just brought in fresh gingerbuns from the Silver Nook Bakery with the paper all crispy and warm.'

Pamela Carby moved closer. She radiated a complex potpourri of bouquets that Boyd could not define. He knew the smell and taste of gingerbuns though.

'Ice cream and gingerbun, yes?' Dennis urged. 'Silver Nook Bakery gingerbuns. Oh, man! Don't worry, we'll play tennis another day. Remember, I'm on holidays now.'

Pamela's enticing arm was about Boyd's shoulders. 'You are such a lovely boy, little Boyd,' she said when she heard his reply.

As he ate his ice cream and gingerbun on the high stool at the bar, Boyd pretended not to see the damask-covered table where Pamela and Dennis had their heads together. Dennis was stroking Pamela's supple thighs, which appeared radiant brown against the white tablecloth.

Two girls in pleated tennis skirts joined Dennis and Pamela, while a waiter in a white calico apron, having just rushed from the kitchen, served them. The girls wore sunglasses with white plastic frames. These were the latest in sunglasses and the senior girls at Hampton didn't go anywhere without them. Barrington, sweaty and excited from his football playing, also joined Dennis and the girls and was now seriously attending to a bowl of steaming beef soup. He had the sweaty brow and look that he had every Saturday at lunchtime when Mavis served beef soup: the look of a little Papa.

Boyd viewed with increasing panic the table reserved for Ann Mitchison. And he dreaded Papa's arrival. He had thought that the tennis lessons and his encounter with Susan would be over long before lunchtime. In desperation, he rushed to the bathroom. When he returned to the terrace, the Mitchisons were already there. Ann Mitchison was wearing a yellow and white flowery frock and Susan a white, puffed-sleeved blouse. Her fine brown hair shone. They had just sat down, Ann Mitchison nodding left and right to their neighbours. Boyd dodged down immediately, keeping close to the back of the terrace, trying to get to the sanctuary of the secluded courts without being seen.

There was a clatter of plates at Dennis's table and the girls laughed, attracting the stares of the men at the bar. The waiter with the white calico apron rushed forward attentively as the girls giggled and hid behind their large winged sunglasses. Barrington behaved like a big boy, like Dennis, laughing rather too noisily. Maybe it was because he was going off to Munro soon, to live in a dormitory with other boys, that he so easily forgot Papa's words. Boyd saw the men look towards Dennis's table and mutter to themselves.

At last he got to the steps and scrambled down them into green space, trying to bring calm to his rattled thoughts. There was no time to lose. Emboldened, he reached into his pocket. The note came up bright between his fingers. Folding the paper twice, he stumbled down the side stairs to the car park, to the Mitchison's Jaguar. Seeing no one about, hearing only the Shhh, Shhh, Shhhing of the steam from the factory, he placed the note in the side window of the car. She was bound to see it there.

At the top of the stairs, he turned back to look. The note stood out, bright white in the sun against the window, unmissable, a public statement of private longing. And it was too late to retrieve it. Other vehicles were entering the car park. Creeping through the fence at the side of the building, stung and cut by nettles and thorns, he limped back to the courts. There he sat on a bench behind a small bush that sprouted lilac flowers. While the minutes ticked away and the sun inched across the lawn, the men drove back to the factory in their Fords and Land Rovers. They would be back at the club in the evening. Boyd waited, knowing that Barrington would come looking for him when it was time to go. At last he heard footsteps. But when he looked up, it wasn't Barrington.

Susan was standing at the side of the court. She stood pale pink against the green. He lowered his head, observing her through the leaves. She'd found the note and had come looking for him, obviously. *Estella, heart-stopping Estella, was waiting in Miss Havisham's garden, waiting for him, waiting to say the words.* His heart thumped for he knew immediately that he couldn't do it then and there. Susan's white blouse was fresh and crisp like Mavis's washing, hair glossier than the mane on Corporal Duncan's horse, Cyrus, on a sunny Sunday afternoon. Although every sinew in his body wanted him to call out, it was impossible. They both remained still while the earth beat. Boyd thought they stood there from one to a hundred but it was only for a second, one to two, and it was over. Someone called out Susan's name. Startled, she ran back up the steps, taking her sun-warmed scent with her.

Instantly, Boyd went back through the hole in the fence, pricked and poked and scratched and torn. Paying no heed to the pain and the spectacle, he emerged running to the side of the building, a sudden sugar breeze lapping at his cheeks. He could see the Jaguar under the Appleton sun, its chrome parts winking. He saw Ann Mitchison come down the steps, her yellow flowery frock in a giddy dance around her legs. Susan followed, her own dress whipped up by the breeze around her thighs. As he watched with bursting excitement, Susan fighting to keep her dress down, he saw a white butterfly detach itself from the car and fly into the air. It flew away, swept up by the scented sugar breeze, over the hedge, across the lawns, towards the canefields, up over them and away to the river. It was his note, words that no one but Susan should see. He watched as the Jaguar went out through the gates, turned left down the Appleton road and was lost to sight.

That night, he went to her, unsettled, aching, wanting her. But Mavis was not in her room. He returned to the amber light of the pink house and to Mama, who smiled away her burdens and showed him a special handwritten note from Miss Hutchinson.

CHAPTER 19

Papa rushed home just before dusk and leaped out of the Land Rover, trembling with excitement.

'Where are the boys?' he demanded, not looking at Mama.

'Why do you want them?' Mama asked suspiciously.

'I'm taking them to a political meeting,' Papa said proudly and loudly.

'A political meeting?' Mama was aghast. She associated such things with bad behaviour and violence, critical press reports and condemnation from respectable people. Maybe nice people like Ann Mitchison went to political meetings in England, but in Jamaica it was mostly always the hooligans and poor people who went. She didn't see why Boyd and Barrington should be dragged off to places like that. And she knew immediately that Ann Mitchison had something to do with it.

'Yes, that is what I said, Victoria,' Papa replied with bravado. He wanted to look dangerous. Miss Hutchinson's words, *Liberté, Egalité* and *Fraternité,* were still with him, and in a tiny part of his mind, he imagined himself leading the revolution, *the revolution,* bringing down the old order, the *ancien régime,* as Miss Hutchinson had described it. His boys would attend a political meeting as Ann Mitchison did as a child. He knew it was good for them, long before Ann Mitchison said so, but her words had acted as a catalyst. He would have something to say the next time at the club when the talk turned, as he always made sure it did, to politics. Ann Mitchison would have her impressions confirmed that he was serious about his politics and a force to be reckoned with. And her eyes would say the things that her lips already revealed.

Papa found Boyd curled up listening to the radio, to the slow piano of Beethoven's *Sonata No 8*, the *Adagio*. He was looking out the window, seduced by passions that he could not understand. He did not know what it was that he listened to, but the music brought beautiful melancholy. It also brought Susan's small voice and many references to her. His feeling was one of blissfulness and sadness. She was waiting and he was desperately yearning. He was in that state of mind when Papa rushed in.

'Boyd, get dressed, you're coming with me.'

'Yes, Papa,' he said, rising from the armchair, sadness and bliss leaping out the window. He searched Mama's face for some sign, some notion of what *you're coming with me* meant. There was nothing.

'Where is Barrington?' Papa asked, tramping off towards Barrington's room.

Barrington was considering the merits of two advertised football boots, Puma and Adidas. He wasn't sure, but he thought Pele wore Puma. He couldn't decide which was the better of the two, but he would give up his scrapbook, not eat for two days, take tennis lessons from Miss Chatterjee and look deep into Vincent's pus-filled eye if he could wear the boots. He would even take a whipping from Papa – not one of his vicious whippings, only an ordinary whipping – if only he could play a game in them, just for one afternoon.

'Barrington,' Papa said, appearing at the door, 'get dressed.'

Barrington knew what a political meeting was. It was about the People's National Party and the Jamaica Labour Party, about Norman Washington Manley the Chief Minister, and Alexander Bustamante, leader of the opposition. He had heard men at the club talk, men like the bartender and the watchman. It was where people stood on a platform, spoke through loudhailers and shook their fists. They spoke about trade unions, wages, poor people who were comrades, Britain, colonial rule and self-government. He saw pictures of political meetings in *The Daily Gleaner* all the time. The only people who went to such meetings were small farmers and the sort of men who sat around outside shops and stared at Papa as he got into his car after buying his Royal Blend cigarettes.

They waved goodbye to Mama standing under the light on the patio, Yvonne entwined in her arms, waving too. They drove into the night, their scalps burning from the bristles of the hairbrush and their faces grey from too much Cashmere soap. Papa called them "boys" and behaved as if he were just a big brother, not their father. He stopped the car at a small shop to buy Staggerback, Paradise Plums and Jureidini's cream soda, the best cream soda in the world. They drove on and on into the night, through cane fields and one-shop villages, under star-filled skies.

Papa talked of Norman Manley and his son, Michael Manley, a young man of great promise who would be the main speaker at the meeting. Papa could not disguise his excitement. It showed in the way he abused the cigarettes, sucking at them harshly and flinging them out the window half-smoked; in the way he braked for potholes and steep corners and accelerated out of them; in the way he cut corners, speeded up hills and down slopes. The boys loved it, hanging on to their seats, looking wide-eyed at one another and at their Papa, not believing what was happening. There was Papa laughing away and telling jokes that they had never heard before. But it was the driving that excited them most. Papa was driving like a racing driver, fast, confident and fearless. 'Like Stirling Moss,' Barrington said with pride later. If Mama had been in the car, she would have said, 'Slow down, you're going too fast!' But Mama wasn't there. It was dangerous, but it was more exciting than dangerous. Papa knew what he was doing and they believed in their Papa. The Prefect obeyed him. The boys felt very close to their Papa. While he drove, he had one arm around them. He had been drinking too and the adult rum smell came off him.

'Boys, boys! We're going to see a great Jamaican. A great Jamaican! Let me tell you, this will be a night you will never forget, as long as you live. You will tell this to your children. You, Barrington. You, Boyd.'

Because of the way Papa spoke about the young man, Michael Manley, the boys thought of him as a film star admired by Mavis, or a cowboy who would bring order to a lawless town. He was already their hero, because he was Papa's hero.

Hands sticky from the cream sodas and Staggerbacks, they got out of the car in a small village square. A hundred eyes followed them as they left the Prefect. A couple of Fargo trucks and vans were parked at the side of the road. Bicycles, big, black, muddy things with huge generators and headlight casings, were thrown about. Several old Land Rovers and John Deere tractors littered the scene, caked in mud and festooned with tufts of grass and cane leaves. People were excited at the smallest movement in the crowd, the flash of new headlights, the crunch of tyres. 'Comrade Mike,' someone called out and a shout went up. But it wasn't Comrade Mike. It was new arrivals, looking pitiful and ordinary. Once or twice a few farmers and several men from the estate in big cars drove up. Papa knew some of these men and went over to talk, introducing Boyd and Barrington, who felt as if they were grown-up, especially when their hands were shaken by the big hands of the big men. The boys stood close to the car because the engine was still warm. Already half asleep, the boys wanted to crawl back into the leather seats and curl up. They thought of their warm beds back at the pink house.

It was late when the young Michael Manley arrived. Papa ushered them in among the big men in their farm clothes, smelling of pigs and two-day-old perspiration. It was like a film show to the boys: the waiting, the bright lights in front, the roar of the crowd and then the silence, all eyes riveted on one spot. They fought to keep their eyes open.

Boyd remembered a tall man looking like a big schoolboy with big ears and curly fair hair, which seemed to glow in the harsh light. He was golden under the lights. But it was his voice that identified him – a voice that was brave and sincere, touching the crowd, reaching deep into their hearts. *Brothers and Sisters, we have been divided, but now we are joined. The word is love.* Between slow blinks, Boyd remembered Papa punching the air and roaring magnificently, just like Mr Samms. And he could not be sure but he thought he saw, out of the gloom, the soft-white form of Ann Mitchison with her hot burgundy lips, standing next to Papa. He remembered the voice and the light and the tall, golden man, the adulation, the chill of the night. Then he was falling into bed, warm and dreamy.

Just before sleep came, he saw her again, Ann Mitchison. She was standing by her Land Rover, stopped in the road in the dark, Papa next to her in the white headlights. And a strange thing happened. Mr Samms was suddenly there too, in the darkness and the mystery of the night, outrageously kissing Ann Mitchison, his lips squashed against hers, devouring her. And he was wearing Papa's clothes. But, much later, when Papa finally slid in behind the steering wheel, the car had the scarlet scent of kiss.

CHAPTER 20

'So, my little *peeny-waalie*, Miss Hutchinson wants you over
at her house,' Mama said, smiling sweetly, not knowing
about *Tropic of Cancer*, his and Miss Hutcinson's deepest
secret. 'That's far better than going to a political meeting, and
you won't get sick from too much cream soda and sweets.'

'Yes, Mama,' Boyd said, knowing not to mention about
Ann Mitchison.

And on that special day, Papa, in a moment of
unexpected generosity, allowed him the pleasure of cycling
the two miles to Miss Hutchinson's, waving aside Mama's
protestations.

'He's a growing boy,' Papa said irritably. 'The house is
just across the way. There's no need for me to drive him up
there. You worry too much. Everything bothers you these
days, woman. Jeezas.'

'Bothers?' Mama rounded on him. 'What makes you
think that?'

But Papa had already left the room.

Barrington, performing big brother duties, showed Boyd
how to get the best out of the bicycle, his bicycle, the prized
hybrid Raleigh that took him on adventures round the
estate roads, past Geraldine Pinnock's house, during the
hours Papa was at the factory.

'Don't stay too long, and look out for the train at the
crossing,' Mama called out as Boyd pedalled furiously
away. Yvonne, a solitary figure on the verandah, threw June
Rose blossoms after him with jealous rage, but seeing the
futility of it, returned to dressing her dolls.

Boyd rode down the slope and across the bridge, feeling the bicycle wheels churning the fine sand of the road. The sun drooled. Sugar and dunder odours from the factory streamed over him. The sky was clear, shiny blue. He believed that somehow Susan knew of his intentions and would be at Miss Hutchinson's house waiting, invited there by Miss Hutchinson herself, who knew the whole story. And because he believed this, he pedalled harder, mounting the railway crossing just as the bell clanged and the gate closed. Looking back, he saw the slow train, the puffing black engine and the thirty or so grey carriages full of livestock and machinery. In no time he was on the smooth asphalt of the Appleton road leading up to Miss Hutchinson's house. It was a brilliant-white house with a green roof and green shutters. Creepers were entwined in the shutters and tiny white butterflies danced about in a cluster. Purple bougainvillea shrouded both ends of the house, dropping blossoms on the perfect lawn. In the distance, the rushing steam from the factory warned *Shhhhhhh! Shhhhhhh!* And it alarmed Boyd because it sounded clearer on that side of the valley, and more urgent.

At the end of the path, the maid, Icilda, met him. She had a pile of crispy sun-dried clothes in her arms.

'You want Miss?'

Boyd answered yes. Icilda held blue-white sheets, towels and napkins, still warm from the sun. Boyd wanted to bury his face in them.

'Come wid me,' Icilda said, walking off, in her wake the invigorating pure scent of washed clothing. Boyd watched her bottom bouncing inside the lavender-coloured dress.

They entered the house and Icilda went to put the clothes away before announcing his arrival. Susan was nowhere to be seen. But she could appear at any time. Her scent was in the room.

He sat on the red cushion in a room full of books. There were Penguin paperbacks, hardbacks big and small and lovely red and yellow editions of the Dent & Dutton

Everyman's Library. The polished floor of the room was of dark wood and the walls were white. He wanted to rush up to the books and pick and choose but there were so many, where would he begin? Which one was the *Tropic of Cancer*? The smell of the books was overpowering. He inhaled deeply again and again. He wanted to touch, caress and turn the pages, see the beginnings of chapters, the last words on the back pages.

Suddenly, in the silence, a door opened with such force that the walls of the house shook. Boyd looked down the hall. The door slammed and a tall man in khakis and riding boots appeared. It was Mr Moodie. From behind the bookcases, Boyd saw him walk briskly and boldly in the opposite direction. He didn't get far. A figure in a lime-green shirt, sleeves rolled up at the elbows, shirt-tails falling over naked thighs, barely concealing black panties, rushed upon him. Boyd saw them smash into one another. Their arms and bodies seemed to do strange things. One of Miss Hutchinson's thighs crept up the back of Mr Moodie's leg and massaged it spasmodically. Then they were fighting, Miss Hutchinson's arms lashing out and scratching. Mr Moodie lifted her up off her feet and smashed her against the wall. They were growling and snarling like dogs, heads together. Both Miss Hutchinson's legs were now wrapped round Mr Moodie's waist and she was moaning and groaning like Mama, only louder and with great desperation and anguish. She was crying out like a pig on the butchering block.

Boyd was in a panic. He did not know what to do. He went weak at the knees and dry in the mouth. He wanted them to stop. Mr Moodie was hurting Miss Hutchison, and their voices were savage and desperate. Then he saw Miss Hutchinson tug hard at Mr Moodie's leather belt. Her shirt came off. He saw with a tortured gasp her naked woman's flesh, her smooth skin, her shoulders, the exposed breasts with the dark nipples, her hungry sucking mouth locked against Mr Moodie's. Mr Moodie put her down for a moment, still at her mouth, their heads together like mounting snakes, and let her slip off the wall and fall against him. Amid her grunting and whimpering, he bundled her up and staggered into a room off the hall. Miss Hutchinson's thighs were rippling and falling, her breasts bouncing, one hand clutching her shirt, Mr Moodie's lips still firmly fixed upon her wounded mouth. A door slammed again and the room went quiet. Boyd strained forward to hear the feeblest sound and imagined he heard cries, the muffled death scream of a pig, but no sound entered the room. He felt like an intruder. His own loud breathing was deafening in the room and he tried to suppress it. But the effort exploded his mouth.

He turned round in the quiet among the books. Their titles leaped at him like hundreds of excited tiny voices calling out. Then Icilda appeared, innocent of the incident, but he was already walking past her.

'You don't want to see Miss?' she asked, seeing his resolve.

'No, I have to go home,' Boyd stammered.

'You can use the toilet here,' Icilda suggested, trying to understand.

'No,' Boyd said, rushing out the door and to the bicycle. Miss Hutchinson should never know he'd been in her house. He wished he had never seen them. But he had seen it, the monstrous act. It was the brutal, physical aspect of the encounter that perplexed him so. Confusion arose because he had been curiously aroused by their cries and by what they were doing. He had wanted Miss Hutchinson's probing tongue in his own mouth. He had wanted this pink tongue of a breast, on which Mr Moodie was feasting so ravenously, to feed on himself. But it was terribly frightening with the pig squeals and Miss Hutchinson distressed and hurting. Mr Samms, in his moonlight engagement, had not been so rough, only theatrical. *But where was Mr Samms?*

'Oh, okay,' Icilda said. She glanced out the window, saw

Mr Moodie's red Buick at the gate and understood perfectly. Then she returned grimly to the kitchen to wash and rewash pots and pans, making as much noise as possible.

Out on the road, Boyd pedalled with such force he surprised himself. A bittersweet pleasure gave him unimaginable powers. The bicycle forced itself up the slope with Ten-To-Six-like determination. On exhausted legs he put the bicycle down by the garage and crept lustfully into the deepest reaches of the garden, hot and sweating, his breathing tortured, soft pollen powdering his shoulders and arms.

CHAPTER 21

Soft pollen powdered his shoulders and arms as he slipped deep into the green arms of the garden, where everything was in unadulterated harmony. The only discordant sound was the distant squealing of a pig. In a sudden panic, he left the garden and rushed towards the house, flying past Vincent who was staring blankly into air by the forget-me-nots.

When he got to the kitchen door, he heard stomping, the sound of someone jumping up and down on the wooden floor in the hall. Mavis was in the kitchen walking back and forth, brows raised, hands soapy and wet, unable to do any washing. It was Barrington. Papa had him by the front of his short trousers in the hall. Barrington's feet were almost off the floor, his mouth a violent hole, his screams pig squeals. Mama stood back at one end of the room, frightened, hands rigid, crying, 'Stop it! Stop it!' to no avail. Yvonne stood at the door to her room, her doll in one hand, her other hand fisting the tears from her eyes. Papa was a gigantic figure. He filled the space with his fury, and fire seemed to blaze from his nostrils. His right hand wielded the thick brown strap, hurling violent blows on the plump boy struggling beneath him. Papa's hand slipped as Barrington twisted and turned to evade the brutal blows, *whup, whup, whupping* his head, shoulders, back, buttocks, legs. Papa grabbed down and hard. Barrington's eyes went white and fixed on Mama. He was frothing at the mouth. Mama pushed forward and tried to pull Papa away. She and everyone could see that Papa had Barrington in an iron

189

grip by his teapot. Barrington's screams were like death. Papa blocked Mama's path. It was ghastly.

Boyd stood trembling, watching his brother being held down. It was the coolie pig, the blood, the shameless squeals, the helplessness, the hideous smell of butchery all over again. It was also Miss Hutchinson and Mr Moodie, the savagery, the animal sounds and the peculiar feelings. Papa was a coolie butcher. Boyd glared at him, piercing looks of hatred and started to cry. No one was helping Barrington. His own brother, whose scent and feelings he knew, who, although eleven years old, was still only little, was dying, butchered by their father. Boyd heard Barrington gag, his begging now without dignity, his voice no longer his own.

'Stop it!' Boyd commanded, seeing Barrington lying dead in the centre of a small crowd, his pitiful body strange and still, smelling of death. 'Stop it!'

Papa glanced round but continued with the beating until Mama, drawing strength from somewhere, restrained his hand long enough for Barrington to slip away. Papa stood alone, furious, the strap writhing in his trembling hand.

His voice was hoarse when he said, 'You disobey me again, you little monkey, and I'll kill you! Bringing shame to the family. We are not common people. You hear me?'

In the kitchen, cups and saucers fell to the black and white tiles, shattering into a hundred pieces. Papa's brogued feet thundered about the house for a while then he got into the Land Rover and drove off in a cloud of dust. Poppy did not follow him to the gate as usual but hid wherever he was. Vincent, feeling helpless on the porch, scowled at Papa as he rushed by. And for the first time, he regretted not having begged to go to England with the Maxwell-Smiths.

Mavis entered the room to see if she could help but Mama said it was all right. She took Barrington in her arms. Yvonne stroked his leg. Boyd looked at his sobbing brother and their eyes met. He felt a peculiar embarrassment and wished that he, not Barrington, had received the beating. He wiped away the tears quickly so no one could see. The whole house trembled with fear.

'I hate Papa!' The words burst out of him. But it was mainly because he wanted Barrington to know that he was not alone, that he felt for him.

'You mustn't say that, darling,' Mama said, cuddling Barrington close.

'You mustn't say that, Boyd,' Yvonne echoed, still sniffling.

'I mean it.' He did not face Barrington, who was also looking away.

'No.' Mavis's hand was gentle on his shoulder. 'No, petal.'

'Mama, why did Papa beat Barrington?' Yvonne asked.

Mama continued to cuddle Barrington, saying not a word. But she knew that voices had whispered at the factory. Voices had whispered about a disgusting note being sent. The same voices had whispered that Dennis had sat at a table at the club with a group of girls creating a nuisance and that Barrington Brookes, son of Harold Brookes, had been there at the table with them, slurping his soup. Mrs Dowding mentioned it to Papa, having heard about it fourth hand. She said that people were talking and that Dennis, though his name had been mentioned, never once slurped his soup, never once.

In the afternoon, when the house was quiet, when Vincent had gone away to Lacovia, Boyd went to Mavis's room and sat on her bed. The house was a violent place even with Papa out of it. He could still hear the pig squealing and see the walls of their home splattered with its blood. Mavis's room was quiet and there was no violence there. Pleasant things, her *Essen*, her *Cutex* and her personal belongings were there, and the music from her pretty brown radio with the big cream dials. His anxiety subsided.

Mavis had her skirt tucked down between her thighs,

revealing radiant dark-brown knees. She sat in such a way that she could see herself in the small square mirror while at the same time reach out to the tub of palmolive pomade on the table. She was plaiting her hair with dexterous finger movements. The pomade gave her hair a brilliant sheen and a sweet and agreeable smell. He drew closer to her until he was so close they touched.

'You going to get hair all over you, petal,' Mavis said.

Her body scent was pomade sweet. Little beads of sweat on her arms gave her smooth skin the translucence of rose petals. Boyd could see the slit between her breasts and the sweat like tiny dewdrops suspended there. Her thighs were like brown allamanda. Heat came off every part of her. He wanted to touch and stroke her thighs as he would the allamanda, or any of the silky, fleshy flowers. He felt the urgency that always enveloped him before he bit into the petals in the garden. He wanted her breasts.

'You thinking of Barrington,' Mavis said gently, feeling his quietness, his intensity. 'It was wicked, wicked.'

Boyd's lips trembled. She came to him immediately, wiping her hands on her dress as he reached out to her. She did not feel his hands on her thighs, this sensitive child of her employers, this little enigma.

'Ooh,' she said. 'Don't cry, petal.'

But that only encouraged the tears. She felt his tiny body convulse against her, felt the breath from his sobs, felt his hot cheeks pressing against her breasts.

'Hush petal, hush, hush,' she said, rocking him against her and feeling the maternal instinct rising. 'Hush, hush, hush.'

His hands brushed against her arms as he tried to position himself comfortably on the bed. She felt his hot breath upon her breast. The bed creaked. As she took him properly in her arms, one strap of her sleeveless dress slipped down exposing a plump brown breast. He saw the flesh like a fresh rose and his lips parted. Her nipples stuck and he sucked and she, as if from a distance, saw a mother and child. Under her dress his hands caressed her thighs and she kissed his forehead and stroked his hair. She could see how he had been affected by the brutal beating, for she had been affected too and had been unable to rid herself of the horror still inside her. She continued to let him milk her as the feeling of fulfilment steadily grew and the tension ebbed. It was very quiet in the room, so quiet that even the sound of falling leaves could be heard. The big house seemed very far away.

* * *

It was quiet among the crotons where he lurked outside Mavis's window that night. After the experience at her breast and the scene at Miss Hutchinson's, the strange craving would not go away. That evening, he found himself sucking his own tongue so hungrily that Mama slapped his wrist and said, 'Stop that!'

He wanted to look at Mavis as he looked at the women in the encyclopaedia. He wanted to see her undress just like Mama and Aunt Enid, quietly, when no one was around, when there was no sound to be heard, just his breathing. And he wanted to know what it was like to see another person, like Miss Hutchinson, take her panties down.

But there were stealthy movements in Mavis's room. It was not Vincent with her, as he imagined, but a man with gold teeth; the strange man who had ridden off with her in the night. He had Mavis against the wall and she was not resisting. Boyd heard her crying out like Mama. Her face was against the man's face.

'No!' Mavis's whisper was harsh.

'Shh! Is okay,' the man said, picking her up and taking her bodily to the bed, her dress rising above her thighs, her shoes falling to the floor. As frantic shadows crowded the room, the man wrestled her down on the bed saying 'Shh!' every few moments.

Boyd clung to the windowsill, fingertips burning,

breathing fast. He had not expected the hard-looking stranger in the room. Should he run and tell Mama, or get Vincent? He was in a quandary and felt even more frightened when Mavis started to cry out. But pictures of Mama and Papa wrestling in bed came to him. And the fresh images of Miss Hutchison and Mr Moodie appeared too, dramatic and violent. It was what they did in private, adults, when they thought no one could see.

'No, Barry. I said no! Stop it! I work here. You can't do this.'

'You not going to give it to me?'

'Barry, please.'

'Give it to me, Mavis. Give it to me.'

Boyd stood on one leg and then the other as if the ground was on fire.

'Please, Barry, stop it! Stop it!'

Barry was not stopping it. He was fighting her on the bed, her thighs on either side of him, his hands furious, her hands furious. Barry had her panties off in a flash and his face was upon her face and Mavis wasn't crying out any more. She said things that had no meaning. Suddenly Mavis rose from the bed, titties loose, dress falling around her ankles and turned out the light. Just before the light went out, Boyd saw the patch of dark hair in the space between her legs. Just like Mama's. Just like the pink women. He stayed long enough to hear the bedsprings squeak, then, as the *peeny-waalies* swarmed about, made his way back to the new book lying on his bed, *The Old Curiousity Shop*.

Vincent's one good eye saw everything. He'd seen Barry arrive, watched him biding his time alone in the room smoking his Four Aces. Vincent took a thousand blows as the scene unfolded, felt the pain rear up in him from a deep place. As Barry mastered Mavis on the bed, he'd turned away from the wall. He went out of the room and slumped on the warm grass near the plum tree, watching the *peeny-waalies* in the deepening darkness. The warm night breeze brushed against his grim features and he wondered, with much doubt and self-pity, what a wretch like him would have to do to gain some recognition from Mavis. He came from nothing, had nothing and was nothing. And then, as if commanded, he reached for the strange tobacco that he had been introduced to recently by transient men in the back room of a rum bar in Lacovia. And the rain pelted down.

CHAPTER 22

The rain pelted down all the next day and Vincent kept out of Mavis's way, wounded and despised, like an old dog left behind by a cruel, departing family. He sat behind the garage, watching the young corn leaves, apple-green in the light, listening to the rain. While he listened, a kernel of an idea emerged deep in his head. It was revolting but he did not care. The rain drowned out all sound, and he returned to the comfort of his room and his new cigar. An hour later, in drugged ecstasy, as the rain ceased, he heard the Land Rover's splashy approach. But he did not see Papa walk quickly into the house, slightly unsteady, smelling of drink.

'All your shenanigans will end when I get you out of this house and back to school.' Papa stood with both feet apart, hands on hips, glaring at Barrington, who sat on the sofa in the living room, frozen. 'All your nonsense will stop when you have to do some work at school. You hear me?'

'Yes, Papa,' Barrington stammered, eyes wild, body primed, ready to run.

'You understand, do you? Then you'll be glad to know that I paid the fees at Munro today. You'd better start doing some book work now – arithmetic, science. You've got the books, so get with it.'

'Yes, Papa,' Barrington said, eyes fixed on Papa's gesticulating hand.

'And you, Boyd.' Papa turned his attention to the small, self-conscious figure lying on the floor, head down, looking at a picture in the encyclopaedia, entitled *The Persistence of Memory, oil painting by Salvador Dali, 1931*. But Boyd had stopped looking at the picture the moment Papa entered the room. He had been listening hard, expecting violence, and so when he heard his name, his head snapped up. 'Yes, you,' Papa said. 'Don't think you're out of it. Don't think I haven't seen you hanging about at that fence like a little good-for-nothing. You just make sure you stay on this side of the fence. Don't think that because Mr Mitchison is the assistant general manager it's alright to go over into their garden.'

'But I didn't go over there, Papa,' Boyd interrupted, astonished. How could Papa have found out that he'd been trying to get to Susan?

'I didn't say you did. I just don't want you over there getting into other people's business. I know what you get up to so don't play the fool with me. You stay on this side of the fence where you belong, so that you don't get into mischief. You hear me?'

'Yes, Papa,' Boyd said, thinking that after such a warning, his only chance to meet Susan would be at school.

'You're off to the Balaclava Academy. I've put your name down and paid the fees. Get education into that empty head of yours.'

'What about me, Papa?' Yvonne sprang forward, believing that yet again she had been passed over.

'You'll go to the academy too, but not next term.'

'When then?'

'Next year.'

'Next year!'

'You heard me. Now, don't be difficult.' He gave Yvonne a hard look and continued down the hall to Mama's room. Yvonne's lips and chin trembled so that she couldn't face her brothers. The rain drowned out her stifled sobs.

'Shh!' Barrington said, five minutes later. 'Papa's quarrelling with Mama again.' As one, they all fell silent.

They had always known fear from an early age. But since their arrival at the pink house, the fear they experienced and believed to be the most natural thing that

197

parents, particularly fathers, inflicted upon their children, had taken on a strange permanence. It was there in the house even when Papa wasn't there. It was as if they were just moments away from disaster. The door would open suddenly one day and they would all be put out on the street. And it was because Mama and Papa weren't friends any more.

'I'm going to my room,' Boyd said, struggling with the encyclopaedia. In his room, he put the book down on the bed and climbed out the window. Poppy joined him. They crouched outside Mama's bedroom and cocked their ears up to the window. From their place in the drawing room, Barrington and Yvonne pricked up their ears.

'Why can't you be like other women?' they heard Papa's slurred voice say.

Raindrops dripped from the end of leaves and dropped with loud plops in puddles close to the verandah. Quiet lightning razed the sky. It had been cosy in the amber light of the living room until Papa arrived. He had returned to find Mama in her pink dressing gown, the dressing gown of the housebound, with that bedclothes smell, redolent of everything he would rather not be reminded of. Behind him at the club were women of Mama's age in soft linen, wearing perfume more tantalising than *Evening in Paris,* women who were making their mark, not lazing about with long faces and dark brows.

'You married me,' Mama cried, feeling the tension, knowing the look in his eyes, sensing the background to it. The pressure had been growing before Barrington's beating and she had wondered when it would erupt. 'You told my mother I was the only girl in the parish for you.' She stared at him, trying to quieten her voice. 'Now you want me to be like other women!'

'You're always at home, you never go out like other wives.'

Mama would have laughed if Papa's comment hadn't been so pathetic. It was obviously the drink.

'Go where?' Mama was mystified. 'I thought you wanted me at home. Now you want me to spend my time at the club like other women? I should walk there, four miles away, and then do what? Who would look after the children? You've always said only maids and loose women walk. If you want me at the club, why don't you take me and the children there more often? The only time we ever get to go there is when I complain that you never take us anywhere. You hardly get home before ten, when it's too late to go out. You often get home in the early hours. And mostly you're drunk. As you are now.'

'Me, drunk?' Papa was incensed. His expression declared that a man couldn't talk to his wife calmly about the things that mattered without receiving unwarranted criticism. But that was women for you.

'Almost every Sunday morning,' Mama continued. 'The children know. They see you lying drunk on the bed with the chamber pot full of vomit on the floor. And they sing that Harry Belafonte song, *Mama, Look-A Boo Boo*, making fun of you.'

Papa sprang to his feet, enraged, trembling, pointing his finger in Mama's face. 'Do you know how hard I work?' he growled. 'All this' – he indicated the house, the grounds, the firmament. 'I am responsible for this. You hear me? Without me this doesn't exist. You hear me? You hear me?' He saw Mama recoil at behaviour that was increasingly alarming.

He couldn't hold back. The words tumbled out. Their quarrels had never taken such a ferocious tone before. Mama kept looking at him from under her eyelashes, silently asking him to stop, to not let it go any further, trying to connect, trying to make him understand. He didn't want to understand. His guilt saw to that.

Mama stood back, breathing hard. She felt that she was partly responsible for the state of things. Secretly she believed she deserved it, creating tension with her suspicions. In her heart she believed that her husband was as straight as an arrow, not given to anything underhand. She believed that his only faults were his impatience, idiosyncrasies and his belief that he was always right. All the men in her life, her father and brothers, anyone of note, behaved in that way. But she never quite understood Papa's revulsion when they argued. This was something new.

She just wanted things to go back to what they were before the Mitchison's arrival. It was all because Ann Mitchison was a live wire and had been to college, drove a Land Rover, did this and that about the estate and frequented the club with her pearls and perfume and political talk. Papa wanted her to be like Ann Mitchison. He didn't say so but she knew. He wanted her at home yet he wanted her out and about. He wanted her to be a woman of the world yet he refused to let her even contemplate establishing her design work. What he wanted, or what he imagined he wanted, was impossible. He was just confused. She was sorry for him in a way, but felt terribly bruised because it was so unfair. And his new anger and disdain frightened her.

Papa said nothing. Mama said nothing. Boyd heard nothing. Papa sat back in the chair, contemplating his brogues against the polished floor. The waters drained away.

'All I am saying is that you need to get out more. So what if I've changed my mind? Can't a man change his mind?'

'And do what?' Mama's voice broke in its appeal. 'Where would I go? Get out like other women. What do you mean?'

'Go out for walks with the children.' He said this grimly, without conviction. It was he himself who had laid down the law that no respectable woman should walk about unescorted. The servants should take the children walking. None of the estate wives went walking except in their gardens and on their lawns. Poor people walked, labourers walked, beggars walked and everyone who could do no better walked. And those who walked only did so in the dust of the miserable roads to and from the factory, walked behind slow donkeys to market, to the rum bars and back to their small, wooden, paint-peeling houses. Papa did not mean that sort of walking. Maybe he imagined a wonderful kind of walking that did not take place on the roads of Appleton. Perhaps Ann Mitchison had told him about her walks in the smart squares of London. Maybe he had been listening to Miss Chatterjee talk at the club about how she strolled in Hyde Park and other London parks with suitors in tow on a pleasant evening. Perhaps he heard Miss Hutchinson say she'd regularly sauntered about the streets of Paris and the suburbs and how delightful that was for a woman like her. On her walks she visited bookshops, art galleries, theatres, restaurants and tea and coffee-houses. But Appleton was neither Paris nor London.

'We live miles from the club,' Mama continued. 'We've only been there together as a family about four times. The other husbands take their wives and children out every weekend; to Maggotty Falls, to the cinema, to family and friends, visiting new places, to concerts. The Baldoos are always off to Mamee Bay on the north coast. It's lovely up there – private cottages, private beach.'

'The Baldoos this, the Baldoos that. They are gods!'

'Well, you're forever talking about them,' Mama replied. 'They're your gods.'

Papa sucked his teeth.

'The Mitchisons go out as a family,' Mama informed him. 'Tim Mitchison is as busy as anybody, always away on business, yet he finds the time. They were at Rose Hall Great House only last week, from what I hear.'

'You heard wrong,' Papa said with conviction.

'And how would you know?' Mama retorted, imagining scenarios of every sort.

'That's enough,' Papa suddenly commanded, with new vehemence, the veins at his temples visibly throbbing.

'*We* don't go out, but *you* are always going out, here,

there and God knows where,' Mama said. 'Who knows where you go?'

'I said that's enough!' Papa's eyes were smouldering.

Mama faced him, unable to disguise thoughts now written large on her face. She knew what she wanted to say but couldn't. It would hit low and could be fatal. The Lluidas Vale secret lurked at the back of her mind, and Enid's words, *if he's capable of this, he's capable of anything*, loomed like a fearful warning. She felt a deep urge to say something outrageous, but the belief that that would be wrong was far stronger.

Papa sucked his teeth again and left the room. It was the second time he'd sucked his teeth that evening. He did not care for her. Mama cried quietly in her pink dressing gown, hoping the children did not hear. They would only worry, the poor things. She was amazed at how frightened she became as she remembered Papa's threats, meant for the children: 'I'll put you on the streets to beg your bread.' These were words the children were accustomed to hearing. But they were words that were now meant for her.

Later that evening, Barrington and Yvonne fidgeted in their rooms while Boyd sat in the chintz armchair waiting for Papa to leave the house. Beside him, the Mullard radio droned and buzzed. The news drifted in from the world, the events of that week, but he heard nothing of it. *Russia launches first intercontinental ballistic missile. Heavyweight boxing champion Floyd Patterson knocks out Tommy 'Hurricane' Jackson in New York in round ten to retain world heavyweight title.*

As soon as they heard the Land Rover gurgle to life, they were at the window, tracking the olive-green shape, the red rear lights vanishing down the hill. They went to Mama like frightened rabbits, while the scent of Angels' Tears from the garden filled the room. And they believed their days at the pink house would end soon and that nothing would be the same anymore. Barrington would go off to boarding school, far away from Mama. Outside, the sound of dripping water continued, against a background of incessant night noises. Mama did not speak. The night drew in rapidly, chilly and cruel.

* * *

Much later that night, if Mama could see Papa, she would see a tidy, respectable arrangement on the Mitchison's verandah. The night air was clean and scented, and nocturnal creatures sang in the garden. Papa sat with Ann Mitchison, sipping tea. He would have preferred a double gin and tonic with a slice of lime and a chunk of ice. He hated the tea, although it was light and fresh and without milk and served in an elegant china teacup. Tea only reminded him of the revolting *cerasee*, its bitter leaves growing wild in the back garden, that his mother used to force upon him as a child once a month. It was what some rural Jamaican families used as a laxative, a "wash-out" for their children. The most repellant aspect of *cerasee* tea was the smell. It made grown men tremble. But tea was tea. Yet, here he was with calm deliberation, seeming to relish cup after cup. It might have had something to do with the person who served it because at one point in the conversation he was flattering.

'Excellent tea,' Papa said, with a knowing nod.

Ann accepted the compliment with a smile that squeezed her eyes shut.

They talked quite a bit after that, and if Mama were watching she would see Evadne clear away the tea things as it got late. If she could hear, as Evadne could, she would know that Mr Ramsook and his companions' days of unemployment were over and that the estate would provide them and their children with medical support. They got that out of the way early. Evadne locked the windows in the kitchen and in the pantry and closed the shutters. Then she said goodnight, looked in on Susan fast asleep under the mosquito net and went to her room in the servants' quarters at the back of the house. If she were still looking, Mama would see Papa rise to go because he'd seen the time and wanted to be circumspect. And she would note the subtle, restraining arm of Ann Mitchison and see Papa sink back into his chair.

Papa sat alone smoking and looking out into the night as Ann busied herself in the kitchen pouring late drinks, real drinks. She returned to the verandah with two nine ounce cut glass tumblers, and Mama, if it were possible that she still watched, would see them draw just a fraction closer to talk. Papa mostly listened while Ann spoke. Then they both spoke animatedly after that and had one more drink. Then Papa really had to go.

A chill wind came up from the valley as they left the verandah and walked along the path towards the garden gate. The night noises were hushed. There was no moon. It might have been because Ann pressed just a centimetre closer upon him or because her night perfume touched him in the right place. It might have been because it was a risk he wanted to take, or it could have been because of any number of things. All he knew was that she was in his arms, her breasts against his chest, his hungry mouth upon hers. It was short and urgent. It was the first time at the gate, in the open, on home territory. They broke apart, breathing hard, said goodnight and hurried away.

Papa remembered the shocking silence as he walked off, not once looking back. Ann remembered the short walk back to the verandah, how cool and refreshing the air was, how calm she felt with her child asleep in bed and her husband away from home, the fourth time in three weeks.

CHAPTER 23

Whether it was contrived to make up to Mama, or whether it was a genuine invitation, no one knew. But when Papa made the announcement at lunch, he was noticeably uneasy, speaking in the manner of a man at the centre of a clever scheme to beguile an innocent.

'The Baldoos expect us at dinner on Saturday,' he said.

'The Baldoos?' Mama said, surprised.

'That is what I said, Victoria,' Papa replied.

'Well, that's nice of them.'

'Are we going too?' Yvonne glanced from one to the other.

'No, just your mother and me.'

The Baldoos were respectable people. Mr Baldoo was respectable because he was one third bald, wore glasses, had a bit of a tummy and looked important. Mrs Baldoo was very pretty, as only people of Indian extraction could be. Elegance and restrained femininity came naturally to her. Her lipstick was sparingly applied to a small, attractive mouth. And she wore linen suits and silver jewellery, not the common silver bangles worn by the coolies down the hill. There was nothing fanciful about either of them.

'It's a Humber Hawk,' Barrington said, indicating the solid two-tone car resting under the papaya tree when the Baldoos first visited.

'It's very nice of them to invite us,' Mama repeated, glancing pleasantly at the children. They returned her glance, not looking at Papa, who, observing this and knowing the reason behind it, set his knife and fork down. His hand trembled.

'When I get angry with you it's because I care,' he said, facing them. 'And when your mother and I argue it isn't because we don't love you. We argue because that is what grown-ups do.'

The children continued to look away from him, at their plates, in their laps or at the other end of the table. Coldly, Papa put aside his napkin, rose from the table and walked down the hall to the bedroom. And that night there was another harsh exchange of words, about something Mama had said at supper.

'Are the Mitchisons going to be there?' she asked.

'The Mitchisons?' Papa turned on her. 'Why should they be there?'

'I only asked,' Mama returned, wounded.

'Well, why not the Dowdings or the Pinnocks. Why the Mitchisons?'

'Harold, I just wondered.'

'But why them?'

'I don't know.'

'Liar,' Papa growled, and left the table.

Mama, stunned, saw the shock on the faces of the children and went after Papa, tears stinging her eyes. The children left the table too, chairs tumbling, Mavis suddenly next to them like a mother hen, huddling together on the sofa in the drawing room. They could not make sense of the shouting.

* * *

That Saturday afternoon, Papa sat with Mama on the front lawn in the shade of the house in jacaranda-scented air. Frosty glasses sat on a dark-green wicker table, ice slowly melting. It was the calm after the quarrel. But it was a fragile calm. A million swallows sat on the telegraph wires a hundred yards away and moving shadows were long on the ground. Poppy stayed back at a safe distance while the children watched from behind bedroom curtains. The

206

Mullard radio, in the drawing room, radiated yellow light and Pat Boone, *when the swallows come back to Capistrano*. Vincent observed the scene from a solitary place. He knew whose side he was on.

At the rear of the house, the poinsettia sun in the first act of the evening, dipped, blazing furiously, wonderfully. White birds in formation dipped too, in crimson, making for the river in one swift swoop to join their mates already strung out on the grassy banks, yellow beaks and yellow feet jousting. There were sad birds among them and Boyd heard their moaning for someone lost that very day.

The evening was tranquil, as all Saturday evenings at Appleton were. The sunset was not yet as dramatic as it would be in the second act, with golden streaks and violent pink swathes. It was not yet at that moment when the air became expectant, the sky a grand opera, when dry leaves rose without wind, suspended like the softest feathers, then falling to rest, prelude to some inspiring narrative. The swallows were waiting their moment whilst the white birds kept to the riverbank in civilised intercourse in tight little groups.

Mama's legs were crossed, her eyes looking into the distance but not seeing the deepening shadows. She was dressed in a cream suit, white wide-brimmed straw hat with a low crown and a spotted navy blue band. Earlier in the evening, Boyd had watched as she anxiously applied red-hot lipstick from the black and gold receptacle and clicked her black leather bag firmly shut with that sumptuous click that only came from women's handbags. But in the quiet of the bathroom, he thought he heard her weeping.

The swallows, as if at a signal, made their exit, leaving in two huge waves of shadow, their Kyrie rising heavenward, so remarkable that Mama and Papa hung their heads like children. And the Mitchison's Jaguar chose that very moment to glide down the road. Papa and Mama stared at the receding car and said nothing. As they looked, a

207

rousing wind, unusual at that time of the evening, drove the dead leaves along the foot of the hedge, backing them up in ominous dark mounds. Papa and Mama did not see this.

They retreated, awkwardly, to the Lloyd Loom chairs. Papa poured another drink. Mama had lemonade, giggling and holding her glass away while Papa tried to stiffen her drink with just a wee drop of rum. But they had stopped talking a little while ago. It was a forced performance, put on only for the watching children.

By the time Papa came in to announce that they were leaving for the Baldoo's, the sun had died to purple bougainvillea flashes. And there was a chill in the air.

* * *

Mrs Baldoo said that there was no doubt about it, the Balaclava Academy was the best prep school in all of St Elizabeth and Papa had done the right thing in selecting it. Then she declared that the best children, *the very best*, went there.

'Do you know,' she said, 'I don't know of any labourer's child who goes there. Not a single one. Not that they wouldn't be welcomed. Everybody deserves a chance. And Sister Margaret Mary is as kind and as honest as they come.'

'They couldn't afford it,' Mr Baldoo said gruffly.

Papa's chest had swelled till it was in danger of obscuring his face. He liked the idea that the riff-raff could be kept out, that none of *those people's* children would have the chance to contaminate his own. He wasn't against *those people's* children going to the Balaclava Academy, he just wanted them to brush up first, learn some manners, be a little less vulgar, and he wanted their parents to acquire just a few *values and principles*. It wasn't asking too much.

'The children will love it,' Mrs Baldoo said. 'The garden parties, the concerts, the outings. Sister is very strict and she has good teaching staff: Miss Robb, for instance, Miss

Casserly and Miss Skiddar. And there are several young nuns too.'

'Some of the young mothers are frightened of her, Sister Margaret Mary.' Mr Baldoo smiled. 'She takes no nonsense. A cousin of mine sends his children there. They are boarders at the convent. And they're coming along in leaps and bounds.'

'Will all the children attend?' Mrs Baldoo asked.

'Only Boyd,' Papa said. 'Barrington will go to Munro. He's almost twelve. Yvonne will start at the academy next year.'

'The younger they start, the better, I always say,' Mrs Baldoo scolded.

* * *

After a delightful evening, Mama and Papa were returning home. The Baldoos had talked about education and the importance of achieving one's ambition. These were familiar topics of discussion for them. Mama had been impressed with Mrs Baldoo. Although she was a wife and mother (her daughter, Anya, attended the University College of the West Indies at Mona), she had a full-time job as a doctor at the local clinic. She sat on several committees and had confidence and intelligence in bucketloads. It made Mama think, with renewed confidence, of her own situation. And so, on their way home, she took a deep breath and returned to the subject of her own personal development. Papa sighed bad-temperedly and gave her one of his hard looks. Here he was trying to mend bridges, had gone out of his way, in fact, by encouraging the Baldoo dinner invitation, and there was Mama, as usual, making not the slightest effort.

'I could learn typewriting and shorthand and get a job at Balaclava in a lawyer's office,' Mama pleaded. 'When the children are settled at school,' she added, trying to placate Papa.

Papa repeated that no wife of his was going out to work.

Mama then, bravely, even recklessly, suggested that if she couldn't be a secretary she could actually take up dressmaking because she had a talent for it and it was what she really wanted to do. She would only make clothes for a few special clients. And she could sharpen up her skills at an academy in Mandeville that she had heard about.

'You heard what I said,' Papa growled.

'I would work from home.'

'I've told you a million times what I think about dressmaking. But you never listen, do you?' Papa gritted his teeth. 'Just imagine Miss Hutchinson taking up dressmaking!'

'She's employed in a job she likes,' Mama said bravely.

'And you're not.'

Mama sighed and said nothing for a while. Then, giving Papa appealing little looks, and remembering Ann Mitchison's work on the estate, she said that if it wasn't possible to be a dressmaker, she could do social work with the poor people at Appleton. But only when the children were older.

'And who would pay you for that?' Papa asked.

Mama didn't answer.

Papa's response was to gun the motor and grip the steering wheel hard.

The Prefect hummed along, pistons punching away, taking them home up the dark roads. As they crossed the bridge, Papa glanced swiftly in the direction of the Mitchison's house. He remembered the impossibly charged moments not long passed, the exploding passion and Ann's pliant lips. Her searing, intoxicating image had been in his head all evening. Then he stared at Mama in exasperation. She was sniffling.

'What's the matter now? Jeezas! Here we are just talking and the next thing y'know – Gawd! Buck up, buck up, girl! Jeezas!'

Papa stopped the car. He saw Mama's frightened face as

210

he turned roughly towards her. He knew that he was overreacting but couldn't hold back. The moment dictated his response.

'Are you going to behave like a child? Victoria, answer me!'

Mama's lips trembled and she said nothing. She sensed violence she had never experienced before, never envisaged, and moved away from Papa in slow motion.

'Behave like a child and I'll treat you like one, dammit!' Papa shouted. He started the engine and the car sprang forward. Not a single word passed between them after that.

Mama sat silently, trembling. Disabling fears flooded in upon her.

CHAPTER 24

That Sunday morning, fears flooded in upon Vincent too. His secret plan made him tremble. More than once that day he sought to abandon it. But through the hole in his bedroom wall, the scene before his good eye told him that it had to be done. Not for the first time, he saw Boyd on the bed with Mavis in the afternoon heat, as the dry brown leaves rustled under the window. Mavis had her blouse open and her full titty out, nursing him like an infant, stroking his head and cheeks as he snuggled up to her, lips firmly round her taut nipple, gently sucking. Vincent took what pleasure he could from the scene, watching with his one eye, wiping it when it became too misty and returning it to the hole again and again. Then the *cauchee* sounded, shocking them all. Vincent saw Boyd pull away from Mavis and rush from the room.

Papa did not come speeding up the driveway as Boyd anticipated. The driveway stood empty and bright in the afternoon sun and the blue of the forget-me-nots blazed along the path. Racing hard up to the house, he saw a boy at the kitchen door. The first thing he noticed about the boy was that he wore no shoes. A small, black bow tie hung limply from his collar. His hair had the look that Papa described as "peppercorn", uncombed, each strand of black hair rolled up into a tight little ball. Boyd knew that sort of little boy. They could be seen in the company of *higglers* on their way to market. Sometimes the boys came to the house with the market women, trying to sell red beans. But Mavis always sent them packing.

'Gud eveling,' the boy with the peppercorn head said. He had dry lips and was standing on one leg with a black Bible in his hand.

Before Boyd could reply, a woman stepped from behind the mint bush, wearing dusty, black lace-up boots, a black dress with a frilly white collar and a black hat. Boyd remembered the woman immediately: she had visited their first house on the estate twice and was the only Bible woman that Perlita spoke to politely before slamming the door in her face, twice. She carried a black Bible, a much bigger version than the boy's, and a neat stack of papers. The sun was clean and hot and her shadow lay crumpled on the ground.

'Is your mama 'ome, little boy?'

'Who is it?' Yvonne asked, suddenly at Boyd's elbow.

'Is your mama 'ome, little girl?' the woman repeated, turning to Yvonne, who seemed to her to be more forthcoming.

Yvonne would have replied but Papa drove up very quickly. Both she and Boyd stiffened unconsciously.

'Is God in your 'earts?' the woman enquired. The boy wet his dry lips and shifted on the spot. His shadow seemed uneasy.

'What is it?' Papa came up behind the woman. 'What do you want?'

The woman turned casually. 'Are you saved, sar? 'Ave you taken Christ as your personal saviour? Are you walking the straight and the narrow? 'Ave you been dipped in the blood of the lamb? Is your place secure up yonder?'

'Am I saved?' Papa laughed, annoyed in the extreme. 'Are you saved? Are you going to get your backside off my property? Are you going to do it now?'

The woman seemed not at all surprised and replied coolly, as if accustomed to this type of bad behaviour from all the sinners she had ever tried to save. 'I bring the word of God to this 'ouse, sar. Listen and you will 'ear.' The boy coughed, his shadow furtive.

213

Papa's chest was heaving; the corrugated brows that the children knew and feared were fixed and dark. The boy drew quietly to one side. His eyes were sad. He just wanted to go home to his dinner.

'Get yourself off this property,' Papa said threateningly. He took a step towards the woman who stood her ground. 'I have a good mind to – '

Poppy chose that very moment to pop up from beneath the house, eyes crossed, teeth bared and snarling. Snarling at strangers was a peculiarity of his, developed out of a sense of having to prove his canine capabilities, about which he cared hardly at all. His intention was not malicious but the woman did not know it. She darted away, discarding her stack of papers. *Tracts*, Mavis later called them. The boy was already ahead of her and his shadow was already ahead of him. They ran down the path, Poppy close behind, growling low, surprised at the effect of his performance. Halfway down the driveway, he stopped, nonchalantly chased small grass birds into the hedgerows then bounded back.

'Well, he's not completely worthless,' Papa observed. Then he faced the children. 'The next time those Bible people come up here, slam the door in their faces. That boy should be getting an education, not wandering about the district with a Bible.' Papa glared after the fleeing figures. 'Trying to tell us how to live our lives. You think they know how to live theirs?'

They trooped inside the house, Papa straight to Mama's room. When it grew quiet, Boyd tiptoed out the back door and together he and Poppy crept beneath the thick foliage under Mama's bedroom window. The Baldoos' dinner had not brought the improvement everyone hoped for. If anything, the tension appeared to have worsened.

'Please, Harold,' Boyd heard Mama say in a low, wounded voice.

'Stop it,' Papa retorted. 'Stop it! You hear me?'

214

There was a long, worrying pause, then Boyd heard Papa's stern voice.

'Don't you understand respectability? No, you Pratts have never understood this. Get it into your head, you're not going out to work. We're not common people.'

Boyd didn't hear Mama's whimpering reply. He only heard the bedroom door slam and the sound of Papa's manly footsteps down the hall and out the kitchen door.

As the Land Rover sped away, Boyd saw Mama's face appear at her bedroom window, seeking out the vanishing vehicle. Her eyes glistened. Racing to the back of the house, Boyd saw Papa's Land Rover churning up the dust as it sped away along the valley road, through the green carpet of canes in the direction of Maggotty.

* * *

Ann arrived there first, on the green hillock under the shelter of trees overlooking the valley, the frothy white waters of Maggotty Falls in the distance. The Land Rover was parked a hundred yards away, camouflaged against the olive-green of the Lignum Vitae. She settled in the warm grass and felt fabulous and dangerous, as he would too when he arrived. And she experienced a transient sense of power which brought a smile to her lips, knowing that she was responsible for making him break every rule whenever he was with her. Doubtless, he felt the same. Waiting and wanting, she felt the warmth and the valley breeze up around her thighs. And she remembered Shropshire at the height of an English Summer: the lavender fields at Holdgate, near Much Wenlock; the snap, crackle and pop of the clean heat; the magnificent quiet. She thought, sadly, how they, the people who lived around Maggotty in their straitened little communities, never seemed to appreciate or enjoy the landscape, the magnificent greenery, the valley, the slopes, the grassy little dells and troughs. They were never there, in these little

215

hideaways, enjoying a picnic, lazing about, reading a book, painting a picture, sketching, musing or quietly writhing in perfumed expectation, as she was then. They didn't know, and did not see, the beauty of this paradise that she had found. And that was why she knew, from the first meeting there, that it was utterly safe. It was the last place the local people would have time for.

Ann removed her scarf and, glancing round, saw him arrive, dark in the sun in his sugar-scented khakis. Papa felt like a rampant estate lion, a cane-piece predator, as he mounted the hill. And long before he got to her in that temporary world that they had created for themselves, values and principles meant nothing. She had wanted first to point out the Maggotty Falls again and the rolling fields in the distance, where the sun and the clouds created shimmering waves. She had wanted to be restrained, as she had been in the Shropshire fields as a young girl, and savour the calm and the mystery before the pleasure. But the delights were immense and dramatic. She remembered the winking sun through the leaves, the sweet heat, the lime-scented aftershave and the silly distracting kling-kling birds screeching in the trees as they embraced forcefully like virgin youth.

And just as forcefully they pulled apart. A donkey and a dreadlocked labourer had entered the clearing. Seeing them in their delinquent intimacy, the labourer's eyes, coal-fire red, widened, and he froze as shocked as they were. The man's head dropped self-consciously and he eyed the ground, urging the donkey before him deeper into the bush, his machete held low at his side.

'Christ!' Papa said, more from relief than shock.

'What?' Ann seemed fascinated by the dreadlocks, not having seen hair like that before and imagined that she had seen a human Hydra. The man's hair was matted but styled like coils of rope and rolled up tobacco about his head and shoulders. She gazed after the vanishing figure as if she wanted to detain him.

'Ganja,' Papa said. 'Didn't you smell it? That's what they smoke, these Rastafarians. We'd better get out of here.' And Papa led Ann quickly away, looking over his shoulder, thinking only of the honed machete held so casually in the man's unpredicatable hand.

CHAPTER 25

Back at the pink house, Boyd stroked Poppy and looked down towards the river while the kling-kling birds screeched eerily in the trees. He was more anxious than ever. The fear of Papa's violence had reigned in his scheme on Susan and made even standing by the periwinkle fence a risky undertaking. He imagined that Papa could detect even his private thoughts without looking into his eyes. That was the most frightening thing of all. For several days, he'd been keeping away from the fence and giving not the slightest impression that his every thought featured Susan. Even though Papa was not at the house, Boyd felt as if he was always present and could tap him on the shoulder at any moment.

As he and Poppy looked down into the valley, they saw dust rising from the road, a single cloud of white. It came from the black dot of a figure on a bicycle, bent double, hands braced on the handlebars. It pedalled furiously, outrunning the dust and everything that might overtake – incidents, happenings, the things that men do, fate even.

The flash and wink of light on metal – a machete honed to razor sharpness strapped to the saddle – distinguished the rider, named him. It was Mr Ten–To–Six on his way home early from the factory. Poppy barked. This was unheard of, Mr Ten-To-Six going home at three o'clock. Never had he appeared before his time.

The shocking news reached them when Papa came home. The Bible woman he'd chased off the property had been savagely murdered by her common-law husband, the father of ten children, the man who kept himself to himself, the dark and mysterious Mr Ten-To-Six. Everyone faced Papa, horrified. Mama could not be consoled.

'Her Bible couldn't save her,' Papa told them, remembering his encounter with Mrs Ten-To-Six. 'Now we know she wasn't *walking the straight and the narrow*. Yet there she was trying to tell us how to live our lives. Christ! What is the matter with these people?'

Mr Ten-To-Six had cycled home, bent double, to murder his wife in the heat of the afternoon, in violent ecstasy. Boyd imagined the butcher's blood staining the floor in Mrs Ten-To-Six's home and heard the bloodcurdling squeal of pigs. No one would set time by Mr Ten-To-Six any more. He was no longer wonderfully mysterious, just a vicious killer.

The men at the factory had murmured that Mrs Ten-To-Six had been washing, ironing and cooking for the new man in the district, the mechanic, Carlton Smith. It was all Mr Ten-To-Six needed to hear. Now Mrs Ten-To-Six lay dead, along with her two children, Carlton Smith too, their heads severed at the neck.

'Those eight children, without a mother,' Mama lamented.

'Oh, they have their own mother, ma'am,' Mavis explained. 'Mr Ten-To-Six is their father. He had four other women he used to live with, ma'am. The dead Mrs Ten-To-Six wasn't the first, no ma'am. He killed the two children he had with her.'

Papa raised his eyebrows at this. 'You know what I've always said about *those people*,' he said scornfully. 'And that is exactly what I mean. They have children they can't look after and create problems they can't solve. Killing his own children!'

'He chopped off their heads, Mr Brookes,' Mavis added.

'Severed at the neck.' Mama shook her head, hands outstretched, eyes unbelieving. The news of the violent murder relieved her, temporarily, of the unrestrained thoughts that Papa's behaviour engendered. And she repeated the words like a mantra. 'Severed at the neck! At the neck!'

Severed at the neck was a very bad thing. It was so bad that it was reported in *The Daily Gleaner* and in the evening paper, *The Star*, with neighbours of Mr and Mrs Ten-To-Six providing graphic details of the tragedy. Corporal Duncan rode up on Cyrus to give reassurance that there were no other labourers on the rampage, that this was a one-off. Even though Mr Ten-To-Six had escaped to the impenetrable hill country beyond Accompong, where the Maroons lived, a people accustomed to hiding and fighting and surviving since the days of slavery; Corporal Duncan felt certain that he would be hunted down and brought to justice. But it was out of his hands. The police high command of the parish had taken charge and brought in some tough detectives from Kingston who had a propensity for shooting first and talking later. Mr Ten-To-Six was as good as dead.

'Is bad omen, ma'am,' Mavis told Mama.

'What do you mean?'

Mavis seemed surprised. 'Bad omen, Miss Victoria, ma'am,' she said. 'Bad omen.' It was what she knew and couldn't understand anyone not knowing.

As the children clustered round, Mama saw her own life wrapped up, somehow, in the tragedy, and could already see and feel the gathering tribulations.

Mavis had shocking news of her own from people who knew people at Taunton. Mrs Ten-To-Six, a Jehovah's Witness, had been reading her Bible when Mr Ten-To-Six chopped off her head. The head jumped across the floor, rolled down the steps and lay in the yard, eyes wide open and looking up to heaven. But other people said that Mr Ten-To-Six had caught Mrs Ten-To-Six with Carlton Smith. They had been *fornicating*, Mavis declared, savouring the drama. She said *fornicating* twice with much emphasis, obviously a word she had just discovered, not knowing its exact meaning but knowing that it contained wickedness.

Everybody in the district knew Mrs Ten-To-Six. She was an upright woman. Her little boy, Leroy, still wearing his black bow tie, lay next to his mother and his little sister, Pansey. Mama and the children listened to the animated Mavis with increasing dread.

On the verandah, Papa and Corporal Duncan deplored, in strong language, the frailty of *some* members of the human race. And Papa was heard to say, 'Y'know, I always knew there was something funny about that man, Ten-To-Six. Any man who keeps himself to himself like that is up to no good. Weak and wicked. Pshaw!'

Out in the yard, the children admired Cyrus, tethered near to the silver water tank. They were so taken with him that they missed the stealthy arrival of the bicycle rider and only heard when Mama cried out. It was a cry so chilling coming in the aftermath of the vicious murder that, galvanised with fright and imagining all manner of calamity, they turned and dashed, Poppy one frantic gallop ahead of them, through the house and to the verandah. There they found Mama in hysterics, Corporal Duncan assisting her to a chair, while Papa held a salmon-coloured envelope up to the light. It was a telegram.

'Is bad omen,' Mavis breathed, observing the agitated Mama sipping from a glass of water, remembering her own words earlier. 'Bad news always come in threes, ma'am.' She and Mama exchanged wild looks.

'Well,' Papa said to Mama, 'it's for you.'

Mama lived in fear of telegrams. Only news of death came in them. The last time she'd received a telegram was at Worthy Park Estate, in the days when Papa was obliging and generous. Her father, John Pratt, had died. After reading in the newspaper about the shooting of Mr Lee of Water Lane, Kingston, she had recurring nightmares about her mother lying dead in a pool of her own blood from a robber's bullet. She'd begged Papa to take her and the children to see Grandma Rosetta but he hadn't seemed interested. Now the murder of Mrs Ten-To-Six only heightened her fears.

Papa opened the envelope and read silently, every single eye on him, including Poppy's, whose presence on the verandah in the midst of the excitement had gone unnoticed by Papa. A knowing smile came over Papa's face and he handed the telegram to Mama. It was from Aunt Amanda, Mama's older sister. Her daughter, Polly, had won a scholarship to a prestigious state school. Mama cried out with sheer relief. She forgot all her worries and talked excitedly about the news from her sister all evening.

'Polly's going to be an important person. I see her at the United Nations.'

'Why is she going there, Mama?' Yvonne asked, dumbfounded.

As Mama tried to explain, Boyd remembered their cousin, Polly. On the great occasion when they last visited Grandma Rosetta, Polly had brought a note with unsettling news. It was during the fascinating weeks before they departed Worthy Park for Appleton. He remembered the rambling gingerbread house and Grandma Rosetta lying in the gloom of a great four-poster bed, a furled mosquito net suspended in a huge knot above her head. He remembered her dark, heavy body in the bed, her old smell, old breath, and felt a terrible sadness. He had wanted to tell her to place the brown bakelite Bush radio on the table by the bed so that when she was alone she could hear the music and be young again. He wanted to say that it didn't matter being alone when you had the radio.

'Where are you going, Boyd?' Grandma Rosetta had said, wagging her finger at him. 'Come and sit next to me.'

He had wanted to tell her that in the dark country night, when there was nothing to look forward to, the radio could become her morning, her afternoon, her pleasant evening, lovely thoughts and dreams. But he had said nothing.

He and Yvonne had been sent to the *barbecue*, the terrace at the side of the house while Mama and her brothers discussed family business. The *barbecue* held thousands of coffee berries drying in the sun. The freshest berries were blood-red but the ones that had been there the longest were black, wrinkled and distressed, just like Grandma Rosetta. They sniffed the coffee berries and watched as the country buses with names like The Morning Star, The Mayflower and The Magnet rattled by at the bottom of the hill. All the buses seemed to be going to, or coming from, a place called Kellits.

On that day, cousin Polly arrived in one of the colourful buses, looking very coy, with a small brown cardboard suitcase. She also brought a special book that she held against her chest called *The Student's Companion*. From its pages she had memorised the capital cities of the world, the highest mountain peaks, the active volcanoes and all the major deserts. She put the book aside on the bed while respectfully and dutifully handing Mama the important-looking envelope. Mama had secreted it away in the large pocket of her cotton skirt and behaved as if nothing had happened.

But later, standing just outside the door, Boyd heard Grandma Rosetta say, 'It's that woman from Lluidas Vale. It's a disgrace. He has no right, no right.' And Boyd knew that Papa was implicated.

'We don't know,' Mama had said. 'It's only talk.'

'Amanda knows more than what's in that note,' Grandma Rosetta said. 'Get him to take you up to Amanda so you can find out. Talk to Enid. She knows what's what.'

'No,' Mama replied indignantly. 'No.'

In the end, when Papa arrived after work, when it was time to go in the inky-black country night, they had all gathered at Grandma Rosetta's bed, kissing, hands caressing, not letting go, saying goodbye again and again at the door. Mama had hung back, hugging her mother and behaving like a girl. And when she came out of the room, they could see she'd been crying. They squeezed by Uncle Albert, who pinched their cheeks and said 'Cluck, Cluck,' in their ears while a fondly smiling Uncle Haughton ushered them out. They stroked Christmas, his dog, who had crept out from under the house to stand next to Polly on the verandah. There was a slight delay as Papa tried, fussing good-naturedly, to get Mama's small flowerpots containing assorted plants and numerous cuttings from Grandma Rosetta's garden into the boot of the car. Polly, silhouetted against the lamplight, waved from the verandah, telling them not to forget to write. But when they got to Appleton, with its glorious sugar smell, its *shhing* steam, its dunder, its *cauchee* and its fantasy, they did forget. But Boyd never forgot Polly's note and Grandma Rosetta's comments about the woman from Lluidas Vale who made Mama cry.

Mama wasn't crying now. She couldn't stop kissing and cuddling the children and looking dreamily into the distance. 'Bad omen, is it, Mavis?' she said, smiling.

Mavis smiled too, because it was right to do so. But her instinct, experience and culture told her that bad news was bad news and came in threes, and that poor Mrs Brookes, or the entire Brookes family, or perhaps even she herself, would receive more bad news. It could come tomorrow, or the day after, or next month. As God was her judge, two more pieces of bad news awaited them. Mrs Ten-To-Six was the first.

That night, Mama again begged Papa to take her and the children to visit her mother.

'It's only in Kingston that they rob and kill people,' Papa told her gruffly. 'People don't rob private houses in St Catherine. When was the last time you heard of any crime where your mother lives?'

Nevertheless, Papa felt that it was time he visited Mama's family, time they knew he was a star at Appleton Estate with a house like the manager's and a future to die for. But he wanted to wait until the waters ran smoothly. So all he said to Mama was that when she had the baby, and there wasn't long to wait, he would take her to see her mother, and wouldn't it be a great occasion then?

Mama stopped mentioning Grandma Rosetta, feeling guilty to be such a burden. Mavis's news the following afternoon that Mr Ten-To-Six was still at large and had been sighted near Maggotty Falls did nothing to change her view that she was being a bit of a nuisance. Even when Grandma Rosetta wrote a three-page letter saying she'd not been well of late and that it would be nice to see the children, she said nothing more to Papa.

CHAPTER 26

When the stranger came riding up the driveway, Poppy went to meet him. It had rained heavily during the night and the sound of wet was everywhere. The children, sitting on the verandah, saw Poppy stand back to let the rider pass and were astonished at this peculiar behaviour. Barrington put his *Superman* comic down, Boyd turned his gaze away from the Mitchison's house, shelved his passionate exploits with Susan and watched in silence as the rider approached, splashing through puddles, small birds flitting out of his way.

The cyclist handed Yvonne a salmon-coloured envelope with black writing on it. Then he bowed guiltily and rode off. Poppy did not chase after him but went quietly under the house, head down, eyes to the ground.

'What is it?' Mama asked tentatively from the depths of the bedroom.

Yvonne, anticipating much woe, held out the salmon-coloured envelope. Mama's hand shot to her throat. Fingers trembling, she read the pink letter. Then she uttered a mournful cry that carried throughout the house. Barrington rushed to her immediately, followed by Mavis, arms covered in flour up to her elbows.

'Is everything all right, ma'am?' It seemed as if Mavis could fix anything in that instant, send back the man on the bicycle and above all, drive away the awful sound that Mama had made. It was in their hearts and it represented the dread that was now everywhere and could not be escaped from. Mavis took charge in quicksilver fashion, flour-covered hands flashing, accomplishing multiple actions all at once. She said nothing about the bad omens but she kept count.

Boyd backed away down the verandah steps and into the garden to stand in crystal-clear puddles and count small birds hopping about. The smell was of raw, wet earth, the air pure and cool. But he felt hot and feverish. Mama would never see her mother alive again. Grandma Rosetta was dead.

Mama had begged and begged Papa to take her for a visit. And now it was too late. In the great four-poster bed in that dark room, Grandma Rosetta lay, rotting, like Grandpa Pratt. Her flesh would run purple like the dye from the logwood tree, and it would run into the coffee beans drying on the terrace of the gingerbread house.

He remembered when Grandpa John Pratt had died: the women's perspiration, their sobbing, the men's liquor-breath and moth-balled, chalk-stripe suits and white shirts with sweaty collars. There was a moment when he stood riveted, watching the made-up body of Grandpa Pratt. It was the dead flesh, covered in potions to hide the unforgiving, that had mattered so much. And the smell that he knew was there, of rotting flesh, like the dead frog that he'd found in the garden when he was only three. The body of Mama's father hadn't moved. A fragrant Aunt Enid had dragged him away as if he'd witnessed the forbidden. So he knew from then that death was ugly and old.

He knew that when Papa came home, it would be the same as it had been at Worthy Park. Papa would walk briskly up and down on the wooden floors while Mama wept silently in her room, beyond comfort. And they would make preparations to go to St Catherine, to the gingerbread house among the fruit trees and flowers, where the rest of the family would be gathered. Polly, the scholarship girl, would be there too, polite and observant. Her parents would be there, Uncle George with his philosophic smile, Aunt Amanda, calm and composed, and her many square-jawed brothers and pretty sisters, respectful and studious. But he did not want to go to St Catherine. He did not want to see Grandma Rosetta dead in the front room, powdered and dressed, her old flesh like tree bark. He wandered to the back garden and stared at Vincent, who was picking ripe tomatoes. Vincent, sensing something amiss, took him to the kitchen and handed him over to Mavis.

'What is it, petal?' Mavis put her arms round him.

He snuggled up tight against her, inhaling thyme and scallion, the pure scent of the living. Mavis took him straight to his bed. Mama came in to lay the back of her hand on his forehead. She smelled of camphor from the balls in her chest of drawers because she'd started to assemble funeral clothes.

'You've got a raging fever,' she said.

Yvonne sat on the bed, sucking her thumb and dangling her feet until she heard the splashing of the Land Rover coming up the driveway. Then she dashed away to be the first to tell Papa the news.

Papa stopped at the door and fixed Boyd with a suspicious stare. 'You can't stay here like that,' he said, seeing deep into Boyd's heart.

Boyd trembled when he heard the words and felt the pain thumping in his head. He couldn't face Papa. Papa would see the truth in his eyes. They could not make him go. In his heart he felt a tender union with the Grandma Rosetta he knew, the one with the funny wagging finger, the one who said *Where are you going, Boyd?* only because she wanted him to come to her. He felt guilty because he didn't want his Grandma Rosetta; he did not want death and sorrow and weeping; he did not want duty and responsibility. All he wanted was the sun and Susan, who was warm and fragrant and alive and dying for him. Now that Mama and Papa, Barrington and Yvonne would be away in St Catherine, it was his best chance yet to carry out the act. He knew that his impatience for Papa and Mama to drive off to St Catherine was indecent but could only accept it as a matter of fact. Susan would come magically through the fence in the warm sun the moment they left.

'Mama's not packing Boyd's clothes,' Yvonne told Mavis. 'He's poorly.'

Boyd could feel Yvonne close by the bed, smell her wax crayon scent. He pretended to be sleeping and groaned weakly as if from a bad dream.

'Mama washed him down with Bay Rum,' Yvonne said.

'It will drive out the fever,' Mavis told her.

In the end, Boyd, head deep in fluffy pillows, waved goodbye with a limp hand. By now, his self-induced fever had become real. Mama kissed him with red lipsticked lips and felt the heat at his temples. Her eyes were weary, and when she looked at him, it was so long and so deep that he thought she too could see into him. Papa, still suspicious, warned him not to get up to any hanky-panky, sick or not. Barrington gave him a funny look, as if to say, *How do you get away with it?*

'Ah take good care of him,' Mavis assured everyone as they left the room.

From the window, Boyd peered at the burnished little Prefect speeding away, Yvonne's face gazing out the rear window directly at him. The feeling of guilt and remorse was short-lived. The house was quiet, the radio his alone, the garden empty and waiting in the radiant sunlight. But his joints and head ached tremendously and the heat radiating from him felt like an open fire. Boyd knew he was being punished for the lies and the pretence. He really wanted to do it in Technicolor while everyone was away.

He met her in the sunlight away from the dead, in fragrant heat, in the perfumed brightness of buttercups and orange blossoms, free from the clutching guilt. Their hearts were free and light, like butterfly wings in warm air, and they went behind the pink house on the crest of the hill like figures in a book. She sat upright in the grass, her scent like cinnamon, drawing him in,

229

her skin radiating heat that wafted about him, her fine brown hair touched with light gold, her lips like strawberry jam, tasty and sweet. Their hearts beat like the wings of big bats, limbs weakened by extravagant expectation, tortured by the feverish waiting, sick with the absence of touch. They would end the sickness and the torture that very day. He entered the cinnamon heat, hidden away from the pink house, using his wet tongue upon the dripping jam, licking, sucking, unable to stop. And music gave them wings, sealed their first touch, marked the spot with memory.

When Mavis looked in on the patient, she saw that he was deep into the pillows with eyes closed, brows terribly wrinkled, body curled up tight.

'Ooh, petal,' she said and clasped him to her. 'Ah get some more Bay Rum.'

Boyd opened his eyes. 'Are you going away?' He felt the closeness of Mavis, heard the rustle of her dress. They were alone in the house. He wanted to surrender to her.

'Going away?' Mavis feigned shock. 'And leave you here on your own? Ah never hear such a thing. Ah looking after you, making sure you are good and well when your Mama get back. In the evening, after me shower, ah coming to keep you company. Not letting you out of me sight. No sir.'

Mavis undressed him. 'Lawd, have mercy. You so hot.'

'And wear lipstick like you're going out?'

'Wear lipstick like ah going out.' Mavis laughed and gave him a look. 'You just get into bed, you hear me. Ah want you better.'

'And *Essen* too.'

'*Essen*? What about *Essen*?'

'Wear *Essen* and lipstick like you're going out,' he told her.

Mavis laughed again. 'You are a funny lickle boy, y'know. A funny lickle boy. You going to buy me lipstick and *Essen*?'

'I have money in my purse,' he said, pointing to the chest of drawers.

Mavis propped two large pillows against the mahogany

bedhead. 'You keep your pocket money,' she said, contemplating the little face looking up at her. And she touched the tip of his nose playfully after applying the Bay Rum. 'Now you stay right here and read your book. If you want anything, just ring the bell.' She pointed to the little silver bell with the black handle standing on the bedside table and left the room. And Boyd, wanting so desperately the pleasure of the garden and Susan, found that he could not leave his bed, dragged down as he was with a fever, pain and delirium.

And that afternoon, for the very first time, Susan rode up the driveway of the pink house, perspiring lightly in the heat, a zephyr fanning playfully at her hair. Both her parents were away at Monymusk, only Evadne and Adolphus were at home. She was dying for Boyd to appear at the window, on the verandah, by the side of the house or at the periwinkle fence. But only Poppy appeared. He came to her quietly, head down, running low on the ground, tail in a spin. And she stroked him and patted him and watched as he rolled over on his back and gave her his belly to tickle. But she wanted Boyd.

She wanted him to come out to play. She wanted him to chase her into the trees, chase her into the forest, the Forest of Arden. She wanted him to come to her like Orlando, ride her bicycle and read her books too. He could come over to her house. She knew he wanted to. She would wait just a little bit longer. Maybe he would appear at any moment.

Susan saw Vincent emerge from behind the house and walk down the path to the driveway. She turned her bicycle round and Poppy followed her back to the gate.

As Susan rode away, Mavis stood in the doorway watching Boyd sleep, the silence in the room and her own questioning stillness intensifying the feeling of unspoken yearning. She returned to him later that evening when the swallows were strung out on the telegraph wires and the scent of ginger lilies filled the room. Her lips were red and moist. She wore *Essen*. He giggled when she sat down on the bed. She giggled too.

'Ah keeping you company until eight o'clock. After that, ah putting you straight to bed. You feeling better?'

'My head still hurts,' he said, touching his forehead.

'Oh, petal,' she said, placing warm fingers across his forehead. 'Let me get you some more Bay Rum. Ah want you better by the time your Mama and Papa come back.'

Boyd clasped and stroked Mavis's arms. He was warm in the bed. She was warm next to him and she wasn't going away. Her Bay Rum-covered hands caressed his neck, chest, cheeks, forehead and arms, and the deep, pink part of him that no one could see.

'Shh,' she kept saying every time he opened his mouth to speak. The Bay Rum, *Essen*, lipstick and the late evening smells from the garden sent encouraging signals. Mavis was wearing a creamy cotton blouse buttoned down the front that Mama had given her. His hands undid the buttons unhurriedly as if it had been agreed in advance.

'You bad lickle boy,' Mavis breathed repeatedly, pinching and caressing his cheek. She knew what he wanted, but first she would see to it that the front and back doors of the house were closed. She didn't want Vincent to suddenly appear, not that he ever entered the house, but there was always a first time. She put the lights on in the living room and the verandah and returned to him, breasts taut. Outside, the sky was fuchsia-pink. She drew the curtains, subduing the crickets, took off her shoes and drew up close to him on the bed. His hands reached out as if to take something that his mouth watered for. She slapped him playfully but deliberately, taken aback by the ferocity of his hands. He pouted.

'Behave yourself,' she said, placing a finger on his lips. 'Behave.'

'I want to,' he said, pulling at her arms, trying to get at her blouse.

'Ah know you want to, but not so rough. You are bad, very bad.'

But she relented and drew even closer to him. She helped him with the blouse. The last of the buttons was undone. His seeking hand stole under her dress up to her thighs. And the cool evening air slipped in behind the drawn curtains as she eased one firm, warm breast out and guided it to his waiting mouth.

It was well past eight o'clock when she left the bed. Boyd was asleep, breathing softly, knees up. She pulled down her dress which he'd lifted above her hips, slipped her brassiere back on, squeezing in her burning breasts, buttoned up her blouse and studied her face in the round bevelled mirror of the bureau. She saw the face of a young woman, well developed for her age, with eyes that were not regretful, not furtive, not suspect, but tranquil, responsible, dutiful. She returned to the bed and lay awake for a long time, breathing the scent of wilted roses.

CHAPTER 27

When Mama and Papa returned from St Catherine, they were full of the smell of death.

'Did Boyd behave himself?' was the first question Papa asked Mavis.

'Oh, yes, Mr Brookes,' Mavis replied sweetly. 'He behave himself very well. He was a good boy, Mr Brookes, a good boy.'

'I'm glad to hear it,' Papa said, giving Boyd, who stood meekly nearby, a hard look.

Mama was weepy all through the next day and kept to her room, Yvonne her only companion. Barrington went off on his bicycle and, brazenly, stayed out late. Papa was more impatient than ever, betraying a restlessness that couldn't be contained. He left the house early, missed lunch and dinner and returned in the wee hours, like a man hunted, stumbling into bed exhausted. The following day was the same, except that during the magical part of the morning, during the *Housewives' Choice* hour, Yvonne ran up to Boyd.

'Susan's at the gate on her bicycle,' she said. 'And Poppy's with her.'

Boyd, his senses reeling, was filled with a sudden boldness but pretended that the news meant nothing. Then, as Yvonne left, he looked round to see that no one was about and ran to his bedroom window. He was too late, getting there just in time to see Susan riding away and Poppy looking about mystified. Elated in the extreme, Boyd knew that he would have to go to her that night and do what he had to do.

In bed that evening, Susan put away her *Lambs' Tales from Shakespeare*, opened at a certain page. She thought of the picture of the Forest of Arden, where Orlando lived, of the moment at the pink house with Boyd's little spotted dog, of the feelings that defied explanation. She saw the pretty blackness outside the opened window and breathed the scented night air. The small hand of her bedside clock pointed to eight.

It was so nice to wake up every morning and feel the crimson feelings. Tomorrow she would ride her bicycle yet again up the driveway of his house and hope to catch a glimpse of him, forever hiding in the shadows, watching her. She could always tell if he was hiding in the bushes because his little dog made yapping noises. He was bound to come out this time. She'd never had a playmate in her life, not in England, not in Barbados and not at Monymusk. The other children had been so silly, like everybody, not magical like Boyd. She knew he wanted to play. She was desperate to play too.

At eight o'clock, Boyd got out of bed in his day clothes and clambered out the window to join Poppy. Together they crossed the periwinkle fence in the moonlight and, frightened but exhilarated, continued up the road in the dark. Poppy led the way. Susan's scent was strong and Boyd started to run, blind to every obstacle. They crept through the Mitchison's fence and got to Susan's window, where the curtains quietly danced. Boyd was about to stand on a low ledge to get up to the window when shadows appeared. Rigid in the dark, they saw Papa and Mrs Mitchison come down the path to the gate. For the first time, Boyd recognised Papa's Land Rover, parked under the trees. He squatted low down, his heart in his mouth. Then, fright giving him wings, he hurt himself dashing back to the house and through his bedroom window before the headlights of the Land Rover lit up the driveway.

That night, Papa stayed up late on the verandah smoking fiercely, flinging the cigarette butts into the darkness, ill at ease. Boyd heard him when he finally went to bed, slamming the French windows. And Boyd heard him when he locked the bedroom door. But the locked door could not keep out the tumult that night.

The children woke up thinking the worst. There were dreadful noises coming from Mama's bedroom. They heard Mama say, 'Stop it!' Frightened, they stumbled out into the hall, Yvonne in crumpled crushed cotton Peter Rabbit pyjamas. Barrington stood by the door to his room, glaring at Papa.

'Get back to your beds!' Papa bellowed, and they scattered like rabbits.

The following day, there was much activity. Nurse Lindo, State Registered, was sent for. She arrived in her little pastel cream and green Morris Oxford, bought in England where she'd studied. Nurse Lindo was like polished ebony. Her perfect skin, pink tongue and white teeth set against the white of her dress and shoes made the children think of Sunlight soap and Colgate Palmolive toothpaste. Displaying professional calm, she spoke to Papa, who listened earnestly with his hands behind his back. After she'd gone, Papa called Mavis to him.

'Get Mrs Brookes' bag,' he told her.

Mavis had no time to apply *Cutex* and *Essen* or put on her new shoes to look presentable, but was bundled into the Prefect with Mama. And Papa drove away without a word. The children were left on the verandah, biting their fingernails, Vincent looking on from the front lawn, his sharpened machete in his quivering hand.

* * *

It seemed that Mama had been away for a whole year when Papa packed them into the Prefect and drove along the winding roads to the Maggotty Nursing Home run by Nurse Lindo, SRN.

As he entered the nursing home, Boyd looked across the street and saw a modern house with a double garage at the end of a wide driveway. His eyes travelled along the radiant bougainvillea and past the garage doors to the front door, where a small girl in white shorts emerged into the sunlight. Following behind her was another figure in powder-yellow shorts. Boyd blinked, certain that this was no other than Susan. But the girls were Ann-Marie and Dawn, two pretty Chinese girls who attended the Balaclava Academy. Their father, Mr Michael Chin, drove up in a red and cream Studbaker Champion, brand new from America. The girls got in and the car drove off. Papa and Mr Chin exchanged purposeful waves.

Nurse Lindo gushed with charm and efficiency as she welcomed them into her house of women and babies. She wore brilliant-white, crepe-soled shoes and spoke in a low, firm voice. She led them down a corridor, the *swish, swish, swish* of her white nylon dress and stockings the only sound. The children could see that Papa was nervous because he kept his hands behind his back and sweated.

The white door at the end of the hall opened and Nurse Lindo stepped back, beaming. Papa entered, a plastic smile upon his face. He was very awkward, tripping over a rug by the bed. Mama smiled and started to cry, glad to see them 'Come in, come in.'

Boyd stood back, wanting everyone else to go first. He felt tearful, especially when Mama said, 'Boyd, here, come here,' pointing to a spot near her.

When Nurse Lindo opened the door, the smell of floor polish gave way to baby smells – Johnson's Baby Oil, Johnson's Baby Powder, freshly laundered baby nappies. Yvonne had exuded those same smells not long ago, but now she just smelled of crayon. Mama's room was large and airy. A big sash window brought the sparkling sunlight in and showed a small pink baby in her arms, fast asleep, its dark curly hair slicked back, eyes funny like baby puppy eyes.

'It's a girl,' Mama said.

They stood looking at the baby for a long time, barely

breathing, not knowing what to say. Yvonne eventually reached out to touch the tiny figure, glancing at Papa as if she expected him to stop her and giggled when he didn't. She touched the little bundle twice, each time reluctant to take her hand away.

'She's the new baby now,' Nurse Lindo said, massaging Yvonne's arm fondly as she left the room.

'I was never a baby,' Yvonne retorted, pulling away, lip trembling.

The daffodil-yellow sun came through the window and crept up to the baby, who shifted in Mama's arms and yawned, lips seeming to form into a silent operatic note, one arm reaching into the air, tiny fingers groping. Boyd reached out and touched the baby then. It was pink and soft and fragile with wrinkles around its neck, like the baby mice he once found in a drawer in the storeroom. He touched its little fingers while Barrington stayed back like Papa.

'Go sit on the verandah and behave yourselves,' Papa told them. 'You can play with the baby later.'

They kissed Mama, stroked her arms and looked at her as a long-lost friend returned with impossible gifts. She smelled of bed-things and baby, an achingly beautiful scent. She radiated intrinsic goodness. And they knew why Papa had been so affected. They hoped desperately that he and Mama would be friends again.

* * *

When they arrived back at the pink house, they saw a pretty woman in a yellow polka-dotted dress on the verandah, sipping lemonade. Mavis was in animated conversation with her. Mama burst into tears again for it was Aunt Enid. Mama was crying so much she couldn't get out of the car and Mavis rushed out to attend to the baby, cooing and aahing and crying too. Papa stood to one side awkwardly. The children couldn't wait to get to Aunt Enid and galloped into the house. Boyd hugged Aunt Enid and caressed her silky, ample woman's arms. Aunt Enid kissed him on the lips, nose and forehead and hugged him close, her eyes closed.

'Hello, my little darling,' she squealed.

Boyd wept.

Then the two sisters were together in a tender embrace. Papa, trying for something appropriate to say, muttered obliquely to the children, 'They're like twins, y'know.'

The tiny baby lying on the bed in Mama's room, watched over by Mavis, opened her eyes and started to splutter. Aunt Enid rushed to the bedroom, closely followed by Mama and the children. Papa brought up the rear in slow motion. Aunt Enid took the baby in her arms and rocked it gently back and forth, humming. The baby, arms and legs bicycling, eyes wide open, gurgled and kept on gurgling.

'We'll call you Babs,' Aunt Enid said as the baby clapped its little hands. Who could refuse an aunt like Aunt Enid, standing in the centre of the room in summer yellow, holding a baby so clean, so pure, so new, everyone looking, waiting, expecting.

Papa and the children were banished from the room while Aunt Enid and Mama chatted. Papa took refuge on the verandah with a glass of rum and ginger and a packet of Royal Blend, but not before he motioned Vincent over.

'Give the Prefect a good polish,' he said. 'And use that new wax. I want to see my face in the paintwork.'

'Ah always use the new wax, sar,' Vincent replied quickly.

'Well, use more of it,' Papa told him impatiently. When Vincent hesitated, intending to offer his congratulations on the birth of the infant Brookes, trying to find the right words to do so, Papa's reaction was a gruff 'Well, get on with it, man!'

After Vincent sloped off, feeling terribly slighted, Papa sipped his rum, spewed cigarette smoke and surveyed the gardens. The significant events developing so rapidly could sink a less able man. It was a dangerous position to be in but one he accepted as an indisputable challenge. Thoughts of Mama and the baby, such a wonderful little thing, his own flesh and blood, the fruit of his loins, were partly crowded out by white-hot images of Ann Mitchison. *He wanted her at that very moment.* And he felt ashamed. She assailed his veritable maleness. Her image was in Appleton heat, impossible to deny. He was the wet sugar in the centrifugal drums at the factory, falling and spinning and sucked dry into the honeycomb walls. The process was dangerous if not managed. He would let events dictate and act decisively and manfully at the appropriate moment. There was no question that his father would have opposed his shoddy behaviour, in no uncertain terms, even though he was a philanderer himself. Papa would oppose it too if it were another man. But it was a unique test, and only he knew how it mattered, what it really meant. The situation was fully under control. His chemistry saw to that. He poured another rum and ginger, measuring the rum carefully. The Dowdings were visiting for a celebratory drink and he wanted to be on tip-top form. He expected Ann Mitchison to visit too.

Aunt Enid's gentleman friend, Theolonious Washington, an American, was driving down from the Melrose Hotel in Mandeville to take her back to Waterloo Avenue, Kingston that evening. He had delivered Aunt Enid to the pink house ('In a fishtail American car,' Mavis gushed) while the children were at Maggotty. When Mr Washington arrived in the afternoon, he cut quite a figure in a milk-chocolate-coloured suit, cream and brown shoes and a wide tie with pictures of horses on it. He said very little for an American. Aunt Enid did all the talking and, over drinks on the verandah, described Mr Washington – Theo – as a realtor who lived on Sugar Hill, a rich district in Harlem, New York. He had taken Aunt Enid to concerts at the Apollo Theater and to the Newport Jazz Festival, where they had heard Ella Fitzgerald sing. He knew about Richard Wright, who wrote the bestselling novel *Native Son* and had attended the Josephine Baker celebrations at the Golden Gate Ballroom on Lenox Avenue. He knew, or was acquainted with, Eartha Kitt and Harry Belafonte (Everyone drew breath at this).

'We are nothing in America,' Aunt Enid suddenly said, after shocking everyone with the impossible news that they actually knew people who sang on the radio – *the radio*. 'Over there we're worse than the coolies.'

Everyone gasped at this because they knew about coolies, *dark people*, whose blue cooking smoke rose lazily into the sky every day – coolies like Mr Ramsook, with their dirt and awful butchered pig smell.

'If you only knew the things I've gone through.' Aunt Enid shook her head slowly, a bitter smile turning into a look of outrage. 'Me! Enid Pratt! Treated like dirt, treated worse than *dark people*.'

'Drink your drink,' Papa said in an attempt to console her.

Aunt Enid sipped her drink contemplatively. Her lips were pursed. 'I couldn't go to the Cotton Club,' she said, shaking her head, 'just because I'm black.'

'But you're not black,' Papa said sympathetically. 'You're coloured.'

'Coloured? Don't be a fool, Harold. I'm a black person. I'm *coloured* black, as you are. You see, you don't understand, like those who describe blacks as *people of colour*, forgetting that white people are coloured too.'

'You're nice and brown,' Papa told her cheerfully, not understanding.

Aunt Enid sighed, regarded Papa pitifully and shook her head. She was overcome with something they could not understand: foreign experience. She told them that the Cotton Club in Harlem, New York, was a famous club run by white people where all the great black American entertainers performed, including Duke Ellington and Ella

Fitzgerald. Theo couldn't take her there because black people weren't allowed in the club as patrons. White people didn't allow black people in hotels, theatres, restaurants, schools, universities or in residential areas. And the law permitted it.

'To think that I,' she poked her breast, 'was treated as inferior, as a second class person, without any respect.'

'Barred from the universities?' Papa felt sure this was impossible.

'They wouldn't let that black girl, Autherine Lucy, enter the University of Alabama,' Aunt Enid raged. 'Her case was in the news. There are hundreds of thousands of black students who are turned away each year from universities only because they are black. It's such a way of life that black students don't even bother to apply to universities. And the police arrested that dressmaker, Mrs Parks, because she wouldn't give up her seat in the bus to a white man. Can you believe a thing like that?' Aunt Enid paused, noting that Theolonious Washington was about to speak. All eyes turned to him. It was a special moment.

'There are a great many things you can't do in the United States if you are a Negro, if you are black,' he said slowly and profoundly. 'In years to come, people are going to wonder why black people can't do such and such, why they haven't achieved this or that. The answer will be because they were prevented, barred, kept out, locked out for hundreds of years, by law. It will take a long time to catch up. At least another hundred years, and it will only happen if they end racial discrimination now, and that's not about to happen.'

The verandah grew quiet. The American accent, so distinctly from another place, was a radio voice. It came straight out of WINZEE, speaking troubling words that Boyd didn't understand. Birds warbled in the trees and somewhere in the valley a donkey brayed lugubriously. A hundred years seemed like eternity, Boyd thought. It was difficult to think that the America he knew about from the encyclopaedia, from the songs on WINZEE and from the comics, was the same place that Aunt Enid and Mr Washington spoke about.

'For all the problems he has to face,' Aunt Enid informed them when Theo excused himself and left the verandah, 'he is a very successful man. You don't realise what is happening in America. You live in paradise here, *paradise*. Jamaica is paradise. The English people out here are nothing like the white people in America.' She turned to Papa. 'What would you do if you went up to the club tonight and they told you that you couldn't enter because you are black?'

They all stared at Papa. He looked horrified.

'It is so wrong,' Aunt Enid said, quite emotional. 'So wrong.'

They had never seen her like this before. She had never been to America before. Boyd saw the fierce light in her eyes, her passion so ravishingly displayed, heard the hurt in her voice, caught the candy scent of her. He shifted in his chair uncomfortably because everything was so confusing, so shocking, so impossible, but must be true because it came from his pretty Aunt Enid's lips.

The most uncomfortable thing on the verandah was the silence. Then Miss Hutchinson arrived and there were kisses and cries of amazement and wonder and the tension went away. Then Mr and Mrs Dowding made their entrance.

Later that evening, Ann Mitchison visited with presents for Mama and the baby, just as Aunt Enid and Mr Washington drove off into the sunset. Boyd observed Ann Mitchison as she sat on the verandah with Papa and the other guests, smoking and laughing beautifully. When Ann Mitchison arrived, she had looked in at Mama, the baby, Miss Hutchinson and Mrs Dowding. In her interlude with the women, she stroked the baby, cooing gently, her fleshy lips moist, exotic. And Boyd, hovering nearby, heard her say that Susan couldn't wait for school to begin. Hearing the name, *Susan*, from her mother's own lips, almost sent him into apoplexy.

'A lovely man, Mr Chin,' he heard Ann Mitchison say. 'He's promised to pick Susan up every day in his Plymouth when she starts school. He drives up with his own children, Ann Marie, Dawn and Junior, and a few others from Maggotty, then to Balaclava and back again in the afternoon. A wonderful person – and a first class businessman too.'

'Delightful,' Mama said. Mr Chin had offered his Plymouth station wagon as a school bus. Taking Boyd to school each day would have been a huge strain on Papa, the factory requiring his attention crucially between seven and nine in the morning. No one was more pleased than he when Mr Chin offered his services. 'He's a brick,' Papa declared. 'We need more men like him in Jamaica.'

But the reality of finally going to school in the company of strange children created powerful anxieties for Boyd, and suddenly he didn't want it to happen. He wanted to remain at home and dream of meeting Susan alone behind the house where no one could see. He wanted the waiting to continue, this beautiful waiting that was so painfully sweet. School would put an end to it.

Unfamiliar feelings settled upon him; what with the new baby, Susan's mother in the house, Susan near yet so far away, thoughts of school and troubling images of Aunt Enid hurt in America. In the end, Mavis rubbed him down with Bay Rum and put him to bed, where he fell instantly asleep. So he did not see Papa, finally and inevitably that evening, alone with Ann Mitchison on the verandah in the low light, speaking in dull tones. Mama and the baby were asleep too. The Dowdings had left and so had Miss Hutchinson, "to spread the news at the club". Boyd did not see Papa eventually escort Ann Mitchison to the periwinkle fence, vanishing among the smooth-touching leaves and caressing trees, kissing her forcefully in the dark. Only Vincent saw it with his one eye, secluded in the blackness, breathing in the peculiar fumes of his strange cigar, his resentment of Papa growing by the minute.

* * *

Mr Samms left Appleton. He left without a word, a note, or a sign to anyone. The last time he was seen was at the club. He was at a table with Mr Moodie, Miss Hutchinson and Miss Chatterjee when he suddenly stood up, bowed gracefully to Miss Hutchinson, kissed Miss Chatterjee's hand, nodded to Mr Moodie and walked away, straight-backed, hair glistening, highly polished shoes dazzling. No one saw him again.

'Took the train back to Kingston,' Papa said grimly at dinner. 'He just needs an ordinary decent woman. Cynthia Hutchinson is far too sophisticated for him, *far too sophisticated*. He had other hopes too, but,' and Papa shook his head sadly, 'Manjula Chatterjee is out of his league completely.'

'Manjula Chatterjee!' Mama exclaimed. 'You mean – ?'

'Yes,' Papa said and calmly left the table.

CHAPTER 28

Manjula Chatterjee stepped out onto the balcony of a small, private hotel in an exclusive part of Kingston, West King's House Close. Her hair, black and wet, was steaming as she towelled it while looking out over the gardens and the pool that she had just vacated. The Sunday afternoon heat delighted and invigorated her. A faint breeze blew over the gardens from the direction of King's House, the Governor's residence. The first time she spent a weekend in Kingston, they'd wanted the Myrtle Bank Hotel, whose advertisement boasted that it was *the rendezvous for Jamaica's social smart set*. But, because of its colour bar, they'd settled for the Mayfair instead, a more elegant and welcoming place. They'd spent three weekends together there already and several clandestine evenings at her house at Appleton. But it was tricky at Appleton and so the weekends at the Mayfair were set to continue. She always took the diesel train in from Appleton and back rather than make the long, exhausting journey by car. It was better in every respect.

What Manjula liked most of all when they were together was their conversations. They spent most of the time talking. She liked his quiet listening, the attention he paid to her every word, the absence of guile and the fact that he reminded her powerfully of her father, to whom she had been extraordinarily close. The conversation was mostly about her. And always there was that steady gaze: the boyish, fun-uncle eyes full of goodness and patience, never lacking in openness and honesty. He didn't know it but she'd been swept off her feet that first time. She had seen him watching her after a tennis game when she was hot and beads of perspiration stood out on her forehead and on the tip of her nose. When they were introduced, she'd expected the usual going-over – the evasive eyes like hidden hands up her dress, the suggestive mouth, the appraisal of her shape and form – and braced herself for it. But his eyes never left hers. There had been no innuendos. They had perfect eye contact; he had seen into her and she had seen into him and so they built a bridge between them. That night, going home, she stopped the car as the full impact of what had happened sunk in. He had walked across the bridge and into her very being.

'Cocktail, Manjula?'

'Yes,' she called back. 'And join me out here.'

She stretched out easily on the lounge chair, noticing the faint ripple of flesh along her burning thighs while positioning the tortoiseshell sunglasses over her eyes. The scent of mint from the garden and his Old Spice tantalised her. Then he joined her, a cocktail glass in each hand, and bent to kiss her lips, a slow, lingering, tender kiss. But she was aroused, her lips parting, urgent tongue darting out, mouth and chin raised, exposing a firm, elegant neck, one hand circling and guiding his head down. He grunted, expertly balancing the cocktail glasses and lightly tongued her smooth neck. Manjula loved these moments, the clean heat, the mint scent all about, the cocktails that charged her tongue and her senses and the slow sex in the long afternoon. Much later, when it was all over, when the sun was still a strip of pink over the Blue Mountains, she would begin to think of the long train ride back to Appleton, the return to work on Monday morning. She hoped it would be a smooth journey back. There had been troubling news on the radio that hooligans had disabled a train between Kingston and Appleton.

The news was all over the radio that night, in the newspapers the next morning and the following days and ran as the main item for weeks. The newspapers reported it as *The Kendal Train Crash*. An overcrowded excursion train had arrived in Montego Bay on the Sunday. On its return journey to Kingston, passing through Kendal, a small Manchester town, the train left the rails and hurtled down an embankment, killing almost two hundred people. Up to a thousand more were injured. Mama read every bit of news about it in *The Daily Gleaner* and *The Star*. And she told the stories over and over again.

'Dead bodies were scattered everywhere, hanging from the upturned carriages, armless, legless, headless,' Mama said. '*Headless!*'

'Lawd-a-mercy!' Mavis cried out. 'Is the third bad news, ma'am. At least you out of it, ma'am.'

Mama paid no attention. 'One woman returned to her home in Kingston that Sunday night and her mother let her in. The following day, the mother found out that her daughter, *her daughter*, the woman she'd let into the house the night before, had died at Kendal.'

'Lawd Jesus,' Mavis shrieked, wild of eye. 'Is her *Duppy!*'

'No, Mavis,' Mama corrected her. 'Her spirit returned home.'

The children trembled. Mavis still had a wild look about her, reflecting their own fear.

'People at the scene said that the dead bodies were like minced meat. *Minced meat!*' Mama shook her head in horror, daring them to believe it. Then she folded the paper grimly and returned to the bedroom and to her baby, with a cup of ginger tea to settle her nerves. She saw tragedy and horror everywhere.

* * *

In the evening as it grew dark, Boyd, hidden in his usual spot in the tall grass watching the Mitchison house, heard Mavis and Evadne speaking.

'Mr Mitchison gone to Kingston again,' Evadne said. 'Second time this week. Mrs Mitchison have the house to herself.'

'Mr Mitchison live in Kingston!' Mavis laughed sardonically.

'Him is a busy man. Sometimes three days pass and him don't come home, whole weekends too. Then they talk and Mrs Mitchison get upset and hang up the telephone. Ah never know that white people could behave so bad. Them behave just like *Neaga* people.'

'You would get vex too if your hubby never at home,' Mavis said.

'Hmm,' Evadne agreed. Then she raised her eyebrows. 'You know Adassa?'

'Adassa who?'

'Adassa, who used to work for Mr and Mrs Brookes before you?'

'What about her?'

Evadne's eyes widened. 'You know what she tell me?'

'What?' Mavis stamped her foot, showing her impatience.

'She say that Mr Mitchison sleep one night over at Miss Chatterjee.'

'Mr Mitchison spend the night with Miss Chatterjee! When?'

'The night of the Kendal Crash is when. She and Mr Mitchison drive up from Kingston that night. She couldn't come by train because of the hooligans. Is what Adassa say, and she should know. She work for Miss Chatterjee now.'

'The night of the Kendal Crash!' Mavis exclaimed. 'Mrs Mitchison know?'

'You foolish or what? Who you think going to tell her?'

'Lawd-a-mercy!'

'Man up to no good. And is not only Mr Mitchison.'

'What you mean?' Mavis demanded.

'Man up to no good is what ah mean,' Evadne replied cooly. 'Your baas not different from the rest of them. Him is only a man.'

'You leave Mr Brookes out if it.' Mavis pointed a steady finger.

'Heh, heh,' Evadne laughed mockingly.

'Big shot people business is not our business,' Mavis told her severely, 'so keep out of it. Try this *Essen* and give me back the lilac bottle. Ah wearing it out this weekend. My man giving me rock and roll, chile.' And Mavis hurried back to the house.

Boyd followed behind her, unseen. He looked in at Mama nursing the baby and inhaled the delicate scent of Johnsons Baby Oil, the smell of new life. Barrington and Yvonne seem preoccupied at supper and he wondered how it was possible that they did not know about Papa. Maybe they knew but chose to say nothing. Full of secret knowledge, he saw Papa drive over to the Mitchisons, where Ann Mitchison had the house to herself.

They could not prevent it, Papa and Ann. Amid the news of the tragedy and the careful show of distress, it was written, not by them but by fate, history, politics and by every damned thing that existed. It was written before that night, and it was being written as they engaged in their contrived *tête-à-tête*.

Susan was in bed, asleep, where she should be at that hour. People were in their homes, in their beds, doors locked up for the night. The world was asleep. They were alone in the world, Ann and Papa. No one could see them in this warm, dark night.

When it got past ten o'clock, Papa looked at his watch. Ann, seeing this, glanced at hers too. They said not a word as they walked down the steps and into the garden. They walked between oleander and bougainvillea and came to open ground hidden from the house, overlooking the valley and the lights of the factory. Here they sat on freshly mown lawn, still warm beneath them, soft as a woollen carpet, and came together as the moon went behind a cloud. Papa caught sight of Ann's creamy hand removing her clip-on earrings and placing them in the pocket of her skirt, just before he got her on her back on the grass. Ann uttered a short sigh, inhaling the overpowering sugar and nicotine smell of him, a veritable male odour, as he crushed her beneath him. Papa remembered the smooth, hot fleshiness of her raised thighs and their whiteness in the dark. And his fiercely seeking mouth, full of guilt and betrayal, attended diligently to her raised lips.

The kiss didn't last long although it seemed so to Papa, worried about the stupendousness of what they were doing, so close to their matrimonial home, with Mama waiting back at the house with the new baby. And suddenly they broke apart, as if caught in a shameful act. Papa swore that he had glimpsed a shadowy figure.

'It's that gardener of yours,' he whispered. 'Always sneaking about.'

'He's never about at this hour,' Ann whispered back.

'So, who was it?' Papa was uneasy, almost willing the intruder to show himself. 'Who's there?' He called out. He got no answer.

'It's the moon,' Ann said quietly. 'It moved from behind a cloud.'

Papa sighed and took her hand. 'First the Rastaman and now a ghost in the garden,' he said. Ann stroked his arm and they laughed softly.

'Tim's in Kingston for most of next week,' Ann said. 'I'll see what I can do.'

Papa turned to her. 'The new term starts on Monday. What about Susan?'

'She needs more time.'

Shadowy in the moonlight, they walked in silence back to the house and up the still warm verandah steps. And it was close to midnight when, from the inky darkness of the trees, Adolphus watched as Papa kissed Ann goodnight. He thought Papa was going to give it to her good and proper right there. He thought the kiss would never end.

* * *

That Saturday, they travelled past Malvern and up into the Santa Cruz Mountains in silence to deposit Barrington at his new school. Mama baked a fruitcake and put it in among his things. Barrington carried two large brown grips and was dressed smartly in grey trousers. Boyd saw boys bigger than Barrington, young men with light moustaches, the dead stamp of their fathers, standing about in the dormitory wearing George Webb shoes. Dennis was not among them. Before they left, Boyd saw Barrington sitting on his bed, which was covered in a grey blanket with three bright stripes, sharing out his cake. The big boys crowded in upon him. Barrington wouldn't kiss baby Babs as they left so Mama kissed him instead. The big boys still laughed.

'You must write,' Mama said.

'Every week,' Barrington told her.

As they walked back to the car, the young-looking headmaster, an Oxford graduate whom Papa liked, spoke eloquently about the school: the excellent teaching, French, Latin, Physics, the cross country runs, the tennis, the rifle club, the cadet corps, the debating society and, yes, the soccer.

Yvonne and Boyd sat on their knees in the back seat of the car and stared out the rear window at the fast receding buildings of the school. Barrington did not come out to wave them goodbye, although Yvonne was sure she saw him come running out at the last minute. By then the billowing dust of the Santa Cruz roads was all they could see behind them. After that, Yvonne curled up in the corner and sucked her thumb. The car was silent. Mama and Papa did not speak. Boyd did not speak either. One thing had ended and another thing was about to begin. It couldn't be stopped. All his thoughts were about school now, how, at last, he would have to leave the pink house for the Balaclava Academy where the pretty Chinese girls were, and where Susan, his very special Susan, after all the waiting, would sit next to him in class, close enough to touch.

* * *

'Mr Mitchison in Kingston for a whole week,' Mavis said breezily at supper that night, pouring black coffee. 'And poor Mrs Mitchison left on her own in the house. And she give Evadne five nights off in a row. Five nights, ma'am!'

'Thank you, Mavis,' Mama said, as Papa stared, dumb with astonishment. 'Evadne's obviously been gossiping,' Mama whispered as Mavis left the room. 'I'll have a word with her later.'

'I've told you before, it's your job to teach her how to behave!' Papa hissed at Mama. Then he left the table, stiff with rage.

Late that same night, Vincent, in a deep funk, watched Mavis return from her night out with Barry. He cowered in the dark, his machete heavy in his weak hand, unable to deliver the blows that should strike Barry down for good. He heard the anguished urgency of their breathing, the rustling of their clothes. Unsteady on his feet, breathing hard, he knew one thing for certain. He was going to have to take Mavis the only way he knew.

PART THREE
The Ending

CHAPTER 29

That September morning, Boyd was dressed in new khaki shorts and royal-blue shirt. He wore brown boots, so new that the leather squeaked even when he stood still. His eight-year-old body washed and brushed, he felt as excited and anxious as Poppy, tail up, nipping at his ankles. Poppy bothered Yvonne too, climbing up her polka-dotted dress. Hearing her shriek, he nipped back to safe ground at Boyd's feet, feigning innocence. The morning sun was up too and the scent of blue dahlias drifted through the open windows, bringing the sound of Vincent's lawnmower putputting away in dewy grass. Birds were darting about in the trees and butterflies already sucking at the jacaranda. From the kitchen, Mavis belittled Vincent. This was a new day for Mavis too. For the first time, Boyd would be away from her. She was especially fierce with Vincent.

The Land Rover was waiting by the garage. Papa was in the bathroom brushing his teeth and Boyd could smell his lime-green Limacol cologne. Boyd's new brown satchel, with its new leather smell, lay on the table in the pantry where Mama stood pretending to be busy with Yvonne's hair and giving vague instructions to an agitated Mavis.

Boyd wanted to run to Mama, take off his new clothes and watch the sun's rays creep across the bedclothes. The trembling started and the panic. He wanted to run back to yesterday where everything was known and in its place. He wanted to cuddle up to Mavis in her room with her nipple in his mouth, or listen all morning to Vincent's lawnmower and breathe the scent of freshly cut grass. He wanted to sit on the verandah and see Susan coming across the lawn like Pepsi, hair shiny under the sun.

But Papa dashed from the bathroom and they were off, Boyd plucked from Mama in a wicked moment. Down into the blue valley, the air sharp, across the dark bridge, dust billowing behind them, and through the green fields of canes they went. Swiftly and smoothly they sped, along the asphalt road, past the empty railway station where porters with black caps and red flags gazed into air. Up the winding slopes they went, sometimes parallel with the black piston-punching train, seeing people looking out from the gold and brown carriages. Then Papa, engaging the gears, laboured up the winding hill, passing little box houses on stilts clinging to the slopes, with proud cocks crowing with gusto at every gate. Finally the Land Rover approached the Balaclava road, raced down it for about half a mile and turned into the large cut-stone gate, coming to rest outside the aged white building with its redbrick facade. Dew sparkled on the grass surrounding the building. Big trees were everywhere, their leaves a rich green, bathed in morning sun like honey from heaven. One tree stood on its own, heavily laden with apples as bright red as fresh lipstick. It faced the building where the murmur of children's voices played like music from a harmonica. This was the Balaclava Academy.

Two nuns, in blue habit, waited at the door. They wore very wide and very white bibs. Boyd stared and turned to Papa. Papa got out. The green door of the Land Rover clicked that metallic Land Rover click. The nuns were smiling. Boyd had difficulty getting down from the Land Rover and Papa said, 'Here we go,' and lifted him down. They stood staring at Sister Margaret Mary and Sister Catherine, who seemed familiar to Boyd. He had seen them before in the pictures in the encyclopaedia, pious nuns with naked pink babies. Sister Margaret Mary went off to one side to talk with Papa, her creamy face businesslike. Papa seemed benign and polished. His brown brogues reflected the sun. His knee-length socks accentuated his firm calves and short khaki trousers showed off his sculptured thighs. Papa was erect, his skin deep-brown and smooth, smelling of his green cologne, smelling of home. Papa knew what he was about; he would make it all right, make the fear and the anxiety go away, make the school do his bidding.

Mama's doctor, Dr Cadien, arrived with his two girls in his cream Jaguar. He let them out, waved to Sister Margaret Mary and Papa and drove off, leaving behind a pleasant smell of leather, petrol and Colgate Palmolive toothpaste. The Cadien girls went straight into the redbrick building, sunlight catching their light-blonde hair, their brown satchels and creamy legs and arms. Images of Susan rushed in upon Boyd but the Balaclava Academy and Sister Margaret Mary shut them out.

'He'll be fine,' Boyd heard Sister Margaret Mary say to Papa. Her head was inclined, eyeing him severely, and he noted the wrinkled white flesh of her upper lip.

Sister Catherine was smooth and creamy like the Cadien girls and very young. She put her arms around Boyd as he stood in his creased new clothes, with creased back of thighs, creased forehead and creased calves. She smelled like the bedclothes in Mama's room and he instinctively nuzzled up to her. But Sister Margaret Mary had other plans. At her instruction, Miss Robb, an efficient teacher who lived in one of the box houses down the hill, arrived very quickly on the spot. Her purple-black skin, like a sumptuous aubergine, full and tight and perfect, gleamed. Her arms were robust (all the better to manage children in classes), her dark, hobble skirt shining, her bottom rounded and firm. And she whisked him away like a great spider. Boyd heard the Land Rover gurgle into life and saw, over his shoulder, the familiar shape move away to the gate. Down in the valley was Siloah, blue with distance. Beyond the blue lay Appleton, a lone silver chimney finger spouting steam, winking in the sun. It seemed very far away.

He stumbled pell-mell after Miss Robb. Sister Margaret Mary came up behind him rapidly, skirts sweeping the ground, rosaries whispering noisily. Sister Bernadette, another young nun, as coy and as pious as Sister Catherine, with a smooth, dark face, joined them. Boyd stumbled along in his new clothes and new shoes in this new place with the new smells. Sister Bernadette put her thin, tiny arm round him. The new smells were pink, young garden lily smells, the tender pink of nervousness in a new place. And feelings like mountains overwhelmed him. How he wanted to see Mavis's milky-blue smoke curling from the chimney and hear Mama's familiar voice calling his name. Now he wished he could answer and go to her. But it was too late. She was not there and there was no sound of Poppy. At least Susan would be in the classroom and the agony would become ecstasy. Already the scent of her presence came to him.

* * *

At home in the afternoon, Boyd could not get the words out as he tried to tell Mama *everything* that happened on that eventful day at the Balaclava Academy. He spoke about the pretty Chinese girls, Ann-Marie and Dawn; Robert Jureidini, the boy who sat next to him; Adrian Lees, the boy with the milky-white skin whose sister, Carol, also with milky-white skin, ate sugar and butter sandwiches. He spoke excitedly about Diana Delfosse who sang "Don't be Cruel" by Elvis Presley in the school bus; his teachers, Miss Casserly and Miss Robb, the two young nuns, Sister Catherine and Sister Bernadette. And Sister Margaret Mary. She really was the holy mother of God. Sister Margaret Mary was all the parents moulded into one. Her word was final, her powers absolute. And everyone knew the Holy Ghost was with her. She was Alpha and Omega, and only the Pope, Pope John the 23rd himself, represented more power and authority at the academy. But Boyd could not speak about the most important person who was missing that day, whose absence felt like a stake through his heart.

'You'll have Susan for company next week when she returns from Mandeville,' Mama said encouragingly, noticing Boyd's disquiet. It had been the same at Worthy Park Prep, the reluctance to leave her each morning, the difficulty in making friends.

Boyd could not speak, hearing the news.

At lunch that day, Yvonne had said to Papa, 'Susan won't be at school with Boyd.'

'Where did you hear that?'

'Mavis told Mama today.'

'She's a delicate child,' Papa said. 'I hear they're keeping her in Mandeville for a week. It's cooler up there and good for her.'

'What's the matter with her?' Mama had asked.

'I don't know,' Papa replied, shrugging.

Boyd said nothing at dinner that night, thinking that any comment he made about Susan would immediately expose his secret. He wanted to tell them what he knew about Susan, knowledge that would fill an encyclopaedia. Her very thoughts!

'At least she won't be a stranger,' Mama told him, noting his reticence. 'Not like the other children.'

'And Boyd could play with her, Mama,' Yvonne remarked joyfully. 'And she could play with Boyd!'

In bed that night, as his eyes closed, the commanding scent of the day was of new exercise books, new leather satchels, sharpened pencils and the ubiquitous girl smell, like jacaranda in the sun. There was the lunch room scent of packed lunches: cheese and currant bun, brown bread and bologna sausage, *animal biscuits*, guava jelly and ripe bananas in wicker baskets. And there were the Chinese girls with batting eyelids, all coy and pretty and virgin. But overshadowing everything was the constant fear, deep in his marrow, of this new place full of new people. Fear of Miss Robb with her smooth skin and her sharp ruler, Sister

Margaret Mary with the rosaries and severe manner. And there was the nervous smell of the classroom but most of all the weepy sadness of absence.

* * *

Sister Margaret Mary ran a healthy regime. Every morning, Miss Casserly, the prettiest of the young teachers, assembled everyone in a semi-circle as the sun came up through the trees, as the dew sparkled on the grass, as they breathed the scent of apple blossoms. Miss Casserly, skin like honey, hair shiny and curly, was very good at callisthenics and never slapped anyone with a ruler. She appreciated every effort as one's best. *Stretch and pull. Point and pull. Up and down. Waddle like a duck! Feet out. Feet in. Up and down. Arms out. Arms up. Down. Up. Down. Up. Down. Waddle like a duck!* The children liked it so much and Miss Casserly was so entertaining that they did not want it to stop. But it was meant to be short and sweet, to get the blood into their cheeks and their brains alert. Sister always stopped it with the ringing of the big brass bell. And they all trooped back into the classrooms – some still waddling like ducks – to sit behind little desks (at the right hand of God the Father). Boys in royal-blue shirts, khaki trousers, brown socks and shoes, and girls in royal blue tunics, Daz-white blouses, white socks and brown shoes, all eager, all small, all glowing, as they made their way into the school building to learn new words and other things to wonder at.

Many of the words came from the lips of Sister Margaret Mary but some also came from Sister Catherine and from the green catechism book and from other places. The days were full of *Magnificat, Nunc Dimittis, the Apostles' Creed* and *the Beatitudes (Blessed are the meek, for they shall inherit the earth).* The days whispered *Born of the Virgin Mary, suffered under Pontius Pilate, was crucified, died and was buried.* Even the creamy, pretty, painted statues in the corners of the classrooms proclaimed *Holy Eucharist, Sacred Heart,*

Immaculate Conception. Every day Angels' voices said *Hail Mary, full of grace, the Lord is with thee. Blessed art thou among women and blessed is the fruit of thy womb, Jesus.* And always, somewhere, voices murmured *Thy will be done now and forever amen.* Boyd wanted very much to be at the right hand of God the Father and to say the wonderful words. He already knew that Susan was the Virgin Mary with her pink lips and knowing look, waiting with goodness and mercy, waiting for the moment.

* * *

Beyond the low walls of the school, the people of Balaclava thought it was a great blessing to have such decent, well-behaved children attending that fine establishment in their midst. Mr Tecumseh Burton, the local tailor, he of the black Chevrolet and American accent, yards of gabardine across his knees and pins in his mouth, certainly thought so.

He and the nice people of Balaclava looked forward to the school's garden parties, fêtes, concerts, maypole dances and fundraising activities. Sister Margaret Mary and her staff excelled in the organising of these events. The Balaclava people knew that, even with the Harvest Festival that Pastor Nind at the Anglican Church managed so well; there were pitifully few social occasions in the town when they could dress up in their best frocks, single pearls and flannels, drink light rum-punch, eat homemade cakes and ice cream, stand in rapt attention at infant theatre performances and, as the string lights came on in the evening, sit in awe before a little string quartet atop the wooden stage on the lawn, long after the Jaguar and Prefect-driving families had left, knowing that they had been properly entertained.

At the beginning of term, the Balaclava people and the parents received the usual notice. It was typed on an Olympia typewriter with the symbol @ in a pretty border round it and run off in the dozens by the school's Gestetner machine. The notice proclaimed that the staff and boys and girls of the Balaclava Academy would be presenting *H.M.S Pinafore* (*or, The Lass That Loved a Sailor*), a Gilbert and Sullivan operetta. Recipients of the notice were beside themselves.

Mr Burton learned his trade in Harlem, New York, and knew what an operetta was, even though he had never been to one. He saw the possibilities immediately. An operatic production meant clothes, costumes and design. He was the master of all three, even if he did say so himself. It was also an opportunity for him to introduce his nephew, Edgar, whose education at a fourth rate private school in Kingston qualified him for nothing. Who knew what could come out of a meeting with Sister Margaret Mary? He believed in creating opportunities. He was teaching the boy how to cut cloth and manage the bookkeeping but his heart was not in it. Like every young man in the town, Edgar fancied a job at Appleton Estate. But he was at the back of a very long queue. Mr Burton did not know socially any of the senior people at the factory who could pull a few strings for him. It didn't help that Edgar spent most of his time loitering at the club with questionable young women and generally giving himself a bad name. The moment he got a job, Edgar would be asked to pack his bags. Mr Burton had already made up his mind about that.

The day after he received the leaflet, Mr Burton put on his suit (made in America of worsted wool) and his brown felt hat, worn squarely on his head. With Edgar reluctantly in tow, he visited Sister Margaret Mary.

While the negotiation progressed by the front door of the school, Edgar took a peek into a classroom. The place smelled of children, newly sharpened pencils and vulnerable young women. He knew their scent. He saw the pretty young teacher, her skirt caught on a nearby desk, revealing the soft curve of delicate and private flesh behind her knees. She caught him staring and pulled her skirt down in one swift motion. But he had seen enough.

'Can you make sailor suits?' Sister asked, oblivious of the communication between Miss Casserly and the young man at the door.

'I can build the ship, Sistuh,' Mr Burton replied with a charming smile, shoving Edgar before him. 'Wit a littuh help from me nephew here.'

Sister took off her spectacles, fierce horn-rimmed things, and peered hard at Edgar, who took one step back and looked away.

CHAPTER 30

That eventful day, Sister Margaret Mary took Boyd's class. Her bib was crispy white, just like the Holy Sacrament the boys received on their tongues from Father John the Baptist at Our Lady of Sorrows up the road. She stood before the class, writing in her perfect hand on the lined blackboard. There was much to-ing and fro-ing up at the convent, and the younger teachers like Miss Casserly and Miss Skiddar were like excited young girls. Preparations for *H.M.S. Pinafore* were well underway. In a distant classroom, children practised the songs, and the sound of hammer and saw could be heard as workmen built the stage in the gardens – the school's tiny auditorium would not be able to cope. Sister Margaret Mary expected all the parents from Appleton and Balaclava to attend as usual.

She was demonstrating, for the few whose writing did not come up to the standard, how it was done – straight up in the academy's way, not slanted, the devil's way. She was not impressed with the new ballpoint pens, the so-called *biros*. With these new pens, the students simply pressed a plastic knob and down came a thin cylinder tube with the ballpoint of sticky ink ready for writing. Sister did not allow them at the school because they hampered good writing style. Only properly sharpened HB pencils and fountain pens with black or blue Parker Quink Ink were allowed. Writing had to be round and straight up. *And I copied all the letters in a big, round hand. I copied all the letters in a hand so free, that now I am the Ruler of the Queen's Navee!*

Michael Sanderson, a boy from the senior class, entered

the room from a side door. He was always tipping the balance and made Sister Catherine laugh even when she did not wish to, because to laugh at his jokes was a sin. But he would learn his manners in Sister's presence. So everyone thought. He spoke to Sister and showed her something. Sister's face turned immaculate crimson. The children thought they saw gold in the palm of Michael Sanderson's hand. Sister said something to him and the little lambs, expecting him to genuflect and back away from Sister's presence, were shocked out of their chairs, their hearts in their mouths, to see Michael, eyes winking, snap his hand up and down, whipping Sister's veil off. Then he ran from the room laughing.

At his desk, rigid, Boyd felt as if someone had pulled Mama's dress off in public. Sister bent down carefully, lifted the veil and snapped it back on. Then she left the room and was gone for a long time. The children did not move. Outside there was commotion. Miss Casserly came, breathless, to take the class. There were rumours that Michael Sanderson had fled the premises. Others said he had gone to confession. Still others said that he had been struck dumb and was roaming the streets. Some of the big boys said he had used a word, the word that should never be spoken, to Sister. And he had showed her a very rude thing, the infamous Gold Coin or *French Letter*. Because of that, and that alone, the big boys said he would go to Hell.

The children in Boyd's class had no idea what a *French Letter* was. But Boyd knew immediately. It was, obviously, a letter written in French and had something to do with Mama's perfume, *Evening in Paris*, folded up and placed inside a gold coin. The letter was probably like his note to Susan, not the sort of thing to show to Sister Margaret Mary. One of the big girls, who lived at Balaclava, said that Michael, for all his shortcomings, would never have behaved in such a vile manner to Sister Margaret Mary, if he had not been put up to it. Whispering it darkly to just a few of the Balaclava girls, she said that someone else was behind it. They knew about his rum drinking, his wantonness, his skylarking with Michael Sanderson. That someone was none other than Edgar, Mr Burton's nephew.

It was the end for Michael Sanderson. No amount of confession could save him. He was beyond prayer. He had had the audacity to behave in this intolerable way while the big plans for the production of *H.M.S. Pinafore* were in high gear. The Balaclava Academy was an extraordinary little institution. Nothing would sully its excellent reputation; not the Gold Coin or *French Letter*, not Michael Sanderson, and certainly not the sinful hidden hand of rascals. All the teachers were expected to stand firm against evil influences. Satan was busy trying to get in. They should keep him out.

Sister Margaret Mary returned from the convent, having received divine unction, to the chorus of 'Yes, Sister' following every word she uttered. It was noticeable that the girls now curtseyed when they spoke to her. The young teachers did so too, their eyes full of adoration and deep respect.

After lunch on that memorable day, Sister Catherine, in the middle of a little excited group of big girls on the patio, looked wistful, like a picture of the Virgin Mary; the Virgin Mary of Italian paintings, poised and serene.

In the sweet heat and amid the scent of apple blossoms, pretty Diana Delfosse got out her record player, a red and cream machine with a captivating robotic arm. How she got it into the school no one knew and no one asked, not Sister Catherine, not Sister Bernadette, not even Miss Robb. And everyone wondered when Sister Margaret Mary would confiscate the music. Sister Catherine glanced furtively towards the convent and moved closer to the big girls in their bobby socks and brown loafers. Diana Delfosse laughed, showing perfect teeth, and tried to get Sister Catherine to dance. Shyly, the little boys, Boyd included, drew closer to the magic and the music.

'It's rock and roll, Sister,' Diana Delfosse thrilled.

'What?' Sister Catherine did not quite understand and kept looking from one girl to the other and then at Diana Delfosse's flailing body.

'Jive, Sister Catherine, jive!' Diana called out.

Diana was jumping out of her skin, hands and legs making shocking, electric movements. Her brown loafers made quick, harsh sounds on the ground. The other girls watched in amazement. The circle drew tighter, protectively; in the very centre, the gorgeous Diana Delfosse and the coy Sister Catherine, head down and smiling, Diana encouraging her to make small, faltering movements.

'It's a new dance, Sister.'

'Who is it?'

'It?' The big girls laughed out loud, some literally shrieked. Was there anyone who didn't know who the singer was? He was in their rooms, in the magazines hidden in their bureau drawers, and everyone, absolutely everyone, was talking about him. They saw at once the limitations of being a nun, which was why none of them seriously thought of taking religious orders, except Arlene, who was an orphan and wanted to be a missionary, but she didn't really count.

'Well, who?' Sister Catherine blushed beneath her veil.

'Elvis!' they all cried out as one. 'Elvis Presley.'

'Elvis Presley?' Sister Catherine wrinkled her brow.

She had no idea who this Elvis was. Boyd, watching keenly, witnessed the subtle little impulses and knew at once that Sister Catherine was yearning. She was longing to wear the lovely creamy socks that the big girls wore with their brown loafers and dance. She was longing to dance off the heavy blue habit, dance with the sun on her back and in her hair, dance away the bloody sacred heart; open her heart to romance, suffer a broken heart, dance to bursting like Diana Delfosse and live it up. She just wanted to be led anywhere but to the convent. Sister Bernadette's eyes met hers and they both looked away, thinking the same guilty thoughts.

The smaller girls had all drawn closer, with wide eyes

and expressions of treasure hunters on a desert island, facing for the first time the twinkle and flash of an opened treasure chest. They did not know who Elvis Presley was either. But to be with the big girls, with Sister Catherine and Sister Bernadette, enveloped as they were in the shade in the shimmering heat on the covered terrace, the boys gathering near, hearing the new music that made the big girls giddy with delight, was pure heaven. And the great expectation of sitting in a circle on the polished floor of the music room after lunch, Sister Catherine at the piano for a double period with the lovely *HMS Pinafore* music, was more than they could wish for.

The little boys were there too, with marbles and chewing gum in their pockets. Boyd was there with Adrian Lees, Robert Jureidini and Junior Chin, who was blowing pink bubblegum. They heard the music and mimicked Diana Delfosse, the girl whose eyes they could not meet. She was simply too pretty, too vivacious. They didn't want to get too close, didn't want to be dragged into the inner circle, the centre of everything. Only Junior Chin ventured close.

On that day, Boyd thought of the sun, the plums, the shrieking parakeets high in the pimento trees. He thought of the gathered girls with their peculiar scent that he breathed and dreamed about, Sister Catherine in the middle of it all, vulnerable and shy, looking to Sister Bernadette for reassurance. But most of all it was the special music from the little record player with the black, shiny records and the lovely pain of missing Susan that seeped deep into him that day.

One of the bigger girls – Denise Jureidini, they thought it was – asked whether there were any records by Chuck Berry or Paul Anka. Diana did have another special record in her small pile of 78s. It was Paul Anka's *Diana*. Shouts of approval went up from some of the girls. But Paul Anka would have to wait until after Elvis. And everybody would have to wait until then.

'*Baby, let me be your loving Teddy Bear,*' Diana sang out,

repeating the words of the song.

The other girls joined in and soon Miss Casserly and Miss Skiddar arrived, snapping their fingers and singing, *'Baby let me be. Baby let me be.'*

The moment Miss Casserly arrived on the scene, some of the big girls ran to her, their fingers splayed with great anticipation. Miss Casserly's dark, glossy ringlets played freely about her face. The big girls whispered in her ear and stood back, wanting her to confirm the buzz. They had asked, *What's your tale, nightingale?* But Miss Casserly did not provide the information they wanted to hear, rumours they wanted confirmed or denied.

Sister Catherine's face was aglow after hearing "Teddy Bear". And when Diana Delfosse, flipping the 78 record over to "Love Me Tender", grabbed her about the waist, she ran with an operatic shriek from the group and away from Sister Bernadette, out into the sun. Miss Casserly, happy and gay, went to her, fingers splayed, like the big girls. It was a memorable picture: the tree heavy with apples and the air with apple scent, the lips of the girls apple-red, Miss Casserly and Sister Catherine inches from the shade of the tree in the sweet heat of the lunchtime sun, silhouetted against the white of the school building, laughing, hugging, talking in hushed tones, not everyone understanding. Some of the big girls whispered, and it must have been about wonderful things because their eyes were as clear as the Balaclava skies.

'Love me tender, love me sweet,' Diana sang passionately, eyes closed, an imaginary Elvis Presley in her arms. Some of the smaller girls, like the Cadien sisters, stared at the ground, blushing.

Diana did eventually play Paul Anka's *Diana* and brought the party to its climax. But it was Miss Robb, well pressed, grey hobble skirt tight and shining about her hips, who ended it when she appeared on the tiny gallery of the main school building, glowering, the big brass bell in her hands. She didn't have to ring the bell. Everyone knew it was the end of one thing and the beginning of something else. And Miss Casserly went away from them.

She left the school early that day, seemingly in a devilish hurry, which was unusual for her. *Put a chain around my neck and lead me anywhere.*

The children walked in an orderly file up the hill to the convent for the double period of music. Behind them, the carpenters hammered at the wooden stage. They entered the convent excited about the *H.M.S. Pinafore* songs: *We sail the ocean blue, and our saucy ship's a beauty*. The music room radiated calm and cool, its wooden floors shone like the piano and when Sister Catherine arrived, full of grace, it felt like an ante-room of heaven. The girls kneeled down and sat on their heels, skirts draped on the floor, backs straight up like the writing in their exercise books. The boys sat carelessly behind the girls on the floor, not knowing what to do with their legs, one or two ending up under the girls' skirts, against their bright white bloomers. It was a day of gushing songs, piano music and beating hearts. In the afternoon, after the *H.M.S. Pinafore* songs, they trooped back down the hill behind Sister Catherine.

Miss Casserly had not been there to practise her song, *For I am called Little Buttercup – dear Little Buttercup, though I could never tell why*. Everyone wondered at this and missed her bird-like warbling.

The sun was dying as the calm but agile Mr Chin arrived in the Plymouth station wagon with the power steering and the sweet smell of petrol. The children took their seats and waved goodbye to Sister Margaret Mary. The station wagon went out between the two moss-covered cut-stone pillars at the school gate. Mr Chin, his dark hair falling over his eyes, looked up and down the road. To his left was Balaclava and to his right the road to Raheen, Appleton and Maggotty. He let the power steering wheel pass smoothly through his open palms and Boyd heard it say *Shhhhhh!* He turned right as Sister Margaret Mary watched gravely from the office, a solid figure of blue and white and gold-rimmed spectacles. *I am the monarch of the sea, the ruler of the Queen's Navee.* The Plymouth, full of small, glowing children, went downhill and uphill and across railway tracks in the afternoon light, along smooth unending lanes with apple-green cane fields beyond.

The new words appeared just as they were driving along Raheen, where the road was straight and perfect. One of the big girls whispered it with great wonderfulness and secrecy, and it was repeated. Several of the little girls giggled with ignorance and Diana Delfosse whispered in someone's ear. Soon everyone was saying it in hushed tones. Ann-Marie and Dawn seemed bewildered, not understanding what it meant. Boyd did not know, nor did Adrian and his sisters and the others. What could it mean? It was a mystery of such potency that the big girls had to whisper it. Perhaps Sister Margaret Mary would talk about it at assembly in the morning because it was so important, like the Hail Mary or the Ten Commandments. They heard it but they did not hear it, this adult secret.

The big girls had said it, the mysterious thing. It was the association of the two words that hid its meaning. The whispering and the secrecy gave it a powerful, seductive quality. The only person who seemed to know anything was Diana Delfosse, who got off the school bus among much activity and excitement at Siloah. Miss Casserly was *in love.*

CHAPTER 31

What did it mean? Boyd sat at his desk watching for Miss Casserly, hoping she would take the class so that he could look at her with inquisitive eyes. *Miss Casserly was in love.* The September breeze whispered it. But, as he craned his neck to look, he saw Sister Margaret Mary in conversation with a man partly hidden at the door. Boyd sat bolt upright. It was Papa, standing by the steps like a schoolboy, attentive and respectful.

'Boyd will need a sailor suit,' Sister Margaret Mary was saying. 'All the children taking part will need sailor suits, sailor hats and black shoes. Mr Burton will make the suits. The costume list was sent with my letter.'

'Oh, yes,' Papa said. 'Boyd brought it straight home. He hasn't stopped talking about *H.M.S. Pinafore.*'

'He knows all the songs,' Sister Margaret Mary said with a restrained smile. 'Boyd really gets involved at rehearsals. If he wasn't so tiny, we'd make him Sir Joseph Porter or Ralph Rackstraw, Able Seaman.' And Sister laughed, not like other people with a loud roar and a throwing back of the head, but with a few soft *hmm hmms* from between closed lips.

Papa laughed too, thinking that that was the right time to take the small brown envelope out of his pocket and hand it to Sister, the real purpose of his visit.

'My contribution,' he said, one hand behind his back.

Sister smiled like the full moon. All her ships had come in now. 'We are very grateful,' she said. 'God bless you. Thank you for taking time out from your important job at

Appleton Estate to drive up here with your gift. It will be put to very good use. The teachers are so excited. Our midterm production will be magnificent, God willing. We look forward to seeing you and Mrs Brookes.'

Papa was walking away when Sister called him back. 'Any news about little Susan Mitchison?' she asked.

'Nothing, Sister.' Papa hung his head.

'The poor thing, so sickly.'

'Yes,' Papa said. 'I think it's asthma. She's recuperating in Mandeville, I believe. The air is cooler up there.'

'Well, we'll be praying for her,' Sister said.

Reeling with the news, Boyd saw Papa walk off in the yellow sunlight. Sister Margaret Mary entered the building, face in shadow, her rosaries playing the music of a hundred and sixty-five tiny chained black balls. He was *in extremis*. Everyone knew that Mandeville was where the hospitals were. Susan was there and growing weaker every day. Everyone was hiding the news. She would die suddenly, just like Little Nell, the girl he read about in *The Old Curiosity Shop*. They would receive a telegram and the sun would stop shining, the music would end. She couldn't last. *Everything comes to an end.*

* * *

That evening, Boyd and Yvonne sat with Papa in the Land Rover speeding towards Balaclava and Mr Burton. Every face that Boyd saw in every car they passed belonged to Susan, returning home from Mandeville at last.

They found Mr Burton in his little shop surrounded by bales of cloth. Black and white pictures cut from *Life* and *Ebony* magazines of men in suits hung from every wall. The shop was cosy and amber with lamplight. A Telefunken radio crackled on a low shelf.

'You are very welcome, suh,' Mr Burton said. 'Step into the shop, this way.' He led them into an adjoining room where two young men sat behind ancient Singer sewing machines, their glossy black and gold paintwork long faded. One of the young men was Mr Burton's nephew, Edgar. He seemed fastidious and vain. They had only been in the room a few minutes but he had already combed his sideburns and reshaped the hair above his forehead twice, in swift, slick movements. The action was like someone flourishing a switchblade knife.

'You know mah nephew,' Mister Burton mumbled, waving a hand in Edgar's direction and shaking his head.

Papa nodded in Edgar's direction and said, 'Young people.'

'Tailoring is not in his plans,' Mr Burton said. 'No young man of today wants to do tailoring. They only want to work in accounts, as clerks or some such, pushing paper. He's looking for a job at the factory.'

Edgar rose, yawned and sauntered out of the room. He must have gone straight to the Telefunken radio because moments later, *Whole Lotta Shakin' Goin' On* filled the room.

'Tun the radio down,' growled Mr Burton. Then in his normal voice he said, 'That young man needs to put his hands to something useful. He's helping with the sailor suits. And I am surprised with how he is so quick to visit the school to make a delivery. Before I took him to meet Sister, he never show a ounce of interest. Now he can't wait to get over there. Young people of today, you cannot figure them.'

'You're telling me,' Papa said, furrowing his brow and letting his eyes rest on Boyd. *Young people of today* was very much a Papa preoccupation.

'Let me measure up your boy, suh. I give you a good price since you are a big man at the factory.'

Papa laughed. 'Is that so?'

'Yes, suh.' Mr Burton took his measuring tape from around his neck while the quiet young man sitting behind the battered sewing machine sprang to his feet with pencil and an opened notebook. Boyd felt himself being manhandled, an unpleasant feeling, especially as Yvonne stood around staring pitifully at him.

'Anything going at the factory, suh?' Mr Burton asked casually.

'What's that?' Papa hadn't heard him.

'Any small job opening at the factory? Young Edgar can do it. He knows accounts and figures and has a good fist. He has the best writing hand I ever see.'

From the other room came the sound of new music, a bouncing, thumping tune and girlish voices. Edgar had turned up the volume again.

'It's The Bobbettes,' Yvonne whispered excitedly, '*Mr Lee.*'

'I'll make the suit as a gift, suh, you are a gentleman,' Mr Burton suddenly said. 'Your son will be the best dressed sailor boy in *H.M.S. Pinafore*. You leave it to Burton's Tailoring Establishment, suh.'

'You don't mean that,' Papa said, slightly embarrassed.

'Ah do, suh, ah do,' Mr Burton repeated, spinning Boyd around and patting him on the back. 'All done, young gentleman.'

Mr Lee still came thumping in from the radio in the front room. Mr Burton rolled his eyes and Boyd noticed the other young man immediately hurry out the door to remonstrate with Edgar. After a brief, hushed exchange, the volume went down and Edgar strolled casually back into the room.

'Uncle,' he said, 'I want to take the finished costumes over to the convent. Save you a trip. And I want to know if Sister will let me help with the lighting work for the concert.'

'What you know about lighting? That is a job for the electricians.'

'I know plenty.'

'Heh, heh, you know plenty all right,' Mr Burton said mockingly.

'I try me hand at everything,' Edgar said, glancing at Papa sitting at a low desk, observing Sister Margaret Mary's drawing of a sailor suit on the piece of paper in front of him but clearly listening to the conversation.

Mr Burton waved to Edgar dismissively. 'Alright then. But tek care you don't damage the suits and I don't want you stopping at Carty's bar on the way.'

'See you later, alligator,' Edgar said, grabbing a huge brown paper parcel from a table and stumbling through the door.

'After a while, crocodile,' the other young man called after him.

When Edgar had gone and the other young man seated himself at the front of the shop listening to the radio, Boyd and Yvonne wandered off to join him. They got within a few yards of him before he knew they were there. He was speaking quietly to someone in another room through a partly opened door. The other person was shy-looking, with soft eyes. Boyd saw a familiar face, sniffed distant DDT, savoured Paradise Plums and remembered someone who had gone away. The face behind the door was none other than that of Mr Jarrett, the sprayman, although now sporting a smart moustache. Seeing who had just entered the room, he vanished like a shadow, the door closing quietly. The young man by the radio, sensing the children's presence, moved away too.

In the other room, Papa turned to Mr Burton with his hands in his pockets.

'All young people need is an opportunity,' he said, aware of Edgar's reputation. 'I'll see what I can do at the factory.'

'God bless you, suh,' Mr Burton replied, overcome with gratitude, thanking Papa again and again as he left the shop.

But it wasn't long before Edgar's notoriety rocketed. People were talking about him at the club, at work and over their dinner tables.

'All those men living at the Bull Pen, with one or two exceptions, are up to no good,' Mr Moodie said at dinner one evening. 'Take that new feller, Edgar. His uncle threw him out of the house for all his shenanigans with the young girls at Balaclava. Now he's spreading nasty rumours about the poor man.'

Boyd had been to the Bull Pen once with Vincent. The place smelled of young men – sweat, cigarettes and cheap cologne. The older men there spent their time playing dominos and doing the football pools in the hope of scoring a big payday. Men walked about in stripy underwear and sleeveless, white merino vests. Women were not allowed there, but on the day they visited, Boyd caught sight of a young woman, scantily dressed, being pulled into a doorway. Vincent had winked.

'Nasty rumours, I tell you,' Mr Moodie continued. 'That man Burton is a good tailor. He makes all my trousers and your suits, Harry, so you know. He doesn't live with a woman – so what? I don't live with a woman myself and no one would dare say I'm a, you-know-what. I love women.' Mr Moodie winked at Papa, who gave him a hard stare. Mama pretended not to hear.

Papa kept quiet. But he might have said he was shocked at Edgar's blatant ungratefulness, his indiscipline, his sheer fecklessness.

* * *

Edgar made his way gingerly up the hill towards the convent with brown paper parcels under his arms as the *H.M.S. Pinafore* songs floated down. Miss Casserly appeared at the door. When she saw who it was, she took the parcels hastily, coquettishly, and left Edgar standing on the doorstep. Boyd, seated under the apple tree in the school yard, saw this and wished that Susan would come to the door of the pink house, sit with him in the warmth and silence on the verandah, breathing and feeling each other's presence.

* * *

That Friday evening, he saw into the Mitchison's house, and it was full of music and party things. Pretty girls in pretty frocks and shiny hair were there. A large table was heaped with cakes and puddings, candy, ginger beer and Kool-Aid. Ann Mitchison dashed about, her hair flashing, welcoming everyone and serving ice cream.

'Hello, hello,' she said. 'Come in, come in. How is Mummy and the new baby?'

'Fine,' Yvonne said, not believing that she'd been invited to the party too.

Susan, dressed in a frilly white frock with pink ribbons, red strap shoes and pink socks, served cake from a small tray. She went round to all her friends, girls he did not know (obviously come up from Monymusk and Mandeville) but also Ann-Marie and Dawn Chin and Adrian's sisters, Ann and Carol Lees, who lived on the estate. When she came near, birds sang in the garden.

'Are you the boy from next door?' he thought he heard her say.

He nodded and noted that she had small, moist, quivering, strawberry-red lips. Her eyes – turquoise, like his marbles – fell upon him like a caress, the kind only Mama was capable of. Her eyes conveyed delicate, intimate questions. Boyd's chest pounded. He wanted her alone in the bedroom, or in the garden where there was silence.

Adrian Lees came over to blow a party whistle in his ear, shattering everything. Then they ran off outside to gasp and chase about. They tried to catch lizards, using stalks from long grass at the bottom of the garden and inadvertently frightened a small girl who ran off bawling, the whites of her eyes shocking. Then they ran to the back of the house bathed in red sun, not talking, only feeling.

'They'll be cutting the cake soon,' Adrian said, throwing a stone over the garden fence and into the road. 'Let's get back.'

The sun went down and it grew dark. Lights came on in the house and children were singing, Happy Birthday to yoo, Happy Birthday to yoo, Happy Birthday to yoo-whooo, Happy Birthday to yoo. Then it was quiet as Susan cut the cake, her hair falling into her face. She searched for him with soft eyes and a pouting *mouth. As she cut the cake, there was a crescendo of claps, hoorays and giggles. And Ann Mitchison was again among the throng, a robust reassuring adult presence, handing out more cake.*

Then it was over. He was standing in the garden with a crashing headache from too much cake and ice cream and from running about with Adrian. Ann Mitchison was on the front verandah saying goodbye to the parents. And then the house was silent except for the discreet sound of Evadne collecting the cutlery and glass. Yvonne and a small girl were playing hopscotch on the patio and creating quite a scene. Susan was nowhere to be seen. Then he glimpsed her, gliding through the drawing room. She came to the window seeking him out. But someone was already there with her. It was Adrian. He was standing behind her, pulling at her hair so that she moved back into the room out of sight, not wanting it. The curtains trembled. Boyd ran forward gingerly, the movie music rising in him, Technicolor writing dripping treachery. He ran to the window and peeped in. And he saw them. Adrian was on the bed with Susan. Her shoes were off. He saw her pink socks and her reluctant eyes. He backed away into the gloom. Reaching the garden fence, he went through it and into the arms of Mavis.

'Where's Yvonne?' Mavis asked.

He darted away up the road in a panic and dashed through the little green gate. He made straight for the chintz armchair by the Mullard radio, where the music lulled him into delicious, cruel melancholia.

CHAPTER 32

The following Monday, Susan attended the Balaclava Academy for the very first time. As he entered the school bus that first morning and saw her, Boyd went into shock and had not been able to look at her, and neither could he do it in the classroom. On that day, the sun was like Babycham. It popped and shimmered and sparkled. Yellow plums, hanging heavy in the trees by the stone fence, scented the air.

When the bell for the lunch break went, Boyd bounded out into the schoolyard, out in the sun where his dreams preceded him. He burst with fledgling passions. Every movement of Susan's head in his direction, every sight of her, every toss of her hair, every flutter of her eyelashes caused the most dramatic impact, so much so that during the game of marbles with Adrian after lunch, he lost all his best marbles.

The fight took place in the dust next to the water tank outside the lunch room, beside the barren orange tree. Someone shouted, 'Fight!' long after it started. It was just after lunch, in the heat of the afternoon, when colourful parakeets screeched high in the pimento tree. He and Adrian grappled and tumbled about on the ground while black pimento berries rolled beneath them, Robert Jureidini trying to pull them apart. Fists were flying, hearts bursting, heads thumping while the big boys chanted, 'Go, Little Brookes, go Little Brookes!' And the girls in their bobby socks and brown loafers were enjoying it too – all except one girl standing close to the steps in the sun, in her new uniform. She caught his eye then lowered her eyelids and turned to Ann-Marie sitting next to her. She seemed to disapprove. After that, Boyd's fists flew, wild, desperate, as the big boys whooped, as the dust flew, as his shirt came out of his trousers, as he was deaf to the music.

It was a devastating moment when their eyes met for the first time. He tasted his own blood, salty and hot, like the blood of the heroes in the books on his bed – the *Knights of the Round Table* and Larry Red King in *The U.P. Trail* – and a sudden madness overcame him. In an instant, he had Adrian on his back in the dust; *prairie dust, on the street of Laredo, women and children watching from the hardware store, hard men in black observing from the saloon.*

Miss Robb appeared on the scene in an instant, dark arms gleaming and a ruler in her hand. She hauled them off to stand outside Sister Margaret Mary's office in the hall by the stairs, where the big brass bell lay on the heavy mahogany table. They waited, standing on one leg, next to a pink statue of the Virgin Mary, hands on their heads, the punishment stance. The smell of melted candle and brass polish hung heavy in the corridor.

Sister Margaret Mary came out into the hall, and while they trembled, she looked deep into their eyes. Boyd tried to look away but had nowhere else to look but into her. He saw himself trapped forever in the fierceness and horror of Dante's Inferno.

'You human being,' Sister said. 'You little *human being.*'

Boyd tied himself into knots and wept. He would never be perfect. He was just a human being. Sister said so.

'You stand right there and don't move,' Sister said. 'I shall deal with you later.' And she walked off, deep blue habit sweeping the floor.

Despite being damned, Boyd felt released of his pent-up anxieties. Still trembling, he grinned self-consciously at Adrian. Tears stained their faces. Adrian grinned back, his face apple-red, and drew closer so they could whisper together. Boyd was elated. His blood had been spilled. It was drama and adventure. And Susan had witnessed it.

He did not understand why the game of marbles had ended in such violence. All he knew was that Adrian had been able to do the things he could not, the very things his entire being begged him to do time and time again. He could not say the words. If only he'd had the note that was swept away by the wind at the club during the summer.

That morning, Susan's first day at the school, Adrian had spoken freely to her, spoken endlessly in animated conversation, laughed out loud, made faces, even pulled her hair. Boyd had hung back as strong emotions took hold. Even during lessons, Adrian had continued his chatter, joking, touching and making her blush. Susan always seemed put out. Just before lunch, Adrian had pulled her hair again. Susan seemed distressed but said nothing. It was in that instant that Boyd felt the mysterious rage, feelings that got the better of him. During their game of marbles, every marble he lost fuelled his rage. And his fantasies became reality. *Adrian had been playing with Susan on the bed at her birthday party. She did not want Adrian to. She wanted Boyd.* Just before the bell went, when there was no hope of winning back the special grey-eyed marbles, marbles that were her caressing eyes, marbles that now belonged to Adrian, he had lashed out.

As they stood waiting apprehensively, all they could hear was Sister Margaret Mary's angry rosaries, the swish of her garments and the whistle of the cane as she tested it. Two little boys whimpered as Sister returned. *Blessed are the meek, for they shall inherit the earth. Blessed are the meek, for they shall… Blessed are the meek.*

That afternoon, as the statue of the Virgin Mary looked down upon the class, softly, serenely, small pink fingers across her breast touching a glorious heart dripping in blood, the rain came down. Intense feelings were let loose in Boyd in the classroom of ten small desks. He imagined them, Poppy, Susan and himself, in the orchard in the rain, hot and excited. When Sister told the class to put their heads on the desk, the rhythm of the raindrops like heavenly music, he looked across the room and met Susan's eyes, briefly. They were heavenly eyes. She did not turn away. In the rain it was just their eyes, not a single word spoken between them. The rain did not stop. It played a gentle, continuous drumming rhythm on the roof and Boyd breathed the virgin scent that was in the room and loved school. It rained and they rained too, casting quick little looks over their hands on the desks at one another, wishing that the rain wouldn't stop.

CHAPTER 33

The rain didn't stop. Boyd left the school bus wet and happy that afternoon, enchanted by Susan's lingering presence and definitive scent. He remembered her in the school bus, in the classroom, every image of her: the hem of her dress as she rose from the chair, the buckle of her shoes and rolled down socks as she walked out the door, the back of her knees, the shape of her neck as she turned, her white blouse so different to the other girls'. He would see her that night, and in the morning, and in that place again in the classroom where they would relive the moment they'd shared.

But that night, Papa did not go out. He said he had never known it to rain so. Lightning razed the sky and horrendous thunder rolled. At the first thunderous explosion, followed by a ripping yellow tear in the fabric of the sky, Poppy ran whimpering under the house. The next morning, the roads were blocked and flooded. School closed.

Just before midday, Papa looked out the factory window, away from the litmus paper and test tubes on his desk. He had seen the grey sheet of water in the valley suddenly darkening everything and felt the wind, chilly, threatening, fluttering the litmus paper. He saw the frightened birds flying uncertainly, their cries like those of infant children. Papa knew that at such a time his place was with his family, not in a laboratory stinking of sulphuric acid.

The wind moaned horribly when he started the Land Rover out in the staff parking area. Heavy drops of water hit the dust like bullets, and by the time Dalphus, the gateman, let him through, dark clouds had descended. The windscreen wiper flew about madly. Out on the road, yellow floods were already rushing, taking along twigs, weeds, leaves, hubcaps, old boots, bagasse and dead wood. Papa could barely see ahead. He slowed the Land Rover to a crawl, face up close to the windscreen. The railway tracks stopped some of the rushing debris but only temporarily. Papa crossed the rails and sank into deep water on the other side. On his way home from the club at night, he just bounced across the tracks and shot onto the white gravelly road, speeding towards the bridge three hundred yards away. It was a straight run and he usually floored the gas pedal. Now, from where he sat, he could neither see the bridge nor the furious leaves of cane in their customary place on either side of the road, so he judged the distance and the direction. But he was worried. Appleton people talked about the foolhardiness of trying to cross the bridge over the Black River during heavy rain, a storm, or worse, a hurricane. Anyone who tried would be found weeks later at the river's mouth, at Black River town on the coast, over twenty miles away, bloated and unrecognisable. In a storm, the river always flooded its banks and only giant tractors dared to cross, driven by reckless men without families or loved ones.

Papa had thought that he'd be out of the laboratory, across the bridge and at the pink house well before the existing conditions had any chance of developing. He was wrong. The elements had moved swiftly, stealthily, tricking him. In the dashing rain and the swirling greyness, he couldn't see a thing. He lost direction. His judgement failed him. It was impossible to go back. He did not know where 'back' was. The only thing to do was hold steadfast to the wheel, keep the vehicle in gear and inch forward as best he could. He did not believe the river was flooded yet and that the bridge was impassable. On an ordinary day, the lowest section of the bridge was a good twelve feet above water.

Still, he regretted not having left the laboratory ten minutes earlier. A few minutes could have made a difference.

Eventually the rain slackened a bit, the howling decreased and Papa, senses invigorated, his hopes rising, began to see shapes. He was in the middle of what the road had become, a rushing river of yellow, swirling water. The canes on either side of the road were all flat on the ground, green leaves submerged, the fields an expanding lake. About thirty yards ahead, he glimpsed the black iron bridge, squat and ugly in the rain. It seemed passable. He speeded up, caution becoming his enemy, while making a mental note of his surroundings. And it was at that moment that he saw the Land Rover, a familiar vehicle but in an unfamiliar location, resting in a peculiar position. It was rain-battered and soaked, up to its wheels in the mud, at the edge of the fields, pointing recklessly into the canes. Surprised, Papa drove up, craning his neck to look. He stopped and got out, immediately sinking to his knees in water, his dry khakis turning dark. The driver's door of the vehicle pushed open from the inside and Papa, on tenterhooks, was not as surprised as he felt he should be to see Ann Mitchison emerge.

Her lips moved but he couldn't hear the words. Her eyes expressed distress. Papa stumbled forward and she, reaching out, almost fell into his arms. She was warm, very warm. Their movements seemed to be in harmony, as if worked out beforehand. Ann ended up next to Papa in his Land Rover as the wind and thunder returned, fiercely, as if in jealous rage, bringing hard sheets of thumping rain and a maniacal fog. A dark greyness had crept upon them, and the howling, like the screams and moans of animals and children, drowned out every attempt to speak. Ann was numb with fright, hands grasping at Papa's shoulders. Papa heard voices too, of Mama and his children, but he also heard other voices. He heard Ann's voice, persistent and urgent, rising above the others. He heard his own loud voice, in terrible conflict.

Papa headed straight for the bridge with Ann as his passenger. The Land Rover struggled as it mounted the ramp into the roaring torrent. He realised immediately that the river was in flood, felt at once the hydraulic pressure against the vehicle. Ann too felt the vehicle under stress, saw Papa struggle with the wheel, heard the mighty rushing, the cracking and creaking, the million voices like dying people calling out to their loved ones. All about them the thunder raged relentlessly like beating drums, crashing cymbals. Ann continued to grip Papa's shoulder, as if to draw strength. His body was rigid, eyes piercing, head snapping back at the vicious bolt of lightning striking the bridge, sparks flying out and up and down. Ann cried out, clinging to Papa. He saw, in the sudden light, the hulking shape, the crude metal uprights, the crusty rivets. They crossed the bridge. A final stuttering struggle and they were at the other side. There the mist was not as dense.

Papa pictured the scene on a normal day: a white road ascended from the bridge and continued up the slope between green pastures, ending on a plateau where the roads forked. One road went to the distant Taunton and the other to the pink house and other staff houses on the hill. Now there was no road, just a roaring torrent of yellow water, rushing down towards the river. It was impenetrable, suicidal to try to traverse it. Remaining in the Land Rover was not advisable so close to the metal bridge, a lightning conductor. They were unable to move forward or back. However, Papa knew there was a hut nearby, a two-room office, small and white and fairly sturdy, where the ranger paid wages to the labourers on a Friday. It should be halfway up the slope. If they could get there, they would be safe till the storm blew over.

'We've got to get out!' Papa shouted.

'What?' Ann's lips replied.

Papa indicated his intentions. They left the Land Rover at the side of the road, next to a stricken tree, its trunk broken, exposed and white, and braved the deep waters.

Once they got beyond twenty yards, Papa picked out the ranger's hut in its familiar place on the slope. There the rain came down in straight streaks and the water, rushing down the hill, was clean and smooth and treacherous, like glass. But it was easier to make progress there. Papa felt the weight of fear lessen as they neared the little white-washed building.

* * *

Boyd dashed to the verandah the moment the rain started. He stood looking out, feeling the growing excitement as the wind tore at the trees, as birds dashed about looking for safety. Fruit fell to the ground by the dozen and the sky grew black and foreboding and wonderful. The whirling rain crashed against the house like the drums of the coolies. The thunder rolled and the lightning flashed. Inside him, in the quiet, he shouted with joy, his heart pounding, and he wondered what Susan was doing at that very moment. Mama commanded that all the windows should be closed and shuttered, the verandah chairs dragged into the drawing room. Everyone shouted and waved their arms because their voices could not be heard. Boyd liked the shouting, the quiet shouting, voices competing with thunder and the tremendous thrashing sounds. He liked the rushing about, the impending disaster, the look of concern on Mama's face, the fear in Mavis's and Yvonne's eyes.

'This is the worse I've seen it for years,' he heard Mama say.

'It looking bad, ma'am,' Mavis panted, dragging at the verandah chairs. 'Is Hurricane Audrey come back, ma'am.'

'You mean Hurricane Charlie,' Mama told her. 'Hurricane Charlie destroyed the Palisadoes Airport and Port Royal and killed almost two hundred people. I was expecting Boyd then. It's not the kind of hurricane you want to wish back.'

In his room, Boyd raised the binoculars to his eyes and stared out the bedroom window at the unfolding drama. Down in the heart of the valley it was misty and dark and the heaviest rain seemed to be concentrated there. Unseen forces were at work, battling with earth and sky and wind. He saw figures and his heart leaped. These were familiar shapes, a man and a woman running, struggling through the rain, and he thought he heard their cries. He put the binoculars down. He wanted to tell Mama but knew that that would only make the storm worse. The house grew dark and the lights went on but he remained in the darkness of his room, breathing hard, Susan his only companion.

* * *

The door of the ranger's hut opened with one push and Papa and Ann tumbled in, awkward and close in their wetness. Papa realised that Ann had been holding onto him glue-tight in their desperation up the hill and now, in the relative quiet of the room, he tried to release her but couldn't. He was close up against the creature who, night after night, walked about in his dreams, her lips calling him to her. The storm seemed to wash away all propriety and he didn't care now, even if the neighbours could see. As he turned, pulling the door shut behind them, he saw her crying and clutching at her hair. That did it for him.

Ann started to speak, her lips blood-red.

Papa said, 'Shh.'

The room was dry. It contained a table and chair and a long bench along one wall. In the adjoining room, Papa spied crocus bags and burlap sacks, labourers' paraphernalia. These were the only objects Papa identified clearly, and the only moment that an objective calculation was made. After that, events took their turn, tumbled one into another with unstoppable force, like the storm. Once again their movements, though frantic, had co-ordination and harmony, as if choreographed. This time it was not short and they did not break apart. This time there were no kling-kling birds to frighten them into thinking they were being observed by strangers. This time no menacing dreadlocked Rastafarian appeared, no suspicious figures lurked in the darkness. This time it was long and slow and tight like pure molasses, full of heat, shocking in its intensity. They grew weak. There was only one place to go; to ground. It was hot and sweet there in their steaming nakedness, his flesh against her flesh and hers against his. They took turns on the burlap sacks and on the coarse bags, grunting and panting and crying out, and going at it again and again like labourers, falling like sheaves.

CHAPTER 34

Everyone marvelled at Papa's bravery in rescuing Ann Mitchison from the storm. Tim Mitchison rushed round to shake Papa's hand and to thank him. Papa achieved heroic standing. Mavis viewed him with the kind of expression reserved only for film stars like Joel McCrae and Randolph Scott.

'You are a star, sah,' she told him.

'But where were you during the storm?' Mama was confused, staring at Papa.

'We sheltered in the ranger's hut,' Papa answered quickly, with the sort of look that said he was lucky to be alive and that Mama should be rejoicing not interrogating him.

Boyd had swallowed hard as he watched Mama tearfully try to apply Bay Rum to Papa's chest and shoulders. He couldn't meet Papa's eye. Sitting on the bed, Papa had been strangely quiet. Boyd was quiet too, hoping that there would be school in the morning, that Susan would be seated in the school bus watching for him, that they would exchange the same secret, feverish, longing look as on that first day in the classroom. There were so many things he wanted to say to her, and he was sure there were many things she wanted to tell him. Words were not enough.

But the storm didn't go away.

Unbearably, it was Susan who went away again. Mavis reported it, with equal amounts of secrecy and intrigue. There had been *words* between Mrs Mitchison and Mr

Mitchison after the storm, *harsh words*, and Mr Mitchison had left the house overnight. Susan was now at Monymusk with her father, and Mrs Mitchison was alone at home.

Mama was speechless before the gossiping Mavis.

'Evadne say the quarrel wake her up, ma'am,' Mavis told Mama, eyebrows raised. 'They quarrel all night and Mr Mitchison say things he shouldn't say, ma'am.'

'When is she coming back?' Yvonne articulated Boyd's only thought.

'Who?' Mavis asked.

'Susan. She's always going away. She should be going to school with Boyd.' Yvonne seemed quite concerned.

'Only God know,' Mavis said and carried on with her gossiping.

As usual, Mama listened, embarrassed and wide-eyed like an innocent. Boyd was more anguished than confused. He didn't understand the complexities involving Papa and Mrs Mitchison and Mr Mitchison's going away, but he knew Susan's absence had something to do with them. Would she return? People who went away did not come back.

At dinner that night, Papa made no reference to the Mitchisons but sat stoney-faced. And because he said nothing, Mama kept silent too. The tension was palpable. Boyd, feeling desperate, curled up by the radio till way past his bedtime and heard a slow voice on the WIMZEE station singing, *Don't be cruel to a heart that's true.*

That night, while Papa was still away, Mama came to him in bed. She had pink streaks in her eyes from crying. He breathed her bedclothes smell. She did not speak as he thought she would, confiding in him, sharing with him the sad stories of the many nights, the sad stories of the unknown future. The language was in her touch. She kissed his forehead, touched his cheeks with warm hands and rose from the bed. Looking down at him, she managed another smile then fluttered her fingers at him and left the room. It all seemed so final. His heart sank. *Something was coming to an end.*

And in the morning, the quiet storm raged. The Land Rover came and went, bringing Papa from the factory to the pink house and back in silence. And at night, in the conniving darkness, it crept up the road to Ann Mitchison's house, empty of Mr Mitchison and Susan. At that time, a multitude of dark suspicions rose up in Mama. But she struck them down, every one, desperate to be wrong, desperate not to overreact, desperate to maintain her sanity.

Aunt Enid, recently returned from America and living in Kingston, visited. Mama had written to her. She had drawn apart from Theolonious Washington with grace and much credit. Her investment houses on Kingswood Avenue and Queens Avenue gave an indication of her credit. She came roaring up the driveway of the pink house in a brown and beige Vauxhall Cresta. Accompanying her was one Mr Fenton Fitz-Henley, a former RAF pilot, who had seen action during the Battle of Britain. Mr Fitz-Henley sported a handlebar moustache which fascinated Boyd. He wore a starched striped shirt, grey woollen trousers, highly polished black shoes and was extremely attentive to Aunt Enid. He had refined manners, sitting down only when the women were seated and rising every time Mama or Aunt Enid entered the room. He had serious designs upon Aunt Enid and spoke about his empty but comfortable house in South Kensington, London, where he hoped they would make their abode.

Aunt Enid brought a sunny fragrance to the house but locked herself away with Mama for serious talking. Mr Fitz-Henley sat on the verandah cross-legged, smoking his pipe and doing the crossword. Boyd sniffed at him and liked his tobacco aroma. But Mr Fitz-Henley did not engage with children. He did not see them.

And no one saw Boyd, halfway down the driveway as the morning wore on, put out his hand to take a letter from the cursed estate postman on his rickety red bicycle.

'Mawning, baas.' The postman grinned and rode away.

Boyd hurried up the path behind Vincent's room, past

the small field of ripened corn, to a spot in the shade under a tangerine tree. He was desperate for Mama not to receive more bad news. His intention was to tear up the letter so that no one would ever know what troubling message it contained. But curiosity got the better of him. The envelope was not addressed to Mama as he thought, but to Papa. Unimaginable fears instantly took hold of him, heightened and multiplied when he considered the implications should Papa ever find out. But it was too late. Trembling, unstoppable fingers tore the envelope open to reveal a lined piece of paper full of scrawly writing. The letter was from a woman called Miss Connor and came from Lluidas Vale. Boyd knew immediately that she was the woman that Grandma Rosetta had spoken about, the very woman who'd made Mama cry. He couldn't understand the letter. It was written on both sides of the paper, and the ink was smudged. But one sentence burned into his memory: *If I don't hear from you, I will see to it that your wife knows everything.*

Unsettled by the revelations, Boyd buried the letter and hurried back to the house. Aunt Enid and Mama were still closeted in the bedroom and Mr Fitz-Henley was still reading the newspaper on the verandah.

When Papa came home for lunch, he was greeted by Mr Fitz-Henley with a stiff outstretched hand and faced a string of intelligent questions about sugar production and Jamaica's future. Papa warmed to Mr Fitz-Henley at once and would have laid out his political perspectives in detail had Aunt Enid not come out of Mama's room and spoken in a low, businesslike tone to Mr Fitz-Henley, who said 'yes' a lot. Each day the woman who would become Mrs Fitz-Henley grew in his estimation. She was a formidable woman. He was a mere man.

Aunt Enid spoke to a reluctant Papa in Mama's bedroom and later, when the door opened, she came out alone. The children clung to her as she kissed each in turn, Boyd smothering his face against her reassuring breasts so dramatically and with such abandon that Mr Fitz-Henley stared in amazement.

Everyone stood on the verandah and waved as the Vauxhall Cresta drove away. Boyd returned to his room and waited, frightened for Mama, listening hard to learn what Papa intended to do. He didn't wait long.

Vincent, smoking on his doorstep with his new smile, seeing stars where there were none, heard the rattle of the Land Rover and, unusually for him, uttered a curse. There was trouble up at the house. That was why Miss Enid was visiting. He had heard them talking in the bedroom as he tended to the lilies under the window, and he'd got up and left, not wanting to know the private problems of his employers. But he did know, and could not un-know what he knew. The knowledge brought out all his insecurities. What if everything came to a sudden end? Where could he find another job? Who would want to employ such a person as him? Little things that he had come to take for granted: three meals a day, his little room next to the apple tree, his wages received in the brown envelope every single Friday. Everything could disappear just like that. He blamed Mr Brookes. His fooling around with the white woman, Mrs Mitchison, was the cause of everything. Adolphus told him things he did not want to know.

Once Papa left, Boyd joined Vincent on the steps to his room. Not a muscle in Vincent's body moved as he inhaled the intoxicating tobacco smoke. The smoke made his eye red and villainous. It left him contaminated with a strange scent that settled deep into his clothes, into his skin and into his mind. Boyd didn't speak for a while but he knew why he was there. He desperately wanted to tell someone about Susan and all his feelings, to confess about how devastingly fragile his plight was, to confess to his inability to cope with so much intimate knowledge, so much passion, such enormous urges, so much beauty, so much fearfulness. He couldn't tell Mama, not even Mavis. He could talk to Vincent because he was the Hunchback of

Notre Dame, someone to feel sorry for. Such a person would never ask questions, never have a view, would never look you in the eye and be shocked. Boyd knew he could talk to Vincent because he just didn't count. But even with that knowledge, he didn't know what to say, how to talk about Susan, how to confess. So he told Vincent instead about *H.M.S. Pinafore*, the pretty songs, the forthcoming performance and explained his part in it. Once again, Vincent thanked God. Boyd's news fitted right into his plans for Mavis. He started to count down the hours.

CHAPTER 35

That fateful evening, grey smoke from Vincent's dubious tobacco hid his face but not the piece of paper in his hand. He gazed at the programme Boyd had given him:

Gilbert & Sullivan

H. M. S. Pinafore

A production by the staff and pupils of the Balaclava Academy

The Rt Hon. Joseph Porter (First Lord of the Admiralty) Miss Skiddar

Captain Corcoran (Commanding *H.M.S. Pinafore*) ... Miss Robb

Ralph Rackstraw (Able Seaman) .... Winston Wright

Dick Deadeye (Able Seaman) .... Errol Beckford

Bill Bobstay (Boatswain's Mate) .... Anthony Darling

Bob Becket (Carpenter's Mate) .... Frederick Spence

Josephine (The Captain's Daughter) .... Verna Baugh

Hebe (Sir Joseph's First Cousin) .... Diana Delfosse

Little Buttercup .... Miss Casserly

(Soloists, Chorus and Sailors: Pupils of the Balaclava Academy).

Vincent did not know what was written on the piece of bright yellow paper. If he saw the word *yellow* he couldn't tell that it referred in some way to that same piece of paper. A long time ago, he had worked out meaning and knew that it had nothing to do with words on paper. He knew that Boyd had left for school that morning, excited to bursting. Vincent knew that it was all to do with the piece of paper in his hand, *H.M.S. Pinafore*. He had heard the songs every day, seen Boyd walking around proudly in his sailor suit, seen the immaculate white trousers, the white stars in the corner of the solid blue back-flap, the black patent leather shoes and the sailor hat. *Sir Joseph's barge is seen.* That morning Boyd had carried a small suitcase containing his costume. *I am the monarch of the sea.* He intended to change into the costume in the evening at school. Vincent understood that Papa would hurry home from work, pick up Mama and Yvonne and drive like the clappers to Balaclava, where they would join the other parents to watch Boyd on stage. *Poor Little Buttercup, sweet Little Buttercup, I.*

Vincent was impatient for dusk to arrive. He knew that sometime after the family left, Mavis would put the baby to bed. She would then be on her own in the house. *He would do it then.* A small bottle of the *John Crow Batty* lay on his windowsill. The rum had inflamed him, made him fearless, possessed of a force that terrified him. But Mr Brookes had not yet arrived. That was so typical of him – always letting Mrs Brookes wait. The wilful tobacco returned once more to Vincent's burning lips. It was four o'clock.

* * *

That morning, the telephone operator at the factory transferred a call to Papa. It was from Ann Mitchison. Ann wanted to attend the concert but not on her own. Tim was still in Kingston and Susan at Monymusk. She had made a sizeable donation to assist with the production and, along with a number of the parents, had baked cookies and cakes and made enough sandwiches to feed a congregation.

'If it wouldn't be any trouble,' she said to Papa.

Without thinking, Papa said yes. He didn't really like the idea of Ann telephoning him at work like that. The practice was fraught with all kinds of danger and he always kept the conversations very short and brusque. Later that afternoon, there were problems with the cane shredder and the main roller mills. Some of the men who operated the machines were provoking dissent and agitating for better wages. In addition to that, the cane-feeder table had been blocked, unblocked and blocked again inexplicably. Towards evening, after the situation had been sorted out, small but worrying problems developed in the vacuum boiling pans and the centrifugal machines. Papa realised he might be at the factory all evening, so to be on the safe side, he asked Moodie to drive Mama, Yvonne and Ann to the school concert.

'Of course, Harry,' Moodie said immediately, already experiencing that peculiar satisfaction of driving a car of lovely women to a concert where a dozen other charming women waited to take advantage of him.

When Ann telephoned Papa, Mr Chin's car had entered the driveway. He was there to pick up the cakes and cookies. He would take them, along with those that his wife had made, to the convent at Balaclava and drive back to Maggotty in time to pick up his wife and children for the return journey in the evening. But when he heard that Tim Mitchison had not returned from Kingston, he was put out.

'He's been delayed a couple of days,' Ann said awkwardly.

'How will you be getting to the school?' Mr Chin asked, his dark hair forever falling into his eyes. 'We could stop by and pick you up. It would be a pleasure. Please.'

Ann was about to thank him for the very kind offer and say she had already made other arrangements. But just before she replied, she thought how much more appropriate it would be to travel with the Chins. She had felt Papa's unease when he had agreed to take her, an unease she understood. Mr Chin's proposition offered the perfect way out. So, later in the day, she telephoned Papa again but got put through to the clerk, Dalkieth Hamilton.

Dalkieth Hamilton was good at taking messages. He listened carefully and wrote down, in what his government school teachers would have described as a 'good fist', all the words he heard. It helped that Mrs Mitchison spoke so clearly. He had taken several messages that afternoon and assembled them carefully on the desk before him. Walking into the senior staff offices with the little white square sheets of paper, he left one on Mr Moodie's desk and several on Mr Brookes' desk. Then the telephone rang and he raced back to answer it. He liked his job; answering the telephone, taking messages, dealing with clerical matters and never having to set foot in the cane-piece, where many of his schoolmates would spend the rest of their lives. His was a success story.

At a little past four o'clock, Mr Moodie, wiping the perspiration from his neck with a large floral handkerchief, entered the office intending to pick up some charts and his broad-brimmed hat and then leave early for home. He would then take a quick shower and get ready to escort Mama and Ann Mitchison to the Balaclava Academy. He put the charts under his arm and was walking out the door when he saw the note, in the centre of the large square ink blotter, with a drawing pin holding it down. The note read:

Not to bother about lift to school concert
Going with Mr Chin instead
Mr Brookes.

The note could only have come from Dalkieth Hamilton, clerk and message-taker. But Moodie was disappointed. He had been looking forward to carrying out his neighbourly duties. Papa wasn't in the office when he put his head round the door so he rolled the note into a ball and flicked it accurately into the wastepaper basket. His original plans for the evening were back on the table. At the factory gates, instead of going home, his car turned right towards Maggotty.

* * *

In the drawing room at the pink house, Mama looked again at her watch, the one with the tiny round gold face and the black nylon strap. Across from her, Yvonne sat on the sofa

302

in a white taffeta dress. Her black patent leather shoes, buckled at the side, were drawn up under her. She wore white socks and seemed very bored. Her bottom lip stuck out. They had both been dressed and waiting for over an hour for Papa.

In the kitchen, Mavis dried dishes while two moths flitted about the lampshade. The baby was asleep, lying peacefully on a bubbled rubber sheet in Mr and Mrs Brookes' room. Later, Mavis would place her gently in the pink crib in the corner of the room and adjust the mosquito net to make sure her sleep was not disturbed. Mavis swallowed hard, conscious of the heavy silence in the drawing room. She hoped that the lovely evening at the school concert would drive away the bad feelings between Mr and Mrs Brookes. She thanked God that she had such a good job, really nice people to work for, nice children, especially that little Boyd. She felt close to them, like a member of the family, even with the troubles they were going through. Where she came from, husband and wife, legal or common-law, fought in public. Chairs would be thrown, bottles broken, knives drawn, machetes too; neighbours had to intervene to prise fighting bodies apart, sometimes in the dusty street, and pacify screaming children. Very often there was tragedy, a woman strangled or a man stabbed. But mostly men just walked off into the night, leaving behind a wife and five children. It only went to show how decent Mr and Mrs Brookes were, that their disagreements were expressed only in argument.

Mama looked at her watch again and groaned. Two hours. Yvonne sighed and put her head on the arm of the sofa, a sign that it was close to beyond waiting.

'You looking really nice, ma'am,' Mavis said, appearing at the door. Noticing Mama's weak smile, she continued. 'You'll be the best-looking of all the mothers tonight.'

'If we ever get there,' Mama said.

'Boyd will be on the stage looking for his Mama and Papa.'

Mama got up. 'It's getting very late,' she said. In the bedroom she applied fresh lipstick and bit her lip. And then, not knowing what else to do, powdered her face again, listening with misplaced hope for the sound of the Prefect racing up the driveway.

In the drawing room, Mavis sat next to Yvonne, re-arranging her plaits, but all she was conscious of was the tension and the harsh waiting, Mama rigid and grim in the bedroom, Yvonne sullen, her dress creasing, the clock loudly ticking.

* * *

Boyd had a splitting headache. He hovered by the door watching the musicians tuning their instruments just below the stage. In the afternoon, he had snacked on grape-nut ice cream and Jureidini's cream soda, as Sister Margaret Mary steered teachers and pupils through one last rehearsal. After that, everyone had gone home – the pupils, the teachers, the carpenters, the electricians, the painters, the florists, the keen mothers and assorted helpers – everyone. Boyd felt an unusual loneliness ever since Susan went away that second cruel time. But now he felt a sudden, special loneliness because everyone seemed to have somewhere to go to and had gone to it, leaving him alone in the classroom. Soon they would all return, in their best clothes, bathed and clean.

He had waited in the deserted classroom as one of only half a dozen children who had remained at the school all day. These children, like him, abandoned temporarily, lounged about aimlessly, sometimes kicking at trees in the grounds or at the walls of the school, or peering into Sister's office which, although empty, still carried her powerful presence. They spied into corners, touched pictures of the Virgin Mary, fingered statues and looked about as if expecting Sister to suddenly appear. They wrote on the blackboard, sat at the desk in front of an empty class, drank water from a tap in the lunch room, pulled up their socks, gazed over the wall into the winding road near the school gate and wandered off among the plum trees and the gardens.

Boyd had gradually found himself on his own in the classroom, hoping to detect the scent of Susan and the *in love* Miss Casserly. He wandered about sniffing the air, the desks and the doorway. He touched Susan's chair, her empty desk, the place where she had stood and breathed, and when he was sure no one was looking, sat at her desk, caressing, stroking and sniffing the brown ink-splashed wood, searching for her scent there. The afternoon passed mostly in this way. Soon shadows of trees moved slowly across the lawn. The temperature dropped, signalling the arrival of evening and sudden fright – Mama and Papa and Yvonne would be in the audience watching him; and the Mitchisons and Susan too. She was bound to return in time for the concert. *Sweet Little Buttercup.*

The musicians continued to tune up their instruments. Before them, the audience grew. People were whispering, pointing, taking stock, readying themselves to be entertained. Sister and her staff, the big girls and the big boys and the select few parents who helped out on these occasions, took charge offstage. The smell of stage make-up, new costumes and assorted scent contrived to excite. The mothers' eyes were bright, the sound of the audience a steady hum. When Miss Skiddar appeared in her costume offstage, everyone gasped. Was this the same Miss Skiddar, their teacher, transformed into the tall, handsome Sir Joseph Porter? Little Buttercup was surely not their Miss Casserly, their *in love* Miss Casserly. She was like a pretty woman in a book, who walked and spoke and laughed and sounded like a real person. Captain Corcoran was a real burly captain, with a captain's bearing and manner, not their teacher Miss Robb. How could this be? And Hebe, Sir Joseph's first cousin, was surely not the gorgeous Diana Delfosse with red rouged cheeks. It was as if they were in a real-life film. Boyd and the other children, all sailors, all breathless, stood back against the walls, out of the way of the traffic and the flourishes of the major characters. They were in awe. From the beginning of term they had dreamt about this very evening. It was already more than they had imagined and the performance had not even begun. The sound of the crowd had moved up several octaves. Sister Margaret Mary's rosaries played a symphony. Someone, a sailor, overcome with beauty and passion, or stagefright, was sobbing desperately.

Mr Burton took his place in the audience, dressed in a light woollen suit. He was in a good mood. And it wasn't only because much of his fine work would be on display and that Sister Margaret Mary had recognised and accepted him as a man she could do business with by conferring on him the title of *School Supplier*. It was not only that he believed he had done a remarkable job for the school and the parents at Balaclava and at Appleton Estate, where his name was spoken at the club and at the dinner tables by men of importance. It was not only that he had managed, through his intelligence and his connections, to secure for his wayward nephew a reasonably well-paid position for a young man of his age and experience at the factory. It was true that Edgar had shown little gratitude and, because of some unfortunate recent domestic misunderstanding, was busy dragging his name in the gutter. But he would not allow that little blackguard to ruin it for him. He felt on the verge of greatness. And it was not only because his status had improved since he met Sister Margaret Mary. It was all of those things and a great deal more.

No one had respected him in New York, where they called him Negro and Nigger, words he hated with a passion. Sister Margaret Mary's respect was invaluable to him. It was a certain path to establishing himself in the Balaclava community, not existing at the fringes like some people he knew. Respect, because he was upright, a responsible businessman who could be taken seriously. He had had a refreshing shower, splashed on some Royall Lyme cologne, whistled as he dressed with the radio on and had walked the half mile to the school up the Balaclava road, feeling satisfied with himself. And to top it off, there he was sitting among decent Balaclava people, especially those respectable women to the left and right of him. It was an experience to relish.

Mr Burton delighted in the presence of the women around him. Only women knew how to dress and present themselves in such a way that brought elegance, sophistication and civility to any scene. Some might ask, given such thoughts, why he wasn't married or engaged in some purposeful relationship with a woman. But he didn't think like that. He liked women, regarded them as the very best suits a tailor blessed with talent could make. The suits shouldn't be worn. They were too good for that. Like the finest art, they should be displayed to be admired, coveted, be fascinated by, put on a pedestal and be written about. The wonder of women, their charms, their inexplicability, their essential goodness as the giver of life; these were the things that he adored women for and the things that kept him away from them, because, after all, he could never be good enough for any of them.

Moreover, should he be lucky enough, he knew the resulting union would be his undoing. A long time ago, on the streets of Harlem, he learned that it was men who gave him the kind of pleasure others obtained from women. It was a desire he had tried to keep at bay because it had been so difficult to come to terms with, and he had succeeded, at least until a few months ago. The young man, Jarrett, seeming lost, on the road to the train station and a new life, leaving Appleton for good, had flagged him down for a lift. He had stopped. They had talked. And one thing led to another. But he had no regrets. He had only behaved true to himself. And so had Jarrett. Fate had brought them together.

'Looking forward to it?' the woman sitting next to him asked, with a smile that could only be the product of a decent upbringing.

'Yes, indeed, ah sure am,' Mr Burton replied, his American accent rising to the fore. It was amazing how when he was among women, he always seemed to behave like a young man. It was as if he were back in New York as a youth of twenty, opening doors for well-dressed, glamorous women, tipping his hat, bowing, smiling in acknowledgement across a table, standing back in deference to allow them to pass on the street.

The orchestra started up and there was a sudden movement through the audience, like quick falling leaves, rustling of paper, respectful hissing. The lights dimmed and darkness descended like a warm, gentle cloak.

'Wonderful,' the woman next to him breathed.

'Wonderful,' Mr Burton repeated, acknowledging her and bowing simultaneously to the couple to his left. At the same time, he noted that the lights the electricians had erected around the grounds had also dimmed. Expectation rose in the audience. Necks craned, eyes peeled, every movement, every sudden rustle of the curtain on stage was quickly and eagerly noted. Mr Burton observed the audience, his eyes moving in a 180 degree angle. And they came to rest on a young man he did not immediately recognise, a young man in the shadows beyond the orchestra, in the school grounds, making his way to the back of the main building. It was when the young man appeared to climb in through a partly opened window on the ground floor of the building that he realised who it was. It was none other than Edgar. Mr Burton felt white wrath. The trouble that boy had got him into lately. The Devil take him!

* * *

Papa sat at the bar smoking, physically exhausted. He

enjoyed being at the club among the men, among kindred spirits, especially after a bruising day at the factory. He liked to see the factory in the background, the battleground, hear the distant hiss of steam, feel the heat and inhale the sugar aroma, the rum from the distillery, imagine the constant hum of power and know that he had a responsible role in that world. His role, an integral one, gave him substantial kudos. His nocturnal activities with Ann heightened his impression of himself. A phrase came to him. He couldn't remember if it was the title of a book or a film. *The Power and the Glory*. But that had to be the caption under his smiling picture, the one for posterity.

He was terribly relaxed now, having seen off the troubles at the factory and arranged Mama and Ann's safe transport to the concert. It was not an evening he had been looking forward to, certainly not one that included Mama and Ann in the same company. He felt much obliged to Moodie for standing in as he did.

Papa appreciated the club and the people there, sometimes more than he appreciated being at home, to be candid about it. The club offered pleasures that home could not. The wine-coloured, cellophane packet of his Royal Blend lay on the bar next to his nine-ounce tumbler of rum and ginger, which he fondly caressed. Men at the other end of the bar were in an expansive mood. Most had not been home yet, driving straight to the club from the factory. The tennis courts were empty. At that time of day, it was not the tennis playing crowd that lined the bar and brayed at small tables, puffing away, baring their souls, contemplating the approaching night with faces that betrayed loneliness and conflict. Few women were at the club at that time.

'Harry, you're the man I'm looking for.' It was Moodie, coming out of nowhere. He wore crumpled khakis and brown riding boots. The sleeves of his khaki shirt were rolled up and he had the look of a big-game hunter. He'd been told that before and liked to look the part. 'You need to give me a lift.'

'What the hell are you doing here?' Papa demanded.

Moodie laughed, appreciating Papa's sense of humour. He hunched over the bar, grinning and ordered a drink. 'What the hell are *you* doing here, Harry?' He laughed.

'Is it over already?' Papa asked, not smiling. He was clawing at Moodie in a theatrical fashion. 'Did you get there and back so soon? How was it?'

'What are you talking about, Harry? My car ran out of gas on the road from Maggotty and I'm late for my little rendezvous.' Moodie grinned slyly.

'What? The concert, man, the concert.'

Moodie's grin faded, slowly. 'What concert? Your note said not to bother.'

'What note?'

'Your note, Harry, on my desk.'

'I sent no note,' Papa said, alarmed. 'Are you trying to tell me you didn't pick up the women?'

'Harry, hold on. The note said, *Not to bother, going with Mr Chin instead.* Note on my desk from you.' Moodie stressed every word.

'From me? No, no.' Papa shook his head, thoughts racing. 'The note didn't come from me. Don't you think I'd know?'

'Well, I didn't send it to myself. It was Dalkieth's handwriting.'

'Christ! What did it say?'

Moodie repeated himself.

Papa knew at once that the note was from Ann. 'Jeezas. Why on earth didn't you check with me?'

'Why should I? Your name was at the end of it, Harry. I assumed Dalkieth wrote it at your instruction. You mean you didn't send it?'

'That's what I said, dammit man!' Papa imagined Mama impatiently waiting, her impatience quickly turning to astonishment, then to incredulity, to anger and then finally to revulsion as the hours slipped by. There was no way in which she would have known about the botched arrangement with Moodie. 'Jeezas,' Papa repeated, 'Jeezas.' *Mama was still waiting on him to pick her up.*

'What are you going to do?' Moodie fingered his chin.

Papa glanced at his watch, the gold flashing in the light from the bar, and got off the stool. Moodie heard the Blakeys clip-clop on the heels of his brogues. Papa demanded the telephone from the bartender. It took a long time before Evadne answered it.

'Mrs Mitchison left a long time, sar,' Evadne said. 'In Mr Chin fishtail car, sar.'

'Jeezas,' Papa said again when he put the telephone down. 'God Almighty. Moodie, quick, we're leaving. I'll drop you off at your place. Get a move on.'

As the Prefect roared up the estate road, sugar cane leaves bowing and rearing up in its wake, Moodie tried to tell jokes. Papa was silent. Halfway to Moodie's rendezvous, he knew it was no use driving by the pink house and then on to the school. By the time he got to the house and set out for the school, the concert would have been over a long time and Boyd would be waiting. He hoped that by some miracle Mr Chin, a man too kind for his own good, would have thought to stop by for Mrs Brookes. Ann herself would have thought of it. He grasped at every reasonable possibility. All he could do now was drop Moodie off and drive like hell for the school. Sister Margaret Mary and the teachers would think the Brookeses were philistines if no one turned up. It would be worse than anything Mama could throw at him. And what would the other parents think when the news got out, as it would? The family at the pink house were *Hurry-Come-Ups.* Common people. *Common people!* People unable to appreciate the importance of attending, as a family, such a civilised occasion as a school concert, such a vital moment in their child's development.

When Papa arrived at Moodie's rendezvous, the house was in darkness except for a light over the front door, illuminating green shutters partly covered in luxuriant creepers. It was Miss Hutchinson's house.

'Just a minute,' Moodie said, leaping out of the car.

The front door opened and Papa saw Icilda, Miss Hutchinson's maid, standing solemnly under the light. She had a seductive figure and they could see that her dressing gown was wrapped loosely about her.

'Where is Miss?' Moodie asked her.

'She gone to see a film show, sar, with friends. She not coming back till late. Ah was just going off to my room for the night.'

'To your room?' Moodie hesitated. Papa saw him move forward and speak in lowered tones to Icilda, who laughed out loud, a vulgar nasal snort. Moodie turned and moved hastily towards the car, grinning. He's obviously been drinking before he got to the club. Icilda stood under the light, smooth thigh exposed.

'Harry,' Moodie said, 'leave me here.'

Papa stared at him. 'I hope you know what you're doing.'

'I know what I'm doing.' Moodie smiled broadly. 'Go on, I'll see you tomorrow. Give Victoria my love.' He lurched towards the light and Icilda.

Papa drove off, scattering pebbles in the ruler-straight driveway before turning left into the long road to Balaclava. The headlights of the Prefect shot out in a powerful arc, illuminating the darkness, finding the road black and empty. Papa floored the accelerator and, above the howling of the wind, the throbbing engine, the turmoil within him, he found an intriguing peace.

* * *

'Go and get your things,' Papa said.

At the door to the changing room, Boyd met Miss Casserly hurrying away, glamorous and demure, an elegant scent floating from her. He stood still. When she got a few feet away, she started to run, her skirts and arms frivolous. Mr Burton and Edgar were just inside the room, their first words of argument bursting forth. Boyd thought they made a puffing sound, like steam bursting from a bag. At his approach, Mr Burton turned away from Edgar, the tail of his jacket flaring out like a woman's skirts behind him, and walked purposefully from the room.

'What I do is my business,' Edgar callously shouted after him. 'You live your life, I live my life.'

Just then, away from the lights, by the warm Prefect, Ann Mitchison returned to Papa. A moment earlier, she had thanked Mr Chin for his kindness but informed him that she would be returning with Mr Brookes. In the dim light, as she came to Papa, she was the colour of creamed peach, her eyes reflecting the peeping moon, her lips a rich burgundy. Papa, solid and dark, full of the essence of sugar and caramel, felt her approach. He noted her movements and the moving figures of parents and excited children, a few yards from them but a world away, under the full lights. The Prefect, in the dark, was parked under the apple tree in the schoolyard. Fallen apples lay on the ground, their skins crimson, some whole, some squashed, their torn flesh white and seeping.

'A pity Victoria wasn't able to attend,' Ann said. 'It was a wonderful, wonderful performance. Boyd was such a little sailor, such a little sailor.'

As Ann spoke, she stroked Papa's arm in consolation, for she could see his disappointment, sense his misery. Papa felt disappointment of a kind, and misery too. In that peculiar frame of mind, he manoeuvred her under the dark of the tree where there were no shadows. A large hurrying shape passed by on the other side. Eyes accustomed to the dark saw the compromising figures. Mr Burton, shocked for the second time that night, hastened away. Papa was reckless and felt Ann's own recklessness in his arms as they kissed. They had to stop, they knew it was madness, but neither took the initiative. Little mewing sounds came from Ann.

'Papa?'

313

A small shadow stood by the car. Papa broke away and Ann adjusted her dress. It was Boyd, still in his sailor suit with rouge upon his face. The small bag that he held in both his hands contained his day clothes and his sailor hat, some silver and gold paper, a pink plastic sea urchin and a sea cow.

'Boyd, get in the car,' Papa said boldly, striding forward to open the rear door. 'Mrs Mitchison's coming with us.'

Boyd pretended not to be despondent because Papa had tried to explain it all, but he was. Mama and Yvonne had not seen him on stage and Papa hardly at all. At least Ann Mitchison had been there, and he had sensed Susan's eyes upon him. Ann Mitchison's adult perfume, her unexpected presence and her observations about *H.M.S. Pinafore* kept him quiet in the car, but he felt abandoned.

All that Papa had seen of *H.M.S. Pinafore* was the lighted stage with a lot of pretty teachers in make-up and small children dressed as sailors, Boyd among them, splicing and pulling at imaginary ropes and singing. It was a long wait, after the performance was over and everyone clapped and surrounded the stage, the players receiving ovation after ovation, before he found Boyd. Parents and other members of the audience hugged the makeshift bar, sipping light rum punch while a quintet played classical music. The children and their teachers seemed to be cavorting about behind the curtains and in the dimly lit classrooms. Papa did not see, but Little Buttercup lost much of her lipstick and make-up in the clutches of a throbbing young man in the dark. She had not been able to resist him when he took her under the trees and later in a dark classroom where they thought no one could see. But they had been followed from a distance and the young man stood accused.

* * *

'What time is this?' Mama demanded.

The house was dark and it didn't seem as if anyone lived

314

there when they got home. But Mama was in her room with the light low.

Boyd witnessed Papa trying to speak.

Mama slapped Papa's face, hard. Boyd heard the sharp sound, saw Mama's crushed and wounded face. It was a self-conscious slap, embarrassing for Mama, but she had to slap Papa.

'Victoria, let me explain,' Papa said, massaging his cheek with one hand while the other closed the door firmly behind him. 'It was Moodie, Moodie!'

But Mama was so full of venom that she could barely speak.

Boyd stood still outside the door hearing Mama's voice spitting sulphur. It could not be suppressed. In his room he could taste the rouge and smell the sweet make-up, like chocolate, like the melange of creams and lotions on Mama's dressing table, applied to his face by dainty hands, Miss Casserly's hands, and remember all the beautiful things. His sleepy head was full of red lipstick drama. He had imagined Susan, in a salmon taffeta dress and white gloves, sitting in the audience watching him, felt her there, drew on the essence of her. Papa's own performance, the kissing of Ann Mitchison, confused him at first, but it seemed to be wrapped up with *H.M.S. Pinafore*. He really wasn't sure if he had imagined it, the night being so full of drama. That memorable moment had been devoid of guilt. Yet Papa's head had been bowed at the door to Mama's room.

* * *

Vincent's head had been bowed too, earlier that night. The half-smoked cigar hung from his fingers, no longer a mystery. In a back room at the rum bar in Lacovia, the men, jolly and friendly (he had grown to like them), had let him know that he'd been smoking a certain weed called ganja, which Rastafarians smoked. The men said they really should have charged him more for that special tobacco, but seeing as how he was a regular and – he shouldn't take this the wrong way – he was half-blind, they were willing to be generous.

When Mr Brookes didn't arrive to take Mrs Brookes to the concert, Vincent became agitated. But later he leaned back against the wall in his room, feet stretched full out on the striped mattress, eyes gazing into darkness as the calm overcame him. The small flat bottle of *John Crow Batty* found his waiting mouth again. The hot lick of the liquid was not madly appealing but he was beginning to appreciate it. What he craved absolutely was the impact, the sudden change in his bones, in his gut and in his head. He sipped and inhaled and inhaled and sipped, filling the room with white smoke that hung motionless. It would not be long. He felt a weight being lifted off him, calming his senses.

The notes of reproach he had already dismissed. In his lonely, bitter years, years in which he had denied himself again and again, it had been those voices that he had listened to, bowed and succumbed to. Never again. Right was on his side. It wasn't as if he were one of those raging drunks, wild of eye and heavy of tongue, pissed to the point of unconscious, incapable of reason. He had worked everything out, from beginning to end.

Mavis, once she truly understood what he was about, would be nice to him. That was what women did, put up a fight for show then give in. That was the wisdom he heard frequently at the rum bars in Lacovia and elsewhere, articulated by men, *pasture bull* men, who knew what they were talking about. He had seen that wisdom played out often enough. His one good eye peeled on Mavis's bed and on the two contorted figures there, like two stray dogs copulating, he had learned that lesson. It never ceased to amaze and frustrate him that Mavis always said, 'Barry, stop it! Stop it!' and in the next moment, with Barry in her mouth and up behind her, was ready to surrender herself to him in the most lascivious fashion. He took one last swig of the white rum, put the bottle aside and raised the ganja to his lips. He felt nothing at all.

Now that the moment was near, he was more certain than ever of the righteousness of his objective, more convinced of its legitimacy. Hearing movement in Mavis's room, he rose from the bed on flat, padded feet and peered through the hole in the wall. The light was on. Mavis had entered the room to change into her dressing gown before returning to the big house. She was sitting before the little dressing table, arms raised, yawning. He saw her spread buttocks, partly opened thighs, jutting breasts. He was ready.

When he entered Mavis's room, the radio was playing *Marianne* but he did not hear it. He only saw the outline of Mavis's body shimmering in the yellow light. And Mavis saw his sudden shadow under the light from the single bulb.

'What you want?' she asked fiercely, eyes narrowing, rounding on him, throwing her skirts between her thighs in a single motion.

'What ah want?' Vincent shut the door behind him menacingly.

He did it so surely and so calmly that Mavis froze. He took that as the sign that things were proceeding correctly. Even when Mavis, overcoming her initial shock, shot up from the chair so that it made a clattering noise and bounced off the floor, his composure was total. He had seen that kind of play between Mavis and that man Barry countless times. Mavis, for all her bluster, her feigning, which was quite impressive, wanted only one thing. Had he known it would be so easy, that he was so capable of being a *pasture bull*, he would have made his move a long time ago. Down in his balls he felt the fire and before him saw the yellow haze that was Mavis. She was dazzling now and calling his name, saying please, please, using all the words that turned him on heat.

She was against him, he could feel her, a strong young woman. He met her, man to woman, force for force, slap for slap, wrist for wrist, bite for bite. She was determined to fight hard before giving in. He would have to get her down on the ground, spread her on her back, master her. The bed against the wall was square and bright-white, the only shape of any clarity in the room. Mavis had him against the door, using knees, elbows, chest, her hot, wet breath like compressed steam against his face. She had pimento breath. He got his own knees up between her parted thigh flesh. Those mighty thighs and calves of his got to work; those ripcord-hard biceps and triceps did his bidding.

Responding to the long pent-up power in his loins, he hoisted Mavis up and, feeling the looseness of her dress about her fiercely resisting body, threw her down on the white patch of bed. She bounced. He was upon her from behind. Barry's past performances were encrypted in his head. He was programmed for the final act, the moment when Barry slid off her, perspiring, spent, his black hood slowly withdrawing, shrivelling, growing small and useless. Watching from the hole in the wall, Vincent always thought they looked like curs in the village street where he came from, fucking hard and determined, eyes everywhere and nowhere, seeing nothing, engulfed in that rigid up and down dance to the end, to the last satiated gasp.

But Mavis was behaving strangely. She had not succumbed but was raging. Under him her fleshy buttocks bucked and thrashed, her breasts swung about and she neighed. Vincent was conscious of the neighing sound, the sound of resistance. He heard it from horses in the field. One hand went round Mavis's throat, the other grasped her tongue the way Barry dealt with her. But Mavis neighed the more, full of fight, and might have had him on the ground beneath her, his rod pointing up, away from her, gorged, frightfully yearning but dying on him as she tried to put him in his place. This time he gave it everything. It was his last effort.

He rode her like a pig, driving with his full weight into her, hearing her grunt and squeal. He mastered her, shuddering as the heavens burst, as the stars rushed by, exploding, bursting in yellow, red and white flashes, winking, dying one by one until the sky turned black. As he slipped from her, the big hand round her neck loosened, her head sagged. They fell together on the bed, slow and slippery, down, down, down. The room spun, the light from the naked bulb attacked his eye. Vincent tried to rise but was so weak he had to fight, every muscle, every sinew straining, his eye popping, joints aching. But he made it off the bed, to the door, out the door and into that familiar Appleton night. He felt so weak but so gratified, aching but composed, lost but fulfilled, heading to his single bed with the stained, striped mattress. Before he slipped into a deep sleep, the kind he'd never had in all his twenty-six half-blind years, he heard, fleetingly, *I want you to take me where I belong, where hearts have been broken with a kiss and a song.*

* * *

Vincent just wished it would go away. The coolies were beating their drums down in the valley. The thumping sound reverberated in his room and he could hear their shouting, that flat, raucous sound. *What time was it?* His head throbbed with a harsh pain. Piercing torchlight beams came from the darkness, hurting his eye, streaking against the walls of his room, creating smoke, like the heat from a magnifying glass. The walls burst into white flames and he raised his arms to protect his eye. But there was a wild shadow in front of him, a dark figure in white light. A black *Duppy*. He cowered under the sheets.

'Is drunk you drunk or what?' the dark figure shouted from the white brightness. 'Is past nine o'clock! Mr Brookes going to give you a piece of him mind.'

Vincent squeezed and contorted his eye and barely made

out the apparition. It was Mavis at the door she'd just flung open. She was holding her nose and pointing at him.

'Get up and get to work, you lazy no good! You little drunkard.'

Mavis's shadow went away but the white light and the heat remained. Vincent turned his head and felt the pain. An empty bottle of white rum lay on the floor by his bed, the infamous *John Crow Batty* that only hard men drank every Friday night. An appalling stink reached his nostrils. His bed was covered in vomit. On the floor lay the half-smoked remains of the ganja. A refreshing zephyr swept through the louvres but it would never be enough to take away the realisation that he'd not left his bed since six o'clock the day before or the shame that he had even contemplated carrying out such a vile act on the young maid.

CHAPTER 36

Venom was what Miss Robb was full of that day. Her dark brows told of hidden frustrations, vile vexations, dreadful things. After the gaiety of *H.M.S. Pinafore*, she wanted discipline. And everyone was in their place. Everyone except Miss Casserly.

No one had seen Miss Casserly all morning. She had not taken the daily callisthenics and was sorely missed. Miss Robb had had to step in and put them through their paces, and it left her perspiring. The morning was very warm, even at that early hour, and it was the kind of perspiration that poured from every pore like a silent stream. Like most decent Jamaican young ladies from the aspiring classes, Miss Robb abhorred sweat and would do anything to keep it at bay. She would live in a cold country like England if she could, in order not to sweat.

She had a big, firm build, with large, powerful upper arms that were supple, smooth and shiny. She was prone to sweat, with a body like that, and kept well out of the sun and away from any strenuous activity. But that morning she had the misfortune of having to take the daily exercise classes, all because pretty Miss Casserly had not turned up. Now she was sweating like a pig and felt most uncomfortable. She could not last the day. Her only hope was to go home at lunchtime for a quick shower and a change. Until then it was hell for her and she showed it.

'Miss Robb, just a minute.' Sister Margaret Mary was at the door.

Miss Robb excused herself but returned almost immediately,

glaring. She walked between desks inspecting books and hunting for bubblegum. Her ruler made slapping noises.

'Draw a line under the work,' Miss Robb commanded, and everyone reached for their rulers. These plastic rulers were fascinating, very 1957, in Kool-Aid-red, lime-green and electric-pink, all made in America and bought at Mr Chang's shop at Siloah.

'Yes, Miss Robb,' everyone intoned.

But Miss Robb was called away again before her ruler could slap some more. This time she met Sister Margaret Mary in the hall. They conferred, heads together. Then Sister walked away, her rosaries singing, her blue skirts sweeping the floor. Miss Robb followed, her proud bottom waggling. They stopped at the entrance of the school, where the sun brightened their features. Miss Robb's arms glistened and her hair shone like splintered light. Sister's white bib blazed. They were talking to a man who held his felt hat in his hands and faced down, a sinner repenting. Boyd recognised the man as Mr Burton. Miss Robb's arms were folded. Sister held her's as if in prayer. They moved away from the door and out of sight, but not too far away, for Boyd could see their shadows against the wall.

In the hushed silence, Adrian Lees tugged at Doreen Chang's hair and blew pink bubblegum, bought at Mr Chang's shop at Siloah, made in America and outlawed by Sister. Adrian's behaviour was shocking because that very day he would be taking Holy Communion with Father John the Baptist at Our Lady of Sorrows. Wasn't he conscious of the watching eyes of the Holy Ghost, the all-seeing, all knowing God the Father? He could be struck down!

But it was Mr Burton who was struck down in shame, even though Sister said he was not to blame, that he couldn't be held responsible for the sordid behaviour of his reprobate nephew. Miss Robb thought differently and kept her silence to show it, because she knew what Sister did not know, could never know. She'd never really appreciated Mr Burton. *Him and his American ways.* He could do what he liked in America. Balaclava was a decent place with nice people. Not a place for *buggery.* She said nothing when he left, *pretending* to be ashamed, *pretending* to show outrage, *pretending* to be apologetic, holding his hat in his hand and everything. Well, he could pretend all he liked. He and his nephew were the same. She could see through men like that, always covering up for bad behaviour. He may have Sister fooled but not her. He couldn't possibly remain the official school supplier now. And she told herself that she would make certain that Father John the Baptist knew the facts. Father John the Baptist would know what to do.

Miss Skiddar came to the door of the classroom just then. She was still Sir Joseph Porter, with all the drama of *H.M.S Pinafore.* At the sight of her, the children heard *I am the Monarch of the Sea* and lived all their emotions again.

'Those for Our Lady of Sorrows, follow me,' Miss Skiddar said, moments before Miss Robb took her aside and whispered long into her ear.

'No!' Miss Skiddar said, shocked, two elegant fingers at her mouth.

'Yes,' Miss Robb confirmed solemnly, darkly.

Boys and girls made their way out of the building towards the stone fence at the far side of the school where the spreading guango tree stood. Beyond the stone fence lay a large field full of tamarind trees. Our Lady of Sorrows faced the field, a small brick church with a cross made of multi-coloured glass set into the brick. Full of the facts, Miss Skiddar, guiding the children, did not know it but Mr Burton was making his way to Our Lady of Sorrows at that moment. They would get there before him because they were taking the shortest route across the field.

Mr Burton took the long way, up the Balaclava road, walking slow and dignified. He did not understand Edgar. That boy was determined to ruin him, by every lascivious deed. But he would pray for him.

Miss Robb looked grimly at her watch. It was close to the end of the school day and the trees were beginning to rustle and stir. And something else too. Boyd heard it first, before the other children. Beautiful singing. The sound of heavenly voices and piano music swept down the hill from the convent. The nuns were singing a song of forgiveness and of hope. They sang throughout the afternoon. Even when the children flowed from the classrooms with their brown grips and satchels and said their goodbyes, the nuns' voices floated into the wind. The sisters were still singing when the school bus arrived. Mr Chin was downcast and Sister Margaret Mary's lips were tight and creased and white. The school bus was quiet and Boyd felt the tension of not knowing.

Diana Delfosse and another of the big girls sat behind Mr Chin, whispering. The chill wind that blew through the cane fields in the valley entered the school bus. It made Diana Delfosse furrow her brows.

'Your skin's just like a naked chicken,' someone said, pointing at Carol Lees, who was milky-white with freckles.

'White like salt and speckled like fish,' someone else joked.

'It's goosebumps,' Carol replied.

'Chicken bumps,' the voice returned.

'Shut up,' Carol said.

Mr Chin had spoken not a single word since he drove out of the school gates. He spun the large steering wheel, changed gears, stepped on the brakes and said nothing. He looked right and left, his slick black hair swinging about. He turned on the trafficator, which flicked out like the tongue of a lizard on heat, waited at the railway crossing and said nothing. He accelerated away from the railway crossing, up the smooth asphalt road, telegraph poles flashing by, and still said nothing.

That afternoon, Mr Chin, for the first time ever, drove up a side road (it may have been to deliver a message from Sister). He drove where the frangipani grew wild, where the estate shade trees were not pruned and where Boyd had once been with Vincent.

Mr Chin drove up to the Bull Pen where the bachelor men of the estate lived, where Four Aces cigarette butts lay all day in ashtrays on the long verandah and where the smell of the men hung carefree and suspect. It was the Bull Pen of the unfortunate Mr Dixon, set on fire by the scorned woman, Ruby. The Bull Pen of the rampant Edgar, who had *a baby in every parish*. No one understood it at all. A mist hung over everything. Boyd remembered the shrieking, the arms thrown up, the skirts flouncing, the rushing about, but most of all the pain in the woman's voice. It was Miss Casserly, just visible through the mist on the verandah of the Bull Pen. She was hurt.

The school bus was quiet for a long time. All the splendour and the beauty of *H.M.S. Pinafore,* the lovely songs like *Sweet Little Buttercup*, could not save her. After a long silence, someone, it might have been Junior Chin, uttered two words that echoed into the mist.

'It's Edgar,' he said.

* * *

It was the dastardly Edgar who caused the hurt and the silence in the school bus that day. And they never saw pretty Miss Casserly again. People said she went by BOAC to London, or moved to Kingston like Patricia Moodie. But no one knew. And Mr Burton went away too, after Father John the Baptist learned the facts from Miss Robb.

At first people said he left Balaclava under a cloud. They said he packed up and left for Water Lane, Kingston, to set up a new tailoring establishment in a busy place where people minded their own business and where no one knew his name. He no longer cared to live in a small place like Balaclava, with its lovely white houses, vines running up their walls, its clean air and cloudless skies, which he loved, and the sedate gentility of the place. He no longer cared to be a Catholic. Catholics were fair-weather friends, unconcerned about human beings like him. People said that the young man, Jarrett, who learned his trade from Mr Burton, also set up shop in Water Lane and changed his name. They were not allowed to live together among nice Balaclava people.

In the end, it was Corporal Duncan who brought definitive news. A hideous body, hanging from a rope, was found in the back room of Mr Burton's old house. It was the flies and the stench that finally gave it away. Mr Burton's body had been hanging there for sometime, in the centre of a room full of pictures and mementos of his life spent in New York and Balaclava. The police didn't think there were any suspicious circumstances.

CHAPTER 37

That Friday afternoon, Boyd, in turmoil, his heart hurting for Miss Casserly, his senses consumed with the absent Susan, left the school bus and went straight to Mavis. When the *cauchee* sounded four o'clock, Mama, looking out the window, saw him rush from Mavis's room and enter the house. She pretended not to see him as he went down the hall and into his own room. *He was only a child, just a little child.*

In his room, a feeling of desperation came over Boyd. It was the end of another week and there had been no news about Susan. The Mullard radio reported the death of someone called Christian Dior and sad music accompanied the reports. He was convinced that this time they would receive news of Susan's death. So many people had died: Grandpa and Grandma Pratt, Mr Donald Lee of Water Lane, Mrs Ten-To-Six, the hundreds of people in the Kendal Crash. He sobbed, self-consciously, knowing that it was over.

Eyes misty, he looked out his bedroom window, half-expecting to see another frightful postman come riding up. But the driveway was empty and in soft afternoon sun. No postman appeared. What he glimpsed was a familiar flash of colour on the road through the trees, a fleeting emotion. Desperation flew out the window in that instant. What he saw was the pink figure of Susan. She was on her bicycle, alone. She had returned. His heart leaped and he cried out, unconsciously. Happiness: the taste of lollipops, the sound of music, the scent of lilies assaulted his senses.

Glancing swiftly behind into the hall and seeing no one, Boyd mounted the windowsill and dropped like a stone into the carpet grass. Then he was up and running on weak legs, already breathless, towards Barrington's bicycle propped against the garage wall. Poppy was ahead of him down the driveway, himself feeling the blazing excitement. So furiously did Boyd ride that he came out ahead of Susan down the lane where the roads forked. Barrington's bicycle, made from scavenged Raleigh parts and put together at the factory by one of the mechanics, was old and skeletal, without mudguards, but it could go. As Boyd flew by at unimaginable speed, Susan gave a startled cry, as if set upon by small birds, and braked at the side of the road. But Boyd could not stop.

The bicycle had no brakes and could only be stopped by exerting extreme pressure on the pedals or, as Barrington liked to do, extending one leg on the rear wheel and pressing down hard with his crepe-soled shoe. Boyd applied as much pressure as he could till his calves and thighs bulged and weakened, but could only slow a hundred yards away. By then, he was facing the Mitchison's house, whereas Susan was near the entrance to the pink house in the opposite direction. It would be difficult to turn and ride back, passing Susan a second time. But that was what should be done; it was what his inner voice whispered, what Poppy wanted, bounding back and forth and waiting for him to follow. Seeing her after such a long time, in the heat of the moment, had made him reckless. But the extreme exertion had sapped his bravery. He stood astride the bicycle in the middle of the road. To ride back was impossible. What could he say? What would he do? The only voice he listened to told him not to go back.

Susan now turned and was riding towards him, yellow sun shafting through the trees, stroking her as she advanced. It was as if she rode through yellow bands of flame. Boyd continued up the road away from her, past her house, past the Dowding's house down the lane, past the paddocks where the Dowding's horses were, down the incline to open ground beyond the houses, where large poinciana trees grew. He got off the bicycle under the trees, out of anxiety but also out of exhaustion, and sat on the soft grass among the bright pink blossoms of the poinciana. If Susan should come riding down the grassy slope, which he desperately hoped and prayed she would, he would be trapped, unable to get away; in the perfect place.

If only it were possible to speak the words he could not speak, it would be so easy. He envied Yvonne, speaking so effortlessly. Words simply flew from her, light and gay, like small birds. His words were like muscovado sugar, heavy, crude and slow, demanding so much of him that in the end it was better to say nothing. He knew, from kindergarten, that his words were only feelings. He wanted Susan to be at that place with him where words would not be necessary, only feelings, looks, a gentle touch.

Her scent now descended like falling pollen. She came down the slope at girl-speed, steady and upright, holding the handlebars purposefully, the familiar image of his days and nights. This was not a dream, lovely feelings in a classroom or a distant vision. Around him the scarlet blossoms shifted. They too felt the end of the long waiting. Boyd hoped, a fleeting, cowardly hope, that Susan might turn at the very last moment and ride back up the slope. But there was a silence, the silence of unseen movement. Poppy barked. Boyd glanced over his shoulder. Susan had put her bicycle down carefully nearby and was walking over, her strap-shoes rustling the grass. Poppy went to her as if approaching an old friend, tail in a smooth round motion, and sniffed at her frock. Susan bent to stroke him, and if she blushed it was unseen as poinciana-pink reflected everywhere.

'Poppy!' Boyd commanded. Poppy, chastened, ran back to stand by him, waiting, head slanted, eyes quizzing.

Susan seemed slightly embarrassed, waiting too, lips parted. Boyd, tongue-tied, looked away towards the river, desperate for inspiration. Susan looked there too, hands behind her back. Neither of them spoke. There was a tension, a creeping suspense, a loud silence pounding the air. Still looking towards the river, Susan sat down on the crimson carpet in the way that girls do, carefully, arranging her dress beneath her in a choreographed movement. Poppy sat down too, paws out, head up, eyes inquisitive. And the steam from the factory went *Shh! Shh! Shh!*

'It was the same at Monymusk,' Susan said softly, sitting so that the inner part of her elbows turned out, as girls do. She observed Boyd with full, dedicated eyes.

Boyd turned to face her, bracing himself, squeezing his toes together in his shoes, managing a wan smile. But he looked past her eyes. It was not the same as on that day in the classroom when she had been just a few desks away. To look into her eyes now, close up, would mean seeing everything – and she would see everything too, his naked thoughts. He very much wanted to ask if she was going away again. But he said nothing. He wanted to touch and play with her as he did with Poppy but he did nothing.

'Do you like the sound of it?' Susan's smile was sympathetic, reassuring.

'Yes,' Boyd said. 'It comes out of pipes. The steam can't get out and it's trying as hard as it can, very hard. And the pipes would burst if it couldn't get out.'

'It's talking. It's saying *Shh! Shh! Shh!* Silence! Silence! Just like at school.' And Susan laughed.

Boyd laughed too. 'And when it gets out it makes a big noise. That's when the men go for their lunch.'

'The noise used to frighten me. When I was little. Before I was used to it.'

'It's very loud. Louder than an aeroplane.'

'It's like a big dog barking.'

'No, like cows mooing.' Boyd's brows wrinkled, correcting her.

'Like big cows mooing.'

'Like big cows mooing and mooing because their baby

calf drowned. They turned their backs and the baby calf fell into the river.'

Susan hesitated. 'Sad mooing.'

'Moaning mooing,' Boyd replied in acknowledgement. He felt warmth moving from his toes to his fingertips. The sluggish muscovado sugar was turning to runny honey. He felt the lovely heat radiating from Susan. He saw the poinciana-pink on the ground all around, the buffed pinkness of her, and even Poppy, sitting still on the ground, reflected shades of pink. It was a special moment, emboldening Boyd, making him draw closer, not be afraid. But still the right words would not come. In his hurry he had forgotten the new note of thirteen special words, secreted away in the chest of drawers in his room. But he knew, at that moment, how difficult it would be to present such a thing as a note. How would he do it? It wasn't simply a matter of handing it over.

'Mummy sometimes puts her fingers in her ears when it's very loud. Evadne says it's a siren.' Susan lifted her dress and crossed her legs on the ground, making a space for Boyd as he moved closer, pretending to fuss about with Poppy, who backed away playfully.

'It's a *cauchee*,' Boyd said.

'What?'

'A *cauchee*. It's what Vincent and Mavis call it. And Perlita, our maid, called it *cauchee* too. Papa fired her.'

'Did she steal money?'

'No, only fish. And Papa fired Agatha and Adassa and Melvyna too. Mama didn't like it.'

'Oh,' Susan said.

There was a pause. After a time, Boyd asked. 'When you were sick in Mandeville, did they wash you down with Bay Rum?'

'Sick?' Susan seemed puzzled.

'Poorly,' Boyd said. 'When you were very, very poorly.'

'No.' Susan drew out the word. 'I wasn't sick. Mummy sent me up there but I wanted to come home.'

'Oh,' Boyd said.

Moments passed again, no one said anything. It was a wonderful silence broken finally by Susan.

'I watch the moon, and the moon watches me,' she said.

'Me too,' Boyd replied, excited, having always thought that only he had a relationship with the moon. It looked at him between the pillow and the bedclothes at night. The face of the moon was soft and friendly and it knew his secrets and his thoughts.

'It follows me around at night.'

'And me too,' Boyd said, unbelieving.

'I look at it from behind my bed,' Susan told him.

'And I watch it hiding behind the curtains,' Boyd replied.

'And the windowsill. And it still watches me.'

'And from in the trees when you think it's not there anymore.'

'Sometimes I run round the house and back again, and still it's there,' Susan said, quite animated.

'It looks at me through the window!' Boyd exclaimed.

'And at me too!' Susan grew quiet, breathing rapidly.

Again there was the silence, broken again by Susan, eyes bright.

'I see the flowers wake at night,' she said.

'And I watch the roses open. The pink ones, the red ones and the white ones.'

'So do I.' Susan clapped her hands, breathless.

'I lick the flowers,' Boyd said, head turned to one side, 'when they're all wet with the dew.'

'Lick the flowers with your tongue.' Susan smiled at him, impressed.

Boyd smiled back. He felt as if he'd spoken a million words and that there was no need to say more.

They were sitting close together now, almost touching, and Susan's scent was strong and good, like lawn grass in afternoon heat. Boyd could see the scene as from a distance and found himself looking at her brown hair, the hair he had witnessed shining in the sun that first day. It was fine, straight hair that moved easily, sometimes flying up across her face at the slightest puff of wind. He saw her arms and the tiny, downy hairs there, the shape of her body upright on the ground, and returned his gaze to her hair. He could not bring himself to look at her lips or her eyes, paths to the inner secrets, to the music place, the place of revelation. His gaze went to the ground and moved along it till Susan's shoes, brown and buckled, came into view. His eyes moved upward to the hem of her dress then stopped. All the while, fresh streams of scent came off her, lollipops, Paradise Plums, a sweet drug in the heat. Feelings of distress taking hold, Boyd got up suddenly and ran to the hedgerows where the bougainvillea blazed. He was going to do it at last, without the words. A posy of pretty petals, fresh and bright, filled his hand, their sap wetting his fingers, foretelling delights to come. He approached Susan, her peachy neck reaching up, bent down and gave it to her.

Only he knew the taste and the feeling. Only he knew the ever-present hunger that words could never describe. Only he knew about the licking and the sucking. It was like weeping when the music spoke to him in every secret place. Showing Susan was easier than talking. He did not want to think of Mavis and Barry, Miss Hutchinson and Mr Moodie. Their troubling images threatened to bear down upon him. But Susan was pretty music and lollipops and she prevailed.

The initiation lasted as long as it took the shadows to creep beyond the hedgerows. There was no protestation, only supplication, like taking Holy Communion for the first time. White birds called out on their way down to the river, their shadows passing swiftly on the ground. Some craned their necks to look at the small boy and girl and dog, heads together in the grass. And they heard the *Shh! Shh! Shh!* from the factory.

'Shh!' Susan whispered, showing burgundy lips, fingers dark from the feast.

Boyd, the close contact giving him enormous confidence, fixed his gaze upon Susan's lips now. Lovely music filled his ears. Susan's lips were dark red, in sharp contrast to the speckled pink of her cheeks. Now that, at last, he had reached her lips, he cast stealthy, oblique glances in the direction of her eyes, the final, vital spot. A river wind came up and enveloped them. His hand went down, her hands went out, Poppy barked, and Susan fell, laughing, sideways into the grass. He saw the back of her knees, the crumpled part of her dress, leaves in her hair, and inhaled the sweet heat smell.

Shh! Shh! Shh! said the steam, and in that moment he saw her eyes, appealing just like the prized marbles in his bureau drawer, sheltered under lowered lids, speaking to him, a voice of music, caressing his heart. Boyd, frightened and elated at the boldness of the music, suddenly grew weak and fell forward into the grass, into the poinciana-pink.

* * *

That Saturday, they sat still on the verandah of the pink house, legs dangling from the chairs. Flame-coloured butterflies pestered the forget-me-nots at the base of the verandah. Susan had a crimson hibiscus, like a motionless flame, in her hair. They hadn't spoken for most of the time they'd been sitting there, and Yvonne, eager to intrude, had been banished to the pantry after several unsuccessful attempts; banished in the face of total silence. She could not understand the silence, why they didn't speak to her, why they didn't speak to each other. On her way to the kitchen, she heard Mavis singing: *One, Two, Three, heh! Look at Mr Lee, Three, Four, Five, heh! Look at him jive. Mr Lee, Mr Lee, Oh Mr Lee, Mr Lee, Mr Lee!*

Papa, returning to the factory after an early lunch, paused to take in the scene on the verandah. He nodded to Susan, by now slouching in the chair, lashes low, and gave Boyd a hard look, for reasons only he knew.

'I want you to behave yourself,' Papa said, walking away, brown Nugget shoe polish and Royal Blend cigarette odours flowing from him.

'Yes, Papa,' Boyd said to Papa's departing back, displeased at being reprimanded unnecessarily in Susan's presence.

'Why did your daddy say to behave yourself?'

'He always says that.'

Susan laughed. Boyd giggled and watched the Land Rover take Papa away. When Yvonne returned to the verandah one last time, having sung *Mr Lee* ten times with Mavis, neither Susan nor Boyd was there. Susan's crimson hibiscus lay discarded on the tiles. Yvonne looked across the lawns, far out beyond the periwinkle fence to the beginning of the orchard where all the trees came together. But she could not see them.

They were under the orange tree in the deepest part of the orchard, where Mavis's voice could not be heard, nor Mama's. It was quiet there except for their urgent breathing and Poppy's impatient little barks.

'This is like in the forest,' Susan said, delighted, looking into his eyes, thinking of the Forest of Arden, Orlando and Rosalind.

'In the garden,' Boyd breathed, thinking of Estella in the garden at Miss Havisham's house. He held her hand. *A girl's hand.* He had never held one before. It was soft and warm and strange, a wonderful feeling. They laughed and Boyd ran off. He led her deep into the green closeness of the garden where the pink women were.

'We're in the Forest of Arden,' Susan said. She wanted to let Boyd know that he was Orlando and that she was Rosalind. She wanted to tell him that they'd just found each other and would be friends forever. But she knew that there would be time enough for that in the days and weeks ahead.

They touched in the apple-green sunlight in the orange-warmth, where no one could see them, lips upon lips under

335

the trees as yellow butterflies alighted and departed. Susan spluttered and laughed, her hair in her eyes, and wiped her lips with the back of her hand.

'No, that's not how they do it,' she said. And she attempted to show Boyd how. She had seen ten times more films than Boyd, including *Gone with the Wind*, although she had fallen asleep because it was too long.

But Boyd was not interested in being shown how. He knew how to suck and lick flowers, how to seek out the soft, delicate heart of them. He was in the music now and her strawberry jam lips were within reach, their scent fruity, delicious. Susan, recoiling so that she stumbled backwards into the long grass, thought Boyd was quite taken with his playing. But she was getting used to him. And now that he was beginning to look directly into her eyes with that new look, the one that made her giggle, that look that made her see other worlds in his eyes and lose her bearings a little, she was willing to lie in the grass with him at her side looking up into the trees and into the sky. It was as fascinating and lovely as on that first afternoon in the open space under the poinciana trees when they first did it.

Yvonne, feeling perplexed from trying, after what seemed like ages, to fix Patsy's hair, was singing, *Little Sally Walker, sitting in a saucer. Turn to the east, turn to the west, turn to the one you love the best.* Looking out the window into a patch of lime-green, she saw them. Quickly she put Patsy down on the bed, her pink legs in the air and her corn-coloured hair spread out on the pillow. She saw them rushing behind the house, Boyd grabbing at Susan's hair as he often did at hers. Susan ran, arms thrashing about wildly, her light-brown hair shimmering and tossing, trying to get away. Yvonne knew that her only escape was to run to Mama. But poor Susan did not know. Boyd chased her into the deepest part of the garden. Yvonne skipped down the hall and out the back door, across the porch and out into the sun. *Ride, Sally, ride. Turn to the east, turn to the west. Turn to the one you love the best.* She knew of the inner

336

reaches of the garden where Boyd and Poppy spent a lot of their time. But it was difficult to get to because it meant penetrating deep into the green foliage, behind the overhanging leaves and vines and twisting things. It meant crawling and twisting and squeezing and having scented blossoms brush against her hair and block her path. She saw them disappear into the greenery. Pink and purple flowers fell to the ground in front of her and fresh leaves, from their urgent scrambling, carpeted the ground. She heard them ahead of her, Susan's little squeals, Poppy's barks, Boyd's *Shhs*. But she lost them and it suddenly got quiet. All about her were shadows of the deepest green. She felt afraid and turned back, saplings lashing at her as she ran out into the yellow sunlight where the sky was wide and open. *Little Sally Walker, sitting in a saucer.*

Later that day, as she sat on her bed looking out the window, she saw them again. *Ride, Sally, ride. Turn to the east, turn to the west.* They still chased but had swopped places. Susan was now chasing Boyd and Yvonne could hear their laughter. They were heading straight behind the garage. Poppy galloped ahead of them, his tongue loose and floppy at the side of his mouth. Yvonne knew the spot behind the garage where they could be found. Boyd and Poppy were always there, just sitting and looking into the sky, something she didn't understand. She sprang from the bed, into the hall and out the kitchen door before Mavis could say one word. She rounded the corner by the garage and didn't immediately see anyone. Then she barely made out Susan's pink gingham frock caught in the sun from under the shade of the jacaranda. Boyd was with her, and Poppy too. Poppy's tail wagged. Neither Boyd nor Susan moved, but they were doing something. Susan was giggling. Yvonne could hear the playful, urgent giggling. Boyd was sucking her mouth just the way he sucked the flowers. She had seen him do it before and Mama had said he would be sick because some of the flowers were poisonous but Boyd never listened to Mama. She had seen him do it when he thought no one was looking. She would run and tell Mama. The mouth he licked the flowers with was the same mouth he was sucking Susan with. Just wait. Mama would know what to do about it. Boyd would have to wash out his mouth with Lifebuoy carbolic soap. As Yvonne turned, Boyd turned too. He saw Yvonne's yellow dress vanishing round the corner of the garage, her white bloomers bright in the sunlight. Poppy barked.

'Boyd's sucking Susan, Mama,' Yvonne said breathlessly to Mama in the bedroom.

'What's that, darling?' Mama said, gently brushing pollen from Yvonne's hair and drawing her towards the bed and into her arms.

'Boyd,' Yvonne said, swooning into Mama's warm caress. Mama's cuddles were so pleasurable that Yvonne often found herself falling rapidly into a doze. She sank deeper into the caress and, like a puppy, worked herself into the most comfortable position, stroking Mama's arms and kissing her neck. Baby Babs slept quietly nearby.

'Did you comb Patsy's hair?' Mama asked, enjoying the cuddle herself, feeling the infant warmth of her little calf. She kissed Yvonne's forehead and pulled her close, massaging her back with little rhythmic paddles of her hand.

After a slow, indulgent sigh, Yvonne said, 'No, Mama. She's a bad dolly, a very bad dolly.' And she quite forgot about Boyd and Susan, who were by then no longer behind the garage or in her thoughts.

But Yvonne was not the only person to see Boyd and Susan. Vincent saw them arrive behind the garage from his lookout in the bushes. When he saw their puckered lips meet, he had rubbed his eye in disbelief. The things children got up to. His own mother would have taken the whip to him if she had ever caught him doing a thing like that at their age. It was all to do with that rock and roll music, and *jive* this and *jive* that, and *see you later alligator* business. Just look at Boyd and Mavis on the bed, and now just look at him with that little white girl. Foreign music and foreign people were responsible. He didn't understand any of it, the modern world. Take the white woman, Mrs Mitchison. Adolphus, her gardener, told him, with his white rum breath, that she went to bed every night naked, with not even a nightgown to cover herself up with. Imagine that. Not even a slip or a long shirt. Not even the poorest, most ignorant *Neaga* people slept naked. She drank and smoked like any man, drove a jeep at breakneck speed and never spent any time during the day at home the way that the respectable women like Mrs Brookes did. But Mrs Mitchison wasn't the only one. Young *Neaga* women, the hoity-toity ones, were just the same. They went to *foreign* and came back just like the white women. *Just like the white women*. But the maids, especially the younger ones, were worse than all the white women put together. They were as loose as whoring women, no shame, no self-respect. And yet they behaved as if they were not common people, as if they were better than him. It made his blood boil.

Vincent had seen Boyd and Susan run off towards the back fence where the meadow began and daisies lay like yellow stars against the lush green grass. He had taken that path to get to Adolphus when he didn't want anyone from the house, especially Mavis, to notice. If they carried on along the fence, they would emerge into open ground below the paddocks where the poinciana trees were. From there it was a short walk up the slope to the Mitchison house. When he saw the children creep under the fence and run along it in the meadow, Boyd chasing hard behind Susan, he knew at once that they were taking the roundabout way to the Mitchison house.

Boyd, breathing valley air and feeling the sun brisk upon his skin, glanced at the coolie barracks in the distance and shouted, pointing. Susan, turning and caught off balance, stumbled. But Boyd was upon her in an instant, like Kid Colt Outlaw leaping off his horse at a bushwhacker or like a tiger leaping at its prey. He dived as though watching himself from a distance, as if he were on show, as he sometimes dived upon Yvonne on the lawn in front of the house. Unlike Yvonne, Susan did not scream out for Mama. Susan just fell into the wild daisies and laughed so much that she couldn't speak, while Boyd wrestled with her, more overcome than she was. He could not believe that there was a real girl with him among the daisies under a blue sky with the sun on his back. He had spent many hours at that same spot with Poppy but had never known such delight. It was the sensation of Pepsi a thousandfold more. Their wrestling stopped and they fell backward, arms and legs flung out. The sky was clear, not a cloud anywhere, so that Boyd could see the mountains in the distance. And Susan's breath was upon him, sweet and hot.

'Chase me round the hill,' she said, rising, tugging at him, running still in her. 'Chase me to the trees, into the forest.'

Boyd, wanting her to stay with him in the grass forever, to prolong and give life to the new feelings flowering in him, said, 'Look at the coolies. Look at their cooking smoke.'

'Into the forest!' Susan cried, her scent drawing him to her. When he hesitated, she said, 'Watch me like the moon, watch me like the moon.' It was hopeless to resist.

The thing was, Susan was the radio, a magical being. She was music and sun and rain and everything. She was Mama's caresses, the first taste of sweet potato pudding, a long lick of ice cream in the afternoon, sunshine falling through leaves. She was the smell of evening primrose and a dozen other fragrances. She was all of those things and many others. She was a living sensation, a girl with girl hair and girl looks and girl scent. And she was there with him, within him, throbbing, dazzling, exciting.

* * *

Evadne had had a half-day off from work and was returning

340

just after three o'clock that afternoon. She was late and had taken the back roads, criss-crossing the cane fields, passing behind the coolie barracks and hurrying along the river road with its dried yellow mud and tractor tracks. Looking towards the hill, she could see the white walls of her employers' house. To get to it she would have to clamber under the fence. To do that she would have to gather up the hem of her dress, ease herself carefully under the barbed-wire, walk across the open space surrounded by poinciana trees and up the hill to the paddock road.

Evadne gathered up her floral cotton skirt and wrapped it expertly between her legs. With one hand holding up a rusting strand of the barbed-wire and the other holding down a second strand, she lowered herself in the space between and made it safely to the other side. Then she hurried towards the crimson poinciana carpet below the first tree. She was late, not because some demanding matter had detained her, but because Mr Mitchison was not at home. He was visiting Frome Sugar Estate, a responsibility that fell to him as assistant general manager. Mrs Mitchison, the very best kind of lady to work for, was not demanding or officious in any way whatsoever. If Evadne was late by an hour or so, all Mrs Mitchison said with a warm smile was, 'Oh, there you are Evadne.' There was nothing she wouldn't do for that woman. Mrs Mitchison made her feel, not like an ordinary maid, not like a common labourer, not like an *ol' Neaga*, but like a real person. Evadne was late because Mrs Mitchison, willing even to make her own tea, did not mind. She thought that Evadne's family responsibilities were far more important than returning to work on time.

Evadne heard the birds crying as they made their way to the river. But she cocked her head. Her ears detected another kind of crying. It came in on the warm air. She turned about. It was a voice she knew. There was nothing to see but the pulsing bougainvillea bush, stationery trees, creeping shadows and the green sea of sugar cane beyond.

She heard the cries once more and turned about, squinting carefully at the bougainvillea, past the bleached wooden fence and along into the deep grass. Then she saw them.

She saw them beneath the poinciana tree at the other end of the field, partly hidden by the sprawling bougainvillea bush, in crimson on the ground. It was the little boy, Boyd, the Brookes boy, the one Mavis talked about, she saw first. Evadne could not believe what she was seeing. Boyd had Susan on her back in the grass. Susan's dress, one that Evadne had hand washed often enough, was raised above her legs, and she was fighting. Her legs, golden-brown in the sun, flicked up and down. She was crying out. The small dog was barking and rushing about, his little tail briskly wagging.

The sin of the flesh.

Evadne remembered her church, the ravished lives in the pews and the thundering, warning preacher. Images of her past came to her, images of childhood and adolescence. She remembered the bush and the hot grass and the dust and the pain. She remembered being held down in the cane-piece by boys from the district on her way home from school. No one had heard her cries and she had hollered like a braying donkey, fought like a wild dog. She was only fourteen at the time and attending Teacher Fraser's school at Taunton. So she knew what boys got up to, no matter how young or how old. It was always nasty and vicious. *The eternal lust of the flesh.* They were only after one thing. And big-shot people were no different. *A decent boy like Boyd.* She didn't want to speak about something that didn't concern her but she knew what Mr Brookes, the father, was up to. She had seen him and Mrs Mitchison more than once on the verandah, talking and drinking and getting familiar when Mr Mitchison wasn't there. She blamed Mr Brookes for whatever was going on, not Mrs Mitchison. Nevertheless, it wasn't her business. Big-shot people could get up to whatever they wished. But Susan was a child. *A innocent lickle chile.*

Evadne wanted to run up to the children lying in the

grass and tell them to stop at once. She wanted to invade the scene of fornication and put an end to it. She wanted to shout *Stop it! Stop it!* and drag Susan back to the house. But she felt restrained. A lifetime of service in which her voice didn't count kept her in check. She did not want to make the mistake of involving herself and then have the fathers, Mr Brookes and Mr Mitchison, the ones who would ultimately decide it, round on her. You could never tell what big-shot people would do when it came to their own children. Before she knew what was happening she would be fired, kicked out of the house, put on the road again to fend for herself in an unforgiving world. Maybe if she talked to Mrs Mitchison alone. Mrs Mitchison would want to protect her lovely little daughter. *Such a nice chile, with such nice hair.*

Thirty or so yards from the children, Evadne stopped, concealed behind a tree. When she heard the dog bark, she stepped forward, saw them break apart and rise in one motion, Susan pushing her dress down and laughing. The small dog was upon Evadne immediately.

'Stop it!' Evadne shouted as the small dog sniffed at her dress. 'Stop it!'

'You frightened us,' Susan called out, face flushed cherry-pink.

Boyd brushed dried grass from his hair and clothes. 'Poppy, come here,' he called.

'Chase me up the hill!' Susan cried again. She was as frisky as a pony.

She broke away and ran off, Boyd chasing hard. Evadne saw them breach the base of the hill and start up it. Boyd caught Susan halfway up, grabbed her around the waist and brought her down. They tumbled and rolled a good ten yards down the hill and came to a stop, legs in the air. Then they were up and running again, poinciana blossoms falling off them, arms and legs flailing, their voices like foreign music. This time Evadne saw them vanish up the paddock road in a flash of colour, heading for the orchard.

She wished she could tell someone about what she'd seen. Maybe if she mentioned it to Mavis…

Over at the Dowding's house, Mrs Dowding sat at her window viewing the pink poinciana-strewn field. It was a scene she appreciated, especially when the sun was dying and the whole valley was painted in a pink light. She hadn't been at the window two minutes before she saw the children, and she watched their every move with growing uneasiness. Like Evadne, she knew that any close contact between a boy and a girl meant only one thing. It would be impossible to tell Victoria what she'd just seen. These were children. *Children.* How could she describe a thing like that? She would mention it in no uncertain terms to Gerald, who would mention it to Harold Brookes.

That night, when dinner was over, when the amber light shone from living rooms onto lawns, when the *peeny-waalies* were not yet out in abundance, when maids found the time to gossip, Mavis listened again to Evadne's shocking story.

'Repeat what you just said.' Mavis stood erect, her hackles rising.

Evadne, taken by surprise at Mavis's vehemence, repeated her words.

'Clear off!' Mavis spat at her.

'But, ah'm only telling you what ah saw!' Evadne pleaded.

'Clear off, you ol' nasty *Neaga!*' And Mavis stormed away.

344

CHAPTER 38

A frivolous breeze, low on the ground, made Mama's ferns tremble. Barrington, home for the weekend, sat in his room, dignified, reading a book called *Far from the Madding Crowd*. He would much rather have been at Munro so that he could steal away with one of the boys, ride out to Hampton where Geraldine Pinnock was a student and meet her in a field nearby. He had done it before and intended to do it again.

Boyd, behind the garage, felt the breeze up his legs. He was dreaming of his rendezvous in the garden with Susan. His secret note, rewritten on a fresh piece of paper that night, lay in his pocket. He was going to give it to her to consummate their union. She was expecting it. He had promised it the day before in a moment of breathtaking bravery.

'Did you read *Great Expectations*?' he'd asked Susan out of the blue.

'Pip and the convict!'

Boyd was astonished by her reply, hearing no reference to Estella. But it should have been so easy to say the words. Instead he said, 'I have something to show you.'

'What?' Susan came near.

'Something.'

'But what is it? What is it about *Great Expectations*?'

'I'll show it to you tomorrow.'

'But what is it?'

Boyd smiled weakly. 'Tomorrow.'

'Will you show it to me in the forest?'

'Yes,' Boyd said, knowing that the path was laid at last.

As he waited behind the garage, he saw Papa approaching fast through the gate at the periwinkle fence, mouth hard, brows dark. He knew that walk. It was full of aggression; a walk that would end in punishment for someone, end in the assuaging of Papa's fury, end after a fiery minute of pain delivered by a whipping right hand.

Boyd stayed behind the garage and watched as Papa mounted the steps to the verandah. Something had happened. Papa had heard something, probably at the Mitchison's. What had Vincent done, or Yvonne, or Mavis, that had made its way to the Mitchisons and assaulted Papa so? The last time Boyd had seen Papa so smouldering was the time he came home and gave Barrington a severe whipping for sending notes to Geraldine Pinnock.

He went further behind the garage, kicking at the frangipani blossoms on the ground. Deep inside him, sublime music played but his hands trembled because the music could not obscure overtones of distress.

'Boyd!' Yvonne appeared at the corner of the garage. 'Papa wants you.'

'*Me?*' It was as if he had suddenly slipped over a precipice and was hurtling down onto sharp rocks below.

Yvonne saw the look of alarm, the futile efforts to conceal terror. She knew his body language well, his tricky attempt at disguise, having employed them herself: the looking away, the studied casualness, the feigned appearance of innocence implying that, whatever the matter, it wasn't important because it had absolutely nothing to do with him.

'What did you do?' she asked sympathetically.

'Nothing.' Boyd's answer came quick and defiant. But in that single word a lifetime of Papa-inspired fear expressed itself. Yvonne, full of understanding, patted his arm and stared into his eyes.

'Papa said, "Where is Boyd? Go and get him!"' she said in a gruff voice, imitating Papa. 'Did you let out the car tyres?'

346

'No, I didn't.'

'What then?'

'Nothing.'

'Did you forget to flush the toilet?'

'No!'

'Then what?'

'I didn't do anything.'

'Did you shoot one of the little humming birds with your slingshot?'

'Don't be stupid.'

'Did you break a window?'

'No.'

'Did you throw stones at the kling-kling birds?'

'No.'

'You interfered with Papa's important papers in his desk!'

'No, I did not!' Boyd was especially vehement, remembering the letter.

'Well, Papa's going to beat you,' Yvonne said. 'Papa talked to Mama and they're waiting for you. They're looking very serious. Mama was even crying.'

Yvonne fell silent after that. Boyd sniffed, feeling terribly wronged. Whatever it was had all been decided. He was guilty. Mama's crying put the seal on it. He wondered what it was that he had done to make her cry. They entered the house together, Mavis smiling, not knowing what had happened as they passed her in the kitchen, until Yvonne told her.

'Papa's going to beat Boyd.'

'Beat Boyd for what?' Mavis asked. 'Boyd, what did you do?'

'Nothing. Nothing.'

Mavis dried her hands rapidly with a towel, took off her apron and followed them down the hall, lips pursed, Evadne's outrageous story fresh in her mind.

Boyd stood before Papa in the drawing room, not in the pantry or the dining room or the hall, where Barrington and Yvonne received their punishment. His sin was clearly monumental. Papa was sitting forward in the armchair, very calm, Mama next to him in a corner of the sofa, her face pained, drained, shattered. She couldn't hide her feelings and he could tell instantly that she was under a great deal of stress. The words were written on her face for all to see: *Boyd, what made you do it?* Boyd saw the agony in her eyes and began to cry. He was frightened because Mama was frightened and because everyone knew that he had done something horrible. It was the look of despair in Mama's eyes. He had done something so monstrous that Papa's anger had been restrained. It was so terrible that they were prepared to talk to him first, as if to a prisoner who, in the harsh reality of the moment, is expected to confess to unimaginable crimes before certain execution. What could he have done? He thought rapidly. Pictures in black and white flashed by. It couldn't be about the letter from Miss Connor. No one knew about it. The only thing that he could think of was the day before when he had looked at the pictures of the women in the encyclopaedia while eating Jell-O. Some of the Jell-O, crimson and lovely, had dropped onto the page. He had wiped it away quickly but not quickly enough. A smudge remained on the pink flesh of the women. Was that what they'd seen, the damage to the books, and now knew that he had been looking at the pictures? But why had Papa come from the Mitchisons? Or was it the Dowdings? Was it something to do with the Dowdings? Had Dennis said something about *Tropic of Cancer*? Was it to do with school? He looked from Papa to Mama and glimpsed, through his tears, the blurry figures of Barrington, Yvonne and Mavis crowding in at the door.

'Boyd,' Papa said slowly and sadly, looking directly at him, as if genuinely trying to help, 'I want you to tell me the truth – the truth – you understand?'

Boyd didn't know how to answer. *The truth? About what?*

'Did you hear me?'

'Yes, Papa.' For the first time he glimpsed the dark-brown leather strap lying between Papa's thigh and the arm of the chair, like a resting snake. It had never seemed so thick and capable before. It said *values and principles* over and over in a steady adult voice, the kind of voice that turned innocence into guilt.

Mama was crying. Yvonne came into the room, walking mechanically, head down and cuddled up to Mama. She too was crying.

'Boyd,' Papa started again. This time Boyd could see the deep lines on his forehead. Papa did not look at him. 'What did you do to Susan?'

There was an intake of breath at the door. It was either Barrington or Mavis, or both. They now came further into the room, mouths agape.

'Answer your Papa,' Mama said, eyes red.

'Nothing, Papa.' Boyd's hands were behind his back, wringing, squeezing, twisting. He stood on one leg.

'Are you going to stand there and tell me that you did nothing?'

Boyd stuttered. 'No, Papa.'

'Well then, tell me. Stop crying like a baby. What did you do to Susan?'

'Nothing, Papa.'

'So everybody is lying and you're telling the truth?' Papa picked up the leather strap and made as if to rise from the chair. For the first time, Boyd noticed that the brown of the strap was very much like the brown of the bakelite Mullard radio, silent in the corner.

'No, Papa.' Boyd's stifled whimpering filled the room.

'If Boyd say he didn't do it, he didn't do it,' Mavis said suddenly, stepping forward. 'Look at him, he not lying. If that Evadne say something to Mr and Mrs Mitchison about Boyd, she lying. Ah know the woman, Mr Brookes, she a liar and a fraud. Mrs Brookes, you can't believe a word that woman say, ma'am. She – '

'Okay, Mavis,' Papa said calmly, indicating the door.

Mavis returned to her place at the door, folding her arms, chest heaving.

'Boyd,' Mama said, dabbing at her eyes with a small damp handkerchief. 'Tell Mama, did you do anything to that little girl, to Susan?'

'No, Mama,' Boyd said, crying afresh.

'Nothing at all?'

'No, Mama.'

'Well, what were you doing with her yesterday?' Papa demanded.

'Playing, Papa.'

'Playing? Where?'

'In the garden.'

'Where else?'

'Behind the garage.'

'Behind the garage? I don't know why you cannot play on the lawn in front of the house where everyone can keep an eye on you. What were you playing at?'

Boyd felt that it should be easy to explain what they had been doing but no words came. There were so many words to describe what they had done but he couldn't find the right ones. He could only look helplessly at the faces round about him, waiting to hear the awful things that their questions suggested. Papa took the silence as more evidence of his guilt. He rose fully from the chair this time. Boyd backed away.

'Hiding behind the garage,' Papa said. 'Doing what?'

'We, we, we – '

'Speak up.'

'We…we were looking at the coolies.'

'Looking at the coolies? Oh, so you crossed the fence. Did I not tell you never to go over the fence?'

'Yes, Papa.'

'Then what?'

Again Boyd could not answer. He could not tell about his singular pleasures. He could not tell what it meant to look up into the sky and feel small like a baby in a womb, smell the wind as it came sluicing through the grass, see Susan's eyes like pretty marbles, inhale the scent of her, her arms, her hair, her sweat, see her pinkness and her gingham dress and the green of the grass and the yellow of the sun. It was impossible to tell Papa about his big feelings, his secret thoughts, the inner sanctum where the music came from, the part of him that had gone out to Susan. That was what Papa wanted to know, the very things he himself could not talk about. Even if he wanted to tell Papa he wouldn't know how because he only knew it in feelings, not words.

Papa raised the strap. Boyd saw the ugly writhing brown snake and looked Papa straight in the eye. Papa felt the stare and blinked. He seemed to grasp the meaning but camouflaged his reaction.

'Boyd,' Papa then said, 'I do not want to beat you, but you have to tell me the truth.' He returned Boyd's stare.

'Pardon me for asking, Mr Brookes,' Mavis spoke up again as the tension dipped. 'But what did Boyd do? What evil did the poor chile do?'

Papa looked round the room. Only Mama knew what he knew.

'That Evadne is a liar Mr B,' Mavis spat the words. 'Ah don't trust that *ol' Neaga*. She is a trouble-maker.'

'It's nothing to do with Evadne,' Papa snapped, losing patience. He returned to Boyd, stooping down so that he was at eye level. 'Boyd, tell me. Did you try to molest Susan in the field by the Dowdings' house?'

'Lawd, have mercy!' Mavis cried out.

Boyd stuttered, looking confused.

'Mavis, please!' Mama was exasperated, though Mavis had only expressed Mama's own shocked feelings when Papa first told her the news.

'But who could say such a thing, ma'am? Who could say such a thing, sar?' Mavis was beside herself.

'What is *molest*, Mama?' Yvonne asked in the sudden ghastly quiet, eyeing Boyd with new interest.

351

'Mavis, take Yvonne into the pantry,' Mama said. 'Make her some tea.'

'But Boyd didn't do anything,' Yvonne pleaded as Mavis took her arm and led her away. 'He was only licking Susan.'

Mama and Papa looked up in one sudden movement. Barrington cleared his throat and pushed his hands deeper into his pockets. He had been listening to the interrogation with quiet amusement and knew instantly that the situation had taken a turn for the worse. At first he had been shocked to hear Papa say he did not want to beat Boyd but now he knew that Boyd was dead for certain. He felt genuine pity for his little brother, who was still standing on one leg, looking very small, hands behind his back, fingers writhing, face damp with sweat. There had been no immediate change in his expression on hearing Yvonne's words. But the expression on every other face in the room had changed.

'What was that?' Papa swung about. Yvonne turned round too, not exactly aware of what she'd said. Papa reminded her. 'What did you say, Yvonne? Tell Papa.'

'Boyd didn't do anything, Papa,' Yvonne now said, carefully repeating her words and looking from Boyd to Papa and then to Mama.

'What else did you say? Help Papa, Yvonne. Help Papa.'

'I saw them behind the garage, Papa,' Yvonne said. 'Boyd was sucking Susan and playing.'

'Sucking Susan?' Papa's face turned very dark. He glanced over at Mama, who had a hand to her mouth. 'What do you mean?'

Mavis had come back fully into the room. She stood, arms folded, and stared with astonishment at Yvonne, daring her to speak.

'Boyd was sucking Susan, Papa,' Yvonne said slowly, like a child chastised, as though she were the little culprit standing in the middle of the room. 'He's always doing it in the garden. I told Mama. Mama told him to stop sucking the flowers because...but...but he was only sucking

Susan...' Yvonne's voice trailed off. She realised she'd said too much.

Boyd now faced the floor, not looking at anyone. Something private had been expressed in a public place. He felt as if they had reached in and torn his heart out. Words read at another time came to him, the words of the convict among the graves in *Great Expectations*, who ordered Pip to "get me wittles...Or I'll cut your heart and liver out." He had had nightmares imagining the act. Now they had cut his heart and liver out.

'He's been sucking flowers since Worthy Park,' Mama said with an air of exhaustion.

Papa gave her a long, withering look that said *I blame you for this*.

'He don't mean no harm, Mr Brookes,' Mavis pleaded.

Papa turned to Boyd with a strange expression, as if seeing a fascinating object for the first time. Barrington, too, surveyed Boyd with unreserved respect, not because of the eating of the flowers but because of what he imagined Boyd had been doing to Susan. Now he would have to get a copy of that *Tropic of Cancer*. Yvonne turned from Mama to Boyd in slow motion but Boyd wasn't there. He'd fled from the room. In his sudden flight, he stumbled into Mavis, hesitated, her arms clutching, folding about him, but he resisted the temptation and flew through the dining room.

Out into the green he ran, the glad sun licking his face. The sky was open and wide above him. Friends were in every tree, in the fields and mountains. Birds flew free, unfettered, telling of *liberté* and *fraternité*, of lives untainted, unencumbered by worry, never accused or vilified, never having their hearts and livers cut out, never suffering the tragedy of cold incomprehensible condemnation. He ran with Poppy behind the garage to be out of sight of the pink house.

But behind the garage, Poppy got in the way. His tail and legs, uncoordinated in his excitement, became obstacles. Poppy did not seem to understand, thinking it was about play, thinking that it was just another day. Boyd turned on him. He aimed a vicious kick, with wicked intent, and felt it smack hard into Poppy's soft underbelly, felt the warmth of him there, and felt the instant regret too, but it was too late. The kick raised Poppy off the ground. He yelped in surprise, not accustomed to violence, landed on his feet and looked up at Boyd, a streak of red already breaking the whiteness of his eyes. In his recklessness, Boyd kicked again, not once but twice, catching Poppy hard on his front paws. Poppy yelped, confused, overcome with fright and pain, and stumbled nervously on his side, legs flaying the air. He got up timidly, limping badly, and stood to one side, looking down as if ashamed, as if guilty of some hideous, unspeakable deed. In silence, Boyd saw Poppy look at him as at a stranger, saw him drop his head and limp awkwardly back towards the kitchen and Mavis, who was hastening down the steps in pursuit.

He ran out from behind the garage, the tears blinding him, crawled under the fence, into the meadow, down into the river road, across it and into the canes. He ran into the river, to the mountains and over them to Maggotty, into the white Maggotty Falls and over the hills to Black River. He ran far away and still he was running, to the Parisian night in the Evening in Paris blue bottle, into the pretty pictures in the books and into the music. He ran into the glorious warmth of the Mullard radio where Papa did not exist. He wanted to get far, far away, beyond himself, and deeper into himself, to hide.

Boyd ran to the periwinkle fence, remembering halcyon times spent there when neither he nor Poppy knew the vicious pain of hurt. The Mitchison Jaguar roared by, pebbles smacking its undercarriage, white dust pouring out, forcing him back into the hedge, leaving him space and time only for a transient glimpse of Susan's face at the window, hair tussled from a sudden turn, lips parted, looking back. She waved at him furiously. Mrs Mitchison, seeing this, waved too. As the car sped away, Susan, eyes burning bright, threw herself at the rear window and continued to wave from there. Boyd waved back weakly and, as the car vanished, turned and ran deep into the gardens.

* * *

He returned home late that evening, so exhausted and torn that he was ready to confess to anything. He saw the shadowy figures of his family hanging back, heard his mother's distressed wimpering and Mavis's painful cry. Papa took him to the bedroom without a word and locked the door. All feeling went out of Boyd. It wasn't happening to him but to someone else, someone in a book. And Papa wasn't Papa. He was someone else too. And Boyd viewed the scene from the comfort of the chintz armhair.

A monstrous man wielded a heavy leather belt and a small boy wet his pants. The small boy didn't feel the pain of the blows, only the humiliation. No sound left his lips. And the monstrous man wasn't, in the end, so fearful. He was a comic, dark figure, dancing about the room to rhythmless music, music that the boy had never heard and would never hear again. When it was over, the boy stood in the warm puddle, his legs stinging, desperate to clean himself up before his mother and sister entered the room. And, as the man left the room, their eyes met, and the boy saw the hidden secrets behind the man's eyes. He saw that the man was full of immeasurable guilt.

'Stay in your room!' Papa bellowed. 'And don't ever let me catch you playing around with Susan Mitchison again. You hear me?' And Papa was gone.

Boyd waited. He thought Mama would be the first to rush in and cuddle him. But no one came. Not Yvonne, because she blamed herself for his troubles. Not Barrington, because Papa was in no mood to be trifled with. Papa would be returning him to school and he wanted him to be in as reasonable a mood as possible for the long ride back to Malvern. Not Mama, because she did not want to tilt Papa over the edge and, in fact, the charge against Boyd was quite monstrous. Not Mavis, because she felt she had overplayed her hand and did not wish, for the time being at least, to appear too understanding. She planned to comfort Boyd when she took him his supper. Mr Brookes had already fixed her twice with that calculating look of his, trying to work something out.

The shadows drew in earlier than usual that evening and the air streaming through Boyd's bedroom window was forbidding. He saw no hint of setting sun, only the dreadful chill and the creeping darkness. Not even the swallows were about. There was no sound of their shrieking. And there was no sign or sound of Poppy. Distraught, Boyd wished desperately that he could hear Poppy bark, that the seared picture in his head was not the one of the small dog limping away in pain. The only sound that came into the room came from the Mullard radio: music meant only for him, poignant, compassionate, soothing. He closed his eyes and felt the music's warm embrace. When it was over, he heard only his own close breathing. But the music remained with him, his only companion.

When Mavis appeared with the wooden tray, long after the others had had their dinner, she closed the door gently behind her. They exchanged looks as she put the tray down. Boyd's lips trembled. She went straight to him, caution thrown to the winds, noting his silent weeping, his outstretched hands seeking and took him fully into her arms. It would have been wicked not to.

'Ooh, ooh, sugar,' she said softly, kissing his forehead and cheeks, feeling him snuggling deep into her, weeping stifled. 'Ooh, ooh, sugar. You didn't do nothing wrong. Not a thing. Hush, hush, hush. Mrs Dowding don't know what she talking about.'

Boyd, hearing the kind words, clung tighter.

He wanted comfort sucking, Mavis could tell, for his mouth made little darting movements towards her titties.

'Supper is on the tray,' she said, pointing. 'You must eat something, sugar. Look. Fried breadfruit, ackee and bacon. And nice hot chocolate with Betty condensed milk.'

Boyd had been cold, without a heart or liver. Mavis was warm and near, a soothing place. She felt his hands reaching urgently between her breasts and could stop it. But she hesitated. She knew Mr Brookes had already left with Barrington but his huge presence was still in the house. She knew that Mrs Brookes and Yvonne were on the verandah entertaining Mrs Dowding. Footsteps on the floorboards would be heard if anyone approached the room, giving her enough time to compose herself before the door opened. One brief, tender suck could do no harm.

Quickly, furtively, she hurried her bursting brown breast to his lips, his eyes full of hunger and thirst. He buried his face into the lovely flesh, the heat returning to him. Mavis, feeding his mouth and quite carried away, could not pull back. It was not going to be brief. A wisping sound at the door turned her head. In a panic she saw the slit where the evening breeze had cracked the door partly open. Releasing her breast, she hurried to the door and, looking down the hall to make sure there was no one there, closed it. Then she returned to Boyd. But this time she was more anxious and kept looking over her shoulder. Only one minute more and it would be over, then she would kiss his cheek and be on her way. The evening breeze streamed through the window bringing amherstia and oleander.

Mavis did not see but felt, catching her breath, a shadow enter the room. Looking up, she saw a face at the window, black against the paleness of the evening sky. It was Vincent, silently watching, his one eye fixed upon the scene before him. He seemed strangely drunk, head swaying like a zombie. Mavis swung round. Unsucking Boyd's lips from her breast as tenderly as she could, she walked directly to the window and pulled it firmly down, drawing the curtains across it, unblinking. She shut Vincent out.

Vincent blinked. He had been hoping beyond hope for a miracle from Mavis, some scrap of kindness, pity even, after his disgrace. Time and time again a child had gone where he, a grown man, had never been. He was undone.

He had always been shut out. But he wouldn't be shut out anymore.

Sitting with Mrs Dowding on the verandah, Mama had tried to listen attentively. The older woman had come as a good neighbour. Mrs Dowding talked about how boys would be boys but that they needed careful watching. When her Dennis was just a child, she never let him out of her sight *once* and now look at him. He was a decent young man beginning to take his place in the world and able to respect womankind. But she did not come to remind Mama about sordid things. She had come to talk about her nephew, Andrew, recently appointed to London University as a lecturer. She had the letter with her; red, white and blue airmail, written in purple ink, page after page of it. But Mama was unable to listen. She kept seeing Boyd, standing on one leg, scared to death, repeating, 'No, Papa.' She had let him down. She hadn't sprung to his defence and believed him as she knew she should. She couldn't listen to the sound of his beating and had closed her ears against it. She blamed Papa. He had bullied her, making her believe everything he told her about Boyd and Susan, making her silence her own voice, making her crush her misgivings.

Mrs Dowding's penchant for jumping to conclusions and getting it wrong was well known and scandalous. Mavis had behaved more like a mother should, and yet she, a young, inexperienced woman, had never given birth, did not, could not know motherly attachment to an offspring. Mama felt ashamed. Listening to the dull, prejudiced, interfering Mrs Dowding drone on and on, all she could think of was Boyd alone in his room, his suffering doubled by his incarceration. Abruptly, Mama excused herself, leaving Mrs Dowding to turn her attention to an insistent Yvonne lurking by the door, and walked barefoot on Mavis's highly polished floor towards Boyd's room.

Mama got to the door and, seeing it slightly ajar, hesitated. Like a child, she swallowed hard, peering into the room, bracing herself for the ordeal to come. She did not expect to see Mavis there. But there she was, sitting on the bed, facing Boyd with her back to the door. There was no mistaking the young woman's stance, the position of her body, the movement of her arm. She was cradling Boyd's head to her bosom. Mama stared, understanding at once the private, silent scene before her. She looked away but then returned again to the cuddling figures, making sure she knew what she saw. She thought, bizarrely, that it could have been a painting of a mother tending her child. But it was not a picture. This was no figment of her imagination. Her eight-year-old son was at Mavis's breast. Mama swallowed hard again, and feeling a cold sweat and the onset of overwhelming fear, tiptoed back to the verandah, where she detained Yvonne. She hoped desperately that Mavis would end it soon and that no one else would see what she'd just seen.

CHAPTER 39

At about ten o'clock the next morning, Mavis entered Mama's bedroom.

'Letter for you, Mrs B,' she said. 'And it's in a nice white envelope, ma'am. Not a bad telegram this time, ma'am. It's about time you have some good news, after everything.'

'Thank you, Mavis,' Mama said, as calm as it was possible to be, not facing the young woman. Mavis, smiling cheerfully, left the room.

The envelope was addressed to Mama in a spidery, unschooled hand. She studied the writing, the formation of her own name, the blotted ink, the peculiar placing of the stamp, the postmark. She could never understand why people didn't line up the stamp with the sides of the envelope so that it fitted squarely in the corner. She did not want to open the envelope. The scent of the letter-writer (Mama was certain it was a woman) and all the unwelcome odours of the place she came from would fill the room, contaminating everything. Mama was thinking of a small district in St Catherine, Lluidas Vale, and a woman whose name had never crossed her lips. It had come to pass. Enid had always told her to *confront* him. But Enid never understood her position, neither did her own mother, thinking it misguided. She prayed to God that the letter had nothing to do with the news she feared, coming on top of everything.

Mama sat by the window, where she had an unimpeded view of the driveway. She wanted to make sure she had enough time to secrete the letter and compose herself, should Papa suddenly appear. Her hands trembled as she opened the envelope. Something fell out. It was the picture of a girl, not more than seven years old, smiling sweetly and shyly into the camera. The picture was taken at a photographer's studio in Spanish Town. His details were stamped clearly on the back in embossed letters.

Mama looked towards the ceiling as the flesh of her face dropped and sagged. But she did not gain any solace from the ceiling. Deliverance was not there. The little girl had Papa's defining features: the broad forehead, prominent cheeks, square-cut jaw and strong, even teeth. And she had dimples of the most pleasant kind in her cheeks. She was very pretty. Mama studied the picture. She thought, *Poor thing, it's not your fault*. It was the deceit, the dishonesty, the hypocrisy and the mess that they were now all mired in.

Mama read the letter slowly, trying to understand each word from the strange hand far away in Lluidas Vale. Papa was probably at the factory, or at the club at that very moment, lecturing about *values and principles*, decrying low morals, highly critical of people like Edgar and others of his sort.

Again and again she read the letter, wishing it away. She knew she couldn't possibly talk to Papa about it, not immediately. When things settled down, she would go to him, when he was in a reasonable mood, and hope for a civilised discussion. But she wanted to delay that moment for as long as possible. Turning away from the window, she wished, for one rash moment, that she was Pamela Moodie, asserting her authority as a woman and wife. And for just one more blinding moment she wished that she was reckless and could dance the mambo.

* * *

As Papa got into the Land Rover that afternoon, Vincent approached.

'Ah leaving, sar,' Vincent said, red-eyed.

'Leaving what?'

'The work, sar.'

Papa gave him an uncomprehending look. Gardeners, yard boys and maids did not leave just like that. They were fired, kicked out, and departed with their sordid little *bankras* or grips and the clothes on their backs. Vincent's effrontery was breathtaking.

'Where are you going?' Papa asked, amused.

'Ah leaving, sar,' Vincent repeated, suddenly irritated, feeling rising resentment of his employer for his privileged position, envious of his continuing fornication with the white woman, bitter at his own miserable failure with Mavis.

'Don't be a damn fool, man,' Papa said, slamming the Land Rover door shut. 'Make sure you're here when I get back tonight.' And he drove off.

Vincent was left standing in his own shadow, angry at the offhand manner in which he had been treated, *had always been treated*, by the callous man in short trousers. He had little respect for Mr Brookes. The man was no good. From the very beginning, he had treated him like dirt. He blamed him for everything.

An hour later, at the factory Papa sat with his head in his hands. A letter lay opened on his desk. It was from a certain Miss Connor. She had written to him at the factory, addressing him as *Mr Harold Brookes, Scientist, Appleton Estate* in her stumbling handwriting. Served him right, boasting to her the way he had. She had taken him literally. He had been drunk that fateful night but remembered telling her with a slurred tongue, "I'm the *schientist*, the brains at the factory." But the biggest blow (he'd raised his hands in despair when he discovered it) was that she had also written to Mama. No wonder Mama had been silent during lunch. He'd thought her silence was to do with Boyd and that disgraceful business with Susan. But he was wrong.

Papa got down off the stool and walked up and down

362

the office. The reality was impossible – to stand before Mama and accept that all along he had been one of *those people*, not the man she knew. The *humiliation*. Men who took their lives he had always considered absolute cowards, not deserving of understanding. Now he knew that putting an end to it wasn't so unthinkable.

He was going to have to go home and face Mama. Once he explained everything to her, she would understand. Thank God she was not the unforgiving kind. The very qualities he thought were her weaknesses would now be the saving of him. And while he was about it, he intended to do something else. The business with Ann: he would have to put an end to that too, however difficult. Maybe a transfer to New Yarmouth estate was the answer. Through the laboratory window and across the valley, he saw the two houses against the green hill: the pink house, his home, and the white house of the Mitchisons under its crimson poinciana canopy. He would talk to Ann that night.

That night, Vincent left the pink house. He went empty-handed, just the clothes on his back and a small bag of the Rastafarian weed, the ganja, in his pocket. He had spent the afternoon cleaning his tools, oiling the lawnmower, sharpening his machete till tiny bits of steel littered the ground at his feet, hoping all the while for salvation. But it was no use. Work, the one thing that gave him a sense of purpose and the only enjoyment he knew, could not take away the feeling of worthlessness. He was without respect, pride or dignity, the things some men killed for, or would die for. Mavis's position at the pink house and Mr Brookes' indifference meant that he could have no place there. And yet, his entire working life – and a happy one it had been too with the Maxwell-Smiths – had been spent at this house at Appleton. Poppy limped after him for a time in the warm, cosy darkness, but seeing that his face was set in the distance, returned to sit on the porch, wimpering all evening, as small distressed dogs do.

And that same night, Miss Chatterjee answered a knock

at her door. When she saw who it was, her face brightened, but just as quickly showed alarm. Her maid, Adassa, a deadly gossip, normally gone from the house at that hour, was still about. She was fussing with brown paper bags in the kitchen while her uncle, Mr Gordon, waited patiently on his bicycle in the dark by the porch. Hastily Miss Chatterjee manoeuvred the visitor into her bedroom, dismissed Adassa for the night, locked up the house and drew the curtains.

CHAPTER 40

That very same night, he came out of hiding, looked into the distance and saw no living thing. He came out of the man-made cave in the cane-piece by the riverbank and crawled up the side of the hill. He'd been living on sugar cane, mangoes and oranges, gathered only in the dark. But he craved meat, cooked food, a swig of rum to put the fire back in him. These could only come from the houses dotting the lower reaches of the valley, now in complete darkness, except for one. A solitary light shone, yellow and hazy in the drizzle. This would be his guiding light.

These houses did not have live-in yard boys or vicious dogs, his main threats, only slow-moving maids who would not open their doors in the dead of night. Because he dared not risk using the roads, even at that hour of night, his journey took him over uneven ground, from boulder to boulder, through fence and thicket, deep grass, a cluster of small trees and finally the manicured hedge of the little house. He followed the low-cut fence, head down, to the rear of the building. Here, where it was darkest, the fence petered out. As his eyes grew accustomed to the near blackness, he barely made out, under cover of the trees, the shape of the secluded Jaguar. He wondered why it wasn't parked out in the carport next to the little Austin Seven where the solitary light blazed. It took him only a few steps to find the kitchen door and a second to raise the worn wooden latch from the outside. Not a single star stood in the sky. It was even darker in the kitchen, so dark he had to put his hands out to feel his way. Kitchen odours, roast beef, fried bacon and baked things, excited and propelled him. Hunger, held in suspension for so long, became acute. He salivated, went weak at the knees and had to brace himself against a workshop or table. Whatever it was moved ever so slightly away from him. A receptacle fell over, scattering cutlery. In the resulting din he ducked down, low on the ground, not breathing, expecting white light to flood the room as someone flicked the switch. But nothing happened. As he waited, he counted out time as he had done all his working life, from ten in the morning to six in the evening. Behind him, the night air rose off the valley floor and breezed into the kitchen through the open door. He felt it against his arms, through his shirt and heard the rapid whispers as it swept briskly along the kitchen floor. Just a flicker of light, from a flashlight or match, would reveal the contents of the kitchen. It was all he needed. Most of the houses had wood-burning stoves so there was bound to be safety matches about. Rising slowly in the prickly dark, he stroked the table top, feeling every inch of it. Edging to the side of the room, he felt the warm metal of the Caledonian Modern Dover stove and worked his way back, reaching out into corners and ledges. The rattle of matches was astonishingly loud as his searching fingers came upon a box. He saw the first match splutter and go out, revealing horrible shadows, limbs outstretched, eyes white and accusing. And he heard, from a far-off place, sickening screams, felt the sudden power in his right arm as the machete went up and down with blinding speed. He heard the *thuck! thuck! thuck!* of hard steel biting into flesh and bone. The motion of his hands had imitated his feet, that quick up and down action against the bicycle pedals, on that terrible day.

The second match burst into yellow flame. This time he saw bread and butter, the small *bankra* atop the refrigerator in the corner, the door that led off into the pantry and the dark part of the house. Before the third match went out, he was upon the bread like an assassin, neck bulging, jaws aching, bursting with the intensity of sudden energy. In the refrigerator he found a jug of lemonade, a slab of roast beef and sweet potato pudding. The match went out. The fourth match flared, an elongated flame shot out, sulphur catching his fingers, taking hold, burning into his flesh. Out went his hand like a whiplash, clean and swift and sharp, flicking in the air. Up went the burning match, up and down and out against the window. Into the *bankra* in the darkness went the bread and roast beef, a carving knife and one or two other items, and he turned quickly to get away. He got to the door and, unusually for a man who wasn't given to looking over his shoulder, glanced round. The kitchen glowed red. Dark figures writhed against the walls. He stumbled and backed away, cowering. Bright red blood covered the kitchen. It came off the ceiling and floor and washed up, frothing and bubbling, against the windows. Again he heard the cries, saw the figures writhing and thrashing about. Blood poured out the door and splashed his arms and clothes, dripped off his cheeks, into his eyes, discolouring his sight.

It was still drizzling but it would be dry in his cave, hidden deep among the canes by the river. With an animal grunt, he closed his ears to all sound and set his face towards his refuge. He wanted it to rain hard, to deafen him and drown out all the voices, the animal sounds, the devil utterances.

* * *

Papa knew it was late but he couldn't tear himself away from Ann's fleshy clutches. The meeting was meant to be business-like and sensible. But he had never known deeper, more consuming passion than he felt that evening. It obliterated everything: the letter, his impending meeting with Mama, his own decision, taken at a sober time, to end the affair. At that moment, in that place, with Ann in his arms, he wanted the past, the present and the future to be of no consequence. He did not want to think. He kissed Ann again, softly at first then deeply and hard. He liked this intense, instinctive, aggressive love-making, this total passion, completely absent from his relationship with Mama. Ann moaned and moved into the kiss, giving him her tongue, clasping his hands into hers. He wanted it to last forever. But she broke away.

'You have to go now, I know. It's late.'

'It's past eleven.' Papa drew her towards him, not wanting to release her.

'Is the club open this late?' Ann asked.

'Yes. People like Moodie live there, drinking the night away.'

'And you spend many a late night there yourself.' Ann laughed, regretted it immediately and turned away, embarrassed.

'I do,' Papa said calmly.

'Doesn't Victoria ever telephone to find out when you're coming home?'

'There's no telephone at the house. I thought you knew.'

'No telephone?'

'No. They took it out before you arrived and installed it here instead.'

'Here? You mean in this house?'

'Yes,' Papa laughed. 'Tim is the assistant general manager, y'know, and there are few telephones to go round.' Papa pulled her to him again, seeing her discomfort. 'It was the right decision. If I were the manager, I would expect the same.'

'You would not, Harold,' Ann said, pulling away.

'I would.' Papa coaxed her back into his arms, stroking the soft of her neck, his hand meandering down to her flanks, pleasing her, not wanting it to end.

* * *

Vincent hadn't returned even when it was past seven o'clock, the latest he had ever been away from the house.

Mama put it down to the weather. But she felt sure that Mavis, who had gone on an errand, would return on time. She was a dependable girl. If Mavis said eight o'clock, she meant eight o'clock, even with the weather so uncertain. But eight o'clock came and went and no one heard Mavis's shuffling feet at the door, only the quietness, the thin falling rain, the consistent plop-plop of water from the roof. Mama just wanted someone to run and fetch Papa. She was beginning to panic.

Baby Babs was ill. Since four o'clock, she'd been moaning and groaning and her little face was contorted, wet with perspiration. Mama had no idea what to do. She'd tried everything she knew, used every medication, held the baby in every possible position, crooned and whispered and soothed and stroked and tried to work her maternal magic, but to no avail. She wanted Papa to take the baby to Dr Cadien at Balaclava. Boyd and Yvonne gathered round her, frightened too, biting their fingernails. They had been pinning all their hopes on Mavis, who always found a way to fix things.

'Where could your father be?' Mama despaired. 'He's usually home in bad weather.'

Boyd struggled to speak, agitated, feeling Mama's distress. He felt a great compulsion to say what he knew, everything, from the very beginning, but pulled back.

'He's at Mr Mitchison,' was all he said.

Mama swung round. 'Mr Mitchison? How do you know?'

'I saw him driving by in the rain,' Boyd said, pointing in the general direction of the road and looking extremely stressed.

'When? How do you know?'

'When you were in the kitchen.' Boyd's demeanour reflected such uncertainty that Mama had the distinct impression he was making it up.

'How do you know it was your father? It could be anybody.'

'Boyd knows, Mama,' Yvonne said confidently.

'But how? Did you see him?'

'I saw the jeep – '

'Land Rover,' Yvonne corrected.

'From the verandah? In the dark?'

'From the fence.'

'From the periwinkle fence?'

'Yes.'

'In the rain! Boyd, you know you shouldn't. What were you doing there in the dark? Are you sure it was Papa?'

'Yes, Mama,' Boyd said. 'It was just a drizzle. I wasn't wet.'

Mama frowned, observing the diminutive figure in front of her. She was more concerned about his psychological state than the meaning of his words. But she knew what she had to do. She patted his cheek, quickly put on her mac and got out the rarely used butterfly-patterned umbrella. They'd have to telephone Dr Cadien from the Mitchisons'.

'Stand by the baby,' Mama said to the two children. 'I'm going to get Papa. If Mavis comes, let her know where I am.'

And Mama went down the verandah steps, across the lawn to the periwinkle fence, through the gate there and up the road in the dark. Water droplets twinkled and sparkled from trees under the fledgeling moon. Boyd was right. It wasn't raining, only drizzling. After-rain smells of washed leaves, wet earth, snails, slugs, worms, frogs, virgin blossoms and the scent of raw anxiety permeated the night. Only Mama's footsteps broke the silence, footsteps that were slow and tentative. She did not really want to call Papa away from his business with Tim Mitchison but she knew she had no choice.

* * *

Beyond the Mitchisons' verandah, a clean brightness like silver covered the lawn and the sorrounding trees. The lawn was squidgy and all around the house, water settled in clear puddles, reflecting the moon.

'Did you hear that?' Papa, suddenly alert, asked Ann.

'What?'

'Footsteps,' Papa breathed.

'No,' Ann said.

'There it is again!'

Twice during the evening, Papa thought he'd heard footsteps in the wet. Stealthy footsteps, like someone creeping up. Twice that evening he'd looked up, expecting someone to appear out of the darkness. He felt unseen eyes upon him. Ann heard nothing. Papa asked about Adolphus, feeling sure the aged gardener was at it again.

'People like that always eavesdrop,' he said. 'It would be hard to find a gardener on the estate who didn't get up to that kind of mischief. Peeping Toms. Up to no good. Keep your curtains drawn at night. At least Vincent, my gardener, can't get up to much. You know he has only one eye.' Ann was shocked and assumed Papa was making it up until he said, 'This is no joke, Ann. They have nothing better to do, you see.'

'You're imagining things,' Ann said. 'You know you are.'

With the moon out and the rain falling gently, there was less reason to imagine intruders, voyeurs and other creatures of the night. And so, in the last moments remaining to them, Papa and Ann walked to the edge of the verandah and looked out over the valley at the thin mist, at the droplets of rain like silver stars, flickering everywhere. Papa kissed Ann again, as he had done so many times before on that same spot. This time it was a longer, passionate kiss, more meaningful than all the rest. Ann responded, surrendering, limp in his arms. Papa did not see how he could put an end to this, although he knew he must. In a moment he would walk briskly down the steps to the vehicle parked in the shadows and drive the few hundred yards down the road, turn left into the driveway of the pink house, roar up it and be home and in bed in a matter of minutes. But it was different that night.

Ann saw it first, a glow of fiery red across the valley.

* * *

When Mama, cold and trembling, returned to the pink house and mounted the verandah steps, she glanced over her shoulder with misty eyes and saw the red glow too. Someone had lit a fire. Terrible images of Mr Dixon at the Bull Pen came to mind but were obliterated as Yvonne rushed into her arms.

'Mavis is here, Mama. And the baby's stopped crying.'

'Ah'm sorry, Mrs Brookes,' Mavis said. 'Ah was delayed, ma'am.'

Mavis appeared from the depths of the drawing room with the baby, whose arms reached stiffly out for Mama. Her cheeks were shining in a gleeful smile and both her legs flicked at the air. Gratefully, Mama took her from Mavis in an almost apologetic posture, and it was some time before everyone realised that it was not raindrops falling from her cheeks. They saw Mama sit down suddenly on the sofa, as if she had lost all strength in her legs. She clasped the baby to her, suffocatingly close, as a grim humiliation settled on her face. She looked straight through Mavis and the children, through the rainy mist, and saw the man and the woman in a close embrace on the Mitchisons' verandah. She had watched them for a long time, mortified, then, on weak legs, turned and walked away. *She had not been confused, not misguided, not been silly, not been wrong. She had been right all along.* She had known it from the very night of Ann Mitchison's dinner party.

In the immediate blur of mystery and tumult, the only thing Boyd heard was Mavis saying, in a clear voice, 'I get you a cup of ginger tea, ma'am.' And she rushed off, cotton skirts fanning out, exposing taut, brown calves. Feeling responsible for everything, Boyd wished the Mullard radio was on, alive with golden light. He wished its vibrant smell of 1957 technology, of warm valves and tubes and Bakelite, filled the dull air; wished the crackling music from foreign places could sweep away Mama's tears.

But Papa broke the silence, racing up the driveway in the Land Rover, water splashing right and left like swans' white wings in the night. He stopped the vehicle by the verandah with the headlights on, bounded up the steps and shouted the most awful news. He was back behind the wheel and out the gate at the end of the driveway before anyone could draw breath. Urgent duties and responsibilities demanded his presence. Miss Chatterjee's house, on the opposite side of the valley, was on fire and burning furiously.

As Papa left, everyone, including Mama, ran for the verandah. Papa was grateful for the emergency. The drama distracted from Mama's pain as it distracted from Papa's guilt. From the verandah they could make out, between dark trees and chilling drizzle, the ominous flames, like the furious tip of a lighted match, and sense the distant violence.

Boyd imagined Miss Chatterjee's screams, her dark flashing hair, her white shorts and her smooth thighs against the red of the flames. He saw her rush from the house in the chilly night air, her scent pretty and light, while the firemen attended to her, some hanging on to her tennis rackets and her lovely clothes. He saw them save her and wrap her in blankets, her fabulous scent driving them on. He knew that the next day she would have to leave the house, just like Agatha. But they would give her a nice new estate house, better than the one before, with a telephone, and she would come to the club and set it alight as always. She was deathless. He held tightly onto Mavis.

'Ah hope she not in the house,' Mavis said in a worried tone, looking transfixed across the valley. 'She and Mr Mitchison.'

'What do you mean?' Mama asked her, astonished.

Instantly, Mavis's hand went to her mouth.

'Nothing, ma'am,' she replied. 'Ah don't mean nothing, ma'am.'

But her eyes gave her away.

'Children, go to your rooms,' Mama commanded.

'Mama, Mama,' Yvonne remonstrated. Flashes of red were already beginning to be reflected in the French windows. Yvonne and Boyd hoped to see much bigger flashes, see churning black and white smoke, see the headlights and hear the screaming sirens of the fire engine and other vehicles racing to the scene to save Miss Chatterjee.

'Get to your rooms!' Mama shouted, seeing them hesitate, the veins standing out in her neck.

As they hurried away, Mavis sat down, staring out at the distant fire.

'Mavis, what do you know?'

'Me, Mrs Brookes?'

'Don't play the fool with me. Tell me what you know.'

'Well, ma'am, ah only know what Evadne told me and she only know what Adassa told her.'

'Which is?'

They talked until the red flames went out and the blackness descended and the air turned chilly on the verandah. They talked until Papa returned, disorientated, eyes bloodshot and so exhausted he could hardly stand.

'Ginger tea, Mavis,' Mama instructed, lips set.

Papa wept in his hands, shoulders rounded. They had found Manjula Chatterjee lying amid the ruins, blackened, burnt and disfigured, unrecognisable, hideous, life and beauty extinguished. There had been someone with her, a male companion, dead too, only a yellow-gold wristwatch to identify him by. A beautiful young woman, the future of Jamaica, was dead. Papa wept like a child. It was because of everything, past and present, things for which there was no redress. Overnight events had shut out the incriminating letter, put off for a time the terrible judgement against him, his certain punishment, which would come in the morning.

CHAPTER 41

In the morning, Papa left the house while everyone was still asleep. When he returned, late in the afternoon, he walked slow. All his swagger was gone from him. He did not speak to Mama and Mama did not speak to him. They avoided each other for two hours.

'Victoria,' Papa said towards evening, finding the strength to face her at last in the bedroom. 'About the letter.' He stuttered like a schoolboy confessing.

Mama folded her arms and set her lips so tight they creased. The bedroom door was closed. Outside, under the windows, crickets peeped.

'I made a mistake,' Papa said solemnly. 'A big mistake. It happened a long time ago. I swear I only knew just before we left Worthy Park.'

'Why, Harold?' was all Mama asked.

'It was a mistake,' Papa told her, hands together, head down. 'A mistake. I wish I could make it right.'

'Make it right? How? She's your daughter.'

'Yes, I know. I'm not denying that.'

'You went to see her?'

'Yes.' Papa tried to face her again but couldn't. 'Victoria, I'm ashamed.'

Mama said nothing.

'I didn't set out to bring shame. It wasn't – '

'You're going to support her?'

'Yes, I have to. It's my responsibility. I ask you to forgive me.'

'Forgive you?'

'I can only ask it.'

'I do forgive you,' Mama said, shocking Papa. Her face showed no bitterness, only hurt. It was just a plain and simple face acknowledging a reality that had come upon them. 'What am I to do? Pretend it hasn't happened? Ignore it? You've said you'll accept responsibility. It's the right thing to do. The poor child is innocent in all of this.'

'Yes, Victoria,' Papa said gratefully, moving towards Mama in a supplicatory stance. Mama moved away and folded her arms across her chest, her back to him.

'Do you have anything else to say to me?'

'Anything else?'

She stopped him. 'Do you love us, Harold?'

'What do you mean?'

'What's difficult about that? Do you love me and the children?'

Papa stepped back and sat down. His posture beseeched Mama to believe him. 'You know I do,' he said, hands shaking. 'How could you ask a thing like that?'

'Love us, Harold? Love us?' Mama backed away as if staring at a frightful monster whose light sleeping she did not wish to disturb. 'After everything you've said. About our future, our lives together, the children's education – you don't love us.' She stood by the window. The curtains parted to reveal wedding-white June rose blossoms catching shafts of setting sun.

Papa was up on his feet and across the room, arms reaching out. 'Victoria, you have every right – ' he said.

'Don't touch me!' Mama hissed. 'I know you – '

'I always put you first, Victoria. You and the children come first. You know that.'

'I don't know that,' Mama snapped. 'You only pretend. All this talk about *values and principles*. You don't mean any of it.'

'Please, Victoria, please,' Papa pleaded, lips trembling uncontrollably.

Mama glared at him, but fear was in her eyes. And she

would have turned away, not wanting to reveal her secret, but she saw Papa stare past her out the window.

'Damn, they're here,' he said. His tone of voice changed instantly. 'Moodie and Cynthia. Victoria, I promise to deal with this properly. Please, don't cast me aside.'

Out on the driveway, the windscreen of Mr Moodie's Buick winked in the late evening light as it roared up the driveway. Miss Hutchinson's little Hillman Minx followed close behind, at speed.

'Forgive me, Victoria.' Papa said this in his best begging voice and reluctantly left the room, lingering awkwardly at the door.

Mama noticed that he hadn't used the word *sorry*, a word that didn't come easily to his tongue. She just wanted to make Papa suffer, make him hurt as she was hurting. But she was scared because she had nowhere to go. Her place, inevitably, was with him. Seeing Ann Mitchison in his arms had suddenly focused her mind, given her the fright of her life, made her come to her senses. She was the one begging, not Papa, but he would never know it. The letter and the business with that woman from Lluidas Vale were irrelevant now. She could come to terms with that. Ann Mitchison was quite a different matter. Mama knew how naive she had been. But she also knew how right she had been. Her suspicions, from the very first moment, had been correct. What had been lacking was faith in herself. She didn't want to lose Papa and everything they had, and she now feared that there was some possibility of that. If she pushed Papa too far, he could walk. What would become of the children? It was a scenario she could not contemplate. She saw how her life was actually pleasant, rewarding, easy even. No more would she put pressure on Papa to let her *take up dressmaking*. What on earth had she been trying to achieve? She had clearly driven him into Ann Mitchison's arms at a time when he needed her most. Did she not have enough responsibility? And could she not derive as much satisfaction and well-being from looking after her children, being a good mother and wife, as Papa wanted? Nothing was clearer to her now than the fact that she had been selfish. She just wanted Papa back. She just wanted to be his wife; she could take the hurt. They would start afresh after Papa confessed, as she knew he would. She joined him in the bathroom, face hard but heart melting, and touched *Evening in Paris* about her neck with a trembling hand.

Boyd, hearing everything, left his place under the bedroom window and beckoned for Poppy, a few paces behind, to follow. He had not been able to look Poppy in the eye since the brutal act. The shame of it would never go away. They made their way round to the verandah by the pink oleander bush. It was already dark. Mr Moodie was sitting alone with Miss Hutchinson, waiting for Mama and Papa to join them.

'They caught that bugger, Ten-To-Six,' Mr Moodie said. 'Cornered the bastard on the riverbank, two miles down from the bridge. Pissed himself begging for mercy. Corporal Duncan said it was a miracle he wasn't shot. Had a machete in his hand at the time, the same one he used to murder his wife and children.'

'That lunatic should be in the asylum,' Miss Hutchinson said aloud and with feeling. 'Poor Manjula. I can't believe it's happened.'

Mr Moodie shook his head, not speaking.

'The maids are talking,' Miss Hutchinson told him.

'Saying what?'

'That she and Tim Mitchison have been together.'

'Impossible. He's always in Kingston on business. If he's been having an affair it's sure to be with a Kingston woman.'

'Do they know who the man was found with her?'

'God only knows. The police are looking into it and we'll get the facts soon enough. Manjula is – was – a young woman with needs like everybody else. Could even be that culprit Edgar, from what I hear. Nobody knows where he is.'

'Edgar, who two-timed Miss Casserly?'

'Shh!' Moodie hissed. 'Don't look now, but Ann's coming across the lawn.'

Boyd turned and saw Ann Mitchison walk swiftly towards the verandah in the soft dark. The moment she started up the steps, Mama and Papa stepped through the French windows. Boyd leaned against the verandah wall, listening with dread.

Ann Mitchison had been on the verandah not more than five minutes when unrestrained shouting tore apart the night, frightening away the *peeny-waalies*.

'Miss Ann! Miss Ann!' It was Evadne, limping through the periwinkle fence. 'Come quick, ma'am. Come quick! The police on the telephone, ma'am.'

'Calm down!' Boyd heard Papa say as Evadne neared the verandah.

'What is it?' Ann Mitchison asked.

'The police, ma'am, the police.' Evadne could barely speak, bent down, hands on knees, exhausted from her headlong sprint up the road. 'They want you, ma'am. They waiting on the telephone.'

'Didn't they say what it's about?'

'No, ma'am. They just say they want to talk to you urgent, ma'am. They say it of uttermost importance. To do with the fire.'

'The fire?'

'The fire, ma'am. Come quick. Come quick, ma'am.'

The pastel-coloured verandah chairs were all pushed back, a tumult of metal scratching against tiles. Boyd heard again the jumble of voices and then an unnatural silence. Ann Mitchison was again rushing across the lawn, soft, creamy, like powder in the night, Evadne making haste behind her.

'God!' Miss Hutchinson exclaimed.

'What can they want her for?' Mama appealed to Miss Hutchinson.

'There could be more going on there than we know,' Moodie said.

'What do you mean?' Mama asked, perplexed. 'Why do you say that?'

No one had noticed but Mama had been quietly drinking gin and tonic, not a drink she favoured and not one she was used to. And her hand shook.

'Believe me, Victoria,' Moodie told her, 'there is more there than meets the eye.'

'You've already said that,' Mama replied irritably, her fingers flicking out.

'Someone should go after her, see what the matter is,' Papa said. He was as taut as piano wire. Mama kept her eyes on him.

'I don't understand,' Mama told Moodie. 'What could there possibly be to know? Is there something you're not telling us?'

'A lot,' Moodie said, feeling like a real gossip.

Papa turned to Moodie in disbelief.

'The maids are talking,' Miss Hutchinson said. 'What I hear is that Mitchison's been sleeping in Miss Chatterjee's bed. My maid, Icilda, came out with it the other day after I caught her gossiping with that imbecile Adassa, Miss Chatterjee's maid.'

'What?' Papa said. 'Adassa, Miss Chatterjee's maid?'

'That's what they say.'

Mama's face showed pure disgust. 'Sleeping in her bed? Rubbish. Maids' gossip. A decent man like that. He has his own wife to sleep with.'

'Gossiping isn't going to help,' Papa advised calmly. 'A tragedy has taken place. We shouldn't just stand about gossiping.'

'This isn't gossip,' Mama said, sipping from her glass.

'What can we do?' Moodie asked, pouring himself another stiff drink.

'We can help Ann for a start,' Papa replied, louder than he intended. 'I'm going over there to see what the matter is. She contacted Kingston but they gave her wrong information. Tim wasn't at the hotel. Only God knows what she's going through.'

'How do you know all this?' Mama asked, watching him like a hawk.

'Victoria, Ann told us herself,' Papa replied, shaken.

'When? I didn't hear.'

'Just now,' Papa told her.

'Liar!'

Mama flung her glass on the table. The slice of ripe lime, like a small yellow quarter-moon, flew out, landed on the polished tiles and slithered into a dark corner. The sound of the glass hitting the table was outrageous. Mama was shaking, her eyes dark, and her breath came in tortured bursts. Moodie and Miss Hutchinson stared, dumbstruck.

'If you go over there, don't come back!' Mama's voice was breaking, weepy but determined. 'Go, and stay there. You hear me, Harold? You hear me?'

It was icy cold suddenly and deadly quiet. Boyd hugged the warm wall beneath the verandah, trembling. On the verandah, Papa did not seem to know what to do with his hands or where to look. Moodie looked from face to face, trying to work out the background to the sudden drama. Miss Hutchinson knew at once and tried to reach out to Mama.

Mama rose from her chair, stumbling, losing all control of her voice. 'Harold, I warn you. Go over there and don't come back. I know what you're up to. You and your deceitful ways and your lies.' She started to weep, her voice now rash. 'No, go to her. Don't let us stop you. You never cared for us, your wife and children, go to your woman, go to your white woman, you lying wretch!'

Papa staggered, desperate to bring control to the sudden catastrophe. He rocked back on his heels, hands gesticulating, composure rapidly crumbling. From the corner of his wild eyes, he could see Moodie and Miss Hutchinson rigid with astonishment. And he saw a small figure appear on the verandah. It was Barrington. Earlier that morning, he'd arrived from Munro, his grip full of unwashed clothes, and had sat in Mama's room digesting the news. He had seemed very grown-up. Now he was facing down Papa.

'Look at him,' Mama cried, completely out of control. 'The man with the bastard child in Lluidas Vale. Did you know?' She turned to Moodie and Miss Hutchinson. 'A seven-year-old child, his daughter, with some common woman in Lluidas Vale. The same man committing adultery with his neighbour's wife under our very noses. The man standing in front of you. This is Mr High and Mighty. And you call this respectability, Harold? Do you? Do you?' Mama's face was like a terrifying wound.

Papa moved forward suddenly, taking two swift steps, and slapped her hard. Mama behaved like a cricketer, upright in the field one moment, suddenly catching a fast ball and tumbling to the ground in a flutter of clothing, grass and dust. Boyd, hidden in the undergrowth, knew that something terrible had happened. In the dark, he drew back from the verandah so that he could see up into it. Mama was on the ground like one of the cows in the pasture, struggling to rise, weakened by pain and shame. Papa was standing off to the side, frozen, looking down at the tiles. Someone was throwing punches at him but the punches were only bouncing off. It was Barrington, his hands in perpetual motion. Papa threw him to the ground against Mama. Barrington was up and at Papa like a tiger, head down and fists flying. He astonished Boyd. But Papa threw him down again, very hard against the pastel-coloured aluminium table. This time he did not rise. And suddenly there were many frightened shadows on the verandah.

Boyd didn't know why he could hear the diesel train so clearly as it sailed up the tracks through the valley, making smooth metallic sounds like a butcher sharpening his knives. But it was because everyone on the verandah stood transfixed, unable to speak, in silence. He saw Miss Hutchinson rush towards Mama in a slow blur, her scarf, bought on the streets of Paris, flowing as if in a sudden wind. She fell to the ground at Mama's side and there was a flurry of hands and scarf and hair. Mr Moodie went up to Papa to try to pacify him but was pushed stiffly away. Yvonne, at the door suddenly, started to cry and wet herself. Mavis's untainted shadow appeared and bent down to tend to Mama and the battered Barrington, who was bleeding from the mouth.

Boyd stood still in the dark and did not know where he stopped and where the earth began. He didn't know how to get from the lawn to Mama lying on the floor in a heap, trying to get to her feet, weeping, sagging on her haunches like the cows in the meadow. But he knew that Papa and they, the Brookeses, were *those people* now. Papa had punched Mama to the ground in the brutal manner of labouring people. He'd turned the entire family into *those people* overnight, shattered their sun-lit, *Essen*-filled, music-from-the-radio lives.

Boyd was cold, the earth moving under his feet, and he was tumbling down, down, down. Someone took him by the hand. It was Mavis. Her hand was warm and steady and good. He embraced it. Then Papa, appearing like a short little man in khakis and brown brogues, was leaving. The car keys were in his hand and he was walking fast across the verandah and down the steps. They saw Mr Moodie remonstrating with the little man in khakis, caught in the headlights of the car. Boyd heard the tyres scatter the pebbles in the driveway as the car sped away. Then they were alone, breathing their own fear, scared of what the little man in khakis and brogues might do next.

That night the music went away. Almost everything that was Appleton died, the crimson feelings and the tranquility, the warmth and the certainty and the living.

CHAPTER 42

Everyone went away. Aunt Enid arrived in the Vauxhall Velox, Mr Fenton Fitz-Henley at the wheel, and took them away while Papa was at work. The Vauxhall Velox was accompanied by a Bedford truck with a growling engine and driven by a man who was the dead stamp of Mr Samms who had gone away.

They went to live with Aunt Enid in her big house on Waterloo Avenue in Kingston. From there, in 1958, Aunt Enid left for London with Fenton Fitz-Henley, to his empty house in South Kensington. And Boyd went too. Aunt Enid begged Mama for three days, saying firmly, 'I will look after him, Vicky, as my own child.' And Mama wept but let Boyd go. She knew he would be safe with his Aunt Enid, who had seen the world and was very capable. Mama remained at the Waterloo Avenue house with the other children. There the bougainvillea was electric-purple and the sprinklers were on the lawn all morning under a champagne sun. Ice cream men on white bicycle carts stopped by the gate every other day at about eleven o'clock, during *Housewives' Choice*, ringing their silver bells, and the children rushed out in the sparkling sun with their pennies and thruppences and ate ice cream with little wooden spoons.

* * *

Papa came home late in the evening to the pink house to find it empty, swallows shrieking on the electricity poles

384

and dark clouds on the horizon. Mavis served him his supper and then she too went away. She went away with her radio and her *Essen* and her *Cutex*, and some very nice clothes Mama had left for her. And she placed the note containing Mama's new address in her bosom. When she got home to Taunton, she locked herself in her room. She recalled Boyd in the room with her and wept as if her heart would break because all the good memories flooded back. When she was all cried out, she looked at the address again. She folded the note carefully into her purse while her little radio wailed irreverently, *Whole Lotta Shakin' Goin' On*. A month to that day she would take the diesel train into Kingston and meet up with Mama again, and learn how to run a Kingston house. For her it was like taking the BOAC to England.

Papa, feeling the cold emptiness of the house, hurried over to Ann Mitchison in the quickening night, wondering whether, in spite of everything, there might be some hope. Ann needed solace. But Ann Mitchison wasn't there. Evadne, on her way out, her heart heavy, her future blighted, met him at the door.

'Dr Cadien come to the house to see her, sah,' Evadne said. 'He take her to the clinic and now she gone, sah.' And Papa knew it was hopeless. He was on his own.

Ann Mitchison had left that morning, packing as much as she could into the Land Rover. Dr Cadien's diagnosis had come like a bolt out of the blue. But she was a strong woman and knew how to cope. She went away to Monymusk sugar estate to be with friends and from there, early in the New Year, travelled to England by BOAC.

That same night, Papa drove to the club and met up with Moodie. It was a sombre place. They got blind drunk and created quite a spectacle. Someone mentioned that Edgar had been located, in a Mandeville hospital, beaten half to death by the husband of his latest conquest. But no one wanted to talk about the latest tragedy – grown men did not have the heart. Ralston served more drinks that night than at any time in all the years he'd worked at the club.

When, at last, the dew heavy on the grass, the tennis courts dark and empty, it was time to go, Papa started to cry. He didn't want to go home to an empty house. He didn't want to go home to a house where no one would hear his footsteps on the floorboards, where Poppy would never bark again as he drove up like an estate lion in the dead of night, to the house where all his dreams had died, to the house that *could be the manager's house*. Regrets lay heavy in his heart, on his head, in every step that he took. He was just another one of those innumerable Jamaican men who couldn't manage it; full of talk and plans, full of bluster, but not possessing the steel to see it through. He was like the rest of them: *lacking*. And for the first time in his life, he did not feel in control.

But that night he was not alone. Someone, returning home to the only place he knew, breathed Papa's sugary scent and saw his broken figure slumped on the darkened verandah. He entered the house through the silent kitchen, machete in hand. Papa did not see the muscular shape rising up from the dark of the drawing room behind him, his scent alien and rank, and might have confused flashing steel, in that split-second before it struck him, with the gentle flash of Appleton moonlight.

* * *

That last morning, Boyd ran to the periwinkle fence, silent voices calling him out, events making him forgetful of Papa's warning. Poppy joined him, nervous at first, one leg off the ground. Boyd patted him, softly, tenderly. Wispy blue smoke still drifted up from Miss Chatterjee's house across the valley. Susan, lips full and red, waited for them at the fence, tingling with shock and news.

But Papa said they shouldn't play.

They went deep into the orchard, into the forest, summoned by voices that they could not disobey. Saplings lashed at them as they ran but they didn't care. Boyd wanted to run hard, run far, run and not come back. They came to an open space where the sun shafted down on a soft carpet of lime-green. It was the place of the pink women. They lay down on the grass and orange blossoms fell from Susan's hair. There were a hundred things on their lips that they wanted to talk about. But they knew and so did not say.

'There was a big fire,' Boyd finally gasped.

'Mummy knew the person in it,' Susan replied, breathing hard.

'Miss Chatterjee. The firemen rescued her with all her tennis things. My Papa was there, putting the hose on the fire.'

'She died,' Susan said, in a small, hesitant voice.

Boyd didn't answer. It was nice sitting next to Susan among the green leaves under the sun in the quiet, inhaling the trembling scent of her. But it was difficult to sit still. They had not seen one another since the heat and the pink in the grass, not since Boyd's painful episode with Papa in the drawing room, not since Poppy's hurt, not since their frantic waving, not since the music stopped. He didn't want it to end.

Papa said they couldn't play.

They wanted to run wild in the meadow, race down the slope and throw themselves in the grass. They wanted to roll about and wrestle in the fallen blossoms, faces turned to the sky, and cry out. They wanted that day to be like the first day in the grass under the trees. And their hearts beat as if they were in the heat of the midday sun; the faint scent of boiling sugar in the air, the warm wind soft against their cheeks. They didn't want it to end.

'We're leaving,' Susan said. 'Daddy's meeting us at Monymusk.'

Boyd's heart leaped but he said nothing even then, although words were piling up behind his tongue; words that could not be spoken at another time.

Poppy nipped at Susan's feet and sniffed at her dress. She shrieked and Poppy ran off, tongue loose, eyes mischievous, tail lashing, his limp noticeable. Susan ran off into the green after him, the sun at her back. Boyd went after her, glad, mad, terrified, the sweet heat smell at his nose. He caught her beneath a navel orange tree, drunk with the scent of her. But she had stopped running by then and wanted to be caught. And they touched again in Technicolor, and felt hot and boisterious, shot through with anxieties and pricking little joys and yearnings, and did not understand it at all. Then they burst through the trees, racing towards the meadow, Poppy at their heels. And Boyd felt something warm and wonderful bursting from him, something that could not be contained any longer.

'You're the girl at Miss Havisham's,' he cried out at last, his voice cracking as he ran. 'Estella! The girl at Miss Havisham's.'

'The girl at Miss Havisham's?'

'In *Great Expectations*. Estella.'

'Oh,' Susan said, giving him a coy look.

'You are the pretty girl,' Boyd said, looking into her eyes. 'Estella.'

'And, are you Pip?' Susan ran hard against him and away from him. They laughed raucously and ran more wildly, their eyes sparkling.

Now that the words were finally out, Boyd felt a glorious freedom. He couldn't prevent the hot tears of joy. The note of thirteen words was no longer necessary: *You are Estella, the pretty girl at Miss Havisham's, and I am Pip.* He laughed, he cried; they were breathless and happy, in the very heart of the music. It couldn't end.

Poppy was ahead of them now, along the river road, stumbling, without his usual rhythm. Susan was ahead of Boyd. They couldn't stop. It was impossible. They ran very fast and came to a quiet place hidden from the road. Once again, Boyd caught Susan, quivering and hot, not wanting to let go. Panting noises came from them. Susan's eyelids fluttered and kiss was like a crimson lollipop on Boyd's tongue. But they knew they would have to get back. Papa could arrive at any moment and end it all. Boyd could hear Mavis calling out and Susan could hear Evadne. But she didn't want to end it.

'I have something to tell you too,' Susan said, breathing fast, facing him. But she didn't say it and broke away for one last frenzied run. 'Chase me into the forest,' she cried.

'What is it?' Boyd asked. But he'd seen the look in her eyes, seen deep down into the secret pinkness where the music came from. That was enough for him.

'Chase me!'

Boyd heard, *Kiss me*!

And they gave chase, Poppy and Boyd, running with madness and abandon. They came quickly to the grassy bank of the river, saw the fast-flowing waters at their feet and stopped abruptly, teetering on the soles of their feet. But Poppy, rushing madly ahead and unable to stop, fell in. Eyes wild, searching for Boyd, his paws paddled furiously. He barked once, a half gurgle, and went under. Instantly, Susan went in after him, hair flashing in the sun, arms and legs flailing. Boyd, seeing Susan flounder, hearing her cry out his name, seeing everything in slow motion, went in after her. And there was much splashing and thrashing about. This went on for about half a minute and Boyd saw Susan sink beneath the water. Through blurred vision, he saw her on the surface, like *Ophelia*, floating stiffly away, her arms stretched out. Then, after what seemed like hours, he found himself alone, clutching fast to the root of a tree. He struggled and rolled over exhausted on his back on the riverbank. He couldn't understand the silence.

It was Mrs Dowding who last saw them, watching from her window.

'It's those children again!' She shot up from her chair, gesticulating to Mr Dowding. 'My God!'

'What is it?'

'The Mitchison girl and Boyd Brookes.' She grabbed him

by the arm, positioning him so that he had a clear view of the running children. 'They're heading for the river.'

'Let them play, for Christ's sake,' Mr Dowding said irritably.

She turned on him. 'Are you out of your mind? After everything, let them play!'

When she returned to the window, the children had already snaked under the fence by the poinciana trees and were now running frantically along the river road, their cries shocking, scarlet poinciana blossoms falling off them. This time Poppy led the way, bounding without balance. Boyd chased Susan hard, both hands outstretched. Mrs Dowding saw them vanish down the road amidst the green leaves of the canes and her middle-aged, cynical face furrowed. She didn't leave the window but stood there flexing and unflexing her fingers. And she didn't wait long. Moments later, a small figure, dripping wet, came stumbling back up the road as if the devil was in pursuit. She waited, expecting to see the other child and the little dog close behind. But it was just the boy, and now she could hear his muffled cries as he flew past the house. After that it became very quiet in the room.

EPILOGUE

Fifty-nine year old Boyd left his flat, took the lift down to the ground floor and walked three hundred brisk yards up the King's Road in the autumn Chelsea sun. London was beautiful at that time of year and lovers and residents thronged the streets, sightseeing, popping in and out of restaurants and boutiques, the champagne sun on their glad faces. Boyd observed this with more than a touch of envy. Throughout his adult years he'd not known love or happiness. Three times married, three times divorced and without children, he knew only memories and regret. And guilt weighed upon his drooping shoulders like an unforgiving mountain. But it wouldn't be long now. *He was to blame. He had no right to life. The long years of torture would end, and it would end that night back at his flat.*

Glancing at the tiny tables and chairs set out on the pavement outside Thierry's, the French bistro, he turned left into The Vale and, kicking at early yellow leaves on the pavement, turned right into Mallord Street. Aunt Enid's house was halfway down the road. She sat in the drawing room all day, every day, alone, surrounded by black and white family pictures in silver frames. Fenton Fitz-Henley was dead, now three years passed, and that on its own, had killed her too. She no longer wrote to Mama, at eighty years old weak and frail and living in a residential home in St Andrew; or to Barrington (partner at the Jamaican law firm Brookes, Babcock & Weston) to thank him for looking after her so well. And she no longer, with feigned indifference, asked about Papa. Severely disabled from Vincent's machete attack, he'd turned to God and was now a "brother" in the Open Bible church, married to a "sister" half his age. His persistent tracts exhorting her to take Jesus Christ as her personal saviour were summarily dispatched to the wastepaper basket. (Vincent, serving life in the Black River penitentiary, received his tracts too, every month). Aunt Enid was dying.

When Boyd visited, every single day, they communicated with their eyes. Her eyes, still young, reflecting bougainvillea and sunny days, widened and flashed in contrast to the dark, old face. Boyd did not want to be in the room with her, for he could not bear it, knowing that this was his last cowardly visit. This was, after all, *his* Aunt Enid, his second mother, the guiding hand throughout his English upbringing. Dr Hyslop-Elliott, at the Chelsea Westminster hospital, unacquainted with this glorious past, was only alarmed that she was still alive. He knew she would be dead by the end of the month. Maybe he wouldn't be so sure if he could see the sunlight still in her eyes, feel the music in her pulse.

Aunt Enid beckoned Boyd over with a weak hand. And she whispered in his ear. He heard the name *Ann Mitchison*. Aunt Enid pointed to *The Independent*, the Saturday edition lying on the floor, opened at the Obituaries page. And she clasped his hand in hers.

Back at his flat that night, Boyd rushed off an email to Yvonne and got to work tracking down his past and his future, his suicidal plans firmly abandoned. If life was about beginning and end, he wanted very much to be part of this beginning. He would give it everything he possessed; make it a present to last. And he drank the wine that would have been his undoing, seeing in deep focus the face of the girl he already knew.

In a New York suburb, Yvonne opened her Friday morning emails. There was one there from Boyd. She opened that first, keeping a perceptive eye on her two small children from a second marriage playing Blind Man's Bluff in the garden. Sixty-nine year old Mavis, her housekeeper, kept a sharp eye too from her place in the kitchen. Later that morning, the children's aunt Babs, Barbara Brookes, the mezzo-soprano, would be visiting with presents and they were all a bit excited.

Boyd's email shouted. Yvonne scrolled down quickly, reading fast, ending abruptly. The news about Aunt Enid was not unexpected. It was the other news.

Yvonne gazed out into the apple-green garden where her two children played and fancied that she saw them again, Boyd and Susan, in that faraway place, the garden of the pink house at Appleton. Amid the green leaves, the face of Susan Mitchison appeared in sun, young, still only a child of seven. Yvonne remembered the day she and Poppy were found, washed up on the banks of the river near Maggotty Falls. The *Black River Gazette* reported it in bold headlines: *English girl and dog found.* According to the paper, Poppy had dragged the unconscious Susan to safety and waited by her side until rescuers arrived. Susan would have been fifty-eight years old if she'd lived.

Ann Mitchison had been beside herself that day, tearing her hair out, weeping uncontrollably when she arrived at the hospital. But it was too late. In the end, they had to drag her away from the small, still body, prizing her cold white fingers one by one from where they were glued solid to the doorframe of the sombre room. When they finally tore her free, she slumped to the floor, helped up by a dozen nurses.

'I'm her mother,' she kept repeating, 'her mother, her mother.'

Poppy became quite a hero. His picture appeared in several newspapers and puppies up and down the country were named after him. And when he died in 1972, run over by a fire engine, the same year that Michael Manley became Prime Minister of Jamaica, it made front-page news. But it was the last they'd seen of Ann Mitchison.

I'm sure it's the same Ann Mitchison. There's mention of her living in the West Indies and in Jamaica, during the 1950s. Last year she was made a Dame in the Queens's Birthday Honours for public and voluntary service – "tireless campaigner for the rights of women and minority groups". She died last week, aged 79, in Holgate, Shropshire. Yvonne, I hope you're sitting down for this. She is survived by her daughter, Suzanna Brookes.